To

Jocelyne.

Best wishes.

Christiane Barbo.

Amelia's Prayer

Christiane Banks

AMELIA'S PRAYER

iUniverse books may be ordered through booksellers or by contacting:

iUniverse
1663 Liberty Drive
Bloomington, IN 47403
www.iuniverse.com
1-800-Authors (1-800-288-4677)

ISBN: 978-1-4917-7982-8 (sc)
ISBN: 978-1-4917-7983-5 (hc)
ISBN: 978-1-4917-7984-2 (e)

Library of Congress Control Number: 2015953748

Print information available on the last page.

iUniverse rev. date: 5/21/2018

To my husband and all our boys, with love.

And in loving memory of my parents.

When love speaks
The voice of all the gods
Make heaven drowsy with harmony

—William Shakespeare,
Love's Labour's Lost

Acknowledgments

To the editors who have collaborated on the manuscript through iUniverse—thank you all for your gifts. You have worked wonders with my "beads," creating an extraordinary "necklace" (courtesy of Frank McCourt).

To Margaret Brady for typing and reading each and every word many times over.

To Victoria Mininni—deepest thanks for using your talents to help create the perfect cover for Amelia's Prayer.

To Joyce Holms, author, for validating my ability to write.

To editorial consultant Kathi Wittkamper for her wise counsel.

To my husband, Gary, for listening patiently and cheering me on to the end. Your unwavering support and belief in me have given us *Amelia's Prayer*. You are my hero.

To all my family and friends who have shared in this journey, offering me constant encouragement, I thank you, I cherish you, and I am indeed blessed.

—1—

Sebastian Lavalle stepped out the front door into the warm sunlight on an autumn morning in 1934. He did not stop to saturate his senses with the beauty around him, nor did he look at the old stone house nestled in the beautiful orchard overflowing with apple trees. The apples hung in multitudes—red, ripe, and juicy, waiting to be plucked and bitten into. Sebastian loved biting into apples and feeling the warm juices drip down his chin. At that moment, he also did not think of the magnificent mountains towering high above the village, looking over it and protecting it like the arms of the gods.

He did not consider his weeping mother, his father, or his younger sister; his mind was set upon adventure. Sebastian was fifteen and leaving home to join the navy. He was tall—six foot two—and slender, and he had thick, wavy dark blond hair; strong bones; a square jawline; and sapphire-blue eyes with dark eyebrows and eyelashes framing them. His family followed him out the front door to bid him good-bye.

"Au revoir, Sebastian; be safe. You look so handsome in your uniform," said his mother.

"*Merci,* Maman." Sebastian waved, turned, and walked away from his home, family, and village toward a new life—a different world—and he could not wait.

The navy was everything Sebastian had imagined it would be: fun, exciting, and full of travel. He joined as a junior sailor and worked his way up through the ranks over the years to lieutenant. He traveled all over the world, lived, laughed, and enjoyed life with his fellow shipmates. Sebastian was part of the engineering team and worked in the bowels of the ship, looking after the engines. All the sailors had battle-station positions and regularly practiced. On September 3, 1939, France and England declared war on Germany after Germany invaded Poland. As a result, the cruiser *Jeanne d'Arc* later became part of the Free French forces in response to Charles de Gaulle's appeal. Sebastian and his shipmates were at war and fearful of the unknown. He was twenty.

Two years into the war, the *Jeanne d'Arc* was part of a convoy sailing from England to Archangel Port in Russia. All the crew were on battle watch, and everyone was at his post, anxious. The *Jeanne d'Arc* was hit, along with several other ships that were part of the convoy. Several were severely damaged and sank. Sebastian could hear the terrifying sounds of the explosions. It seemed to be silent for a moment after. Running to see what damage had been done to the engines, Sebastian dodged the shells. He watched in horror as his shipmate's head was blown off, hit with a shell. He heard screams coming from every corner. Sebastian was not sure if they were coming from himself or the others. He slipped on the deck and fell on top of a sailor who'd had his legs blown off. Flesh, blood, stench, petrifying screams of his friends—the chaos that ensued was insane. Broken bodies were scattered across the ship; wounded men were everywhere. Men he had lived with, eaten with, drunk with, and worked alongside over the past six years were blown to pieces in front of him. Sebastian cried out, holding on to himself—the screams were coming from him.

As he staggered from one wounded man to the next, trying to help them, he was numb with shock. Smoke, fire, and dust hindered Sebastian and his shipmates as they ran around trying to help see to the wounded and put out the fires. They worked all night, and when at last the fires were out and the wounded men attended to, Sebastian stood in the eerie silence, looking around him at the devastation, destruction, and madness of the war.

Placing his hand over his mouth to stifle his sorrowful cries, tears pouring from his eyes, Sebastian longed for home. He ached for his mother's arms, the taste of a juicy apple, and the sight of the mountains, for he was sure he had arrived at the mouth of hell.

The *Jeanne d'Arc* was not completely destroyed, as some of the ships that took the worst of the attack were. Hundreds of men were lost or wounded, and several ships sunk that night.

On July 12, 1941, the *Jeanne d'Arc,* with some other ships, slowly made its way to the northeastern coast of England, to the city of Newcastle upon Tyne. They were heading to Hadrian's Shipyard, where they would stay for an indefinite time in order for the *Jeanne d'Arc* to be refurbished and the men to have some much-needed rest and recreation.

The captain had told them that the Romans had settled in Newcastle for five hundred years, leaving behind some of their culture and artifacts. The Tyne Bridge was a great sight and arched across the river connecting the two cities—Gateshead and Newcastle. As the *Jeanne d'Arc* sailed under the bridge toward the shipyard, Sebastian could see the locals selling fish on the quayside. As he stood on the deck with the sun on his back, he thought he would enjoy getting to know this ancient city.

The captain had promised the crew that he would give them time off the next day, July 14, Bastille Day—a French national holiday celebrating the country's independence. The boys who were able would go into town, as the local women's volunteer group were holding a tea dance in the city to keep up the spirits and morale of the fighting men and to give them some comfort and a small taste of home.

Amelia was excited, as she and her older sister were going to the monthly tea dance in Newcastle that day. It had been months since they had been to a dance, as the last one had been canceled after the bombing of houses just two streets from where she lived with her parents and sisters. Dozens of families just like hers were affected when the bomb fell. The bombers had meant to hit a supply depot two miles away, but they'd missed, and the bomb had fallen on the houses.

Amelia looked out the window to the street below. She could see two young lads kicking an old can around like a football. They were wearing worn-out wellies in the middle of summer. They did not seem to notice or care, as it was either that or bare feet.

"I can't stand this. I can't do this anymore!" Deidre jumped off the bed, holding onto the stocking she had mended for the umpteenth time. "Do you know Victoria Smith, the girl I work next to at the armory factory?"

"You mean the one with the big chest and the loud voice?" Amelia said.

"Yes, hard to miss. She was telling me that she went to Catterick Camp last weekend with some American GIs—some dance. She said it was fantastic. She danced till she was ready to drop, and she came home with silk stockings and chocolate." Deidre waved her mended stockings in the air. "Silk stockings! What I wouldn't give for that. It's been at least a year since I had a new pair, with the rations coupons and all."

"I wonder what she had to do to bring silk stockings home," said Amelia, raising her eyebrows.

"Oh, Amelia!"

Amelia turned her head back to the window and was quiet.

"What are you thinking about?" Deidre asked.

"The bomb."

"Oh, that—it's just too horrible to think about. Do you know our Helen told me that when she went down to help, she walked along the street and did not recognize it? Big piles of rubble the size of hills. She said that some of the houses were split in half and you could see into the rooms upstairs; all the walls were blown away, and the bed was just sitting there. Helen cried and cried when she told me she saw a little arm hanging on a branch of a tree—blown off a child. It was terrifying—body parts all over, blood running down the street into the gutters like rain. She said that one family hid in the broom closet under their stairs. They were not killed by the bomb, but the chimney stack fell through the roof, and the rubble from it blocked them in, and they suffocated. They found them leaning up against the door, clinging to one another—all five of them. Helen said when she and Charles got home afterward, they carried young Aiden from his bed so that he could sleep between them. Helen was so shaken and distressed that she held Aiden in her arms all night."

Deidre jumped up from the bed. "I don't want to talk about this anymore. Let's just offer a prayer to the Virgin Mary, and then we can get dressed up to the nines, thanks to our clever sister's magic fingers. I can't believe what Helen did with that gold satin curtain from the jumble sale. Who could have imagined she could make such smashing dresses?" Dee held hers up against her tiny frame; she was like a doll with short blonde hair and big blue eyes. "I am going to wear high heels that I borrowed from our mam. They are too big, but I am going to stuff them with newspaper so that I am as tall as you are, Amelia."

Amelia and Deidre left the house, arms linked, walking along the cobbled streets past the terraced houses.

"You look like a film star," Deirdre said.

"So do you. I heard there is a contingent of ships just arrived, some with French sailors. Maybe they will be at the dance. I wonder if they will be good-looking."

"I don't mind if they are not. I will just close my eyes and listen to their beautiful accents. Oh, they could have two heads, but I could dance until dawn if they just whispered sweet nothings in my ear," Deidre replied.

Amelia giggled. "Oh, you are so funny, Dee," she said as they headed out together to the dance hall.

Amelia and Deidre arrived at the Crystal Palace ballroom. As they were volunteering, there was no charge. The entrance fee was normally six pence for afternoon tea and dancing to a live band. Amelia loved it and looked forward to the opportunity to feel normal while having fun and helping out. They had arrived early, and they began setting up the tables.

"I love this room," Deidre said. "Don't you?"

Amelia smiled. "Shades of the Victorian era."

"Never mind that," Deidre replied. "I love the enormous dance floor with the fantastic spring in it. Helps me dance longer." Deidre giggled. "I see they have the crystal chandelier still up. I heard they were going to take it down because of the bombing."

"I'm pleased." Amelia looked at the chandelier as it hung majestically over the dance floor. The crystals caught the light like a million icicles in the winter sunshine. The ten-piece band was playing, and a female singer was crooning out a familiar song: "Bluebirds over the white cliffs of Dover ..."

"They must be expecting a big crowd," Amelia noted. "I see they have opened up the upstairs."

Sebastian and some of his shipmates arrived at the Crystal Palace. There was a queue, and they stood outside in the summer sun, enjoying the fresh air.

"This must be a popular event," Sebastian said to his friends. "One that will be much welcome. To hold a woman in my arms and dance …" He nodded along with the rest of his group.

"Something so normal, yet I am aching to get in there," one of his mates declared.

Sebastian understood his comment. The dance would be a contrast to the horror they all had experienced only days ago. He could still smell the burning flesh in his nostrils and hear the screams in his mind; he could see the blood and gore when he closed his eyes. It would not leave him. He needed a distraction desperately; they all did.

"Next, please." He looked at the woman behind the glass window of the ticket box.

"That'll be six pence, pet," she said, smiling.

"Merci. Thank you." Sebastian gave her the coins.

"Have fun," she said, winking at him.

Sebastian checked his hat, and with their tickets, they all went into the glorious ballroom. There were plates of sandwiches and cakes on the tables, and the band was playing. People were moving around the dance floor, and music filled his ears. As Sebastian cast his eyes around the room, a young girl came up to the door to greet them all.

"Hello! Come in, have a seat at any table you find empty, and someone will bring some hot tea."

"Merci." Sebastian smiled at her. She was sweet. "I am going to walk around and look at the *magnifique* ballroom."

"Huh?" said the girl. "Oh, yes, that's fine. I love your accent," she said, giggling.

"Merci. I also like yours." Sebastian left his mates and wandered around the large room. The female crooner was good, and the words to the song were mellow: "We will meet again. Don't know where; don't know when." He went upstairs and sat on a luxurious velvet couch in one of the cubicles. He took a sandwich from the plate on the table; the bread was disgusting, like cardboard, and the filling was Spam. He could not eat it, and he put it into his napkin. Looking down from above was wonderful; he could see everything, as if he were a bird soaring through the sky. Sebastian watched his shipmates find dance partners and move around the floor cheek to cheek to the crooning of the song.

Then his eyes found her. She was moving around the tables with an enormous pot and pouring tea, floating from table to table like a dancer. He stood up and went to the balcony in order to get a closer look. She was tall, and the dress she wore moved in gentle golden waves as she swayed to the music. Her dark curls cascaded onto her shoulders with golden highlights, and her face was exquisite. She had delicate features and fine lines like a perfect sculpture—she was extraordinary. Sebastian had never in his life witnessed such beauty. He knew he had to ask her to dance, for to hold on to her for one moment would be enough to get him through the rest of this horror-filled war—just one moment.

He ran down the stairs, not taking his eyes off her for one second. He flattened his hair with both of his hands, pulled himself up to seem taller, checked his collar, and with every sinew of courage within him, moved toward this vision of loveliness. His heart was beating so loudly that he could not hear the music. Sebastian stood in front of her.

"Bonjour, mademoiselle." He smiled. Looking down, he could see she was even lovelier close up. She had glowing skin and eyes so dark that they were like black velvet. She looked at him and smiled, her teeth white and lips ruby red.

He felt the warmth of her smile on his face like an early sunny morning.

"May I have this dance?" he asked.

"Of course you may," Amelia replied. "Today is Bastille Day, isn't it? Come—let's celebrate."

Amelia put down the teapot. Taking her hands, Sebastian walked her to the dance floor. She looked up at him.

"What is your name?" he asked.

"Amelia Sullivan," she responded.

They started a slow waltz. Holding her in his arms, he breathed in her perfume and felt her soft skin; she filled all his senses. As he pulled her gently closer to him, her silken hair touched his cheek. As he led her around the ballroom floor, he felt their heartbeats become one. He was aware of nothing else; everything left his mind except for Amelia dancing in his arms. Was this why he was born? Had the horrors of this war brought him to this place to encounter such grace and beauty? He had been sure the moment he'd laid his eyes upon her that he had met the woman of his dreams, the girl he was going to marry.

They danced together all afternoon into the early evening, talking, laughing, and enjoying the freedom of being young and alive. When the last waltz ended, Sebastian brought Amelia to a table.

"*Merci beaucoup,* Amelia, for the most wonderful dance of my entire life."

"Oh, you Frenchmen—full of charm. My sister warned me about you with your wonderful accents. I must say she was right."

Sebastian grinned. "I would very much like to escort you home, Amelia."

"I would like that too. My sister is with me, and we must help with the cleanup."

"I will escort you both, and my shipmates will help with the cleanup."

"That would be great. Thank you," Amelia replied.

When all the work was done, several of Sebastian's shipmates walked with the girls. They all stopped off in a pub and bought a bottle of cheap French wine, a loaf of bread and some local cheese. They sang French songs. When they arrived on the street where Amelia and Deidre lived, Sebastian steered Amelia off to one side.

"I have had the most wonderful time—a Bastille Day I shall never forget, Miss Amelia."

"Me too." Amelia smiled.

"I would love to see you again," Sebastian told her.

"I would like that too, Sebastian. How long are you here?"

"I am unsure—maybe ten days, possibly two weeks. It depends how long it takes to fix our ship. I hope to see you every single day."

"That's not possible, but some of the days definitely."

"May I come tomorrow?"

"Yes, you can, seeing as it's Sunday. After Mass, we can take the bus and go to the beach if you like, and I will show you one of my most favorite places."

Sebastian kissed the back of Amelia's hand. "I shall count the seconds until I see you again. *Adieu*."

Amelia lay on top of her small bed. The window was open, and the soft breeze was blowing through the room. She was listening to Deidre prattle on.

"I can't believe you danced all afternoon with that gorgeous hunk of a Frenchman. I met him at the door; my legs were like jelly when he spoke. He's the best-looking, best-sounding man I have met in my whole life. You lucky thing, Amelia!"

"He's coming to see me tomorrow after the ten o'clock Mass. I told him we could go to the beach on the bus. I think I will take him to King Eddy's Bay."

"Oh, dreamy—snogging with him in the sand dunes. What a vision to fall asleep to," Deidre teased.

"Yes," said Amelia with a sigh. "Sweet dreams, Deidre!"

—2—

Amelia was putting together a few bits and pieces for a picnic. She packed a thermos of black tea. There was no milk or sugar, but she did have some cornbread and some homemade cheese her mother had received from a friend who owned a farm in the country.

"I'm not all that sure about you walking out with a French sailor," her mother said as she was packing up the picnic.

"He's really very nice, Mam—polite and smart."

"You know how your dad feels about foreigners, don't you? Best keep it to yourself just now."

"Oh, it's just a bit of fun, Mam; that's all."

"You just watch yourself, lass," her mam said. "Remember your place—do you hear me?"

"Yes, Mam, I do." She kissed her mother on the cheek and left with her basket to meet Sebastian at the bus stop.

Sebastian was prompt and looked even more handsome than he had the day before. They sat on the bus and talked about his home in France, including how much he missed his mother, father, and sister; the food; the wine; and the apples in his orchard. She loved to listen to his voice; it was like music.

When they arrived at Tynemouth, they got off the bus at the end of High Street. They walked along the cobbled road, looking at the houses, shops, and churches running up and down each side of the street. The shops were closed, as it was Sunday, but because of the war and rationing, there was little to purchase anyway. Sebastian took Amelia's hand, and they walked together along the ancient street, past the town clock, and arrived at the entrance to the castle and priory.

"This is one of my most favorite places," Amelia told him. "It overlooks the North Sea and the River Tyne. It has a two thousand-year history. Anglo-Saxons settled here first, and it was known as Venerable Crag. It changed a lot, and then it eventually became a priory run by Benedictine monks. Then the priory was destroyed by Vikings. Eventually, King Henry VIII kept the castle. So queens have lived here, and kings have been buried here. I love to stand inside the ruins of the cathedral, because you can still see where the high altar was and the shape of the windows. I can almost hear the monks chanting their Gregorian words as the North Sea pounds the rocks below and the winds howl around the building through the cracks in the windows and walls."

"Ah, *oui*," said Sebastian. "You paint a very good picture."

"Currently, they are using part of its artillery fort to protect our coastline. I think it is a very sacred and beautiful place," Amelia said.

"Then I cannot think of a more perfect place to kiss you." Sebastian took Amelia in his arms; she closed her eyes and allowed him to hold her close. With his strong arms enfolding her, he kissed her tenderly as they stood entwined together, surrounded by the broken-down walls of the Norman chapel, ancient headstones in the graveyard, the cliffs, and the sea. Amelia felt like a queen, as though she were in a dream.

"You are the most beautiful woman I have ever seen, Amelia," Sebastian said as he released her.

She smiled shyly. "Come—I want to show you King Edward's Bay before it's too dark. We cannot miss the blackout curfew."

They looked down into the bay and watched the waves crash onto the rocks, leaving their white foam behind. They reached the top of the cliffs and put out their blanket.

"I know the weather could be nicer for July, but I love to come here before a storm. See those seagulls? They are inland, squawking and looking for food—that's a sure sign there's bad weather coming. When the tide is in, sometime you can feel the spray on your face. The sun setting behind the priory has an eerie stillness."

Amelia set out the picnic. "I know these are meager offerings; it's just that we are so limited with the ration books."

Sebastian took her hands. "I feel like I am in Buckingham Palace with the queen because I am with you."

They sat together, looking out to sea. Sebastian brought out a bar of chocolate and gave it to Amelia. She jumped up.

"Oh my goodness! I have not seen or tasted chocolate for a year. Thank you!" She bent down and kissed Sebastian on the cheek. "Wait till Deidre sees this!" she exclaimed.

"I would walk across oceans to bring you chocolate, Amelia, if it makes you feel this good."

As the sun started to set and cast its shadows across the Tynemouth Priory, they lay together on the blanket, and

Amelia closed her eyes, giving herself up to the handsome Frenchman and his kisses.

The following Saturday, Sebastian and Amelia walked hand in hand along the quayside, passing the fishmongers and the farmers. It was market day, and the side was buzzing with excitement. The merchants were calling out, Kippers! Kippers! Fresh fish! "Tomatoes!" and "Apples! Fresh Apples! Come and taste a juicy apple." Sebastian stopped in the queue and bought two shiny apples, red and juicy looking. People were pushing and shoving, anxious to be served, as supplies were short and limited. After purchasing his two apples, he gave one to Amelia and, with anticipation, bit into his own. It was nothing like the apples from his orchard at home. These were dry, not juicy. They were dull and did not burst with sweetness.

"This is the Tyne Bridge," said Amelia. "See how it reaches across the river and connects to the city of Gateshead? It's actually a copy of the Sydney Harbour Bridge. People from Newcastle are very proud of this bridge; it is, in fact, a landmark. Let's stop at the shop at the bottom of the road and see if they have caught any fresh fish today."

They sat together under the bridge, eating fish and chips out of newspaper, watching the world go by and the ships sail slowly up and down the Tyne River. Everything seemed normal for a moment, Sebastian thought, as if there were no war.

"I like these chips and fish very much indeed. *Tres bien,*" he told Amelia.

They finished the food and walked together up into the city along Dean Street. Sebastian was impressed and amazed at the beauty of this street—how it curved upward toward the city center, cobbled all the way, sweeping gracefully up to Grey's monument. Four-story buildings with domes, spikes, and pillars lined the street. Amelia turned sharply to her left.

"Look at this," she said. It was the narrowest street Sebastian had ever seen—dark and dingy. Amelia giggled. "Look at the name of the street." She pointed.

"Certainly two people could not walk beside each other down this street. Fat Man's Squeeze—oh *mon dieu!*" Sebastian laughed until tears ran down his cheeks.

"Come," said Amelia. "I have one or two more wonders to show you."

They stopped in a small park, near part of a wall about three feet high and less than six feet long.

"This is part of Hadrian's Wall, the Roman wall that Emperor Hadrian himself built thousands of years ago."

"I can't imagine how it still stands," Sebastian said. "It must have been like a mountain, strong and protecting the city—*non?*"

"Yes, that's right." Amelia smiled. "It was built AD 120. Imagine. It makes me feel like a grain of sand in time—I mean small in such a world, compared to everything that goes on around us. Do you understand?"

"Ah, yes, oui, I do," Sebastian replied.

"The wall stretches for miles and miles across Northumberland; this truly is God's country. Maybe I will show you one day."

"I look forward to that."

They walked down Dean Street toward the river, down that magnificent, winding street. "I'm going to walk you up to the castle keep, also old, though not as old as our Roman wall. It is almost a thousand years old, built by William the Conqueror's son. We can climb to the top and look over Newcastle."

They climbed up the stairs of the castle ruins and stood together with their arms around one another, looking out over the beautiful city.

"What are you thinking about?" Amelia asked him.

"Ah, about how I am immersed in beauty in this ancient city surrounding you, Amelia. The view from up here is breathtaking, and I would like to say something to you. I would like to explain something, though my English is not very good, so the words may not be what I would like them to be or express what I feel inside."

Sebastian looked into Amelia's eyes. "I love you. I know it seems not possible in a short time—but I do. We have been given our orders to move out on the *Jeanne d'Arc*. It is almost finished; within the next seven days, we leave. I don't know where or for how long or even if I will survive this."

"Don't say that," Amelia said with a gasp. "Say a prayer quickly. Ask Mother Mary to protect you."

"You say it for me, Amelia. Please listen to me. I want you to marry me before I leave."

"Oh, Sebastian, I don't know—"

"Do you love me?" he asked.

"Yes … yes, I do love you, Sebastian."

"Then that's all I need to know. This is our time; we may not get another chance."

Amelia touched Sebastian's face gently. "I love you too,

Sebastian. What are we to do—stuck in the middle of a world war?"

"*Je ne sais pas*, but I do know we love each other. What else is there in wartime? It's not like peace time, when we would have the luxury to get to know each other. This is our moment."

"I do love you, Sebastian," Amelia said. "Yes, let's get married."

"Then you have made me the happiest man in this world," he said, and he swept Amelia up into his arms.

Six days later Sebastian married his beautiful Amelia on a Tuesday morning at ten o'clock at All Saints Church in Gateshead in the presence of Amelia's parents and two of Sebastian's shipmates. Amelia's sisters could not be there, as they could not change their schedules at the factory. Sebastian wore his uniform, and Amelia wore a navy-blue suit and hat with a small veil over her face and carried pink roses her neighbor had picked from the garden.

She borrowed her mother's ring, as everything else gold was in short supply. After the ceremony, Sebastian escorted Amelia outside into the sunshine; it was a glorious day.

The wedding group went to a restaurant down the street from the church and had a celebratory lunch of what food was available, cake, and white wine. As Sebastian and Amelia left the restaurant, some of his shipmates threw confetti at them. Amelia kissed her mother and father on the cheek.

"Bye, Mam."

"Good luck, Amelia," said her mother. Her dad said nothing.

"See you bright and early in the morning!" one of his shipmates called. "We leave at zero seven hundred hours."

"Don't remind me," Sebastian replied.

"I have booked a room in a hotel close to the shipyard where the *Jeanne d'Arc* is docked so that we can spend as much time together as possible," he told Amelia.

They checked in at the hotel and went for a walk to the local park, where they sat together under a weeping willow and shared ice cream.

"Come," said Sebastian, taking Amelia's hand. "Let's go back to the hotel and enjoy our short time together."

Amelia awoke and lay still in the dark room, unsure where she was. Then she heard Sebastian breathing next to her and felt his warm skin. She tingled. Suddenly, she remembered she was married—Amelia Sullivan was now Amelia Lavalle. She could hardly believe it; it had all happened so fast. Still, Sebastian was right; all they had was the now, and she would not have given up that night of love for anything in the world. She turned over and looked at the clock. It was five o'clock—they had two more hours together. She leaned over and kissed Sebastian on the lips slowly. He opened his eyes.

"Ah, good morning, Mrs. Lavalle." He smiled at her. "What time have we?"

"It's five," she replied.

"Then come to me, *chérie*; we must cherish every second."

At six thirty Amelia stood on the dock beside the *Jeanne d'Arc* in the early morning light, watching the activity of the trucks loading up supplies, smelling the fish, seaweed, and diesel fuel. Sebastian had his arms around her.

"I will write to you as soon as I can, and I will not stop thinking of you for one second," he said.

"Please come back to me." Amelia was crying. "Promise me."

Sebastian held Amelia close. "No matter what happens, chérie, I will take you with me deep inside my heart." He gave her one more tender, lingering, blissful kiss and boarded the *Jeanne d'Arc* on July 28, 1942. She left the port at seven o'clock as Sebastian and the other sailors waved and blew kisses to the girls they were leaving behind. Amelia waved at Sebastian, tears running down her face, wondering if she would ever see her husband again.

"What's it like?" Deidre asked. "Oh my gosh, you are married to that gorgeous man! What's it like being married?" she whispered across the bedroom they shared. It was dark because of the blackout curtains on the window, and it was late, after eleven. "I mean, do you feel different? Did it hurt? You know. You must have cried when his boat left."

Amelia lay on her bed and listened to the constant stream of Deidre's questions, not wanting to answer any of them. She was exhausted and sad and wanted to be alone with her thoughts—not that she was given much of a chance.

"Listen to me, Deidre. I don't think I'm much different. I'm still sharing this dark, dingy room with you, listening to you go on and on. And I'm getting up early tomorrow—if we are not blown to bits by the bombs tonight—to go work in the armament factory and assemble guns. Besides the ache in my heart, no, it does not feel that much different."

"Oh, I'm sorry, Amelia. I'm just excited, you know."

"Yes, I know. It's like it was a dream, except for our honeymoon. It was so beautiful, Deidre. I can't say much more, because it feels almost sacred to me, like it belongs to Sebastian and me alone—our secret."

"Oh, Amelia, I understand. You are so lucky. If the bomb does drop on us tonight, at least you died knowing what it feels like to be in love and to have done it."

"Oh, go to sleep, Deidre," Amelia said as she turned over and closed her eyes.

—3—

It was the week before Christmas 1942, and Amelia, Deidre, and Helen were decorating the spindly, small Christmas tree given to them by their mother's friend who owned a farm and sometimes supplied them with cheese and other goodies.

"Helen, you are such a genius," Deidre said. "I love these ornaments you made from that button box of Mam's."

"Well, we all have to make do," Helen said.

"The rhinestone ones look so pretty. They twinkle."

Amelia was quiet, observing Helen's ability to create beautiful things with her hands. Physically, Helen was ordinary. She did not look like Amelia or Deidre. It seemed to Amelia that Helen was the personification of average—average height, average weight, and average brown hair and eyes.

"Have you heard from Sebastian yet?" Helen asked her.

"No. I am worried about him."

"Oh, I wouldn't be. The post is impossible, you know, as you can imagine."

"I know. The thing is, I can't send him a letter until I get an address or something."

"A letter will show up soon," Helen said. "You're not alone, you know."

Amelia was aware of that. She wondered sometimes if Sebastian had been a figment of her imagination. It seemed so long ago that they'd shared their night of love. She carried on with the decorations, putting out the nativity display that belonged to her mother, who had received it from her mother.

"I love to see that come out," Deidre said. "I like the tradition of it, don't you? Really makes it feel like Christmas."

"Yes," said Helen. "I have some apple cider and shortbread. Charles is bringing Aiden over later to finish decorating the tree. We can put the fire on, listen to carols on the radio, and drink our hot cider."

Amelia smiled at Helen. "That's a really nice idea. Christmas is all about children."

There was a knock on the door, and Amelia went to answer it. It was the postman.

"Hullo, Fred."

"Amelia, I have many letters. I thought I would hand them to you instead of pushing them through the letter box. Looks like a backlog."

Amelia took the envelopes from Fred. "Oh," she said as she read the top one, addressed to Mrs. Amelia Lavalle. The one underneath was also for Mrs. Amelia Lavalle. "Oh, thanks, Fred!" Amelia held the envelopes against her heart; she had tears in her eyes.

"Oh, you're all right, pet; I wanted to see your face when you got them. Go in the house and read them now, and have fun. Tara!" Fred said, and he left.

Amelia closed the door and leaned up against it, offering a prayer of thanks to Mother Mary. She ran up the stairs to her room, sat on the bed, and opened the first of the three letters.

Ma chérie Amelia,

It is evening, and the weather is calm. A full moon shines upon the ocean. I cannot tell you of my location, but I can share with you my thoughts. They are of you—only you, my darling—for it is those thoughts that bring me the courage to survive. Every moment we are apart, I imagine you waking, working, sleeping. Every second of the day, I dream of our reunion, ma chérie, for I will take you home to my native France, to my parents and sister. Oh, they will love you. We can sit under the trees, eat apples in the orchard, and climb mountains together, feeling the soft breeze on our faces and the warm sunshine. I shall make love with you endlessly in the lush green grass.

Chérie, I have been reading Shakespeare in order to improve my English. His words have inspired me to write you a sonnet, darling.

Let me cast my eyes upon you,
Calm the storm within this
wandering soul,
Lay my shadow next to yours
That we may blend in harmony
Like earth's warm tones
And together look toward the sunrise,

Lest it be only in my dreams.
You are my life, my very breath,
And I am yours until death and into eternity,
My chérie, my love.

It is the simple thoughts and dreams that help me face my daily fears, of which there are many. You too must hold on tight to the day of our sweet reunion, for as sure as the sun rises, it will come. This war cannot go on forever. I close this letter and close my eyes; I can see your radiant beauty both inside and out and feel your warm and tender kisses upon my lips. It fills me with a glorious pride and joy. I love you, chérie, with all my heart.

Sebastian

Amelia wiped the tears away as she read and reread the same letter. The next letter included an address for her to send her letters to—some town in Madagascar. Amelia spent the rest of the day and night reading Sebastian's letters and writing a reply.

Darling, how overjoyed I was when Fred, the postman, brought me your words to hold onto and place against my heart. Sending you thoughts of love and prayers to bring you back to me soon. My sisters and

I are decorating the house for Christmas, and what a fantastic gift—three letters from you, my love! I have read each one twenty times, and I shall continue to do so every day until we are reunited.

I have little news to send except the war goes on, and we survive, making the best of things. We are about to celebrate another meager Christmas, though my thoughts of you will warm my soul.

My job in the factory stays very much the same, except the king and queen came to visit last week, which created a bit of excitement. The weather is miserable; the days are short, and the nights are long. The rationing continues, which makes it difficult to prepare a Christmas feast. Deidre and I still help out at the tea dances. She is looking for a gorgeous Frenchman of her own. However, I think she is out of luck, as I have him! I don't dance, Sebastian—I just serve tea. I remember the day you came to me and we danced all afternoon.

We will go to Mass on Christmas Eve at the church you and I were married in, my darling. I will light a candle for you. Think of me wherever you are, for the flame will cross the distance between us, warming your heart and guiding you home to me safely.

Sebastian, I have read and reread your wonderful poem a thousand times. It is beautiful, and I shall treasure it always, my love.

I long to hold you in my arms, Sebastian, my darling, and kiss away your fears. I feel your tender touch and long for the day we can make love in the green grass of France. Hold on to me in that thought.

Your chérie, Amelia

Sebastian's letters were sporadic over the next eighteen months. Amelia never knew where he was. She prayed every day for his safe return, just as the other women in the United Kingdom prayed for their men, and kept the home fires burning. This war had gone on for almost four years, and it felt like an eternity. Finally, on May 8, 1945, peace was declared. Winston Churchill's radio address announced that hostilities would end officially at midnight.

Deidre and Amelia danced around the living room, crying with joy.

"I can't believe it's over! Finally, I will get new silk stockings!" said Deidre.

Several days after Churchill's announcement, Helen came to visit and joined Amelia in the kitchen.

"Hello, Helen. I didn't know you were visiting."

"Mam asked me to come." Her voice was shaking. "I have a telegram for you."

Amelia looked at the envelope, not sure what to do—rip it open or hide.

"Oh, Helen, I'm so scared!"

"Would you like me to read it?"

"No," said Amelia. "Give it to me. I will open it."

"Maybe it's good news," Helen said.

Amelia's hands trembled as she opened the envelope, pulled out the telegram, and read the words.

"Oh!" she cried. "He's safe; he's well. He's coming home!" She immediately excused herself to write back to him.

> My darling, I received your telegram telling me you are on your way home. I am delirious with joy and cannot imagine the moment we will see one another for the first time after two years apart. Everyone has been dancing up and down the street for two days and two nights, singing, waving flags, throwing streamers, and celebrating like ten thousand Hogmanays rolled up into one. The world is giddy with joy because of the end of the war. I too am giddy, and I danced and sang with the rest of them, filled with joy because you are coming home to me. I love you, darling.
>
> Your chérie

"I am pregnant," Amelia whispered as she lay in Sebastian's arms under their favorite apple tree in the late-afternoon sunshine of an October day in 1947.

"Amelia, chérie, did you say? Did you say?"

"Yes, yes, I did—I am pregnant!"

"Magnifique!" Sebastian jumped up and took Amelia in his arms, waltzing around the orchard with tears in his eyes. "Besides the end of the war, chérie, this is the happiest of moments in my lifetime. I am overjoyed."

Later that night, when Amelia was sleeping next to him, he lay awake, full of thoughts about the day and becoming a father. He recalled how his own father had died of a heart attack during the war, and his dear mother had followed him eight months later with pneumonia. Sebastian had not found out until months later, when his sister was able to contact him. He and Amelia were now living in the family home, and he had a good job in Strasbourg—a diplomatic post with the French government with a lot of opportunity to advance. However, he was feeling a mixture of joy and sadness, for he would have loved to share this news with his parents, telling them they were going to have a grandchild.

Sebastian was aware of everything he had in his life and was deeply grateful. He knew he must take extra-special care of his beautiful Amelia, for she was not adjusting to France as well as he had hoped. He believed that given time, she would learn to love it as much as he did. He turned over, pulling her closer to him. He laid his hand upon her soft belly, feeling their baby, and closed his eyes with a smile upon his lips.

Amelia kissed Sebastian on the lips and watched him walk along the street to the bus stop. It was seven o'clock in the morning, and he would be gone until seven o'clock that evening at his job in Strasbourg. She would be alone all day—summer, winter, spring, autumn. That was how it had been for the past two years, except on the weekends. She could not learn the language; it was too difficult because she could hardly read. Everyone talked quickly. The neighbors and everyone else in the village were old, and she did not like the food. Rabbit in white wine, fish soup, snails, frog's legs—it all made her feel sick. The isolation was breaking her. She thought about her sisters, mother, and father and was heartsick. She missed everyone every minute of the day.

Deidre was married to a Scottish army major and living in Edinburgh. She too was expecting her first baby. Helen was raising her family. They were all busy with their lives, and they all envied Amelia for living in France, nestled in an orchard surrounded by mountains, but it felt like a prison to her. She hated it and wanted to go home. She couldn't tell that to Sebastian, as she knew it would break his heart, but a big part of her did not care. She was starting to feel nothing, as if she were numb. When her baby kicked, it was just a kick rather than an amazing thrill that used to send shivers of wonder through her whole body from the top of her head to the tips of her toes. She used to be in awe that she, Amelia Lavalle, was going to have a baby.

She did not eat, for she was not hungry, and she didn't cook or clean. She felt tired all the time. She sat in the window and cried, waiting for Sebastian to come home.

It was evident to him that something drastic had to be done. Amelia was fading away in front of his eyes—she was gaunt, thin, and pale. He was distraught for her and for his unborn child. Amelia was six months pregnant.

Sebastian had taken her to the doctor one day after the neighbors told him they were concerned, as they had witnessed Amelia through the lace curtains, sitting in the window and crying day after day. Sebastian understood that Amelia had not adjusted over the past two years; however, this reaction was extreme. The doctor had strongly suggested Sebastian take Amelia back to England, where she belonged.

Sebastian placed the last of his and Amelia's belongings into the boxes that would be transported to Gateshead; he closed the cases and sealed the boxes. He watched as Amelia helped him without any light of life dancing in her gorgeous eyes. Sebastian prayed that this move was the answer. He was giving up his life, but what was the alternative?

"Are you ready, Amelia?"

"Yes, I think so."

"We have a very long day ahead with two buses, a train, a boat, and then another train—twenty hours of traveling until we reach Gateshead."

"That's all right. I can sleep; I don't mind," Amelia said. "And then we will be home tomorrow."

"Bien," Sebastian replied, picking up the cases. Amelia walked ahead of him out of the house without looking back. Sebastian stood in the living room of the house that he had been born and raised in. It tugged at him; he felt his eyes sting with tears. Closing the door behind him, he stepped out into the warm sunshine and stopped to saturate his senses with the beauty that surrounded him. He was twenty-eight and leaving the only home he had ever known.

—4—

Five years later Helen was sitting in Amelia's house. She went to visit her regularly. Amelia now had four bairns—Andre was almost six, Eugene was five, Leah was four, and Camille had just turned two. One bairn was lovelier than the next. The eldest boy, Andre, had dark hair and eyes like his mother's. He was an amazing little bairn for the age of six and as protective of his mother as a twenty-year-old, helping her whenever she asked, mostly with the younger ones. Eugene was the image of Sebastian; his good looks were evident even at the tender age of five. He was a little devil, getting into all sorts of things. Amelia needed an eye in the back of her head when he was around. Cammie and Leah were two of the bonniest lasses on the Tyne—what Helen wouldn't give for a lass.

"You look peaky, Amelia—are you sick? What is it, Amelia? You look exhausted."

Amelia continued to keep her head down and concentrated more than was necessary on folding the damp clothes.

"I am pregnant."

"Oh dear God," said Helen.

"I'm so worried. I don't know what to do," replied Amelia.

"Have you told him?"

"No, I haven't. He will go out of his mind. We can barely make ends meet now."

"How far along are you?" Helen asked.

"Six weeks or so. Oh Helen, will you come be with me when I tell Sebastian? I must have someone with me; maybe he won't lose his temper as much if you are here with me."

"I cannot do that, Amelia. It's between you and Sebastian."

"Oh, please help me," Amelia said desperately.

Amelia knew that Helen would love to have another baby. Helen had one son, Aiden, and had almost lost her life while having him. The doctor had told her absolutely no more. She would have been delighted to have a little girl.

"Helen, you will be with me when I tell him, won't you?" Amelia pleaded.

"Yes, I'll come if it means that much to you," Helen assured her.

The desperation lifted from Amelia's voice, and she placed the damp clothes in the old cupboard to the side of the large fireplace.

"Then I shall go make us some more tea," Amelia said, "and we will discuss what we will say when he comes in and the children have gone to bed."

Sebastian walked along the path, which was cracked and covered with green moss in places, neglected and overgrown and in need of some effort and time, of which he had neither. He stopped and chased two scrawny cats off the six-foot wall that divided the two backyards from each other. He made his way along the yard to the water tap. Sebastian stopped and washed his hands almost ceremoniously before he went into the house—a ritual of his that gave him some time alone before he went into the house. Today was different. As he washed his hands, he was worried, having been told he would be laid off from the factory for several weeks and maybe longer. There were no orders after next week in his department, nor were any expected in the days ahead. Sebastian opened the back door, which led into the old scullery at the back of the house. Amelia was making his supper.

"Bonjour, Amelia."

She looked up. "Hello, Sebastian."

He walked over to her and kissed her cheek. Looking into her eyes, he could see her tiredness. He knew how hard she worked; they both did. Amelia turned her head away. The stress was telling on their marriage—there was no doubt about it. Sebastian had little time to spend with Amelia or his children; he tried his best, but it was not good enough. Most of the time, he was exhausted after a twelve-hour day in the factory, and he had no patience with the children when he came home from work.

Tonight he was glad to be home, as he was feeling extremely tired. He opened the cupboard door and took out his ledger, and sitting at the kitchen table he looked at all his bills for this month and knew he would not be able to pay them all. His wages and rental income totaled just under twelve pounds. With expenses of almost four pounds for food; two pounds for the mortgage; about one pound for coal, electricity, and gas; train and bus fares; shoes and clothes for the children; and everything else, he could not make ends meet. He placed everything back in the ledger, put it back in the cupboard, and wondered what he could do. Amelia brought his dinner to the table—cabbage and mutton pie tonight. The night before he'd brought in a rabbit someone had given him at work. They'd cooked it with onions, garlic, and a little white wine. There hadn't been much meat on the bones, but it had tasted good—and it was a free meal.

After finishing his supper, Sebastian walked over to the radio, lifted the cat, and placed him on the floor. The cat, which was more of a mouser than a pet, slept on top of the radio, as it was the warmest place in the house. He attempted to tune the radio, trying to find the French station; sometimes he could get it if the weather was clear. Sebastian listened to the news announcer.

"*Ici* Radio France. Here is the news. Although General Eisenhower has declared that defeat of Communist aggression in Southeast Asia is vitally important to the United States, he declines to deploy US airpower to relieve the siege. Eisenhower has likened the situation to a domino game. When you have a row of dominoes set up, if you knock over the first one, then they all go over very quickly. The eight-week siege of Dien Bien Phu has ended with the surrender of the garrison." The Radio France station faded, and the ring of the doorbell broke his concentration.

He listened to Amelia as she answered the door. He heard a familiar voice—Helen, Amelia's meddling, well-meaning sister, had come to visit. He found the visit odd, as it was seven thirty, and he wondered what was going on. Amelia came through the kitchen door with Helen close on her heels.

"Hello, Helen. Is everything well?" Sebastian asked.

"Yes, Sebastian. I was passing and thought I would drop in and visit."

"It's nice to see you, Helen. I'll pop the kettle on," said Amelia, "and make some tea."

Helen sat down. She seemed uncomfortable, and Sebastian noticed. She fiddled with the handle of her handbag and fidgeted in her seat.

"Are you sure everything is okay, Helen?" he inquired.

"Yes." Helen cast her eyes downward. Amelia came back with the tea and some homemade cake, and as they drank their tea, Amelia dropped the news.

"I have something to tell you, Sebastian. I am pregnant," she said. As the news came out of her quivering lips, the words were feeble, but they hit the silence in the room like a thunderclap. There was a stillness, and then Sebastian leaped from his chair toward Amelia. He could feel his face flushing and his eyes flashing. He was sure he would explode. Sebastian thrust his face close to Amelia, and she backed away, putting her head down. Taking her chin into his hands so that she was forced to look into his eyes, he spat his words out, overcome by his inability to handle this news of yet one more mouth to feed. His fear and concern manifested themselves in the worst possible way—rage.

"I have just been told there is no more work until further notice. No more orders—that means no money. You need to get rid of this little bastard."

He could see Amelia was horrified and shocked. Helen jumped out of the chair to say something.

"Shut up and sit down, you stupid, interfering woman. This has nothing to do with you. What are you doing here?"

Helen obeyed, and Amelia started weeping.

"Save the tears for the four children you have upstairs that are going to starve if things don't change." He stormed out of the house, slamming the back kitchen door so hard that it shattered the little scullery window into a million pieces across the floor.

Helen went immediately to Amelia and put her arms around her.

"What are we to do?" Amelia sobbed.

"Don't cry, Amelia; we'll think of something." Abortion was out of the question—Helen knew it. They sat quietly together. Then Helen said, "Maybe if this baby is a little girl, Charles and I could adopt her."

Amelia stared at Helen with a look of disbelief. "I don't know, Helen. That's rather drastic."

"It's a wonderful idea; you won't have to worry. Sebastian would be relieved, and I would get the little girl I have always wanted."

"Well, if you think so, Helen. I'm too exhausted." Amelia put her head in her hands and wept some more.

Seven months later, in the maternity ward, on a warm spring evening in April, Helen held the baby Amelia had given birth to two days earlier, a little girl.

"Oh, look at her, Charles; she is a precious angel."

"Yes, she is that, Helen. I suggest you give her back to Amelia, as I must talk to you."

"What is it, Charles?" Helen asked, feeling irritated.

"Come sit down here."

"What for?"

"Sit down," Charles commanded. Helen did as she was told, as Charles was rarely this formidable.

"You know, Helen, I was never happy with that plan the three of you hatched of us adopting Amelia's baby if it was a girl. Right from the onset, I did not agree."

"I know that, Charles, but I thought—"

"Don't interrupt me, Helen. You thought wrong. I forbid you to go ahead with this half-crazed scheme of yours. It will never, ever work, Helen," Charles said, "and I will not support you through this. The child will grow up always being drawn back to the home and mother you are snatching her from. You cannot fight nature; it's doomed from the start, Helen."

Helen was devastated. She jumped up and attacked Charles, beating him on the chest with her fists.

"No, she is mine—she is mine, and I want her! You bastard, don't you dare stop this!"

Charles took her wrists in his hands to calm her. "This baby girl is not yours to want. She is your sister's baby, and moving heaven and earth is never, ever going to change that." Charles was adamant and refused to go along with the plan.

Amelia took her baby girl home. They named her Abigail. Helen spent many hours at the house, helping Amelia as much as she could in order to be as close to baby Abby as possible. She still thought of Abby as her baby.

—5—

It was wash day—a Monday in the summer of July 1955—and the old black pot was boiling in the backyard. Amelia was dipping all of the family's white clothes into it with big tongs. When the clothes were gleaming and spotless, she dropped them into her cold starch pot, rang them out with her old hand wringer, and displayed one long line of brilliant, starched, clean white clothes for all the world to see. They looked like farewell flags blowing in the early morning sunlight. Doing the laundry was an enormous task. She started at six o'clock in the morning and did not finish until the sun went down. She was fortunate that it was a warm summer day.

The children were still sleeping; she wanted to get as much done as she could before they got up. She could hear Sebastian moving around. He was in the scullery, shaving over the kitchen sink, as the one bathroom in the house was saved for the paying lodgers, while the family used the outside toilet and the kitchen sink. They all bathed in a large tin bath in front of the fire on Friday nights.

As Amelia was pegging the clothes on the washing line, she felt nauseated and dizzy. She leaned up against the wall to stop herself from falling over. She wondered what was going on and thought maybe she was hungry. She decided to go into the house to make herself some tea and toast. As she went inside, Sebastian was coming out of the kitchen.

"I see you were up early. Wash day, is it?" said Sebastian. "It's a good day for it."

"Yes," said Amelia.

"I won't be home till later this evening—a little overtime coming my way," Sebastian told her.

"Really?" Amelia asked. "That's very good, as we could use the money."

He did not kiss her. There was a distance between them, and they were growing further apart. It seemed to her that they were just going through the motions. Amelia turned away, thinking there was no evidence of the overtime—no money for extras.

"Good-bye," he said. Amelia watched Sebastian walking away along the backyard, away from her—that was all he seemed to be doing these days.

She put the kettle on and placed some bread under the grill. She started a big pot of porridge for the children. Andre came downstairs first, dressed, with his hair stuck down to his head with Brylcreem. Abby was toddling around behind him.

"Ray? Ray?" She couldn't say the name Andre, but she followed him everywhere.

Andre picked her up and put her in her highchair. He looked after her as if she were his own; he'd taught her to walk and talk. He enjoyed her. Leah, Eugene, and Camille came downstairs also.

"Can I have the cream off the top of the milk, Mam?" yelled Eugene.

"No, you can't. Share it."

"Ah, I don't want to," he said, groaning.

They all had breakfast, and the four oldest children went off to school, where they stayed all day and had a cooked lunch. It was provided, which was a blessing, as jam and bread fed them at teatime. Amelia waved them all off at the door, holding Abby in her arms. She went back out to the backyard and put Abby down. As she went to finish the washing, Amelia stepped on the back stair and passed out.

When she awoke on the concrete yard, she opened her eyes and could hear a baby crying as though it were in a tunnel. She sat up. Abby was sitting beside her, stroking her face and crying, "Mama!" As soon as Amelia sat up, Abby crawled into her lap. She held Abby close to her and started to count the weeks back in her head. Then it struck her: *Oh my God, no. I'm three weeks late.*

"Pregnant?" Sebastian screamed at Amelia. He looked horror-struck. "So much for your goddamn Roman Catholic contraceptive rhythm method. It's got you pregnant six times. I just hang my pants on the chair and you're pregnant, and of course, abortion is not even an option. It's just a dirty word to you. Just what do you suggest we do—fill the house with little Catholic babies? Where can we put them? How will we actually feed them?" He screamed the words in frustration and fear at Amelia. She kept her head down.

"I don't know," she whispered. "I feel so sick with this one. It isn't like the others. Day and night, I'm vomiting, and I've passed out four times. I'm only four weeks, and none of my clothes fit. I think it's a very large baby." She looked up at Sebastian, and he could see her pleading eyes. "Please, please, don't yell at me, Sebastian. I can't bear it. I did not do this alone, you know."

Sebastian sat down and put his head in his hands, exhausted. "Ah, oui, *vrai*, you are right," he said. "I suppose somehow we will find ways to manage—we have so far."

"How?" Amelia asked.

"I could look for more work—that's one thing. We could put the four older children together in one room and bring Abby's cot into our room. That would free up another room for us to rent. That would bring us five pounds a month. It will be a struggle, because you won't consider the alternatives."

"We have managed before. We will manage again."

"Go and see the doctor. Find out when this one is due and why you are so sick."

Amelia breathed a huge sigh of relief. Sebastian could see her offering a whispered pray to Mother Mary.

One week later Amelia sat in the doctor's waiting room with several other people—some coughing and sneezing, some with sore legs, and little children crying. The hard plastic chairs were uncomfortable, and it was hot and stuffy in the little room. She looked at a hole in the wall where the plaster had fallen away and hadn't been fixed yet; it was a dull, ugly room. She was the next one in line to see the doctor, and hopefully he would have the results from the tests she had done, including blood work and X-rays.

The nurse broke into her thoughts. "Mrs. Lavalle, the doctor will see you now."

Amelia went into the doctor's surgery, which was not much bigger than the waiting room and didn't look much better either. However, she liked Dr. O'Malley. He was a nice Irish Catholic doctor, and he had been their doctor for ten years or so. He was a kind man and good with the children. The doctor came into the room, looking at her over his round horn-rimmed spectacles.

"Well, hello, Amelia. How are you feeling today?" Looking at his notes, he continued. "Are you still feeling as nauseated?"

"Yes, I am. In fact, I've never felt like this with any of the other five," she replied. "Do you think there is something wrong, Doctor?"

He smiled at her. "No, not at all, Amelia. All the tests are back, and all is as it should be. You are indeed pregnant, approximately eight weeks."

"Why do I feel so ill? Is the baby all right?"

"Yes, it would seem everything is very good. In fact, the reason you are feeling the way you have been—you are carrying more than one baby, Amelia."

She looked at the doctor, feeling dumbfounded.

"Oh my God," she whispered. "Twins?"

"No," the doctor said, smiling. "Not twins. You are expecting triplets."

Amelia had known she did not want to hear the doctor's

news today, but she had never dreamed it would be what he had just announced.

"Oh my God, what am I to do? How will I ever tell Sebastian? We will never manage. We cannot cope now. He was out of his mind when I told him about this. He thought six babies was enough—but eight!'" She was close to hysteria.

The doctor called in his nurse. "Make some tea—hot, sweet, and fast."

Dr. O'Malley tried to calm her. "There, there. I know this is a shock, but you will manage. We will find ways to help you."

The nurse came back with the tea and gave it to Amelia. "Sip it. Sip it slowly," she said.

Dr. O'Malley said, "The first thing you must do, Amelia, is look after yourself. You are carrying three babies now, and you need rest and nourishment and certainly no stress."

"How can I do that with five children at home all under the age of ten?" she wailed.

"Amelia, you go home and share this news with Sebastian. He must know as soon as possible. You both need to work out some way to find help with the children, as I will be admitting you into the hospital when you are five months. You cannot carry these babies to full term at home and be the sole caregiver to five children."

Amelia held onto the teacup as if it were giving her some secret strength.

"Do you understand what I am saying to you, Amelia?"

She nodded, placing the cup and saucer on the desk and drying her eyes with her handkerchief. "Thank you, Doctor."

"I want to see you in a week, Amelia, and we will make arrangements for you. Now, go talk to Sebastian."

Amelia stood up and immediately passed out on the doctor's floor.

Sebastian and Amelia stood outside the dark, gloomy-looking building—Pickering House. It was the sixth foster home they had looked at in two weeks. She hated it on sight—it was a large Victorian Gothic building like something out of a Dickens novel. The last five had been even worse from the outside. This one looked the best. A small lady opened the door. Inside, it was damp and cold, even though it was August and warm outside. There was a strong smell of damp moss, seaweed, and dead mice. It made Amelia gag.

"This is it," said Sebastian under his breath. "We really have no choice left—it's the last one."

As they walked around together, Amelia felt like crying. The matron had short hair, looked rather masculine, and did not give out much warmth or maternal feeling. They followed her up a winding staircase that creaked as they stepped. She opened a door halfway along the hallway. They looked into a large room with two beds and a cot.

"They will sleep in here. One room—two girls in one bed, two boys in the other, and the little one can sleep in the cot. It will save you quite a bit of money, and the four older ones are in school all day. Just the two-year-old to watch."

"And what will you do with Abby?" Amelia asked.

"Nothing. She will play outside like all the others who don't go to school. Do you want this service or not, Mrs. Lavalle?"

Sebastian spoke up. "We will take it. Thank you very much."

Three months later Sebastian and Amelia, with all five children, arrived at Pickering House.

The matron opened the door. "Come in, and follow me." She looked at Sebastian and Amelia. "I strongly suggest you leave now. We don't want them howling and disturbing the others. I'll give you a minute."

"Mam, do we have to stay here?" asked Leah.

"Yes, you do, for a short time."

"It stinks," Eugene said. "Like poop." He held his nose.

"Behave yourself." Sebastian smacked Eugene on the ear gently.

Andre was holding Abby in his arms. "Don't worry, Mam. We will be fine—really. We will come and visit you on the bus when we can."

Amelia started to cry; she could not help herself. Sebastian turned away. Amelia hugged her children one at a time. "Behave yourselves—all of you!"

Abby squirmed in Andre's arms. "Mam, Mam," she said, reaching out her arms to her mother.

"Go, Mam," Andre said. "I'll look after her."

Sebastian rushed Amelia out the door, and the last sounds in her ears were her Abby's cries and screams.

Several weeks later Andre stood at his mother's bedside, shifting from one foot to the other and running his hands through his thick, wavy black hair. Amelia could tell he was embarrassed as his eyes scanned the mothers feeding their little ones, looking at their breasts as their babies suckled.

"I can't stay long, Mam. I left Abby down in the courtyard. They won't let her in—you know, 'cause she's so little. She's misses you and cries a lot. Do you think you can open the window and wave, maybe shout hullo? The other kids are at the door, waiting to wave to you. I'll go ask the matron."

Amelia watched her eldest boy as he politely asked the matron—the nurse with the biggest hat, as he called her.

"Please may I open the window and help my mam say hello to my little sister Abby down in the courtyard? She misses my mam a lot."

The matron looked at him and seemed to ponder his request for a while. "Yes, I will allow that, young man. But do be careful, and only for a few minutes, Mrs. Lavalle. Your other children can wait in the hallway outside the ward, and I will allow you to wave from the doorway only. I shall inform them that you will be along presently, young man."

The nurse, in her big starched hat, walked stiffly and efficiently and showed Eugene, Leah, and Camille the door.

Amelia looked down into the courtyard through the window and shouted, "Are you being a good girl?" She could see Abby nodding using her whole body. As Amelia watched her in her blue coat, she thought she looked like a little soldier desperately trying to communicate. Amelia thought Abby must have felt as if she were a thousand miles away from her mother.

Abby frantically waved both of her hands. "Are you coming home soon, Mammy?"

Amelia heard her trying to make her tiny voice clear. If Amelia had heard one more word, she might have wailed like a banshee. She'd been cooped up in this ward for the past five weeks and was not leaving, apparently, until she delivered her three babies. Amelia looked down at Abby waving up at her. Amelia waved back with both hands.

"You be a good girl. Do you hear me?" She closed the window, and she could still hear Abby's faint voice say, "Bye-bye, Mam." She gently kissed Andre and watched him walk away. It seemed to her he carried the weight of the world on his back. The rest of her children stood at the entrance, waving good-bye. Amelia felt as though someone had sewn five separate stitches into five different parts of her heart—each stitch knotted to a long thread and each thread attached to one of her children. Every now and then, she would feel the knot pull in her heart—sometimes one, sometimes two, and sometimes even three. The ache would radiate through her body until she felt only the knots. Today all the stitches were pulling in every conceivable direction. The wrenching was so great that Amelia put both hands over her mouth to stifle her cries until Andre had left the ward and was well out of earshot. Amelia let out a sob.

So melancholy was the sound that some of the other mothers went to her to try to console her. How she longed to open her arms, gather up her children, and hold them close to her, just like the three who were growing inside of her now. At least they were safe for the time being.

Not knowing what else to do, Amelia moved her lips in prayer. "Mother Mary, bless this day ..."

—6—

"Give one more push, Mrs. Lavalle."

Amelia did not have much left in her to give.

"I can't!" she said.

"You must. One more—come on," said the doctor.

With everything and anything left in her, Amelia let out one last cry and gave one last enormous push with all her might. She felt the last of her three babies slip away from her and heard it struggling to take its first breath.

"Good work, Mrs. Lavalle—another boy. Congratulations! Triplet boys, all healthy and very good weights. That does not happen very often here, let me tell you."

Amelia lay on her pillow with her eyes closed, thinking that she had pushed each baby out of her body with just gas and air along with her strength and faith. Later that morning she sat up in bed, drinking her comfort tea and praying to thank Mother Mary for the safe delivery of her three healthy baby boys.

Sebastian was dreaming of France. In his dream, way up in the mountains, he could hear church bells ringing in the distance. Slowly, he woke to the sound of the front doorbell ringing; he had overslept.

"*Merde*!" He jumped out of bed, dressed himself quickly, ran to the door, and opened it. His sister-in-law, Helen, stood on the front step.

"I have been ringing this bell forever! Don't you ever answer your phone? We have been trying all night."

"I am sorry, Helen. I overslept. I have been working many hours and—"

"Never mind that," Helen interrupted, pushing him into the vestibule. "Let me in."

Sebastian did as he was bid. He stood in the hallway.

"Both the hospital and I have been phoning you all morning."

Sebastian turned around. "Is Amelia all right?"

"Is she all right? You mean, has she successfully given birth? Yes," Helen retorted.

Sebastian was frozen to the spot.

"In the early hours of this morning. Three boys—strong, healthy boys."

Sebastian did not know what to do—fall onto his knees and thank God or cry. He was overflowing with mixed emotions.

Helen pushed at him again. "Come on. You look like you could use some hot, sweet tea."

Sebastian followed her into the kitchen. *I need a whole lot more than that,* he thought. Sebastian drank some of his tea and then stood up. "I must go, Helen, and see Amelia."

"Not this morning—they won't allow it. They are pretty strict on visiting times in the maternity ward. Maybe later. Six to eight thirty is the visiting time."

"But I want to see Amelia."

"Never mind Amelia. Have you been to see your other children lately?"

Sebastian hung his head in shame. "No, I have not. I tried several times, but it always ended up with them crying at the door, wanting me to bring them home, especially the little one."

"Do you mean Abby?" Helen snipped. "Well, I was there last Sunday, and they are all sick with that dreadful influenza that's going around. All five of them locked down in that disgusting, dingy room. When I went in, Abby was lying in her cot, covered in shite from her nappy. Burning fever, all of them. I really played war with the staff—gave them a piece of my mind. They told me the doctor told them to keep them quarantined. 'Is that what you call it?' I asked them. 'It looks more like cruelty to me.' I had them bathed to cool down, had them put in clean pajamas, and had all the beds stripped with clean sheets on them. And also lots of water, orange juice, Lucozade, and biscuits. It was absolutely disgusting, Sebastian!"

Sebastian felt numb; he could not stand much more of this.

"I told them in no uncertain terms," Helen continued, "that I would be back often and would not tell them when I am coming, so they should make sure that every one of those children is well taken care of, or I would report them to the authorities." She slammed her cup down hard on the table.

"Maybe I should go to them?" Sebastian said.

"No," said Helen. "They are quarantined; besides, you can't take the risk of taking that influenza to the new babies."

Sebastian stood up. "Helen, if you don't mind, I must get ready and go do something useful. Thanks for coming. I will show you out."

"Good enough." Helen looked shocked at being cut off.

Sebastian did not care; he needed some time to think, and he wanted to see his Amelia.

Ten days after giving birth to triplet boys, Amelia walked through the front door of her family home four months after leaving. She was carrying two of her boys, Sasha in one arm and Nathan in the other. Sebastian followed behind with Noah. Helen had arrived the day before to help.

"Welcome home, Amelia. Good to see you. And look at those beautiful bairns—what a miracle!" said Helen.

All three were fast asleep. Helen had lined the five children up to see their new brothers.

"Oh, Mam, can I hold one and give him a bottle?" Leah asked.

Amelia nodded. "Yes, Leah, you can. That would be a big help."

Abby jumped up and down like a jack-in-the-box. "Mammy, you're home! And you brought new babies. Can I play with them? Please?"

Amelia was beginning to feel overwhelmed. "Yes, Abby, you can when you are older. Right now, you must be very gentle with them. Do you understand?"

"Yes, Mammy. I'm glad you're home."

Camille asked, "How come when my friend at school

asked for a new brother, her mam told her no because they can't afford one, and you come home with three of them? Why don't we give one of ours to my friend, Mam?"

Amelia smiled faintly, and Sebastian interrupted. "That's not how it works."

Eugene spoke up. "I've seen the babies. Can I go out and ride my bike now?"

Sebastian nodded.

Andre stepped forward. "Mam, give me Sasha. I will hold him." Andre lifted the baby gently from Amelia's arms into his own and held him close. Amelia had tears in her eyes. Sebastian noticed.

"Go out and play, children. Your mother looks tired and must lie down."

Amelia looked at her five children, longing to cuddle each one and tell them how happy she was to be home and to see them all again. Alas, she did not have the energy or strength to do so.

Helen was a godsend as far as Amelia was concerned. After the boys came home, Helen showed up regularly to help. Today they were preserving strawberry jam in the back kitchen.

As they were placing lids on the jars, Helen remarked, "I can't believe Abby's had her fourth birthday."

"And she's such a great help," Amelia added. "She's in the back room with them now, giving them their bottles."

"I don't know how you do it," Helen said.

"I have no choice. Day and night blend; weeks and months blend. I find it hard to believe they are five months old. I work twenty hours out of twenty-four, and when they sleep and the others are at school, I catch forty winks. It works. It seems the sacrifice is Sebastian and me—our life together is suffering."

"How?" asked Helen.

"He works all day—twelve-hour shifts. And I work all night. We hardly sleep together anymore, and when we do—well, you know, our backs are to each other. I feel really sad about it, but I just want to sleep."

"If it makes you feel any better, it's often what happens. Charles and I don't even share a bed now. I sleep in the other room because of his snoring."

Amelia laughed. "Now Sebastian has a part-time job three nights a week, teaching a French class to English adults—conversational. He seems to love it. I hear him singing on the nights he is going out to teach."

"Oh," Helen remarked.

"I am pleased for him; I am pleased for all of us. The extra money comes in handy, and now we are renting the back room. It makes a big difference. I must go check on Abby and the boys."

Abby helped her mammy every day with her new brothers. She could feed them all by herself now that they were five months old. Mam propped the three babies up in the cot and put the bottles in their mouths, with a nappy under each bottle, holding them up. Abby's job was to see that the babies drank all the milk and then to burp them. Amelia had given her an orange crate to stand on so that she could reach in and help her little brothers by patting and rubbing their backs. Abby was singing to them:

> Dance ti' thy daddy, sing ti' thy mammy,
> Dance ti' thy daddy, ti' thy mammy sing;
> Thou shall hev a fishy on a little dishy,
> Thou shall hev a fishy when the boat comes in.

"How are you getting along, Abby?"

Abby told her, "I love this job, Mammy. Look at Sasha—he is trying to sing with me. He loves it when I sing."

"How do you know that's Sasha? I still have to look at the ribbon sometimes to tell them apart," Amelia said.

"Oh, it's easy, Mammy; his eyes are like yours and Andre's, and he's always smiling at me. He kicks his arms and legs as well. Nathan is always trying to put both of his hands into his mouth, and he smiles a little bit."

Amelia laughed at Abby.

"And Noah is always asleep. Even when he's drinking his bottle, he keeps his eyes closed. Look. I like to pick Sasha up and hold him, 'cause he tries kissing my cheek. It feels tingly in my tummy. Daddy said that's called butterflies."

"Did he?" said Amelia. "Well, I would say you are a very good helper, Abby, and I am lucky to have you at home."

Abby jumped down from her crate, ran toward her mother, and hugged her as tightly as she could. "Don't go away again, Mammy. I don't like it when you are gone."

"No, Abby, I won't," she said, patting her on the head. "Let's get back to work; there's much to do."

It was a cold, bleak night in January 1957. The north winds howled around the house, and sleet lashed up against the windows. Amelia was in the kitchen. It was after ten o'clock, and she was baking bread. All the children were asleep in bed. The triplets had just had their first birthday, and Amelia had hardly noticed that first year slip past her. She did, however, notice Sebastian's absence. Most nights he was not home until well after ten. Amelia appreciated the time to catch up. Her time alone was when she achieved the most—ironing clothes, scrubbing the floors on her hands and knees, washing nappies, and making bread.

Amelia was so caught up in maintaining the well-being of her eight children and looking after the house that she thought little of where Sebastian was. She only cared that he showed up with the housekeeping money, looked after the lodgers, collected the rent, and did outside work around the house. That was the extent of their communication these days.

She was about to pull a loaf of bread out of the oven when Sebastian came through the back door.

"Bonjour," he said. "There is an enticing smell of baking bread making its way along the backyard. Is there some ready?"

Amelia placed the loaf on the countertop. "Yes. I will make tea for us and bring you a slice with butter and jam."

"*Tres bien,*" Sebastian said as he went into the kitchen.

Amelia came in with the bread and tea; Sebastian was rekindling the dying embers with a shovelful of coal. By the time Amelia served the tea, the fire was roaring, and there was warmth around the room.

As he sat in his chair, Sebastian sighed. "Ah, it's good to be home."

"How was your class tonight?"

"It was very good. I have a very diverse group of students. They are interesting and interested and want to learn the language. It excites me."

"Tell me about them," Amelia said.

"They are various ages, most of them quite young. I have a young man who is engaged to a French girl, and he wants to learn the language so he can communicate with her family when they visit France. Also, I have a group of young people wishing to embark on a six-month trip across Europe. A good grasp of the French language will be a good start. There is a twenty-year-old girl leaving for Paris to be a nanny to an American family. There is a young widow—she says she is looking for something interesting to do to fill the lonely void in her life since her husband died. She seems to be enjoying the challenge and hopes to go to the Riviera next year to try out her newfound language."

As Amelia listened to Sebastian, she noticed his tone change when he named the young widow. "How extraordinary!" she said.

"What is that?" he asked.

"The young widow—that she's actually looking for something to fill a void in her life, when I can hardly find a minute in the day to brush my hair. How different our lives are."

"I understand how busy you are, Amelia, and how little time you have for yourself. We have become distant, but we are managing financially surprisingly well, with me working my twelve-hour shifts in the factory, teaching French, and renting the back garage and the back room upstairs. We are collecting four pounds a month extra. I alone am working to support ten of us. It is the way things are and have to be right now."

Amelia stood up and took the dirty dishes back to the scullery. "I'm going to bed, Sebastian; I am absolutely exhausted."

Sebastian enjoyed working at the college and teaching his native language to the English students. He found it to be the most rewarding part of his life, and he counted the minutes to each class.

"Okay, ladies and gentlemen, for homework this week, I want you to review the days of the week, months of the year, and numbers to five hundred. And also time telling. We will have an oral test next week. Thank you for your attention, and *bonne nuit.*"

As the students were leaving, Sebastian started cleaning off his desk. The young widow, Sarah, approached him.

"I wonder, Monsieur Sebastian, if you would consider some private lessons after classes on Monday, Wednesday, and Friday nights? There is a small café outside of the college we could go to."

"I don't know, Sarah. We finish quite late here, and I—"

"I'm willing to pay you very well." Sarah smiled at him.

He was aware of her attractiveness. Sebastian sensed she was flirting.

"One pound per week, Monsieur Sebastian. And if we do three lessons a week, I will give you a bonus."

"We can try; we can start next week on Monday," he replied as he thought about what he could do with that extra money.

"That sounds very good to me, Monsieur Sebastian. I look forward to it."

The next week, when Sebastian came home from work, Amelia gave him his dinner. They hardly spoke to each other again.

"I will be late this week after teaching," he told her.

"Why is that?"

"I am teaching a private lesson to a student. One hour after class—if I do three hours, I will make almost two pounds. We cannot turn that down."

"That's a lot of money to fork out for French lessons. Who is it—the rich widow?" Amelia said with half a smile.

"*Oui*. In fact, yes, it is. We will be going to a café. I'm going to try it this week to see how it works out."

"Okay," Amelia said, and she left him alone to eat his dinner.

The private lessons worked well. Over several weeks, Sarah picked up the language quickly; however, the café changed its hours and started to close at eight. Sarah suggested they continue the lessons in her home, as it was only a ten-minute drive from the café.

"Well, I don't see why not," Sebastian replied.

The following Monday, Sebastian arrived at Sarah's house for the lesson.

"Come in," Sarah said. "Make yourself comfortable. Have a glass of wine."

"I don't mind if I do." Sebastian noticed it was Châteauneuf-du-Pape, which happened to be his favorite French wine. "Very nice. I have spent some very pleasant times in Avignon, Provence, in the south of France. A beautiful old-world city with wide, tree-lined boulevards; lazy, open cafés; and a magnificent view of the Palace of the Popes commanding its place over the walled city. And, of course, the famous Sur le Pont d'Avignon, the bridge."

"I look forward to seeing that one day," Sarah told him.

Sebastian relaxed into a chair and sipped the wine. Looking at Sarah, he observed that she was everything Amelia was not. She was present, and she had blonde hair, blue eyes that shined as if she had a secret behind them, perky little breasts, shapely hips, and long, slender, sexy legs. She was enticing at that moment. He put his glass down, thinking of his life and how at this moment, here with Sarah, his life felt sane for the first time in a long while. As they sipped wine and listened to Edith Piaf on the record player, Sebastian noticed the exquisite perfume Sarah was wearing.

Sarah smiled at him. "I love your accent, Sebastian; you sound like Maurice Chevalier. You know, the sexy singer—'Thank Heaven for Little Girls.' I am not going to ask you about your life, Sebastian; I don't wish to know. You are here with me now. I have been widowed for two years, and I nursed my husband for eighteen months before he died. I suffered the pain and sorrow that is part of losing a loved one slowly. I need you, Sebastian; you make me want to feel beautiful once more—something I thought I had lost forever. I feel like a desirable woman instead of a sad shadow of my former self. Would you like more wine?"

"Non, thank you." Sebastian put his glass down and moved closer to Sarah. Edith stopped singing. All Sebastian could hear was himself breathing and the beating of his heart against his ribs. He reached out and pulled Sarah into his arms, placing his lips softly on hers and kissing her with a deep, tender passion, closing his eyes to blot out the image of the lovely girl who'd stopped him from breathing so long ago.

Amelia looked at the clock on the kitchen wall; its white face and black Roman numerals seemed to scream, "Eleven fifteen—it's late!" Sebastian was still not home. He was teaching that night, and he had his private tutoring session after class. It was excellent money, and she was happy to have it; however, Sebastian was working long hours. The children were now all sleeping through the night, and that too was a blessing.

Amelia walked past the mirror that hung on the wall. She avoided looking into mirrors these days, as their reflection shocked her. Her face was thin and gaunt looking, and her deep-set brown eyes looked like dark holes in her face, with black circles underneath them. Her teeth were loose and decaying, and her once-beautiful cascading, wavy curls were limp, wispy, and thinning. Amelia sat down in her chair and sighed as she sipped her comfort tea and cried at the sight of herself.

I must do something, she thought. *I will call Helen tomorrow and ask her to help me.*

At eleven thirty Sebastian opened the scullery door and entered. Amelia jumped.

"Oh, you are home. I've been worried—you are late. You must be exhausted. Where have you been?"

"Amelia, I am going to bed; it has been a long day." Sebastian did not look at her and kept walking. As always, Amelia was looking at his back.

"Can't you even stop and look at me, Sebastian?"

He stopped at the kitchen door for one moment and dropped his head but did not turn to look. "I am going to bed. Good night," he said, and he was gone.

Two days later, Helen showed up with her large carpetbag.

"I am so glad you called me; I was planning on coming over to see you this week. Are the bairns napping?"

"Yes," Amelia replied.

"Then we can get to work!" Helen placed her bag on the table. Amelia was in awe. "Did you do as I asked you and wash your hair?"

"Yes, I did."

Helen placed a comb, a plastic cape, a pair of scissors, almond oil, mascara, lipstick, blush, baking soda, and a toothbrush on the table and pulled out a new dress from her bag. "I managed to run this up for you."

Helen went to work snipping, shaping, clipping, and styling, pushing Amelia's hair about until everything was where she wanted it to be.

"You are so clever," Amelia said.

"You've been neglecting yourself for far too long," said Helen. "You look like an old woman these days. Can't let yourself go like that." Helen finished with the scissors and massaged the almond oil into Amelia's head. "Now, here—take some of this; rub it into your hands, face, and neck; wrap a towel around your head; and leave it for a while. Go use that toothbrush with some baking soda—see if you can brighten up your teeth a little. I'm going to put the kettle on and make some tea. I brought some cake for us to have. What time does Sebastian get home?"

"About six o'clock," Amelia replied.

"I have decided that I am going to stay here and look after those bairns with Andre and Leah's help; I'm sure we'll manage. You are well overdue a night out—just a couple of hours. Go for a drink to the pub, and walk home, and have some fish and chips. I know you can't afford it, so I will give you some money. There!" Helen pushed a pound note into Amelia's hand. "That should cover your expenses. It's time for you to get out of here, Amelia."

"I realized that last night when I looked in the mirror—it frightened me. I looked so old!"

"We will see how we do tonight, and if it works, I can do it again sometime. Now, let's wash that oil off your head."

Thirty minutes later, Amelia was looking at her reflection. Her hair was short and shiny, with soft curls framing her face and curls on the nape of her neck. Her skin looked brighter and her teeth whiter. Her eyelashes were longer, and her cheeks were pink, with the help of the mascara and blush. The dress was periwinkle blue with a white belt and a collar to match.

"Turn around for me," Helen said. "Well, if I say so meself, you look smashing, Amelia!" The babies were just waking up, and the children were coming home from school—all were hungry.

"Mammy, you look like a princess!" said Abby.

Andre's eyes were wide. "You look so nice, Mam."

"Did Auntie Helen do that for you?" Leah asked.

"Yes, she did, and I'm going out with your father tonight. Auntie Helen will stay with you and babysit, and I want you to help her like you help me—do you hear me?"

"Yes," Leah and Andre answered together.

"And the rest of you, behave yourselves, or woe betide you if I hear differently."

"We'll be good for Auntie Helen. You go out with Dad and have a nice time, Mammy," Abby told her.

Sebastian came home a little earlier that evening.

"What have you done, Amelia?" he asked her.

Amelia half smiled. "Helen did it—do you like it?"

"It's fabulous. You look lovely, Amelia."

"Helen's going to babysit, Sebastian; she gave me a pound so we can go out to the pub and have a drink, buy fish and chips, and eat them on the way home."

"How nice, Helen. Thanks," Sebastian said. "I'll wash up and put on a clean shirt."

Amelia hugged Helen and looked at herself one more time approvingly before she and Sebastian left.

Sebastian was concerned; he thought Helen and Amelia might suspect what was going on. He was unnerved by Helen's gesture of kindness.

"Are you enjoying your drink?" Amelia asked.

"Ah, yes, it's a long time since we were out on date together, non?"

Amelia giggled. "It feels like a date, doesn't it? I felt better in those days. The boys are so grown up now, toddling around all over the place. Nathan got into the coal shuttle yesterday, covered himself with coal dust, and ran to me screaming and frightened, all covered in black."

Sebastian laughed.

"Maybe when the weather improves, we can take them all out on a picnic to King Eddy's Bay on the train," she suggested.

"*Oui*, that would be nice." Sebastian fell silent.

"Would you like to get some fish and chips?"

"Let's do that," he said. Walking home, they shared their fish and chips, with Sebastian holding them wrapped in newspaper. They were hot, fresh, and crispy.

"This is fun—reminds me of one of our first dates," Amelia said. "Let's try and do this more often, Sebastian."

"Absolutely," he agreed as they arrived home.

"The bairns were good as gold," said Helen. "Fell fast asleep in their beds. Let me know, and I will do this again for you."

Amelia hugged Helen tightly. "Thank you for everything you did for me today. Good night, Helen."

"Thank you for your help," Sebastian added.

Amelia and Sebastian stood at the door and waved Helen out. They went to their bedroom and looked at their four youngest children, who were sleeping soundly. Amelia went over to the bed, took off her new dress and her undergarments, and slipped in between the sheets.

"Come to bed, Sebastian," she whispered. For one shining moment, he could see a hint of the old Amelia, though distantly. Moving toward the bed gently so as not to disturb the sleeping babies, he threw his pants on the back of the chair.

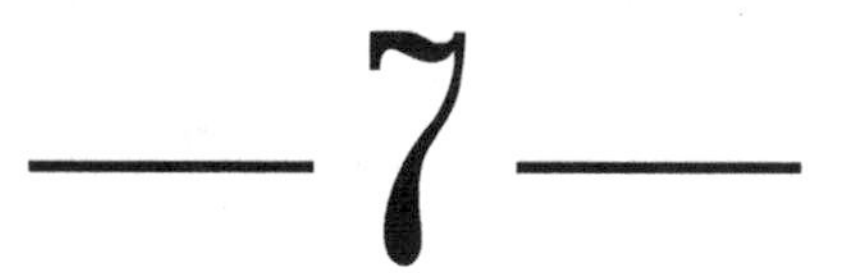

7

"Get rid of it!" Sebastian screamed at Amelia a month later when she announced that she was pregnant.

"I will not!" Amelia yelled back at him. "It's a human life! You are asking me to commit murder, and I won't!" She had thought of gin and a hot bath, but her conscience would never allow her.

"This is the last straw; our marriage is fragile enough with all those responsibilities. It's impossible to find the time—"

"I understand, Sebastian, but I'm pregnant, and it's ours. How can you think of killing it?"

"Because we can't manage another mouth to feed. When does it end, Amelia?"

Amelia attempted to reach out to Sebastian. "We will manage—don't worry. We always do."

Sebastian charged past her toward the back door. "Not this time," he said, slamming the door behind him as he left.

Amelia and Sebastian grew further apart and barely spoke to one another. They just moved around, trying to survive, with Sebastian working day and night and Amelia cooking and cleaning. Sebastian had rented the back room to a young lad from Scotland, Tom, who was doing a plumbing apprenticeship and courting a lass called Maggie. Amelia was delighted to have the back room rented, and Tom and Maggie were a nice couple. Amelia was folding clothes one day when there was a knock on the kitchen door.

"Come in."

Maggie entered. She was tall and had long brown hair and a friendly face. "Hello, Amelia. How are you doing today?"

"I'm draggin' my feet a bit today, pet."

"I came down to ask if Tom and I could take the young ones to the seaside today," Maggie said.

Amelia was thrilled. "Oh yes, they would love it. Thank you. You and Tom have just been a godsend to me."

"We thought it would give you a rest, and we love taking them out."

"Hold on, and I'll pack a picnic."

"No," Maggie said. "Don't bother; we'll feed them. Little Sally is outside with them. We can take her along too. She's a lovely little girl, such a pretty little thing."

"Did Abby ask you to bring her along?" Amelia asked.

"Yes, she did."

Amelia smiled. "They are good friends, really fond of one another. Sally is an only child—and also a lonely child, I think. She lives in the house over the road with a multitude of doting Italians—all adults. They run the ice cream parlor and the vans. Sally runs over to us whenever she can to play. She's like one of my own."

"When I left, she and Abby were playing with the buttercups in the garden, holding them underneath the boys' chins to see who likes butter," Maggie said, and Amelia and Maggie laughed.

"We'll be off then," Maggie said.

"Come home at teatime. I'll have a high tea ready. I can't thank you enough. Have a wonderful time."

Amelia prepared high tea with egg and tomato sandwiches made with fresh homemade bread, fluffy Madeira cake, fruitcake, and jam tarts, and she suspected Sally would be bringing in ice cream. She was sipping her comfort tea, enjoying her quiet time. The baby started kicking; Amelia smiled.

"You are an active one," she said, placing her hand on top of her large belly. "What are you getting up to in there? I wonder if you are a little boy or girl—I suspect a boy, the way you are kicking, and I think maybe a football player." Amelia kissed the palm of her hand and laid it on top of her unborn child. "See you soon, little one," she whispered.

"That looks good," Sebastian said, looking at the table full of food as he came in through the door. "It won't look like that for too long. Are Tom and Maggie staying?"

"Yes, they are—and Sally," Amelia replied.

"As if we don't have enough of our own kids to take care of. You are a glutton for punishment," he said.

"She's no bother to me. Will you be staying for tea, Sebastian?" Amelia waited for the usual no.

"Non, I will eat mine and go, as always." He was probably thinking of the next thing he had to do—Amelia understood that. They had not had a night out together alone since their pub night seven and a half months ago. They slept in the same bed; however, they never touched one another. Sebastian sat down for a moment, picked up a sandwich, and bit into it.

He asked Amelia, "This one's due soon, isn't it?"

Amelia looked at him. "I'm very surprised to hear you even ask; it's the most you have discussed with me in the past seven and a half months—the first real interest you've shown in this child. It's felt for me like an immaculate conception."

Sebastian appeared to ignore her comment.

"I may need to go to France for a few days," Sebastian said. "My uncle Philippe, who lives in Marseille, is rather sick and needs a little help getting his house in order. He has requested that I go over and help him. I thought if I left on a Friday evening after work, I could be back by Sunday evening and not miss work."

"When do you plan on making this trip?" she asked.

"Around the end of the month—as soon as I can arrange it and before this one arrives." His eyes went to her growing stomach.

"Do what you must," Amelia told him. "We'll be fine. I have all the children to help—and Tom and Maggie and, of course, Helen and Charles. Besides, I have six weeks to go."

Sebastian popped a jam tart into his mouth as he stood up. He swallowed it and then licked his fingers. As he walked away with Amelia looking at his back, he said, "I will let you know when I have made the arrangements," and he left her alone.

Sebastian arrived at Sarah's home with wine and flowers. She was cooking for him that night, and together they were going to plan a weekend in Provence, France. Sarah opened the door; she looked gorgeous. She took the wine and flowers and put them in the kitchen. Sebastian followed her, taking her into his arms and kissing her deeply. After a sumptuous meal, it appeared to Sebastian that Sarah was moving things along, and she escorted him to the bedroom. He always felt hesitant before they went to bed, yet when Sarah aroused him, there was no stopping.

With shimmering skin and hearts pumping, their tongues and lips touched. Their body fluids blended, yet their souls did not. Hands reached out, breasts leaning against strong golden chests as each body worked, moving desperately yet passing over one another and not truly connecting. Sebastian knew he was working separately to attain and reach a satisfying climax, and he did so, as did Sarah. They seemed to move not as one but as two separate souls, reaching deep into the other to retrieve what each one needed and wanted to maintain its own desires. In his mind, he knew they were making love without love. It felt like motion without poetry—both holding something back, guarding it inside themselves for different reasons.

After they made love, Sarah brought Sebastian a glass of red wine.

"You know, Sebastian, I feel the need to protect myself, for I understand you are saving yourself for one very special woman, and I realize it is not me. It seems to me you carry your isolation very deep, where you think no one else can see. As I look at your handsome face, it makes me sad because I know this will not last. I really want this trip to France, and I am looking forward to it. But you know, for both of us, I almost feel I would like to hold it off a little while long longer because I really believe the trip will be the beginning of the end of this relationship."

Sebastian did not respond. He knew Sarah was right; this could not continue. He intended to enjoy the trip to France and not think about anyone or anything else.

Four weeks later, it was a Friday night with heavy gray skies and pouring rain. It was suppertime. Sebastian rushed in through the scullery door, saturated and in a feverish hurry.

Two of the triplets, Nathan and Sasha, were standing at the door, holding an old Matchbox car with all the paint chipped off. "Look, Dada," they said, proudly showing their father their little toy.

Sebastian put down his bag, took off his coat, and shook off the rain. He took the car. "*Tres bien, tres bien,*" he said.

"Hello, Dad," Abby said.

"Hello, Abby. Where is your mother?"

"She's in her chair with her feet up. Her feet won't fit in her shoes. I'm playing with the boys so Mommy can rest, and Andre is helping Leah make some tea. We're having sausage, eggs, beans, and chips—my favorite, Daddy!"

"That's nice." Sebastian patted Abby on the head. "Now, take Sasha and Nathan out of my way. I'm in a big hurry. Tell your mother I'm home."

Abby took Sasha's and Nathan's hands as they left.

"Daddy is home," Abby told her mother.

Amelia looked at her children all playing around her. "Oh, is he?"

"He is getting washed and changed and leaving in fifteen minutes."

"'Yes," Amelia said, "I know." Amelia stood up slowly. She stretched herself, putting her hands into the crook of her back and massaging herself. She was so tired—only three weeks to go, and the next one would be here. *Thank God,* she thought.

"Hello, Amelia," Sebastian said.

"Hello, Sebastian," she replied. "You look—and smell—good."

"I don't have much time. How are you?"

"I'm okay," Amelia said wearily.

"Now, you know I will be back late Sunday, early Monday morning. You will manage?"

"Of course we will," said Amelia. "Helen and Charles are taking the children to the seaside on Sunday for the day, picnic and all. It's perfectly fine for you to go look after your uncle Philippe and give him the help he needs from you."

Sebastian dropped his gaze; he leaned over toward her and kissed her on the cheek.

"I'll see you then. Bye-bye, children. Be good for your mother." They all jumped up and ran around him, stopping him from getting out the door. He almost panicked. "Move," he said. "*Merde! Sacré bleu!* I will miss my train."

Amelia called the children; they all ran to her. Sebastian opened the door and was gone.

Amelia watched him walk away from her; as she did, she shivered, as she had a strange feeling of foreboding. Her lips moved as she offered her silent prayer: *Mother Mary, bless this day. Keep us safe.*

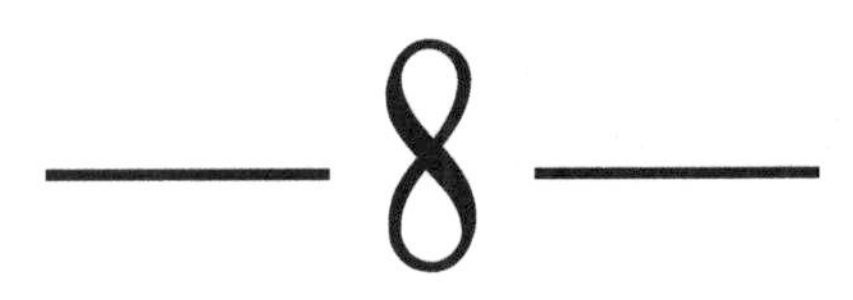

When Sebastian awakened it was still dark out, and the room felt cool with the early morning breeze. He lay still, savoring the sound of the ocean waves. He climbed out of the bed and moved quietly across the room so as not to disturb Sarah, who was still sleeping soundly. Sebastian stepped out onto the balcony of the apartment they had rented in the village of St. Pierre, looking over the medieval town. It was not clear; it was still dark, as if there were a veil in front of him. What a majestic moment—a full, bright, round silver moon hung in the star-filled sky, floating over the ocean, spilling its light upon the sea. The reflection created a silver pathway to an uncharted space, inviting one to follow it. It was a splendid sight—one did not often witness a full moon over the Mediterranean. Sebastian sat quietly and enjoyed the stillness.

As he looked to the east, he could see dawn peeping through the clouds. The soft, warm glow of pink, orange, and mauve was lovely, promising the greatness of a brand-new day. Looking back at the moon, Sebastian could see the first light filtering onto the ocean, giving a different look from the horizon. The colors were a myriad of different shades and were extraordinary—pewter, lavender, silver, pearly pale blue, soft pink, turquoise, and indigo, all blending like a prism. The sight was truly something to behold as the cool morning sun stretched and reached up toward the sky while the moon slowly, quietly slipped away.

The veil had lifted, and Sebastian saw the village clearly now as he looked across the red roofs of the old town, with its distinctive church and bell tower in the center like the medieval villages of the back country. The narrow cobblestone streets sloped steeply down toward the sea. He saw the quiet little town square beside the church and a wooden bench circling a beautiful, big tree.

Sebastian missed his homeland, especially Provence. How he longed to move back to his native France. He knew it was impossible, as it would not work for Amelia and his eight—soon-to-be nine—children. He felt life would be better for them all in France. Things could have been worse in England, but still, it was difficult. He had to act for the greater good of all. He was outnumbered.

He closed his eyes as though to block out that part of his life. This weekend was about his wants and needs, his desires and dreams. He smelled the aroma of croissants baking as the breeze floated past his nose. Sebastian felt his mouth watering.

He tiptoed through the bedroom, slipped on his clothes, and made his way to the street. Following the delicious smell, he walked to a bakery, passing shuttered windows with window boxes filled to the brim with flowers of every color showering him with the natural perfume of Provence as he passed them. The street was still sleeping, as it was Sunday morning. As he opened the door, a small bell rang in the back to announce his entrance. An older lady popped up from behind the counter.

"Bonjour, monsieur. *Ca va?*" she inquired.

"Oui, et vous?" Sebastian replied. *"Deux* croissants, *sil vous plait,* madame."

"Bonne." She wrapped them, and then he was on the street again, heading back with the warm croissants in his hand and the gentle heat of the sun on his back, looking forward to making café au lait and waking Sarah so that they could enjoy breakfast on the balcony and watch St. Pierre slowly awaken.

"I am astonished at the difference in you, Sebastian, from the moment you stepped on French soil. It is as if you shed a skin and another person emerged. You have been lighthearted, enthusiastic, and clearly proud of your homeland," Sarah said.

"Yes, I want to show you every corner of the Côte d'Azur."

Later, they walked along the beautiful Promenade des Anglais, which stretched along the sea front. They stopped at the magnificent Hotel Negresco for an expensive espresso before meandering through the old Nice, enjoying the boutiques, galleries, restaurants, and fascinating flower market.

"I feel quite at home here," Sarah said. "I loved last night—that quaint little restaurant on the harbour front. Tell me about that soup again, Sebastian."

"The soup de Poisson is the local specialty, almost a sacred ritual. There is the soup, toasted baguettes, grated gruyere cheese, and then the secret ingredient, roux, a pink-looking mayonnaise. You float the baguette on top of the consommé, then the cheese, and then the roux. It is heaven on earth!" Sebastian told her.

"I am besotted with France—the ambiance, the food, the French people, the wine, and, most of all, you."

That morning, they enjoyed breakfast on the balcony. Afterward, they went back to bed, where their lovemaking was feverish and exhilarating.

—9—

Helen and Charles arrived as promised that beautiful Sunday morning to take the Lavalle children on an outing to the seaside. There was so much noise in the kitchen that it sounded like a kindergarten. They were all excited. Amelia eventually got them all lined up, with the four older children holding the hands of the four younger children. Helen and Charles walked in front, carrying the famous carpetbag, which was filled to the brim with goodies for a picnic. Amelia waved them off with a sense of sadness, wishing she were leading in the front with Sebastian at the back. As she was about to close the door, Maggie arrived.

"Hello, Amelia. You are looking really tired," she said.

"I'm fine. The bairns have gone to the seaside for the day, and I am about to get on with some tasks. Sebastian is in France, visiting a sick uncle. This is a great time, and I'm going to take full advantage of it!"

"Do go easy, Amelia. You look like you have dropped a little, and the baby is lower than the last time I saw you."

"I think you might be right, Maggie."

"Can I help you today?" Maggie asked.

"No, thanks. You go see your young lad. I'm just fine." Amelia went into the backyard and started some of the dirty laundry to get a jump start on wash day. She went back to the scullery while it was soaking, and she baked bread, cakes, and meat pies. Satisfied with her efforts, she went back outside and hung the clothes on the line. It was a wonderful day for drying. She was full of energy and had accomplished Monday's work as well as Sunday's by three in the afternoon. She would now reward herself with a nice cup of tea and a piece of cake. She sat down to put her feet up and relax, as everyone was going to be out till at least six o'clock that night. They would all sleep well. Sebastian would be home late, and she would be glad to see him, although he wasn't around much. She wondered to herself if his trip had been a success and if he'd been able to help his uncle. Amelia knew Sebastian would revel in being in France, and she understood what he had given up for her all those years ago.

She closed her eyes to shut the thought out and reopened them to pick up her cake. She had left it in the scullery. Pushing herself up with both arms for support, she looked down in horror—her water had broken.

"Oh my God, you are too early—three weeks too early! I'm not prepared for this." Moving around the kitchen, holding on to chairs, she made her way to the bottom of the staircase and sat down on the bottom stair.

"Maggie! Maggie, can you help me? Are you up there?" she called.

"What is it? What's wrong—are you sick?" Maggie rushed down.

"My water's broken. Do you think you and Tom can get me to the hospital?"

"Of course we can."

Tom also came rushing down the stairs. "What's happening?" he asked.

Maggie replied in a high-pitched scream, "Amelia is having the baby! Tom, go get the ambulance. Be as fast as you can. Please hurry. Don't worry, Amelia; they will be here quickly."

As Tom ran through the kitchen, Maggie continued frantically, "Amelia, why don't we move you to a chair or something a bit more comfortable?"

"No, don't move me—don't touch me! I'm not standing up until the ambulance arrives."

"I wish it would hurry. Tom! Tom, where is the ambulance?"

"This one feels so different. I'm afraid to move." Amelia moaned.

"Don't panic, Amelia."

"Don't tell me not to panic—I've had eight of these!"

"Just try to breathe," Maggie said, trying to soothe her.

"Don't tell me to breathe. I am afraid that I am going to have this baby right here on this floor. Oh my God, where is the ambulance?"

"It's on its way," Tom said, coming from the kitchen. "It will be here in a few minutes."

"Try not to worry, Amelia. We will all work together and look after the bairns. We'll be just fine. I can stay the night," Maggie said.

"I'm sorry I screamed at you; I'm so scared. Bless you, Maggie; you are truly heaven-sent," Amelia told her as they heard the sirens of an ambulance approaching. Amelia was rushed off to the Princess Margaret Maternity Hospital. She relaxed a little as she was whisked off to the delivery room, as she knew she and the baby were in good hands.

"You are crowning, Mrs. Lavalle," said the midwife. "Breathe and push. There's gas and air to be taken when needed."

Amelia seemed to be pushing for a long time with no results. She was sweaty and exhausted and was starting to get concerned. Again, this delivery was different.

"What's going on?" Amelia asked the nurse. "I've done this several times before, and I can't feel the baby moving. It should be out by now; I've pushed and pushed. I know something is wrong. Why is this so difficult for me?"

"Don't worry, Mrs. Lavalle; we just think it's maybe stuck, and we need a bit of help. The doctor is going to come use the forceps."

"I've never had forceps!" Amelia screamed. "I don't want to be cut. I've had eight babies and always delivered them myself."

The doctor came into the room. "Now, now, Mrs. Lavalle. Let's get this head out. Try to relax. One more push now."

At long last, Amelia felt the head and the rest of the baby's body slip out.

"Is it a boy?" she whispered. She could hear the familiar slap, followed by a fraction of a second of silence. She did not hear the familiar crackle of the fluid and the air or the cry and rush of life into the baby's lungs—sounds that were music to a mother's ears every time. All she could hear was a dark, bleak, empty silence.

"Why is my baby not crying? Give him to me. Is it a boy? I want to see him and hold him."

"I'm sorry, Mrs. Lavalle," the nurse said. "We lost the heartbeat several minutes before he was delivered. I am afraid we've lost him—he's gone."

Amelia screamed, "What do you mean he's gone?"

The nurse dropped her eyes to the floor and shook her head slowly. "I'm sorry, Mrs. Lavalle."

"I don't believe you!" Amelia said. "It's not true." She looked up and could see the young nurse swiftly moving toward the door of the labor room with what looked like a small bundle of sheets and towels. With all the strength she could summon, she pulled herself up and demanded in a surprisingly strong voice, "Stop! Bring back my baby!"

The young nurse froze in the doorway and slowly turned around, looking at the woman on the bed with her arms open.

"Bring him to me now," Amelia said. "Please."

The young nurse did the unthinkable—she walked over to Amelia and placed the bundle in her arms. Amelia took the baby and slowly pulled away the sheets; they were like swaddling clothes. As they fell away, she could see him in his entirety.

"Look at him," she said to the nurse. "Every little part of him is perfect—his head, eyes, nose, ears, and lips. His hands, fingers, and fingernails. Legs, feet, toes, and toenails. He's like a sleeping angel."

Amelia looked at the nurse pleadingly. "What in God's name happened here? What happened to him?" She could not control her sobs.

"We're not exactly sure, Mrs. Lavalle. We think he asphyxiated on his way down the birth canal. You appeared to be very stretched from your previous deliveries. He was perfectly healthy, but the cord was tangled around his neck and stopped him from breathing. I am so sorry."

Amelia sobbed again and held her baby to her. Searching around, she picked up a small cup of cold tea that had been left on her bedside. She dipped her thumb into the liquid and started blessing the baby on his forehead, eyes, lips, and heart.

"I bless you and baptize you as Malachi, which means 'angel of God.' May Mother Mary take you to paradise in her arms, where you will be safe until we meet again my boy child, Malachi." Tears poured from Amelia's eyes; she clung to him and rocked him back and forth as though to bring him comfort. She stared at him, saturating her senses with every part of him and inscribing his image upon her soul. Amelia could not endure the agony and the ache inside her.

"I am sorry, Mrs. Lavalle. I have never seen anyone do what you have just done, but I must take him now. I promise I will be gentle."

"One more minute, please," Amelia begged.

"I must do my job." The nurse held out her arms.

Amelia pulled Malachi closer to her breast and kissed him lovingly upon his forehead. Handing him over to the nurse, Amelia let out a heart-wrenching cry, and then she watched as the young nurse held Malachi close and walked through the door of the delivery room slowly, closing it behind her.

— 10 —

It was Sunday evening and raining when Sebastian and Sarah arrived at the Central Station.

"I will make my own way home," Sarah told Sebastian. He found a taxi for her, and they kissed gently.

"Your home in France is totally enchanting and delightful, and I shall never forget the weekend we have spent together there. When I grow old with little or no use or purpose, I will rummage around in my memories for the days I spent in Provence with you, my beautiful Frenchman. My soul will smile—I thank you." Sarah kissed him again on the lips and climbed into the taxi, and Sebastian watched as the car disappeared into the distance. It was over; he was sad, yet a major part of him was relieved. He and Amelia's life together was fractured—his marriage was not far from ruins. Feelings of guilt and shame overrode his other emotions, including the rational part of him that had justified his relationship with Sarah and his behavior.

Traveling home on the train from London that day, Sebastian felt heavyhearted. It was as though he could hear

Amelia inside his head, calling his name. Amelia would have explained it as a premonition. He smiled in spite of himself; her Irish superstition was one of the things he loved about her, along with many other special things she did, such as patting the loaves of bread she baked before she cut them and shaking the milk bottle to distribute the cream so that the children would not fight over it. He had stopped noticing; he had stopped looking. He had lost sight of the blessings of his Amelia and all his children. Making his way home on the bus, he resolved to make this marriage work and to make a better life for Amelia and the children. The new baby was their common bond—the thread that would bring everything back together. Sebastian sighed. *This baby might be the answer.*

Helen and Charles arrived back at the house on Sunday night with the children after their long day at the seaside. Everybody was exhausted and excited, looking forward to telling their mam stories of their adventures. Maggie dashed out of the kitchen to meet them in the hallway.

"Hello," said Maggie. "Did you all have a good time?"

They all started chattering at once.

"Oh yes, we went swimming, jumped the waves, and had ice cream!"

"We made sand castles, picked winkles, and climbed rocks!"

"We had a lovely picnic! It was so much fun."

"One at a time, one at a time," Maggie said with a laugh.

"Let's get you into the kitchen and start getting you ready for bed. It's late. Then I can hear all your stories."

"Where's my mammy?" Abby asked.

"We have a big surprise for you."

Helen looked at Maggie. "What would that be?"

"Mammy left to go the hospital to get your new little brother or sister."

"She's early! What happened to her?" Helen said in a panicky voice. "Why? When?" Helen dropped her bag, went to Maggie, and shook her by the shoulders.

"She's fine," Maggie assured her.

"Calm down," Charles added.

"When she left in the ambulance, she was in good hands, and I promised that I would stay and let you know. We need to look after the children," Maggie said.

"No," said Helen. "I am going to her. Is she at the Princess Margaret?"

"Yes. A little while after the ambulance left, I tried to phone, but they would not give me any other information other than to say she had arrived safely," Maggie told her.

"Charles, you stay here and help with the bairns," Helen told him as she left for the hospital to find out what was going on.

When she arrived, she found the nurse at the maternity ward. The nurse told her the story and showed her to Amelia's bed. Helen was shocked at the sight of her sister; she was deathly pale and had swollen eyes with black circles underneath them.

"I'm so sorry, pet," Helen said as she went to Amelia.

"He died," Amelia sobbed. "I managed to baptize him as Malachi. I feel so empty."

"There, there, pet," Helen said. "We'll look after your bairns; don't worry. I'll come back tomorrow." Helen left feeling numb.

Deciding to get home as fast as she could, she went to the Central Station to catch a taxi. She went inside to use the bathroom, and as she came out, she looked down to make sure her handbag was closed. Looking up, she could not believe what she saw: Sebastian was walking through the central concourse with a suitcase in one hand and his other arm around an attractive blonde woman's waist. She also carried a case as they walked together, chatting and nodding. Helen hid behind a large pillar and leaned against it for support. She followed them with her gaze and watched as they waited in the taxi queue. Sebastian put down his suitcase to place the woman's case in the backseat of the taxi. She leaned over and kissed him on the lips as Helen watched in disbelief.

She could hear the PA announcing the departure of the nine o'clock train and wished she could run to the platform and jump on it—any train going anywhere was better than being left here. She did not want to witness this, but she continued to watch as the woman took Sebastian's hand in hers and whispered in his ear. Helen felt dizzy with anger and disbelief. She spoke out loud under her breath. "Brazen bitch. Hussy. Whore!" Helen normally never used words like that. The blonde kissed Sebastian, climbed into the taxi alone, and was gone, out of sight. Sebastian picked up his suitcase and walked to the bus stop.

Helen ran out, got in a taxi, and was back at the Lavalle house within twenty minutes. She knew Sebastian would be at least another twenty minutes on the bus. When Helen arrived, everything was quiet, and Charles was sleeping in a chair.

"Wake up, Charles; I want you to go home. I am going to stay the night, and I will explain everything tomorrow. Please don't ask me any questions."

"Well, I have to ask the obvious, Helen. Is Amelia okay?"

"Yes and no. She lost the baby."

"Good God." Charles put his head down and blessed himself.

"I don't want to talk about it, Charles. Where is Maggie?"

"She's upstairs with the children. They are all fast asleep. Don't worry, Helen."

"Thank you. Now, go home, Charles, and I will catch up with you tomorrow."

"If that's what you want." He kissed her on the cheek and left.

Helen went into the scullery and put on the kettle to make some strong, hot, sweet tea—she needed it. What was she to do? Should she confront Sebastian? She wasn't looking forward to breaking the news about losing the baby. *I'll just deal with one thing at a time,* she thought. *Filthy, rotten Frenchman running off for a dirty weekend with his tart and leaving Amelia eight months pregnant with eight children. How could he even think of doing such a thing?* Helen felt physically sick; she ran to the scullery sink and vomited. After splashing her face with cold water, she stepped outside to take some deep breaths of fresh air. What a day she had had, though nothing like her sister's. She knew she had to protect Amelia and those bairns.

As she went back into the kitchen, she heard the door opening and footsteps coming down the long hallway.

Sebastian came through the kitchen door looking both weary and surprised to see Helen.

"Hello, Helen. What are you doing here at this late hour? Is there something wrong?" he asked.

"You could say that," Helen replied. "I have some bad news for you, Sebastian."

"Is Amelia all right?" Sebastian had a hint of panic in his voice.

"She's going to be fine. She gave birth to a baby boy tonight—a stillborn. Perfect in every way. He asphyxiated going down the birth canal. Amelia was on her own, Sebastian; I've been to see her, and she is utterly devastated. She looks like she has been to hell's gate and back." Helen felt a sense of satisfaction as she watched Sebastian turn ashen white, the color draining from his face. She watched him clutch the table to support himself. He went to the cupboard and poured himself a cognac, knocked it back, and poured himself another quickly. Helen felt hatred toward Sebastian, and if she could find a way to make him suffer, she would do just that.

"Can I see her?" he said.

"Not till tomorrow."

"Do the children know?" asked Sebastian.

"No," Helen told him. "No one does outside of Charles."

"I must tell them first thing. I cannot believe this," Sebastian said as he sat slowly on a chair.

"I'm sure," said Helen.

"I want to go to her."

"They won't let you in; it's too late."

Sebastian put his head in his hands. "So there's nothing to be done till tomorrow?"

Helen fired another vengeful look at Sebastian. "That's right. And I have decided that I won't tell her."

"Tell her what?" Sebastian asked.

"What I witnessed tonight at the Central Station." Helen could hear her own voice quiver. "You miserable bastard, if it were not for Amelia and those wonderful bairns, I would swing for you."

"I swear to you, Helen, it's not what it looks like." Sebastian jumped up. "And it's over—I promise you."

Helen leaped at him. "Don't you lie to me!" she screamed. She went to slap him, but he caught her arm.

"Calm down, Helen, or you will awaken the household. It's truly over; we broke it off. We will never see each other again."

"So the shapely blonde I saw you with was your sick uncle in France?"

Sebastian hung his head. "Yes," he whispered. "You must believe me, Helen. If I'd thought for one second Amelia was to have this baby when she did, I would not have left."

"And that makes it better, does it?"

"No, of course not. I can't ask you or anyone else to understand. I was overwhelmed. I needed to get away for a few days."

"Oh, shut your lying mouth, Sebastian, and you listen to me. My wish for you is that the gates of hell open and the flames swallow you. However, I think that might be too good for you. And I want to protect Amelia and her bairns. She needs someone to support her. You will live with what you have done for the rest of your life. It shall be on your conscience. The death of your child was not expected—that I understand."

Helen glared at him with venom. "But you should have been with Amelia. God will find his own ways to punish you. I shall never utter a word of this to a living soul, but I swear to you, Sebastian, if you do not do everything humanly possible to help Amelia and those bairns live a decent life, I will come after you myself." Helen looked at the broken man before her, turned, and walked out. She went to the room where Abby and the three babies were sleeping and climbed into the bed next to Abby, where she cried herself to sleep.

Helen awoke the next morning feeling somewhat disoriented as the sun streamed in through the windows. She wondered at first where she was. There was an overpowering stench in the room, and she realized where it was coming from: the smelly nappies. The little boys were all awake and jumping up and down on their cots with their nappies around their knees and poop all over them and their sheets. It seemed everyone had overslept. Helen looked at her watch; it was past eight o'clock.

Abby was sitting up. "Hello, Auntie Helen. Where's my mammy and daddy?" She climbed over Helen to her brothers. "They need to have a wash and clean nappies, and if you'd like to help me, I can show you exactly what to do and where everything is kept. My daddy must have gone to work, because he's not in bed, but he doesn't do the nappies. It's my mammy and Leah and Andre who do the nappies, and I can fetch the clean ones, put the powder on, and hold the safety pins. My mammy loses them, and it's a very important job to hold the pins and give them to her one by one so that she has them when she needs them. Where is my mammy, Auntie Helen?"

"Come on, Abby. Help me look after these little brothers, and then we will have some breakfast."

"But where is my mammy?" Abby asked again. As Helen was making her way over to the boys, there was a knock at the door, and Sebastian came in.

"Good morning," he said.

"Yes?" Helen replied. She could not look at Sebastian.

"I have the older ones in the kitchen. I've told them this morning about their mother. They are all upset. Do you think you could give them all breakfast once you clean up the little ones? Andre and Leah will help you. I must go to Amelia."

"Yes. Sebastian?" she said, calling him back. "You must find an alternative arrangement for these bairns because I can't do this indefinitely."

"I know, Helen. I understand."

"There's a convent affiliated with my church, Sebastian. It's an orphanage run by the Little Sisters of Home in Jesmond. I know about it because of the Catholic Women's League I am involved with. I do know the mother abbess quite well. I could take them up there. Maybe they will help."

"I would be most grateful," Sebastian replied.

"Where is Mammy, Daddy?" Abby demanded.

"Don't worry, Abby; your mammy is fine. She's just gone away for a few days."

"Why?" Abby said. "Will she get the new baby?"

"Yes, that's it. Now, be a good girl. I must go." He put her down, kissing her on the nose.

"Good enough," said Helen.

Sebastian went back to the kitchen; the four older children were subdued.

"Can we come with you to see Mam?" Leah asked.

"No," Sebastian told them. "Not for a while. She must have lots of rest. I want you to help Aunt Helen. She's going to take you all to a house in Jesmond, where you will stay for a few weeks with some nuns."

The children looked at him.

Andre asked, "Can we not stay here? Leah and I can look after the babies until Mam comes home."

"Non, you must all be looked after, go to school, and be clean and fed. Do as you are told. Now, go help Helen. All will be well. Bon jour." He was gone.

11

Leah stood inside the open gate, pushing her brothers in the pram. As they began their walk, the gate reminded Leah of a wide, open mouth, and the winding driveway was like a long, crooked tongue. When the gate closed it was as if the mouth closed and swallowed her—she was not able to get out. It was dark like night because of the tall trees, yet it was still daytime. Leah prayed they would soon find the convent. After going around one more bend, she saw it—a big, ugly black building. It looked like an enormous, evil palace with a large black door and an ugly face on the door knocker. It had many windows, all little, and the house was covered with slimy green moss. Leah could see black bars on the windows of the top floor. Leah wanted to run.

"Do we have to live here, Auntie Helen? It's dark and mean looking. I hate it."

Leah's little brothers looked at her and all started crying, as did Abby.

"I want my mammy!" Abby wailed.

"Behave yourself, Leah. The last thing we need is these bairns bawling. Tell them it's okay—do you hear me?"

Leah bit her bottom lip, stopping herself from feeling terrified. "Oh, look, boys," she said as she pointed to a big tree. "It reaches all the way up to the sky!" The little ones looked and stopped crying. "Maybe Jack and the beanstalk or the giant are up there."

"I would like to see the Reverend Mother," Helen told the nun who came to the door.

"Yes, come in. Who is calling?"

"It's Mrs. Kennedy."

"Wait here," the nun said as she walked away.

Leah looked around her. The building was beautiful inside and completely different from the outside. There was a huge stained-glass window of the Virgin Mary holding baby Jesus in her arms. The light filtering through showed off all the colors and shined onto a sideboard that held a crystal vase filled with flowers. As they stood in the entrance waiting, Leah could hear a *clickety-click*. As the Reverend Mother entered, Leah could see that the rosary beads hanging from her belt were making the noise.

"Hello, Mrs. Kennedy. What have you here? Visitors?"

Leah watched the nun look at each one of them.

"Would you all like some milk and biscuits?" she asked the children.

"Yes, please." Leah nodded. "My little brothers will be hungry."

"Then follow Sister. She will look after you all."

Helen sat in the Reverend Mother's office. It was luxurious and elegant. A large cherry desk sat in the middle of the room, with two burgundy velvet chairs in front and a leather chair behind the desk. The most striking feature of the room was the picture window, which faced south toward manicured gardens. It was late August, and the roses were still blooming, providing an abundance of color. In the center of the garden was a stone grotto with a small replica of the Lourdes Virgin Mary appearing to St. Bernadette. The windows were open, and the sounds and smells of the garden trickled into the office—the nightingales and sparrows singing, the tinkling sound of the water running through the grotto, and the scent of the roses.

Helen sat in one of the chairs and sighed. "How lovely!"

"Yes, it is," the Reverend Mother agreed. "This is my space where I come to work, think, and pray. How can I help you, Mrs. Kennedy?"

Helen related the events of the past two days, leaving out the part about Central Station. The Reverend Mother sat back and listened intently to Helen.

"How long do you think the children will need to be with us?" she asked Helen.

"I'm not sure," Helen replied. "Amelia is still in shock. They gave me the impression last night that it will take some time for her to make a full recovery. I think months rather than weeks. I realize it's a lot to ask, Reverend Mother, but we have no choice or alternative. I cannot take them myself, and there is no one else."

"I see your dilemma, Mrs. Kennedy. Hope House is here to help in situations such as this. We have varied facilities to accommodate all the children. There is a boys' dormitory on the grounds, and we accept boys up to the age of fifteen. How old is the eldest boy?"

"Almost thirteen," Helen told her.

"That's fine then. The girls' dormitory is within the convent. And the youngest girl?" the Reverend Mother asked.

"Abby is six years old."

"She's too old for the nursery, which is on the second floor, where the three little boys will live. We take them from newborn to five. While the older children are expected to go visit and volunteer to help with their little brothers, they will also have tasks and responsibilities in their own dormitories. Hope House runs like a well-oiled wheel, Mrs. Kennedy."

"How many children are here?" Helen inquired.

"We have more than one hundred and fifteen when we are full, and the children themselves actually run the house. They are responsible for kitchen, laundry, garden, housekeeping—they are supervised, of course. Then there is their spiritual well-being, and we encourage prayer and worship. We devote approximately two hours a day to chapel, prayers, and rosary."

"That seems like a rather strict regime for little children."

"It's what we expect," the Reverend Mother told Helen.

"Is there a fee?" Helen asked.

"No, not exactly. It is charity and runs on corporate and private donations. The government does give a small amount per child. Mr. Lavalle may donate whatever he can, if he can. It sounds to me like the poor mother will need a long recovery and convalescence. I do suggest that you leave now, Mrs. Kennedy. They are in the dining room. We must get them settled into the new surroundings."

"Oh, I thought I might come back with some of their pajamas, toys, and clothes."

"We have everything required here, Mrs. Kennedy; don't worry. We do find through experience that it is advantageous if they are left to do their adjusting without visitors for the first few weeks. Children are adaptable and extremely resilient. I bid you good day, Mrs. Kennedy."

"Thank you very much, Reverend Mother." Helen walked out the door breathing a huge sigh of relief.

— 12 —

Sebastian walked into the maternity hospital at approximately nine thirty on Monday morning. He felt nervous; his mouth was dry, and his hands were clammy. He wondered what he would say when he saw Amelia. He was sad at the loss of their baby, but a part him felt relieved, which made him feel guilty. Sebastian knew Amelia would be devastated. She had carried that baby for nine months, feeling it grow and kick; then she had endured the full labor and delivery. His grief was real; he was not going to get to know and love the child they'd lost. He felt tears on his cheeks and wiped his face with the sleeves of his jacket. He could not let Amelia see him like this. All he could do now was be strong and help her recover physically and mentally as best as he could from the sad loss.

Sebastian decided he would contact Amelia's sister Deidre to ask her if Amelia could come stay with her to recover. He hoped Helen had had success at the convent, as it was essential to get help to care for the children. He could not see any other option—no one person could look after so many children.

Arriving at the desk, he said, "I am Mr. Lavalle, and I am here to see my wife."

"Ah, good morning," the matron said.

"I apologize for the delay; I did not arrive back until eleven thirty last night. This morning, I was attending to my other children. I would like to now see my wife. How is she this morning?" Sebastian asked.

"Mr. Lavalle, your wife has had a physical and mental breakdown, I am afraid. It is the loss of the child that has brought this to a climax, but it would appear it has been a long time in the making. Tests have shown her to be undernourished, low in iron and hemoglobin, and other physical symptoms indicate fairly severe neglect. We can help in the hospital with iron injections and some good nutrition. Within two or three weeks, I would think she will be physically strong, but I must tell you that mentally, she really needs rest and recuperation, and it is essential for her to have at least three months' rest. She cannot go back to taking care of all those children."

"I understand," Sebastian said.

"She is up this morning, and we gave her a bed bath. She looks a lot better, and she has been asking for you. Please do not stay too long—short, regular visits at this time, Mr. Lavalle. Here we are. We have left the drapes around the bed for privacy and so that Mrs. Lavalle does not have to watch mothers with their babies." The matron pulled the drapes back. "Your husband is here to see you," she told Amelia.

Amelia was sitting on a chair in the corner of the space created by the drapes around the bed. Beside her was a table with some unfinished tea and toast. He felt overwhelmed;

he was not sure he was able to do what was required. Amelia ran to him. Sebastian was startled, as he had expected her to be in bed.

She was crying. "My God, the baby is dead—he was so beautiful. And now he is gone!"

Sebastian held on to her. She looked childlike and heartbroken. "Ma chérie, I cannot stand to see you so sad. I understand how you feel at the loss of our boy, but you must not cry so."

She fell against him like a rag doll. "Oh, Sebastian, how could this have happened to us?" She continued to sob.

Sebastian thought of his conversation the night before with Helen, and he could hear her words echoing in his ears: *God will find his own ways to punish you.* She was right.

"Come. Let me put you into bed. Lie down, and I will tuck you in, chérie." Sebastian walked her over to the bed, laid her down gently, and covered her with the blanket. He had never seen her so fragile; it scared him. She always seemed strong and capable. He sat beside her bed until her sobs started to subside.

"What are we to do, Sebastian?" She looked at him.

"We need to get you strong and back on your feet. Matron told me you will need to be in the hospital for a couple of weeks. Then she suggests that you go somewhere quiet. I thought maybe we would call Deidre, and you could spend some time with her in Scotland."

Amelia just stared at the ceiling. "Whatever you think is best, Sebastian."

Standing up, he kissed her on the forehead. "I will come back later and be with you, ma chérie. *Je t'aime beaucoup.*" As he was about to leave, he realized Amelia had not asked him about their other eight children. He turned back to her and saw that she was lying fast asleep in the bed.

Outside the hospital, Sebastian realized he needed some time to think before he went home to meet Helen. He walked into the city to a French café called La Baguette, which he used to frequent with some of his old navy friends when he was based in England during the war. The café au lait was delicious as he sipped it; it slipped into his belly and warmed his bones, giving him much-needed energy. It was important to find some strength and resilience in himself and to get through the next few months. After finishing off the last few drops of café, he left.

Walking toward his bus stop, he passed the Cathedral of St. Margaret Mary, next to the old keep. It wasn't his intention to go in, but he found himself walking through the ancient doors into the sanctuary. The cool, dark silence was peaceful. He walked up the aisle and found himself stopping in one of the side chapels. He lit two candles in front of the Madonna and Child for Amelia and the baby's soul, dropped to his knees, covered his face with his hands, and gave in to his overwhelming emotions. Silently weeping, he could not forget Amelia's face when he had first seen her.

"Lord, forgive me; help me forgive myself. Lift this heavy cloak of guilt from my body so that I may move forward and be a better husband, father, and man. Give me strength, heal my weaknesses, and control my desire to take what is not mine, as in doing so, I betray those I love the most. Help me sin no more." Sebastian made the sign of the cross, blessing himself, and stood up to leave. He was startled to see an old priest standing behind him. The father looked at him and smiled.

"Good day, Father." Sebastian bowed.

The priest made the sign of the cross over Sebastian's head. "Go in peace, my son. All will be well. The Lord be with you," he whispered.

Sebastian walked from the cathedral into the sunshine with a new sense of strength he had not entered with. He ran to the bus stop with a new resolve, knowing he would make it through this difficult time. They all would.

— 13 —

Leah looked around her. The room looked like the dinner hall at school—big, with lots of tables and chairs—and smelled like it too. It smelled like old cooked cabbage. The odor made Leah feel sick.

"Pick up your plates, and place them in the dirty dish bin," the sister instructed Leah. "And help your little brothers. This is to be done after every meal; then you will set your place for your next meal. Do you understand?"

"Yes," Leah answered.

"I am Sister Edwina, and you will address me as Sister. You older children will be given a timetable with your duties and responsibilities. Now, all of you follow me."

Leah and Andre took the little ones by the hand and ushered them toward the door, keeping up with the nun.

Andre mouthed to Leah, "Bossy Boots."

Leah smiled. The hallways were long and dark. It seemed to Leah that there were a thousand closed doors. Eventually, Sister opened a door. The room was large and bright and had chairs and tables and a piano in the corner.

In the center of the room was a big table with boxed games on top, including Snakes and Ladders, tiddledywinks, and Monopoly. There were people in the room who were not nuns.

Sister called over to a lady in the corner, "Peggy, come here." A large lady walked toward them. She had long, stringy hair and wore crooked glasses. She stood in front of them. Leah thought she smelled like old pee and fish. Leah also noticed that some of her teeth were missing, and others were black. When she walked, she dragged her left leg.

"Yeth, Thithter?" The lady spoke with a lisp.

"Peggy, these are the Lavalle children. They will be with us for an indefinite time. Please take the three little ones upstairs to the nursery. Sister Mathilda is expecting them."

Leah stepped up. "May I go with them, please?"

"What is your name?" Sister asked sharply.

"Leah, Sister."

"Yes, you may. The rest of you stay with me, and I will show you where you will sleep. You two older boys stay here, and someone will show you the boys' dormitory, which is on the grounds. You will come to the main convent to eat your meals and go to chapel. Girls, follow me."

Abby stared at Sister Edwina and burst into tears. "I want my mammy!" She rubbed her eyes. "Let me go home. Where is my daddy? Where is my auntie Helen? I want to get on the bus with my brothers and sisters and go home to my house!" Abby wailed with a wide-open mouth, feeling tired in this cold, big, strange space. "Where have the babies gone? I want to see them."

Andre came over to her. "Shush, Abby. You will like it here."

"No, I don't," she protested.

"It's only for a little while till Mammy gets better; then we will all go home together."

"I don't like it here," Abby said. "It's scary, and that lady was smelly."

"Come with me now, and I will show you your dormitory," Sister Edwina demanded.

Cammie held on to Abby's hand. "Come on. You will be all right. It's just like home, and we will sleep in the same bedroom."

Abby and Cammie followed Sister Edwina, walking to the rhythm of the *clickety-click* of her rosary beads. Abby looked up at the large, wide staircase; there were so many stairs that she wondered if she would ever be able to get to the top.

"Let's count the stairs," she said to Cammie. "One, two, three ..." She got to ten and stopped, as that was as high as she could count. She started again. "One, two, three ..."

Sister Edwina stood at the top of the stairs, hands on her hips, tapping her foot impatiently.

Abby said to Cammie, "I counted to ten and then to ten and then two stairs—how many is that?"

Cammie stopped and thought for a moment. "Twenty-two."

"That's a lot of stairs."

"Come. Follow me," Sister Edwina ordered.

As they did so, Abby passed a statue. "Look," she said

to Cammie. "St. Francis, like the one at the church at home. He's got all the little animals at his feet." She stopped. "He's smiling." She sat down and stroked the figure of a kitty. "Hello, kitty." She was about the pat the puppy, when she heard Sister Edwina.

"Come along. Make haste—we have no time to dillydally."

Cammie ran back and grabbed Abby's hand. "Don't do that, because we'll get in trouble." They both ran to catch up to Sister, who turned into yet another doorway. She lifted the top part of her long black dress and pulled out a bunch of keys. Abby could see her looking at all the different keys. Sister chose one long silver one and unlocked the room.

"This is the storeroom," Sister said. "Here we keep all our supplies—sheets, towels, soap, toothpaste, clothes, socks, underwear. I am going to get you some sheets for your bed and a towel, facecloth, and toothbrush. It is your responsibility to look after them. Your towels will be washed once a week on Saturday, and you will be given a clean one. Every Saturday, your beds will be changed, and you will be given clean sheets." She dropped the sheets, pillowcases, towels, and washcloths into Abby's arms. Abby almost tipped over.

"Hold on, Abby. I'll help you," said Cammie.

"Oh, I'll get them."

Sister Edwina interrupted with a sharp voice. "Follow me. The large girls' dormitory is full; therefore, you will be in the sick bay." She walked into a room where Abby counted six beds—three along one wall and three along the other. They were made of iron and painted green, with skinny striped mattresses and little pillows. Beside each bed was a wooden chair, and a wardrobe and chest of drawers stood at the far end of the room. Through two big windows high up, Abby could see the treetops outside. The only other item in the room was a large portrait.

Sister Edwina pointed at it. "This is a picture of the Sacred Heart of Jesus. You must bow your head and make the sign of the cross when you stand in front of him. Do you understand?"

"Yes, Sister," Cammie replied.

"I don't like it!" cried Abby. "It stares back at you!"

"You are quite correct. The eyes of the portrait follow one everywhere within the room. It's quite an optical illusion. It's a gift to the sick bay—a blessing so that everyone in a sick bed has the eye of Jesus looking upon them," said Sister.

Abby hid her eyes and stood behind Cammie so that she wouldn't have to look at it. "He's still staring at me!" she wailed, and she ran to hide behind the wardrobe. Sister went over and pulled Abby out.

"How dare you make such comments, you ungrateful child! I can see you are going to be a problem. I will have no such behavior!" She pulled Abby by her arm and stood her in front of the picture. "Now you will kneel down in front of the Sacred Heart of Jesus and say twenty-five Hail Marys—do you hear me?"

Abby knelt and nodded.

"You reply, 'Yes, Sister,' when you are talking to me!"

"Yes, Sister." Abby had a big lump in her throat.

Sister Edwina turned to Cammie. "You will make the beds for your sisters—both theirs and yours. Then report back to me. I will be in the storeroom, finding you a school uniform."

Abby looked at Camille from her knees. "How do I say a Hail Mary? I don't know how to say it." She was crying.

"Don't worry; just mumble some words under your breath for a little while. When you get to the end of mumbling, say, 'Amen,' really loud."

"But I can't count to twenty-five."

"Do what you did on the stairs—ten and ten and five," whispered Cammie.

"Will I go to hell for hiding from Jesus?" Abby asked.

"I don't know—I'll ask Leah when she comes back."

Sister Edwina walked past the door.

"Amen!" Abby said loudly as Cammie opened up the first mattress to start making the beds.

Leah and the boys followed Peggy Schilling up the stairs to the nursery.

Sasha sat down and said, "No more. Me tired."

"Come on," said Leah. "Just a few more stairs. Help me count them, Sasha. Hold on to my hand—one, two, three, four, five!" shouted Leah. After two more, they reached the top stair. At the top was a big, arch-shaped wooden door. Peggy Schilling turned the knob and pushed the heavy door slowly; it creaked as it opened. She held it open so that they could all walk in past her.

"Stay there, and don't you move till I come back," said Peggy.

A nun appeared. "Ah, Peggy, here you are. I believe you have some little ones for me to meet."

"Yeth, Sisther."

"Oh, look at you—triplets no less! Well, I never. Bless

my soul. We have never had triplets—twins, yes. Three sets at one time—one set of identical girls, one set of identical boys, and a boy and a girl. Let me see. What is your name, my dear?"

"Leah, Sister."

"I'm Sister Mathilda. Oh goodness, don't look so frightened. I know this is a bit confusing. You will all be just fine, and your little brothers will be very happy with us in the nursery. You will be expected to come help in the nursery each day and take care of the little ones."

She's nice, thought Leah. Sister Mathilda was short and round, but she had nice skin, big brown eyes, and a nice smile, and when she looked at Leah, Sister made her feel like smiling back.

"Ah, well then, come along with me, Leah, and bring those trips with you. Thank you, Peggy; you may go now."

Leah could smell baby powder, which was familiar and comforting. She walked with the boys beside her. Sister Mathilda was in front, chatting on and on about twins and triplets. She turned into another room.

"Come along this way, little boys, into the playroom."

They all followed Sister Mathilda into the big room, which was full of light, laughter, and children from a few weeks old to four years old. One of the staff was playing a record on the record player, and all the little ones were singing along: "Six green bottles hanging on the wall, and if one green bottle should accidentally fall—" They all fell down with their legs and arms in the air. Giggles and hoots of joy and laughter filled the room. The triplets wanted to join in the fun.

"When this song is finished," said Sister Mathilda, "I should think they all need a nappy change. Come along with me, Leah, and help. I will show you where we change the little ones and bathe them. I expect you are very good at that."

"Yes, I am, Sister Mathilda."

Sister smiled, and Leah had a strong urge to give her a big hug.

"Come along, trips," she said. "Follow Sister Tilly. That's me—Tilly for short." She pointed to herself and skipped out of the playroom with the four Lavalle children behind her. Sasha was skipping along beside her; she took his hand, and they went through another big door. This time they went into a large bathroom made for little people—a baby bathroom all in white. Leah counted eight sinks, eight toilets, and four bathtubs in the corner. There was an oblong table with a towel laid across it in the middle of the room, and piled on the table were nappies, safety pins, a tub of barrier cream, and a big tin of baby powder, all nearby.

"Well, here we are," said Sister Tilly. "You know what to do. Show me your stuff."

Leah went about changing her brothers efficiently, and they were soon all clean and ready to go play.

"You must be a wonderful help to your mam."

"Yes," said Leah. "My mam says she doesn't know what she would do without me and my brother Andre helping with the babies. All of us help; it's just that we are the oldest boy and girl, so we do the most." Leah went quiet.

"I am very sad to hear about your new little brother, Leah. He will go straight to heaven, you know."

Leah dropped her head. "My mam said if it was a boy, she would call him Malachi because I liked the name. I read it in a story at school—about Malachi and the leprechaun. He won't need a name now."

"Well, of course he will," said Sister Tilly. "You know his name, and you will remember Malachi. Don't be sad. Your mam will be back with you all very soon, Leah. You can come up and help me on the nursery floor whenever you have time. We would love to see you."

"Can I bring my sisters?" asked Leah.

"But of course, the more the merrier. Now, run along. I think those trips are just fine, don't you?"

Leah looked over, and they were doing the "all fall down" part of "Ring around the Rosy." The three of them were lying on top of one another, hugging and giggling with their arms and legs in the air. Leah wished she could jump in the pile and stay with them up there in the nursery. It felt nice there—different from downstairs, where she would stay with her sisters. She left the nursery, and as she was walking along the corridor, she looked at the wall. She stopped and looked in amazement. She rubbed her eyes and looked again.

Painted across the wall was a mural of a beautiful rainbow, and at the far end was a pot with gold coins overflowing from the top of it. The leprechaun from the story was sitting beside the pot. Leah ran up to the painting of the leprechaun, looked at him, and smiled. *Yes,* she thought. *I like it up in the nursery. I'm going to come here as often as I can.*

— 14 —

Dinner at Hope House was a disciplined ritual. The Lavalle children all sat around one table.

"It's cold in the boys' dorm; it's just a big room with twenty beds and a bathroom with sinks and toilets. I hate it," said Eugene. "I want to go home, even if Mam is not there. I can take care of meself."

"Shhh," Andre said. "If Sister hears you complaining, she may put us all out. We must behave ourselves and do as we are told until Mam gets well and comes back to us. We can be together at least at meal times and on Saturdays and Sundays, when we are not at school. Don't be unhappy, Eugene."

Eugene scowled at Andre, and they started to eat their food: toad-in-the-hole with peas, carrots, and lumpy mashed potatoes. *A lot like the school dinners,* thought Andre. *It definitely smells the same.*

Eugene said, "This food is awful, but I am so hungry. I will hold my nose so that I can't taste the carrots. The lumps in the potatoes are making me feel sick."

Sister Edwina, unfortunately, saw him, and she came over to the Lavalle table in an instant. "What are you doing, boy?"

"Holding my nose," replied Eugene.

"How dare you! How dare you be so ungrateful, you thankless boy. Get up from your chair at once! Do you know how many starving children around the world would fall on their knees and thank God and all the angels and saints for a plate of wonderful food such as this?"

"No," he said quietly.

"No, *Sister*!" she yelled at him.

"No, Sister."

"Tell this ungrateful boy how many starving children there are around the world." She looked at all the children in the dining room eating the same dreadful food.

They all replied together, "Thousands of hungry children around the world."

"And what must we do?" Sister said.

"Pray for them, and clean our plates." They all spoke like parrots in unison.

"You understand? Do you?"

"Yes," said Eugene.

"Yes what?" Sister demanded.

"I understand," said Eugene.

"Yes, I understand, *Sister*!" she ordered him.

Eugene replied as Sister Edwina had demanded.

"Now, get down on your knees at this table, and you pray twenty-five Our Fathers—out loud so we can all hear you as we finish our meal. Your dinner will be divided up between your brothers and sisters. That way, you will understand minutely the feeling of what it is like to be hungry!" She pulled him off his chair and threw him onto the floor with such force that he fell on his face and hit his nose on the floor. It started bleeding. She shoved a hankie into his hand.

"Use it!" she barked at him. Eugene was crying.

"Our … Father … who art in heaven," sobbed Eugene.

"Louder!"

"Hallowed be thy name," Eugene continued.

"They cannot hear you in the back of the room."

"Thy kingdom … I want my mam. I want to go home."

"Shut up and pray!"

Andre could not stand to watch a minute longer. He stood up quickly from his chair.

"Please, Sister Edwina, may I kneel and pray with my brother? I think he is very sad, and he is missing our mam. Can I help him say Our Fathers? I know he did not mean to be so ungrateful. I promise on his behalf he will not do it anymore. Will you, Eugene?"

"No!" Eugene wailed. "I promise."

Leah, Camille, and Abby all stood up.

"We will all say the Our Fathers with him, Sister. It will be nice and loud, and all the children will hear," said Leah.

"Very well," she said. "Get on with it."

They all knelt in a circle around their table and supported Eugene in his prayers. "Our Father, who art in heaven. Amen," said Abby loudly.

Leah lay in bed, thinking about how several weeks had passed since they had arrived at Hope House. They were getting used to the routine. Saturdays were for cleaning—all hands on deck. However, the children were allowed to sleep for thirty minutes longer, as there was no school. Sister Edwina awoke them, as she did every morning. Leah could hear her marching along the corridor, her rosary beads *clickety-clicking*; she could always hear her coming before she heard her voice. She would open all the dormitory doors with a cry of "Hail Mary, full of grace, the Lord is with thee!" Then she would start all over again.

All the children fell to their knees on the hard wooden floors by their bedsides. They had to say ten Hail Marys before they were allowed to go to the bathroom. By the end of the second Hail Mary, Leah's knees were stinging. She shuffled around a bit, lifting one knee off the floor and then the other. By the time she finished her prayers and stood up, her eyes were watering from the stinging of her knees. Her knees were marked with welts, dints, and little white bumps from kneeling on the hard wooden floor. The next morning, Leah pulled her towel onto the floor before she knelt—what a relief that was.

The children then rose, made their beds with hospital corners, and made everything neat as a pin. Then they dashed to the bathroom, where the floor was like a cold winter morning after a hard frost. It made Leah shiver from head to toe. All the kids hopped from one foot to the other to try to keep warm. The white sinks and taps were old; Leah had to twist them and twist them to make them move, and they squeaked awfully once turned on. The first water of the day was always dirty, brown, and icy cold, and it took a long time for it to run clear. Most of the children didn't wait, so Leah brushed her teeth in dirty, cold brown water while standing on one leg, shivering on the icy-cold bathroom floor.

They would then file out quietly and walk to the chapel for Mass, all before seven o'clock on weekdays and seven thirty on Saturday mornings.

Leah thought the chapel in Hope House was outstandingly beautiful. It was not large, yet it felt grand as one entered the doorway. The high altar was hand carved, and there was a statue on each side, one of the holy family and the other of the Immaculate Heart of Mary. Mary's head had a halo around it, made up of tiny lights, and on special occasions, it was lit up. The stations of the cross adorned the walls of the chapel. On the north and south sides of each chapel wall were three stained-glass windows, all six depicting different stories from the Bible. On the white marble stairs was a deep turquoise carpet that was the color of the ocean on a lucky day.

The visual effects of Chapel Hope were stunning, yet the children liked it primarily because of how it made them feel inside. The children were encouraged to go to the chapel in their free time, and many of them used it as a place of solitude, peace, and warmth. It was a special oasis in an institution where there was little chance for respite.

After chapel, the children would file out to the breakfast room.

On Saturdays, they stripped the sheets from their beds and took all their dirty linen to the laundry, along with the one towel each child received for the week. They then pushed the beds into the middle of the dormitory and then swept and washed the floors. All the children, approximately twenty or so, lined up across the length of the room or hallway and held hands, and each of them placed an old pair of nappies or sheets cut into small dusters under his or her feet and moved in unison across the floor. They were human floor polishers, and they were efficient. Every corner of the convent had to be clean, twinkling, and shining before they were allowed to go out to the playground behind the convent for one hour of free play. Leah noticed that the hour was like playtime at school; little groups got together in corners, some boys played football, and the girls played hide-and-seek or played on the swings and monkey bars, chattering about events that had taken place.

No matter the weather, they were sent out for their hour of free play and fresh air. This event, to many of the children, was not unlike time in the chapel; it was free, and they were allowed to be themselves. They were then brought back into the convent for their lunch, which consisted of a Spam sandwich, raw carrots, and a glass of milk.

"We have finished all our jobs, Sister. May we go to the nursery?" Leah asked on her sisters' behalf. Sister Edwina marched around their dormitory, checking their beds, making sure the floors were polished, and checking the sinks and toilets in the bathroom. She looked as hard as she could, but she could fault none of it.

"You may go," she said, "but you be back in time for Benediction at four o'clock."

"Yes, Sister Edwina," the three girls said in unison. They joined hands, ran off, and jumped up the stairs, counting them as they went.

The most difficult time for Leah was the end of the day—bedtime. All the children congregated at the bottom of the stairs. There was a head count, followed by prayers. They were then each given a plastic beaker. Sister Edwina had a large aluminum jug filled with watery hot chocolate, tepid at best, and she doled out rations to the children as they stood in front of her. Unlike with most treats, Leah kept her fingers crossed, hoping Sister would give out less liquid rather than more. On rare occasions they would get nice biscuits or pieces of jelly roll; however, most times they received only the dreaded bedtime drink. When the hot-chocolate ritual was done, they all went up the stairs quietly and slowly. Sister Edwina kept a rule of silence at most times, unless one had a good reason to speak out. They went to their dormitories, where they took off their Saturday clothes, put on their white flannel nightgowns, put their dirty clothes in the laundry hamper, set out their Sunday best, and then went to the bathroom, where they brushed their teeth and went to the toilet. They said more evening prayers, and then they were allowed to go back to their dormitories, where they prayed one more time on their knees at their bedsides. At last, they climbed into bed.

Leah enjoyed climbing into bed on Saturdays, sliding into the clean, crisp sheets. As the blankets and sheets became one and embraced her tired little body, she lay awake in the dark. She could see the tops of some of the trees through the high windows in the sick bay, and in the distance she saw neon lights flashing from the street in the world outside of the convent walls. The neon lights came from a red sign that spelled out the name of the Punch Bowl, a pub. Leah felt sad and lonely. She and her siblings had been at the convent for two weeks, and no one had come to visit them or tell them where their mam was or how she was. Leah felt sad about baby Malachi, yet it seemed as if nothing had happened, as if Mam had gone on a trip or something.

She longed to break the gates and run as fast as she could home to her mam and dad. Eugene and Andre had once done just that by jumping over the wall. They had gone home after the event in the dining room with Sister Edwina.

Even if her mam and dad weren't there, Leah knew that together, her brothers and sisters could look after one another. She prayed someone would visit tomorrow.

The Punch Bowl's light flashed on and off. It was comforting to Leah; it helped her feel better somehow, like watching the ocean move in and out when she went to the seaside. She decided to count the flashes—one on, followed by two off—and as she did so, she tried to fall asleep. Her tears fell onto her pillow; she moved her head around to find a dry patch as she finally drifted off to sleep.

On Sunday, Sister Edwina started her Hail Marys at six thirty in the morning. Leah was up and dressed in her Sunday best for the seven o'clock mass. High Mass on Sunday was an event, and the chapel looked spectacular. The altar displayed an array of beautiful blossoms depending on what was available in the garden, which was based on the season. The garden was still full of roses at that time—pink, white, red, orange, and dark pink—and they had a delightful aroma. Leah put on her mantilla, a lace head covering; blessed herself with holy water; genuflected; and went to help Abby put on her mantilla. All the girls had been assigned a lace head covering, as it was compulsory for them to wear one in church or chapel. Sitting in their designated pew, the girls listened to the choir singing a nice hymn. Our Lady's halo was lit up.

"Look," said Abby with a big smile. "She looks just like a princess."

"Oh, don't be daft," said Camille. "She's Our Lady, queen of heaven, not a princess."

"I think she looks beautiful," said Abby. "Like Cinderella."

"Shhh!" said Leah. "Or Sister Edwina will be after us."

Mass started, and Leah stood and knelt, said her prayers, sang hymns, and listened to Father Shaughnessy shout from the pulpit. He yelled about sin, damnation, and the flames of hell swallowing them for eternity if they did not keep themselves in an eternal state of grace.

Abby looked at Leah, terrified. "What's grace? Can you get me some?"

"It's all right," said Leah. "Don't worry."

Leah longed to see her mam and ask her when she was coming home. Last night, the girl in the dormitory next door, Maureen, had told her she had no mam and dad. They were dead, she said. She didn't have any brothers or sisters either. She had no one to come take her home ever. Suddenly, Leah did not feel so bad. She stood, and at last, Father blessed them all and left the altar; Mass was finished. They sang some more hymns and headed out of the chapel into the dining room for some more prayers and then breakfast. The time between getting out of bed on Sunday morning and breakfast was approximately three and a half hours. Some of the children fainted regularly in the chapel, so much so that there was a nun on duty to take care of them. She would lead them outside for fresh air, march them around, give them a sip of water, and send them back into chapel.

After breakfast, the nuns set the tables for Sunday lunch. The children did not work in the convent on Sunday. They kept their best clothes on all day, most of which was dedicated to prayer, Mass, and Benediction. The children had a little free time between breakfast and Sunday lunch. They were allowed to go to the common room, to the chapel, or, if the weather permitted, for a walk on the grounds. Hope House was blessed with two acres of beautiful land, most of it old oak, ash, and chestnut trees intertwined with evergreens. There was a rose garden behind the convent. Children who were interested worked with a part-time gardener to maintain the grounds, raking leaves, pruning some of the bushes, and, of course, keeping the Virgin Mary grotto in tip-top condition.

The main event was Sunday lunch; the nuns' perception of it was far beyond its reality, which was gristly, overcooked beef; lumpy mashed potatoes; mushy cooked cabbage; peas and carrots that were not cooked; and awful, lumpy gravy—all in all, somewhat of an insipid offering. Most of it was stone cold by the time it reached Leah's plate; however, it was a cooked meal, and the children were made to understand how fortunate they were. Sister Edwina walked around the tables, watching them hack and chew and grind at their beef. Leah tried with all her might, along with her sisters, to grind it to a pulp in order to swallow the food; no matter how hard they tried, they could not.

Most of the children would spit it out and leave it on their plates. Some dropped it onto the floor, hid it in their handkerchiefs, or pushed it up the sleeves of their cardigans or jumpers—anything to make it disappear from Sister Edwina's evil eye. At the end of Sunday lunch all the plates were collected, and the remaining food was scraped into a big white tureen, gristle and chewed meat included. Then the nuns redistributed it to each and every child in the dining room, even the individuals who'd managed to clear their plates. No one left the dining room until all the food was eaten. It was agonizing. Leah thought of dinners at home; they did not have nice food, such as beef, or as much to eat. Her dad did not allow them to leave food on the plate, and he was strict, but he would not have made them do this.

Maureen suddenly jumped up, and her chair fell back. It sounded as if she were choking. Sister Edwina dropped what she was doing, ran over to her, and started smacking at her back with her fists and telling her to cough it up. Maureen was turning red in her face, and her eyes bulged from their sockets as she heaved, groaned, and coughed, struggling to get the obstruction out. She looked as if she had stopped breathing. Sister Edwina continued to beat on her back, and a piece of gristle sprang across the dining room floor as everyone watched in horror.

"Sit down, Maureen," said Sister Edwina. "And drink some water. The rest of you children say your grace after the meal and clear up the dining room, and you may go to the common room for some free time until Benediction this afternoon at three thirty. Some of you will have visitors this afternoon, and they will join you in the room." Leah and the girls left feeling grateful they did not have to finish their scraps.

When she turned to leave, Leah saw Maureen sitting at the table, sipping at her water. Leah wasn't sure, but she thought she saw Maureen wink and then smile. Whatever had happened, Leah was relieved that they did not have to finish their scraps.

The biggest excitement of the week was the sweetie shop. Sister Edwina had a walnut cupboard with endless little doors, drawers, nooks, and crannies filled with different kinds of treats and sweets. If she was in a good mood, she opened the shop on Sunday afternoon for fifteen minutes, and the children purchased some sweeties with their pocket money. The sweetie shop was amazing, because the children could buy a lot for a penny or a halfpenny, as they were not allowed to spend more. The shop had sherbet fountains, jelly babies, dolly mixtures, and more; the children were, for a small moment in time, able to behave like children.

Visiting hours that day were over.

"I hate it here!" cried Abby. "I want to go home. Where's Mammy? When is she coming? Or even Aunt Helen?"

"I don't know," Leah said. "I can't tell you—maybe Saturday."

"When's that?" Abby asked.

"It's the no-school day when we clean and clean and then go out and play."

Abby was excited to hear that; she had a big plan for Saturday, and she was going to keep it a secret. Her mammy used to tell her when Abby was helping out at home that if she was a good girl, washed her face, combed her hair, turned up the cuffs on her cardigan, looked smart, and didn't forger her manners, then Mammy would get her a surprise—sometimes a sweetie, sometimes a biscuit, and sometimes a halfpenny.

Saturday arrived, and Abby did all her jobs and worked hard with her sisters. They finished early, and it was playtime.

Abby quietly washed her face, brushed her hair, rolled up the cuffs on her cardigan, and went outside to wait on the old tree stump for her Mammy to come take her home.

Cammie and Leah came up. "Aren't you coming to play?"

"No, thank you," Abby replied, remembering her manners. She continued to wait until Sister Edwina called everyone in. Her mammy did not come.

Abby decided to try harder the next Saturday; she was sure her mammy would arrive, but she did not. She did the same for the next two Saturdays after that. Abby sat on the tree stump with her washed face, brushed hair, and turned-up cuffs, saying please and thank you to no avail. One Saturday, Abby stopped.

No visitors arrived the following weekend. On Sunday afternoon, the girls were in the common room.

"I am going up to the nursery," said Leah. "Do you want to come with me?"

"No," said Abby. "I like this book. Can I stay?"

"If you like. Are you coming, Cammie?"

"No, I will stay with Abby."

Leah made her way up to the nursery, counting the stairs as she went.

She walked slowly past the rainbow wall and touched the leprechaun, and as she did so, she made a wish in her head: *Please make my mammy better.* She felt like crying and leaned up against the wall and closed her eyes. "I want to go home," she whispered. She heard the familiar clicking rosary beads coming down the hall. Leah looked up, and Sister Tilly was facing her.

"Hello, Leah. Have you come up to help us?"

"Yes, Sister," Leah replied.

"Well, what are you doing in the hall alone?" Sister asked.

"I was looking at the rainbow and the little leprechaun."

Sister Tilly smiled. "Did you make a wish?"

"Yes, I did," Leah replied.

"Good. You keep it a secret, and I hope it comes true. You look a little sad, my dear."

Leah broke down. "I waited in the room for someone to come see us—my dad or my brothers or even Auntie Helen. I kept waiting and looking, and no one came. Will we ever go home, or have they just forgotten us?"

"Come. Come with me, child." Tilly put her arm around Leah and took her into a little prayer room and office, which was small yet bright. Tilly sat Leah down and gave her a glass of water.

"Now, you listen to me, Leah. Hope House has a lot of rules. That is how it works so efficiently—there are many children to take care of. Some of the rules are good, and others are not. Reverend Mother insists on absolutely no contact with the family in the first few weeks in order for you all to adjust to your new home and surroundings and get into a good routine. It can take time. I expect no one explained this to you downstairs. Your family have not forgotten you, my child. They will definitely bring you news of your mammy. I'm sure that the hospital is taking very good care of her, and she will be getting stronger every day. I know that she will not be worrying quite as much knowing her Leah is with her little ones."

"So now that we have been here for two weeks, maybe next visiting day? I miss my mam very much, and she must be feeling so sad that Malachi died."

"Yes. Now, dry your eyes." Tilly handed her a handkerchief. "I have someone I wish you to meet."

Leah followed Sister Tilly out of the office, wiping her eyes and blowing her nose on her nice clean handkerchief, which smelled like lavender from the garden. Leah caught up with Tilly. "Are we going to see my brothers, Sister?"

"No, not just now; they are in their bedrooms, resting. It's quiet time in the nursery. I am taking you to a part of the nursery that you have not seen yet." Sister Tilly opened a door, and they were in a bright, beautiful room. Leah thought it was pretty; the walls were yellow, blue, and pink. One wall had a window looking out over the tops of the trees and the grounds of the convent. Over the wall, she could see buses and cars. A lady was feeding a baby in a rocking chair by the window. Leah knew it was a baby girl, because she was wearing a pink cardigan.

Leah moved to the baby like a magnet. "Hello. Ah, she's lovely. What's her name?"

"This is Susie," said the lady feeding her. "She is three months old now, and she has been with us from birth."

"She is so sweet," said Leah. "And little."

"Come," said Sister Tilly.

Leah stood and stroked the baby's head. "Bye-bye, Susie. I'll come back to see you later before I go." The big room was full of babies of different ages; some were crawling and playing in playpens, and some were sleeping in cots. Sister Tilly went to a cot and lifted out a tiny baby dressed in a blue bonnet and a little hand-knitted coat.

A little boy, thought Leah. Tilly placed the new baby in Leah's arms.

"There you go. Now, support his little head. That's very good, Leah. Come over and sit in one of the rocking chairs with him."

Leah walked slowly, holding on to the baby, unable to take her eyes off his face. "Who is he, Sister?" she asked.

"That's a very good question, Leah. Like a lot of our new residents, we don't know. He was left outside the convent, on the steps outside the front door last night. He was wrapped in an old, torn red dress with no message. Sometimes the mothers or fathers can't look after their babies for various reasons. The mothers can't tell their own parents that they are pregnant, the fathers don't want the mothers or the babies, they are frightened, there is no money or no work—there are a thousand and one different reasons. Hope House has a no-questions policy; if they leave their babies, we will look after them. Usually, we can find very good, loving homes for the babies, and most are adopted within the first few months of arriving here. Young Susie, who you just met, will be going to her new home in a few days. We here at the nursery are just a stepping-stone on the way to keep the babies safe, warm, and loved until they find new homes. As you can see, this little fellow is in perfect condition. He's only two or three days old—no more."

"He's so tiny. Look at his little hands." Leah lifted one of his hands onto her little finger. "He's beautiful, Sister; his little fingernails are perfect." Leah had no thoughts of going home or missing her mammy at that moment in time. "What is his name?" Leah asked.

Sister Tilly smiled. "That's the thing—he does not have one as yet. We here in the nursery thought that you might like to give him his name, Leah. What do you think?" Tilly kept her eyes on Leah.

Leah pulled the new little one close to her, kissed the top of his head, closed her eyes, and whispered, "Malachi, Sister. I would like to name him Malachi."

—15—

Three months later, Amelia walked along the cobbled streets of the market with purpose. The October winds were blowing, tossing the falling leaves around her feet. Pulling up the collar on her coat to cover her neck and ears, protecting herself from the chill, she shivered. It had been raining for quite some time, but the rain had stopped. The weather was slightly warmer, and she could see steam rising from the cobbles as the water evaporated and rose into the air. The sun was milky behind the clouds, yet the effect was enough to create a rainbow across the length of the Royal Mile.

Deidre linked arms with her sister. "Look at that rainbow, Amelia. Make a wish!"

Amelia smiled. "You too."

"This is like the old days," Dee said. "When we used to go dancing—remember? Walking all the way there and home again. I'm really pleased you asked me to come with you today. I love this walk." They were heading toward Edinburgh Castle to St. Margaret's Chapel. They walked past St. Giles's Cathedral, the law courts, and the Royal Festival Theater.

It was a particularly nice, picturesque walk as they made their way toward the castle perched on the hill. The street meandered its way up.

"I really enjoy going into the chapel. It's always so peaceful there."

"It has helped me so much," Amelia agreed. "When I first arrived, I would sit and look into the air—beyond time, space, and feeling. I couldn't think too much. I felt so down and dark. The ache left inside from the loss of Malachi was so overwhelming there was room for nothing and no one else—only the pain. Eventually, I was forced to feel. Then I would cry and pray. After a while I found a desire to ask for courage to help me move through the sorrow. Slowly but surely, I started to feel."

"Oh, Amelia, I am so pleased you are feeling more like your old self. Do you know that when you first arrived three months ago, I was terrified out of my mind? You looked like a stranger to me. I did not recognize any part of you, and Sebastian didn't look much better. But I think you have proven that old saying—'Time heals all things.'"

"Along with your patience and kindness," Amelia added. She pulled Deidre closer to her. "You know, when Sebastian came on his last Sunday visit with Andre and Eugene, I was actually nervous. I felt awkward and uncomfortable, but the overriding feeling at the sight of my children was to go home and be with them—all of them. It was really wonderful to give them a cuddle and hold them. I realized how much I miss them all."

"I can understand that. You have been apart for a long time."

"When Sebastian comes next Sunday, I am going home with him, Deidre."

"Are you sure you are ready? You shouldn't rush yourself; you've been through a lot, Amelia."

"It's time. I must get my family back together. They all need me, and more than that, I need them."

"Well, if you are sure," Deidre said. "Let's stop right here at your lovely tearoom; I'll treat.

"What about the chapel?" Amelia asked.

"I cannot walk one more step on these cobbles; my feet are killing me."

Tilly sat in the rocking chair, looking out the window and holding Malachi, who was now three months old.

"Look at him," she said. "He is so gorgeous with his round sapphire-blue eyes, curly black lashes, and peachy skin."

Malachi cooed at Tilly like a cherub.

"Have you told Leah yet?" asked one of the nursery workers.

Tilly looked at her. "No, I have not. I shall do it in my own time."

"May I suggest sooner rather than later?"

"Yes, I know you are right. It is just that this adoption has crept up on me."

"You know it's going to devastate Leah when she finds out, Sister. Everyone knows she adores Malachi. It's like they belong to one another. It's been that way since you first laid him in her little arms. She will be dashing up the stairs from school soon to bathe him."

Tilly sat silently listening to the helper chat on.

"I watched her last week giving him a bath. He shrieked with joy and delight. He loves her, you know."

"Enough," Sister Tilly said, jumping up from the chair. She placed Malachi in the crib, and he smiled at her. Tilly looked down at him. "I know you will be going to your new parents soon, and I am happy for you, for you are like a little angel. I shall never regret putting Leah and you together. It has been a blessing to watch you thrive because of one another, no matter what the outcome."

Leah came dashing into the nursery. "Hi, everybody!" she said. "Where's my boy Malachi?"

The baby cooed and giggled at the sound of her voice, his arms and legs kicking.

"Hello, Sister." Leah pushed in front of Tilly in order to pick up Malachi.

"Not yet, Leah."

"But it's half past four, Sister, and I only have thirty minutes to bathe him before dinner."

"Is it really that late already? Oh well. Off you go then; get him bathed."

The helper looked at Tilly, and Tilly left the nursery angry with herself, delaying the inevitable conversation with Leah until another day.

— 16 —

The next time Sebastian came to visit, as they sat in the tearoom, Amelia blurted out, "I am coming home with you; I knew the minute I saw Andre and Eugene on your last visit that I must come back. My babies will not recognize me after three months. That's a long time in the life of a child. I can't and won't stay one minute longer, Sebastian."

"I agree with you," Sebastian said. "If you think you are strong enough, it's time. And I certainly would be happy to have my family home. The boys and I have missed everyone; we've managed well enough whilst you were gone. Helen drops in several times a week with homemade food—vegetable soup, stews, and pies. She picks up the boys' dirty clothes and brings them back all cleaned and ironed. She really has been a godsend. On the weeks I couldn't visit the girls, Helen would. They have quite a rigorous routine at that convent; from the moment the children climb out of their beds until the moment they lay their heads on their pillows, they are busy. Still, it is a fantastic facility watching over our children while you recovered. I think we will be forever in their debt."

As they arrived at the station in Newcastle, Amelia stepped onto the platform, and Sebastian held her hand to help her. She took in the hustle and bustle. It was Sunday evening, and people were coming home from their weekends away. Sebastian walked beside her. They went from the Central Station to the street. It was a cold, dark, dreary November evening; Amelia shivered.

"Are you all right?" Sebastian asked.

"Yes, it's just so damp."

"We can take a taxi home," he said.

"No, no, we must not. We will use the bus; it's fine. Come. Don't worry; I'm fine," Amelia told him. "Let's go home and see the boys, and when you come home from work tomorrow, we can collect all the children from the convent."

"Amelia," said Sebastian gently, "I think it would be a very good idea if you visit with them first. Let them spend some time with you. It will be too much for you all at once. You could bring the girls back first and then, maybe a few days later, bring the little boys."

Amelia broke in. "Don't you think I've waited long enough?" She stopped in the middle of the street, her voice shrill. "They are my children, Sebastian, and I want them back home with me." She started to cry uncontrollably. "I will not let you stop me—I won't. If I have to carry them home on my back one by one, I will do that."

Sebastian put his arms around her. "No one is trying to keep you apart."

"Yes, you are. I can hear it in your voice: 'Wait a day. Visit first.' No, I won't!"

"Amelia, listen to me. You must calm down. Let's go home, and we can discuss it there."

"As far as I am concerned, there is no discussion," Amelia said.

The following morning Sebastian and Amelia sat at the kitchen table, having breakfast with Andre and Eugene.

"It's nice to have you back home, Mam." Andre hugged his mother. "I have missed you."

"Yeah, me too!" said Eugene. "I'm glad you are back; it's not the same without you, Mam."

"I am pleased to be home. I have missed you all. I can see you have grown into young men while I was gone and have become very independent."

"Not now that you are back," said Eugene. "Can't wait to eat your homemade bread."

"We will all be together tonight, as your dad is taking the day off work, and we are going to the convent to pick up the other children. We will be all sleeping under one roof finally."

Sister Tilly sat in her office, staring out the window. She was going to talk to Leah when she came to the nursery after school today. The new parents were taking Malachi home on Thursday, and Tilly had still not broached the subject with Leah. She dreaded the discussion. Tilly heard a knock on the door.

"Come in."

It was Peggy. "Thithter Tilly, Reverend Mother wants to see you in her office."

"Thank you, Peggy." Tilly wondered what the Reverend

Mother wanted. She left her office, made her way to the Reverend Mother's office, and knocked on the door.

"Come in. Good morning, Sister Tilly."

As Tilly approached the desk, she saw the Rushtons, who were Malachi's new adoptive parents.

"Good news, Sister Tilly," the Reverend Mother continued. "Mr. and Mrs. Rushton have all the papers in order regarding Malachi's adoption. They don't want to wait a moment longer and wish to pick up Malachi now and take him home this morning."

"Today?" Tilly asked.

"Yes, Sister. Is that a problem?" the Reverend Mother asked sternly.

"No, Reverend Mother. Um, no. It's a little unexpected. We don't have him prepared."

"What is there to prepare?"

"He's sleeping now. When he wakes, he will need his lunch. He naps for two hours in the morning."

"We shall come back after lunch and pick him up then," Mr. Rushton said.

"Have him ready, Sister Mathilda."

"Yes, Reverend Mother." Tilly left the office; she stood outside and leaned against the door, offering a prayer: *Holy Mother of God, I am at a complete loss and taken by surprise. Please help me approach Leah. She's lost more than enough in her young life.*

Tilly went back to the nursery and instructed the staff on duty to have Malachi prepared and ready for his new parents to take him home that day after lunch.

"Oh, how wonderful," the helper said. "He's going early to his new family. We will miss him. Does Leah know yet?"

Tilly shot her a long stare.

"Oh, I see. We will have him ready, Sister Tilly."

"Pack him some of his clothes and nappies. I'm sure the Rushtons have everything they will need, but you never know. I will take him down myself when they arrive."

Later that day, after lunch, the helper handed Malachi over to Sister Tilly. He reached up with a little hand and touched her cheek.

"You are quite the lad. It's as if you have been with us before." Tilly held him close as he smiled up at her. She was feeling something out of the question—attachment. The outcome was heartache. She carried him down to the Reverend Mother's office, but first she went to the chapel and sat in the back pew, holding Malachi close as she looked into his blue eyes. He was pulling on her nose and chuckling.

"I have never come across such a cheerful child in all my days in the nursery. You smile from morning to night—how could we not love you? Bless you, Malachi, for your presence in our nursery and for passing through and touching each and every one of us. You have brought with you many gifts. May God walk alongside you on your path through life and keep you ever safe, you beautiful boy." Tilly kissed him on his forehead, and Malachi shrieked with delight. He was following the reflection of the noonday sun on one of the stained-glass windows.

Reluctantly, Tilly left the chapel and went to the office where Malachi's new parents were waiting.

"I thought we might go early to the convent," Sebastian said. "There's a pub opposite called the Punch Bowl. They do a really nice lunch. Would you like that, Amelia?"

"Yes, we should get to the convent quickly after lunch, before the boys go for their nap. I want to spend as much time with them as I can. I am sure they will not recognize me, Sebastian."

"Of course they will—you are their mother. Don't worry so."

Sebastian and Amelia sat in the pub, eating their lunch. Amelia picked at her shepherd's pie. It was delicious, but her mind was on the convent across the street. It was past one o'clock. She wanted to be there with her little boys. She needed to spend time with them before the girls came in from school at four o'clock.

"I want to leave, Sebastian. Let's go."

"Okay," he said. He opened the pub door. She ran through the open door and across the road without looking, and a car nearly struck her. Sebastian went after her.

"Amelia, slow down. Nobody is going anywhere; they are safe and warm until we decide to take them home."

"Every second I am not with them is a waste of precious time."

"Amelia." Sebastian stopped in front of her, and taking both of her hands, he looked into her eyes. He spoke as softly as he could. "If you arrive at the convent in this heightened state of excitement, although we all understand how you are feeling—"

"I don't think anyone understands how I feel."

"Maybe so, but I do know this, Amelia: if you rush to bring the children home too quickly, there will be consequences.

You must relax and let them see you are ready to take the children home. They will be looking at what is best for the six children. If you look in any way fragile or unstable in their opinion, based on your anxiety and behavior, they will not release them."

"They can't do that. They are ours."

"I understand that," Sebastian said patiently. "Let's walk. There is a lovely grotto and garden. Come catch our breath. It's a nice, bright day—a change from the usual November damp." They walked past the Lourdes grotto.

Amelia bowed her head. "Mother Mary, bless this day. Keep us safe."

— 17 —

Tilly knocked on the Reverend Mother's door with Malachi in her arms.

"Come," Tilly heard, and she entered holding Malachi.

"Ah, good. Come in, Sister."

The Rushtons were sitting on the edge of their chairs. They reminded Tilly of two budgies sitting on their perches, waiting for the cage door to be opened for them. Their nervous energy was waiting to explode with the freedom and ability to flap their wings and fly out of the cage to new, unexplored territory. They both jumped from their chairs and stood together, nervously moving from one foot to the other. Their unblinking eyes were glued on Malachi.

Tilly did her best to sound jocular. "Well, here's your little boy—all dressed up and ready to go to his new family. Well done!" She handed Malachi over as though she were a little rushed; after all, she did this regularly.

"I have left some notes in his folder regarding his feeding and sleeping schedule, et cetera. If you have any concerns, please don't hesitate to contact the nursery. We will be more than happy to help you. He's a very good baby—content. If that's all, Reverend Mother, I shall leave. I am short staffed in the nursery."

"Yes. Thank you, Sister Mathilda."

"Good-bye, Mr. and Mrs. Rushton, and congratulations," Tilly said as she left.

Sebastian and Amelia were still in the grotto.

"Let's go, Sebastian; it's past one o'clock." They walked together to the entrance of the convent.

"Please stay calm," Sebastian urged, taking hold of Amelia's hand.

The front door of the convent opened, and a man and a woman carrying a baby came out. Amelia's heart skipped. She dropped Sebastian's hand and moved quickly toward the door.

"How lovely!" exclaimed Amelia as she looked at the woman. She could see only the warm blue blanket and the woolly hat peeking out of the top. "May I look at him? It is a boy, isn't it?" she asked.

The woman nodded. Gently pulling the blanket down so that she did not disturb him, Amelia peeked in. The baby's wide blue eyes and smiling mouth greeted her. He gave out a shriek of delight that startled them all.

"He is so beautiful," Amelia said. "May I hold him for just a moment, please?"

The woman looked at Amelia and hesitated for one second. "Yes, you may." She handed the baby over.

Amelia reached out her arms and folded them around the baby as though it were the most natural of events.

"Oh," whispered Amelia. "How old is he?"

"Three months."

Amelia smiled at the woman. "He is so beautiful. You are so lucky and blessed."

"I know," the woman replied.

"What's his name?" Amelia asked.

The lady paused for a moment. "It's Malachi," she said with a smile.

Amelia stared at her. "Did you say Malachi?"

"Yes," the woman answered. "The nursery named him; we liked it, and he recognizes it as his own name."

Amelia could hardly believe her eyes and ears. It was like an omen—the same age and the same name. He even looked like her children.

"We must go now," the lady said, and she took her baby back. "It was nice to talk to you. Good-bye." The man took the lady's arm and hurried her away.

Sebastian came up behind Amelia. They stood together at the convent door and watched the couple walk away with their baby until they disappeared in the distance.

—18—

Inside the convent, several different activities were going on. Being Monday, it was a busy day involving taking stock and replenishing shelves after the weekend. Sister Tilly was in the nursery, putting the children down for their afternoon nap, when she looked up to see Peggy Schilling.

"Why, Peggy, you startled me!" Tilly said with a smile. "Twice in one day you've come up those stairs."

Peggy shuffled, looked awkward, and gave a faint grin. "Thithter Tilly, Reverend Mother wishes to see you in the office as soon as possible."

"She does? Very good. That's fine, Peggy. Thank you for bringing me the message."

"I don't mind; I like you, Thithter. You are kind and always thank me, and I like that. It makes me feel good—special-like and important."

Tilly smiled at Peggy. "You are very important—one of the most important people in the convent, Peggy. Come—there is hot apple cider and warm biscuits in the kitchen. We made them this morning for snack time. I'll walk with you before I go downstairs. Maybe you can stay up here and help get the little ones settled. I'm short staffed today, and I could really do with your help."

"Yes, Thithter, I will help you."

Tilly made her way down to the Reverend Mother's office. It was well after one, and the naps were late; the children would only get an hour of quiet time. *What a topsy-turvy day,* thought Tilly. *I wonder what Reverend Mother wants.* Maybe the Rushtons were calling because Malachi wasn't settling well.

"Come in," said the Reverend Mother in answer to Tilly's knock.

Tilly could see a man and woman sitting in the chairs opposite the Reverend Mother. The woman had a familiar look. Tilly thought she recognized her from somewhere.

"Sister Tilly, this is Mr. and Mrs. Lavalle."

Of course—it was Leah's face Tilly could see. Tilly crossed the room to Amelia and took her hands. "How glad I am to meet you, Mrs. Lavalle—and Mr. Lavalle. You have the most wonderful children."

The Reverend Mother continued. "Mr. and Mrs. Lavalle have come to take their children home. Not all at once, of course. It is their suggestion to start with the girls for a week or so and then bring the little boys home. I myself agree. What is your opinion?"

For the second time that day, Tilly was at a loss for words. "I, ah, don't know."

"What do you mean?" snapped the Reverend Mother.

"What I mean is I can't answer that question, Reverend Mother. It's an upheaval for them. I understand Mr. and Mrs. Lavalle would like their children home as soon as possible.

It's wonderful news to see their mother back, but I can't tell you how they will respond. I suggest moving slowly. I can't add to that." Tilly stepped back.

"Mrs. Lavalle wishes to see her boys immediately," the Reverend Mother said.

"Well, it's nap time," Tilly answered. "They are asleep. Mrs. Lavelle, why don't you come back later when they are all refreshed? Then you can see them—visit with the girls later. It would be wise, I think, to give them all some time to know that you are back and to tell them they are going home—as I suggested, slowly."

Mr. Lavalle appeared to be nodding his head as though he understood. "I agree. Come, Amelia. We can come back later."

Mrs. Lavalle stood quickly. "Thank you, Sister. At what time do you suggest we return?" Her lips were trembling.

"Why don't you come have tea with the little ones in the nursery at about three? And then you can spend time with the girls on the main floor after. They will be so excited to see you, Mrs. Lavalle. I know they have missed you very much."

Mrs. Lavalle nodded. "Thank you." She and Mr. Lavalle left the office, closing the door behind them.

Leah jumped off the bus, grabbed both of her sisters, and held their hands tightly all the way along the wide-mouthed driveway leading to the convent door. She was breathless and excited; she loved Mondays. If she was on time, she could collect Malachi and give him his bath. She was early today as she dropped off the girls on the main floor and went up the stairs two at a time. Sister Tilly's office door was closed. She went into the playroom and saw her little brothers.

"Hello, boys!" They all ran over to her, and Leah lifted them up like a little mother.

Sasha held up his hand to show how he had hurt his thumb by catching it in the door. It had a bandage on it.

Leah kissed it. "There—all better!" She smiled, and Sasha agreed. Then he went back to the big truck he was playing with. "I'm going to give Malachi his bath." Leah turned to leave and was startled to see Sister Tilly standing behind her.

"Hello, Leah."

"You made me jump, Sister!"

"I'm sorry. It's good that I found you; I wonder if you would come with me, Leah."

"I'm just going to collect Malachi," Leah said, resisting. She was expected to be in the dining room by five, and it was now twenty after four.

"Leah, I said come with me now!"

Leah was shocked. Sister sounded angry and upset—Sister was never mean to anyone. Leah fell in line with Tilly, almost crying.

"What's wrong?" Leah said. Tilly shot her a glance as they arrived at the office door. She opened the door and ushered Leah in, closing the door behind her.

"Sit," Tilly said.

Leah sat and then jumped out of the chair. "Am I in trouble? Did I do something wrong? Are you angry with me?"

"Sit down, Leah—now!" Sister ordered. "Please listen to me. First of all, no, I am not angry with you, and secondly, you are not in trouble. Let me assure you there is nothing wrong. I do, however, have something to share with you. I have two things to tell you—very good news." Tilly hesitated. "All round, I would say wonderful. Malachi—" Tilly cleared her throat. "Our Malachi has been adopted."

"What?" Leah asked. "What do you mean adopted?" Leah didn't sound like herself. She was yelling at Sister.

"Lower your voice, and listen to me. It's been in the works for a while now; however, it was pushed forward unexpectedly. I am sorry, Leah, that I did not prepare you, but it's just that I was not sure how to tell you. But I do have some other wonderful news about your—"

Leah screamed, "I don't believe you!" She jumped out of the chair and ran out of the office door and into the baby's room. She went frantically from cot to cot, looking for Malachi, lifting blankets to no avail. As she was dashing past one of the nursery staff, the woman called out to Leah.

"Wonderful news about Malachi, isn't it, Leah?"

Leah screamed again and ran through the nursery floor, looking in every possible place in a desperate attempt to find Malachi, calling out, "I can't believe it! I can't believe he's not here!" Leah ran through the nursery doors and down the stairs, tears pouring from her eyes and mucous running from her nose. She drew her sleeve across her face in order to see where she was going, ignoring Sister Edwina's warning that she should not run. Leah threw open the chapel doors and slipped into the pew she loved the most, sitting at the foot of Mother Mary with the lit halo—the one Abby called a princess. Kneeling at the feet of the statute, Leah wept. She let the tears flow. She did not pray; she simply showed and shared her sorrow, letting it flow freely in the safest of places.

Tilly jumped up and followed Leah but made a wise decision not to interfere with Leah's rampage through the nursery. She followed her down to the chapel doors and sighed with relief when Leah went in. Tilly was aware it was the safest place for her to be. Turning to head back up the stairs, she ran into Mr. and Mrs. Lavalle.

"I am so relieved so see you both. May I have a private word before you go up, Mrs. Lavalle? Mr. Lavalle, why don't you go ahead and see the boys? Prepare them, and tell them that their mammy is coming up to see them. The staff are expecting you. I must speak with your wife."

Tilly ushered Amelia into the stockroom. "I hope you don't mind," Tilly said as she closed the door behind her, speaking in a low voice. "It's just that I must have a word with you regarding Leah."

"Is there a problem? Is she sick?" Amelia asked.

"No, nothing like that. Let me explain. When Leah first arrived here, she was very sad. I decided to put her with a newborn who had just arrived. She named him Malachi, and they have worked miracles on one another. Fortunately for him, he was adopted today, but I was slow in preparing Leah. I have just now broken the news, and she is in the chapel, heartbroken."

Tilly could see that Mrs. Lavalle listened intently and had tears in her eyes. Mrs. Lavalle placed her hand on top of Tilly's.

"Leave it with me, Sister, and I thank you for being a guardian angel caring for my little ones whilst I was recovering. I am back now, and I intend to make up for lost time."

Mrs. Lavalle hugged Tilly with all her might, smiled, and left the stockroom.

Amelia opened the door to the chapel and quietly closed it behind her. Standing like a statue, she looked toward the altar, feeling the peace and safety of the place. Searching the pews, her eyes came to rest on her beautiful daughter kneeling at the foot of Mother Mary and crying gently. Amelia was touched at the sight. Knowing she must be strong in order to help her child, she walked toward the pew, slipped in, and sat down beside Leah. Leah did not move for a moment. She then turned her head to see beside her and looked with disbelief.

Then she cried out, "Mam, Mam!" and burst into tears. Amelia opened her arms for her child to fall into and held her close, listening to Leah's sad story and rocking her like a babe. They were silent for a while as Leah allowed her sobs to subside. Amelia drew back, holding her daughter's face between her hands.

"You know, Leah, I saw your beautiful Malachi."

"No, you couldn't have, Mam. He's gone," Leah sobbed.

"Listen to me. Daddy and I came at one o'clock today. We wanted to see the boys before their nap time. As I approached the door of the convent, a lady and man were coming out holding a little baby. I asked if I might look at him and how old he was. I asked if I might be allowed to hold him. The lady passed him over, and I took him in my arms."

Leah was listening to her mam with wide eyes and an open mouth.

"Holding him very close to me, I asked his name. 'Malachi,' said the lady. You can imagine my disbelief and surprise. I looked at him and smiled, and he shrieked with joy and giggled with glee, kicking his legs in excitement. Everyone appeared to be a little flabbergasted at this response. But now I understand, Leah—Malachi thought I was you. He was saying good-bye. He saw your face in mine—I'm sure of it. He was passing on his love." Amelia continued, "I am so proud of you and the work you have been able to do. What you were able to give to that little boy. It is truly a miracle that you found one another. He is one of the happiest babies that I have ever seen, and it is because of the love you gave him until he found a home with parents who will also love him. There is no greater gift. You will miss him—you will always miss him—but he will be in here." Amelia touched Leah's heart with her hand. "That's the gift. Now, dry your eyes and blow your nose."

Amelia gave Leah her handkerchief, and she did as she was told. They stood up and walked out of the chapel together hand in hand.

"Let's go find your brothers and sisters, Leah. We are all going home."

Abby sat on the floor of the dormitory with her legs crossed, frantically polishing a pair of shoes with a brush, trying to bring up the required shine so that one could see oneself, as Sister Edwina demanded. As it was Monday, all shoes were to be inspected, and polishing them was Abby's job.

Putting down the brush and shoe, Abby counted, "One, two, three ..." up to twelve. Looking up at the portrait, she added, "That's all of them, scary Jesus. You know, I like this job. We get time to talk. Do you remember when I ran away from you and hid? Sister Edwina was mad. I have to tell you about Leah. She's really sad because Malachi has gone home to a new mammy and daddy. Everybody knows how much Leah loves Malachi; she is always with him. We had our tea without her tonight. Sister Edwina sent me up here to do the shoes. That's good, scary Jesus; no one yells at me up here."

Abby held up the shoe to the picture. "Do you think that's shiny enough, scary Jesus?" She was polishing the last shoe when Peggy Schilling came in.

"I've been looking for you."

Abby did not like Peggy; she was smelly and talked funny.

"Reverend Mother wants you to come downstairs to the common room."

"Why?" Abby asked. "Am I in trouble?"

"I don't know; don't athk me. I was just told to find you." Peggy grabbed Abby roughly by the arm and pulled her out of the dormitory. The shoes scattered all over the floor.

"Well, if I'm not in trouble now, I will be when Sister Edwina sees this room."

"Stop dawdling! Move!" Peggy yelled.

Peggy was moving so fast that Abby had to run to keep up. She wanted to hold her breath when she was with Peggy to keep out that bad smell, but the trip was too long for her to hold her breath. Climbing down all the stairs and trying to count, she could turn blue and die, and then what? Sister Edwina would be angry. Peggy continued to pull Abby by her arm until they arrived at the common-room door, and then she let go, took her hand, and pushed her through the door.

The Reverend Mother was at the entrance. "Come in, little one. We have a surprise for you."

Abby's first reaction was to cry from relief; she had been sure she was in trouble. The Reverend Mother never called anyone into the common room unless he or she was in trouble. Abby's tears rolled down her cheeks.

"Why are you crying, child?" exclaimed the Reverend Mother.

Abby was unable to answer between her relief and the stench coming from Peggy. She was unable to speak.

"This is no way to greet your mother, now, is it?" the Reverend Mother said in disgust.

Meet who? Abby thought. *Whose mother?* She looked into the big room, and to her astonishment, there, sitting on a chair beside the old piano, was her mammy, waving her hand in a forward motion.

"Come. Come to me Abby," her mammy said. She was holding a blue teddy bear. "Look—I made him just for you."

Abby stood still as though her feet were glued to the floor, staring first at her mammy, then at the Reverend Mother, and then at smelly Peggy. It was more than she could stand. Plonking herself onto the floor, Abby burst into fresh tears.

"Good gracious, child. What has got into you? Get up this minute," the Reverend Mother demanded.

Abby was unable to move or stop crying. Her mammy jumped up from the chair. "Please, Reverend Mother, kindly allow me to handle this."

"As you wish, Mrs. Lavalle." The Reverend Mother walked away, taking Peggy with her.

Her mammy sat down beside her on the floor. She put the teddy beside Abby.

"Oh, you have grown up so much. You look beautiful, Abby."

Abby was quiet; she could not believe her mammy was sitting beside her, and she did not know why she was crying.

"Why are you so sad, Abby? I have come to take you home."

Abby looked at Amelia and burst into tears again.

"Because I am not ready—I didn't wash my face or brush my hair or turn the cuffs up on my cardigan or even say please and thank you."

Amelia smiled at Abby. "Dry your eyes, and give me a big cuddle. I've missed you very much."

Abby looked at her mammy and threw herself into her arms, wrapping her arms around her mammy's neck as though she would never let go.

—19—

Abby was happy and excited. She jumped up and down in the kitchen and danced around the table like a ballet dancer. It was the first Saturday since they had arrived home, and they were all together, just like in the old days before her mammy got sick and had to go away to get better. There was a lot of work to do, and everyone was helping, even the little boys.

They were all under the kitchen table, and her mammy had given them all dusters—old nappies—and told Abby to look after her brothers and show them what to do. They each had to polish a leg of the table. Their job was to wrap the duster around the leg of the table and pull it toward them with one hand and then the other. They thought it was great fun. They had to do this until the table leg shined like a new penny. However, there was more playing than polishing going on under the table. But at least she knew where they all were, Mammy said. The boys were three years old now and up to all sorts of mischief.

Andre and Eugene were helping Daddy in the backyard, cleaning up some of the weeds. The grass was so long that it was hard to see. The concrete walkway had turned green and needed to be scrubbed with bleach and a brush. It was slimy, and Abby did not like standing on the green bits when she went outside to the toilet. In fact, Abby hated going to the outside toilet; she would only go if she were nearly bursting. When she sat on the long wooden box with the hole in it in the dark room outside with no light and pulled the old, rusty chain that made it flush, she was sure it would swallow her like a big monster. She feared she would never get out alive because creepy crawlies of all sizes were coming to get her.

Often, Abby did her business in the grass instead. It was brighter, and she felt safer. Her daddy said he was going to rig up a light in the old toilet and whitewash the walls so that it was brighter. Abby didn't think too much of that idea, as she would then be able to see the monster coming.

The whole house was busy, as tomorrow was Sunday, their first one together in a long time. Mammy had said things must be shipshape or else. Auntie Helen and Uncle Charles were coming for Sunday dinner after they went to Sunday Mass at their own church. Abby was not excited about going to Mass—it was long, and she didn't understand the priest. He talked funny—not just because of the language, which was called Latin, but because he bent over like an old wizard, and his mouth seemed as if it were broken.

"Why does Father Litchfield speak funny?" Abby asked her mammy one day. "He frightens me sometimes."

Amelia told her, "He fought in a war. Someone shot him with a gun, and the bullet went through his throat into the roof of his mouth."

Abby thought that was horrible. "So that's why he talks funny. That's a sad story, Mammy." Next time Abby went to church, she smiled at Father Litchfield.

"Hello, Father," she said. He smiled back at her, and his eyes shined as though he might start to cry. He came over to her, made a cross shape in the air over her head, and touched her head. She didn't understand the action, but she knew it was something special.

One warm April afternoon Helen stopped by Amelia's with some fresh eggs. She knocked on the front door and pushed it open gently.

"Hello! It's me. Can I come in?" she called out.

Abby was behind the door with Sally, her friend from across the road, playing make-believe house inside the front hall holding their swaddled dolls. Sally's was a beautiful doll with a hand-painted face and a white lace bonnet. Abby held a blue felt teddy bear.

"Hello, Auntie Helen," they both said. Sally was a fixture at the Lavalle home, as though Amelia didn't have enough to do. Still, she was a bonny lass. She had long, shiny black ringlets hanging down to her waist, held back with a pink satin bow matching her pink satin sash. She had black eyes as large as saucers and olive skin. She was a beauty and a canny little bairn to boot. Abby loved her, and God knew they were good for each other.

"We are getting our babies ready for bed," Sally told Helen.

"What are your babies' names?" Helen asked both girls.

Sally stood up and proudly opened the shawl around her baby doll. "Her name is Emily Jane."

"Well, she certainly looks like an Emily. She's very lovely. How about yours, Abby? What's your baby's name?"

"This is Malachi. My mammy made him for me. I call him Micky for short. He is very soft, and I sleep with him in my bed. Would you like to hold him?"

Helen's heart sprang to her throat as she took the teddy from Abby's hands. *Out of the mouths of babes,* she thought. This child was inordinately profound and had such a pure innocence that there were times when Helen longed to steal her away. She was sure the child would not be missed. It seemed to Helen that Abby was always on the outside looking in. Helen deeply regretted in her heart that Charles had not allowed her to go through with the adoption when Abby was born. She would never forgive him.

"Auntie Helen, please, can I have him back?" Abby broke into Helen's thoughts.

Helen smiled. "Of course. You two girls carry on playing. Have fun. I'll go find your mammy."

Amelia was in the scullery, making bread, as usual.

"Hello, Helen. It's good to see you. I see you have brought eggs; thank you. Why don't you pop the kettle on while I finish this off? The boys are in the backyard, playing outside the scullery window, where I can keep an eye on them. Eugene and Andre are in the garage, building a bicycle. Andre was offered a paper-delivery job at the news agency and wants to have a bicycle to do the deliveries. It would be more time efficient, as he says he gets paid by the number of papers delivered. He's quite the entrepreneur. Eugene just seems to hang around watching, not quite as sure or as ambitious."

"You look very tired," Helen said. "Are you all right?"

"I'm fine; don't worry so," snapped Amelia. "We work day and night here to keep things together and make ends meet. We just lost the lodger in the back room, so we are two pounds a week short. Needs to be cleaned up and rented as quickly as possible. If you hear of anyone looking, please let me know."

"Sit down," Helen told her. "I'll put the kettle on. I think I might have just the person for you. Charles happened to mention her yesterday—a niece of someone at work, a student nurse. She lives in Hexham and is looking for a room here."

"Do you know how old she is?"

"I would think twenty-two maybe. I'll let Charles know that if she's interested, she can come look."

"That's wonderful. It needs a lick of paint and a spring clean. It would be really good if we don't have to advertise in the paper."

"Leave it with me, Amelia."

They relaxed in their chairs and sipped their tea. Suddenly, the sky turned as black as night. Helen looked out the window and shivered. There was a flash of lightning and an enormous thunderclap. The little boys came running in from the yard.

"Where did that come from?" Helen said. "I'm surprised."

"Me too," Amelia agreed. As they looked out the window, the heavens opened, and hailstones the size of golf balls fell to the ground, sounding like firecrackers going off.

"Well, I never. I've never seen the likes!" Helen remarked.

"That's really creepy," Amelia said. She didn't know why, but she closed her eyes and whispered her prayer.

"Mother Mary, bless this day. Keep us safe in every way."

Stella looked at the small piece of paper with the directions to the Lavalle home. She was impressed with the look of the place—a big double-fronted Victorian detached home—and it was only five minutes from the bus stop. *This would be perfect,* she thought. She approached the house and lifted the latch on the wrought-iron gate. It was rusty in places and squeaked as she opened it, sounding like a meowing kitten. She closed the gate and stood on the path, looking up at the big old house.

"Hello. What's your name?"

Stella looked down at the young voice and found a little girl holding hands with two smaller boys. As she looked around, she saw a third boy about the same age sitting on a blanket in the grass, playing with some toy cars. Stella was surprised.

"Ah, I'm Stella. What's yours?"

"My name is Abigail—Abby for short. This is Nathan and Noah, and that's Sasha sitting on the blanket. They are my little brothers. Have you come to look at the room?"

"Yes, I have." Stella was still a little dumbfounded. Abby looked like a sweet little child who appeared to be mature beyond her young years.

"They are in the house, waiting for you. Just make sure you have closed the gate and the latch is locked, and I will take you to them." Abigail walked her brothers over to the blanket. "Now, you stay on the blanket until I get back—do you hear me?"

The little boys all looked at her, nodded, and sat down together. Abby came over, looked at Stella, smiled, and took her hand.

"Come along with me," she gently commanded. "This way." Abby opened the front door and then another glass door leading to a long, narrow, dark hallway. Several doors and a staircase ran off it. All the doors were closed, and some were locked. Stella could smell bread baking. At last, Abby paused and pushed open a door.

"Mammy, she's here—the lady to look at the room. Her name is Stella." Once more, Abby smiled. Then she let go of Stella's hand and was gone.

Stella was standing in a room that looked well used and lived in. A middle-aged woman appeared from behind another door, probably the scullery.

"Hello. I'm Amelia Lavalle; you must be Stella."

"Yes, I am. It's nice to meet you."

"I can show you the room and bathroom—just come with me." They walked up the staircase to the landing. "This is the bathroom; you share it with four others."

Stella looked in; it was clean and adequate. Amelia went up three more stairs and unlocked a door. She stepped back and allowed Stella to go ahead of her. Stella was pleasantly surprised at how large and bright the room was compared to the rest of the old house. Scanning the room quickly, she saw a large mahogany wardrobe with a full-length mirror; a black marble fireplace with a gas fire, one burner for a kettle, and a small oven; a sink; and, in the corner, a dressing table. There was a large window looking over the backyard, which gave the room a sense of grandness because of the amount of light.

"Of course," Amelia said, "the gas is run off a meter. You won't need to use too much in the spring and summer—your hot water and gas ring only. Winter will be more expensive, as you will need the fire."

Stella smiled. "I love it, Mrs. Lavalle. I'll take it!"

"You will?" Amelia was clearly delighted. "Very good. When would you like to move in?"

"As soon as possible," Stella replied.

"We need a two-pound deposit—that's your first week's rent."

Stella opened her handbag and gave Amelia eight pounds.

"I would like to pay you a month in advance, Mrs. Lavalle."

Amelia's eyes opened wide, and she took the eight pounds quickly. "Whatever you wish." She handed Stella the keys. "Welcome to your new home. What do you do?" she asked Stella.

"I'm a student nurse. I have eighteen months before I am finished with my RN. I work a lot of different shifts and many hours. I also spend time doing homework in the library."

"I am very pleased," Amelia told her. "You seem like a lovely lass—welcome. I hope you will be very happy here."

— 20 —

Stella moved into the Lavalle house; it was perfect. The room was nice and cozy, and she had everything she needed. It was close to all amenities, including the grocery store, post office, newsagent, and library. It amazed Stella that there were eight children living in the house, but there was never any noise on her floor. Often, when she was coming home from work, she would see the younger ones playing in the grass outside.

One Saturday morning, as Stella was leaving the house to do some errands, the little boys were outside playing on the front path alone, which was unusual. She had just opened the gate and made sure it was closed behind her when she heard a loud scream. Stella turned and ran back.

One of the little boys was sitting on the ground, covered with blood and sobbing, and the two other little boys were looking at him, touching him and trying to help. Stella knelt beside him.

"What's your name?" she asked, but he kept sobbing. "You are okay, little boy. He'll be fine; don't worry," she told his brothers. Stella ascertained quickly that the injury was gash above his right eye. He must have fallen and hit it on the step; he was lucky to have missed his eye. She gathered him up into her arms and asked the other boys to take her to their mammy. The boys jumped up; they looked white with shock. She held a handkerchief to the gash on his head and placed pressure on it. The little boys ran up the dark hallway, screaming for their mammy. The door of the kitchen opened, and Mr. Lavalle stood in the entrance.

"What's going on?" he asked.

"Your son fell and hit his head, Mr. Lavalle." She carried him into the kitchen and put him on a chair. "Please fetch me some cold cloths and some cotton wool and antiseptic. Do you have a first-aid kit?"

"Ah, oui, yes."

Stella looked at the two other boys. "Can you help me, boys?"

Mr. Lavalle handed her the tin and ran to get some cloths. She opened the tin and gave one little boy the cotton and the other the Elastoplast. "Now, hold these for me."

Mr. Lavalle came back with the cloths. Stella took one and placed it on the cut.

"I suggest you wipe the blood off the other boys' hands. I am sure it will make them feel better. This looks like it may need a couple of stitches."

"Daddy, where's Mammy? Where's my mammy?" one of the boys cried.

"My wife has gone to the grocery store," he told Stella.

"Do you have a doctor?" she asked.

"Yes, he's just around the corner."

"Does he have a surgery on Saturday morning?"

"I honestly don't know," Sebastian replied.

Stella took charge. "How about I take care of Sasha, and you look after his brothers? We will get him stitched up, and he will be just fine. It's a shock for him." Stella smiled. "And his little brothers, apparently." The two uninjured boys both sat on chairs, still looking white and holding on tightly to their first-aid supplies.

"My name is Stella, and I'm a nurse. I'm going to take care of Sasha, okay?" Stella took Sasha into her arms, still applying pressure to the wound. Mr. Lavalle held the door open.

"I simply cannot tell you how much I appreciate your help, Stella; I am so grateful you are around. I'm not much good at this sort of thing; their mother does it all."

Stella noticed his bright blue eyes as she looked at him. She had not realized how handsome he was.

"I'll be back soon, Mr. Lavalle; don't you worry." She took off with Sasha, in full control of the situation.

An hour later, Stella and Sasha stepped out of the doctor's surgery. The doctor had successfully stitched up yet another Lavalle child. Sasha had required three stitches above his right eye. He had a large white pad tied to his head and a lollipop in his hand. He was taking long, lazy licks; clearly, no other issue was on his mind. Amelia came rushing up the path breathlessly.

"Sasha!" She scooped him up into her arms as soon as she saw him. "Oh, Sasha, are you all right?"

"Look, Mammy. I have a lollipop and a big bandage on my head."

"Yes, I see." Amelia turned her attention to Stella. "Thank you so very much. Sebastian told me how amazingly helpful you were with all three boys. How fortunate that you were around and heard him."

"It's my pleasure, Mrs. Lavalle. I was only too happy to help. It must be quite a regular occurrence with eight children. Well, I don't mean such a situation—but always some little one with a cut, bruise, or bump."

Amelia went silent and appeared to be pensive. "Yes, you are quite right."

"I know from my nursing experience when I was in emergency. We always had children coming in who needed stitching up. Others had broken arms from falling off their bicycles. Some of them had even shoved marbles up their noses. Ah, the things young ones can get themselves into is nobody's business!" Stella was trying to help ease the situation.

"I should have been there with him," Amelia said quietly.

"Well, if you don't mind me saying so, Mrs. Lavalle, how can you be two places at one time? They also need to eat, and I assume that is what you were doing when this accident happened—out at the grocery store." Stella smiled.

"You know, you are quite right," Amelia agreed. She looked directly at Stella. "I think I'm going to like living with you, Stella. You really should smile more often."

"That's what I'm told." Stella smiled back.

"How about we invite Stella to come have Sunday dinner with us, Sasha?" Amelia said, and Sasha left his lollipop long enough to agree.

"I do not wish to put you to any trouble, Mrs. Lavalle," Stella replied.

"It's no trouble to me at all. Allow me to thank you in my own way," Amelia insisted.

"Of course. I would love to come share dinner with you and your family."

"Good," Amelia said as they entered the front door. "One o'clock—just come down to the kitchen, and we will be waiting for you."

Sunday at one o'clock, Stella knocked on the kitchen door. It opened, and a lovely looking young girl was standing there with two of her little brothers at her feet.

"Come in!" Mr. Lavalle called over the girl's shoulder.

Stella moved into the middle of the room; it was smaller than she remembered. Sasha was staring at her; Stella went to him and knelt.

"How's your head? Does it feel better?"

He nodded. He was bruised around the eye. Stella peeked under the bandage.

"He's healing beautifully," she announced as she looked up. It seemed as if there were a thousand eyes looking back at her. Stella smiled, feeling nervous.

"Come sit down," said Mr. Lavalle, and he showed her to a chair.

"Why, thank you." She sat at the table and was aware this family had little to share. It was evident in the sparseness of the room. There was no luxury, nothing that was not required. Yet in the room's starkness it was apparent they were celebrating a special occasion. The room was so clean that one could have eaten off the floor. Everything had been cleaned and polished until it was gleaming. The table was set and opened up to hold eleven of them. The chairs around the table were a mishmash—some were wood, others were painted, and there were folding chairs and high chairs. There was a place for everything, and everything had its place. The tablecloth was extraordinary—white with embroidered flowers in a multitude of colors. It was striking, and if one had looked at the cloth only, one would have thought it did not belong. Yet the moment she scanned the room, as sparse as it was, she could see it was perfect for the occasion.

In the center of the table was a blue ceramic vase with wildflowers clearly picked from the front garden. The crockery did not match, nor did the cutlery. Even though the setup was a mishmash of different items, the overall appearance was delightful.

Mrs. Lavalle entered from the scullery and placed a skinny roasted chicken on the table. It smelled delicious. She and the three girls went back and forth between the scullery and kitchen table until the table was covered with every possible vegetable and side dish, including brussels sprouts, turnips, peas, cabbage, roasted potatoes, mashed potatoes, stuffing, gravy, and fresh bread rolls with butter. Stella's mouth was watering; she had not had a hot meal in days.

"This looks very delicious, Mrs. Lavalle, and I cannot wait to sample it."

One of the older boys bent his head and said grace. There was not enough meat on the chicken to feed them all, which was probably why there were so many vegetables and bread rolls on the table to fill them all up. It was clear to Stella the children were eagerly anticipating their Sunday dinner. They had their knives and forks at the ready. It was an occasion to be sure. They were all well behaved at the table, and the young ones sat quietly while the older ones helped them put food on their plates. The little ones had no chicken but had lots of other foods. They tucked in.

"Do close your mouth when you are chewing, Nathan," Mrs. Lavalle said.

There was chicken on Stella's plate—Mr. Lavalle saw to it that Stella was served first, followed by himself and all the big boys. Mrs. Lavalle looked thin and tired. It would have been Stella's assessment, if Mrs. Lavalle had been a patient, that she was undernourished and overworked. Stella looked at everyone around the table. The table was full and busy with eleven of them there.

"Please, may I have some more bread?" asked one of the boys.

"No," Mrs. Lavalle told him. "That's for your tea later with some jam and hot tea."

He sulked for a moment.

Mr. Lavalle looked across the table at Stella. "Tell us about yourself, Stella." Everyone looked at her.

"There's not much to tell, really. I'm a student nurse in my final year at the infirmary. My parents live in Hexham. They have a small working farm—cattle mostly. My father is looking to retire in a year or two, sell the farm, and move to a small bungalow."

"Do you have sisters and brothers?" Camille asked.

"No, I don't. I'm an only child," Stella told her.

"Like Sally," Abby said.

"Is it lonely?" asked Leah.

"No, not really. You would imagine it to be lonely because you are very lucky and have lots of brothers and sisters. I didn't have that, so I don't miss it and don't feel lonely.

"My mother was a twin," Stella continued. "She told me the story of her mother, my grandmother, visiting a friend at a nearby house in the country during a snowstorm in December, when she was approximately eight months pregnant. It was just light snow when she started out on her visit. My grandmother was not aware during her visit with her friend just how much snow was falling, and a gale-force wind started blowing, causing the snow to create drifts. When she was preparing to leave, the snow had drifted so high it had blocked off the front door. There were four-foot drifts up against the house; it was clearly impossible to even make the short distance back to her own home the next farm over.

"My grandmother ended up an overnight guest in a beautiful, warm bed with an eiderdown cocooning her as she slowly drifted off into a wonderful sleep, listening to the howling wind outside and the *tap-tap-tap* of the branches up against the window. In the early hours of the morning, she awoke with very powerful pains in her back. She sat up and rubbed her back for a little while and then realized it was the beginning of labor. My grandmother called out to her friend, who came to her immediately. She told her husband to go find the doctor as quickly as possible. The neighbor's husband opened the door, and the snow was piled even higher. He found a shovel and tried to burrow his way through but was clearly unable to do it. The snow was falling so hard and the wind blowing so strongly that the visibility was zero. The only thing they could do was go about delivering these babies themselves.

"My mother was the first one to be born. She had no problems; she came headfirst—strong, healthy, and straightforward. Her twin sister, however, was another story; she was caught with the umbilical cord around her neck, and no one was aware of it. My grandmother was told later that even if the doctor had made it, the outcome would have been exactly the same. No one could have been aware. My grandmother delivered a dead baby girl, perfect in every way—my mother's identical twin.

"My mother always told me that she felt as though half of her was missing. She was just standing by herself, not complete, not even after I was born. I imagine that was a lonely place to be, and not too many people would understand."

While Stella was telling her sad story, one could have heard a pin drop, although Nathan was fidgeting. His mother gave him a stern look and told him to be quiet and sit still.

"That is quite a touching story," said Sebastian as his eyes fell upon Stella.

"We have enjoyed having your company today, and you are welcome to join in with the family whenever you feel the need. I feel a connection to you after hearing your mother's story," Amelia said as she stood and collected the plates.

After the meal was over, the girls wanted to show Stella their bedroom, as it was next door to her room.

"Thank you for the wonderful meal, Mr. and Mrs. Lavalle; it was delicious. I had a lovely time."

"You are most welcome." Amelia put her hand on Stella's arm. "You are welcome here any time."

Sebastian nodded and agreed as he held open the door for her. The girls pushed past to go up the stairs, chasing one another.

Stella looked up at Sebastian and smiled. "Thank you. I shall. Good-bye." As she followed the three girls up the dark stairway, she thought, *What wonderful blue eyes Mr. Lavalle has,* smiling inside.

—21—

In the year that followed, Stella and the Lavalle family were inseparable. One cold October afternoon, Amelia was working in the scullery alone, making vegetable soup. While standing at the sink, she leaned up against it for support, as she was feeling weary. While peeling parsnips, carrots, and other winter vegetables, she thought she would make some extra for Stella. As she was draining the fat from the stock, the doorbell rang.

Amelia went to answer; it was Helen.

"Hello, Amelia. Here I am. I thought I would drop by with some fresh eggs—a dozen extra-large brown from the co-op. They are on sale."

"That's good of you. Have you got time for some tea?"

"Yes, I brought some scones and some shortbread biscuits. I thought we might sit together and have some and enjoy the silence now that you are on your own all day. How do you like it with them all in school now?" Helen asked. "What time do they leave?"

"About eight forty-five I walk Cammie, Abby, and the

three boys over the road. Leah is going to high school now, so she takes the bus. Of course you know Andre started work in September; he's fifteen now and works in the factory with his dad. He's doing a great job and bringing a wage packet in; he hands it over to us every week. In order to make his pocket money, he cleans windows. Eugene—he's a different story altogether. He's still in his last year of school, when he's not playing truant, stealing from the local newsagent shop, or falling out of trees and breaking his arm. He's truly a headache. Seems to need more attention than the rest."

"So it's quiet for you?"

"Well, it's a mixed blessing. Certainly more time to do what I need to do, but I miss them. The little ones are good company. The three of them are no bother, really; they look out for each other. I suppose I am getting used to it. They are just all growing up so fast."

"Are you feeling well?" inquired Helen.

"Yes, I'm fine, thanks," Amelia replied.

"That's good." Helen did not wish to comment on how tired and thin Amelia looked. It seemed a permanent state for Amelia.

"I meant to ask you last time—is that Stella girl still working out for you?"

"She's fantastic—one of the family. Everybody loves her. Even Sebastian spends time with her when he's around."

"Oh?" Helen's ears pricked up. "In what way would that be?"

"She's learning French, and he helps her with the words. She's a great help to me, Helen, especially with those boys around, splitting their heads and falling out of trees. She pays her rent on time and keeps the room squeaky clean.

Her nursing training is finished in the next few months, but I hope she never leaves."

"It's not good to depend on someone that much, Amelia."

"Oh, you worry too much, Helen. Stella is a blessing to us all—like another daughter. I love having her in my home."

"Good enough. I have to get back to Charles and make his tea. I'll be on my way. Thanks for the tea and the chat."

Amelia was about to show Helen out when the kitchen door swung open. A plain-looking girl came in without knocking.

"Oh, I'm sorry, Amelia. I didn't know you had a visitor."

"Come in." Amelia waved. "This is Stella, Helen—our lodger. This is my sister Helen."

Stella thrust out her hand. "Nice to meet you, Helen. I have heard the children talk of you."

"I'm sure." Helen already didn't like the girl; she was a bit too pushy and sure of herself. She should have knocked.

"I'm off, Amelia. I'll see myself out. Good-bye!" Helen walked out to her little car—no, she did not like that girl one bit. Helen intended to keep an eye on things and see what she was up to, especially the French lessons.

Helen and Amelia were working in the kitchen, making toffee apples for the nighttime party in the back lane. It was November 5—Guy Fawkes Day and bonfire night.

"The children were so excited when they left for school this morning," Amelia said. "Sasha and Nathan danced all the way to the end of the street. It was wonderful to see them so happy. They will be delighted to see such a wonderful spread. We are all going to celebrate. Sebastian is bringing fireworks and sparklers. Andre and Leah made a fantastic-looking Guy. Stella is coming with some homemade fudge and cindered toffee. She's such a good help."

"Yes, how is she doing these days?" Helen was stirring the caramel, making sure it didn't stick to the pan.

"She intends to stay with us another year if she gets the job she's after. I'm delighted."

"That's good," Helen responded weakly.

"She's even offered to look after all of the children—with Leah and Andre's help, of course—for the weekend so that I can visit our Deidre up in Edinburgh. What do you think, Helen?"

Helen stopped stirring the caramel. "Is Sebastian going with you?"

"No, he's staying to oversee things. I'd not leave her alone with all that responsibility or even suggest it. I'm tired and looking for a few days away. I thought you would be supportive," said Amelia.

"I am. It's just, you know, I thought you and Sebastian could do with some time alone together."

"Yes, I agree, but he has to work Friday night and Monday morning, and we need the money."

"You know, Charles and I would have come up and helped." The caramel in the pan started to stick, and Helen went back to stirring vigorously.

"I really appreciate all that you do for me, Helen; no sister could be kinder, and I bless you every day for it. However, it's arranged; I'm going to Edinburgh on Friday morning—a ten o'clock train. I should be home Monday night. Stella has a four-day weekend, and she will move downstairs on Friday and look after everything for me."

Helen had a feeling of foreboding; she was sure this girl had an ulterior motive. She removed the toffee from the stove and smacked the wooden spoon on the side of the pan—much harder than required—to remove the excess. Amelia appeared to notice.

"Be happy for me, Helen; I'm so looking forward to some time away. I've not been away since I lost our Malachi four years ago. I deserve it—don't you think?"

Helen gave a feeble smile. "Good God, of course you do, Amelia. I want you to go have a good time." Helen went to look for her handbag and took out two pounds. "Here—buy yourself something nice, or have your hair done, please." She pushed the notes into Amelia's hand. "I must be off now, but I will see you next week when you come home," Helen said as she prepared to leave.

"Thanks so much, Helen." Amelia followed her to the door and waved as she drove away.

Helen's eyes were full of tears, something she could not control no matter how she tried as she drove away from Amelia and her trusting nature.

—22—

On Friday afternoon Stella was downstairs in the Lavalle kitchen. Amelia had left that morning for Edinburgh for the weekend. She had promised Amelia she would tend to Sebastian and the children and watch over them. While preparing tea for the children, who would be coming home from school soon, she thought of the French meal she planned to cook for Sebastian after he came home from his evening French classes. He would not have to be up early the next morning, as he was not working. The children would all be in bed, and even Eugene and Andre would be in bed early, as they had to work at five o'clock the next morning, delivering papers.

Stella felt butterflies as she thought about cooking the meal for Sebastian. She wanted to show her appreciation for all the help he had given her over the past months—not just with giving her French lessons but also with fixing her room and studying in the kitchen when the children had gone to bed. She, Amelia, and Sebastian would sit together, and Sebastian would ask her questions from her medical textbooks. They had become a sort of family. She cared for them all in different ways. Amelia was a caring and nurturing mother, and the children were like nieces and nephews. But she had a strong attraction to Sebastian and had felt it for a long time. For many different reasons she had not acted on her feelings—the biggest, of course, being the betrayal of Amelia's trusting friendship. Then there was the security of this home with them. She shivered as she moved around Amelia's kitchen, getting things ready for the children coming home.

Stella left to pick the children up from school. "Would you all like to play in the park on the swings before we go home?"

"Oh yes, please!" they said. They all ran up the street, through the gates, and into the park, where they ran, jumped, and skipped and played on the swings, slides, and monkey bars until they were tired out.

"Come along," said Stella. "Let's go home; it's time for tea."

When they arrived back home, she found, to her surprise, that Sebastian and Helen were there, and all the older children were home. The kitchen was full.

"Hello, everyone. I thought I was alone this evening," Stella said.

"My classes have been canceled for the night," Sebastian replied.

"And I stopped in to see if I could help, maybe even take Abby and Cammie for the night—lighten the load," added Helen.

"I am going to spend the night at Sally's," Leah piped in.

Cammie spoke up. "Oh yes, please! Can we go?"

"That's fine," Stella said. "If your daddy says it's all right."

"No problem. Thank you, Helen. That's very good of you," Sebastian replied.

The girls dashed off to collect their pajamas and toothbrushes.

"I'll bring them back early tomorrow morning," said Helen.

"Very good," Sebastian replied.

"Good-bye," Helen said as she left with the girls. "I'll see you in the morning."

"Bye-bye, Stella. Good night, Daddy," said the girls, giggling as they ran off together.

The hustle and bustle was over; the little girls had left. Leah and Andre helped Stella feed the boys and prepare them for bed. Leah got her things together and went over to see Sally for the night. Andre and Eugene watched TV before going to bed early.

At last, the house was quiet, and Sebastian and Stella were alone in the kitchen.

"I am preparing you something special to eat. Are you hungry?" Stella asked him.

"Yes, I am. Can I help you?"

"Maybe you would like to set the table. I bought a bottle of Beaujolais, as it's Friday night, and I'm off four days for the weekend." Stella smiled.

"You are most kind to spend your time looking after my children." Sebastian opened the wine and poured two glasses.

"Oh, I'm delighted to be here and enjoying the time with you *all*," she said, emphasizing the last word.

"It smells *fantastique* in here; what are you cooking?"

"Steak Diane."

"Oh mon dieu!" Sebastian exclaimed.

"Do you like it?" she asked.

"Like? *Tres magnifique!*"

They sat down to a feast and conversed, sometimes in French and sometimes in English, and they thoroughly enjoyed one another's company.

"I will make us some beautiful café, and we can have a liqueur. Let me do the dishes." Sebastian stood up.

"Thank you. I'm going to look in on all the boys and see if they are well." She went into the boys' bedroom, where all the little boys were sound asleep. The bigger boys were coming in to say good night and go to bed.

"Do you have an alarm clock, Andre? Or shall I wake you?" Stella asked.

"No, thanks. I can get myself up. I'm fifteen now and don't need anyone to look after me. When is my mam coming home?" he asked.

"Not until Monday."

"It sounds and smells like you had a nice dinner with my dad," Andre said. "We had egg and chips—no meat on Friday. It's a mortal sin, you know, to eat meat on a Friday."

Stella could hear the resentment in Andre's voice.

"I wish my mam hadn't gone away. I miss her. It's not the same around here without her," Andre added. "It feels strange. I'm going to bed. Are you coming, Eugene?"

"Yeah, okay." Both boys headed upstairs to their shared bedroom and did not stop to say good night to their father.

Stella followed them. It seemed to her that if one was a Lavalle child, nothing was personally his or hers; they all shared everything they owned. The boys went into the room and closed the door. Stella waited outside the door and could hear them talking.

"Are you in bed yet, Eugene?" asked Andre.

"Yeah, I'm in bed. I'm going to set the alarm for five o'clock, and I'm switching off the light now."

They fell silent. Stella waited a moment longer and then went back down to the kitchen and joined Sebastian.

"I would like you to know how much I appreciate your helping me these past months with my French lessons, studying for my nursing exams, and keeping my room so nice—all the little extras that you have been doing. I really like living here and sharing your home. Sebastian, you are a wonderful ..." Stella hesitated as she looked straight into Sebastian's eyes. She wanted to say so much more. She ended with "person."

"You most certainly know how to make me feel good, and I do feel good. I can't remember when I last had such a marvelous evening—good food, wine, beautiful company, and the most stimulating conversation. You are a delight to be with, Stella, and it is my pleasure to assist you in any way I can, as we appreciate all you have done to help Amelia and the children."

They fell silent.

"What are you thinking, Sebastian?" She thought he looked almost sad. Stella was flirting with him.

"I was remembering the last time I felt like an attractive, strong man."

"When was that?" Stella asked.

"Oh mon dieu, many years ago in France. I was on a beach, at a restaurant under the warm evening sun. The memory is so clear I can smell the salt of the Mediterranean. It's in my mind's eye, and I could count what appeared to be twenty shades of blues, greens, aquas, and silvers—endless dancing colors within the sea. The wine, the soup de Poisson, and the beautiful woman sharing the moment, making me feel strong and attractive and indeed desirable."

"Are you all right, Sebastian?"

"Ah, oui, I am just remembering—thinking of my beautiful France."

"You must miss it. Do you ever go back?"

"I have not been back for many years, but one day. You know, Stella, everything has its time, and right now, I must concentrate on raising my family. That is all we have time for—or the money. I certainly enjoyed sharing my memories of France with you this evening."

"There's time left—we can do this again tomorrow."

"Oh, I don't know," Sebastian said. "We will have all the children tomorrow. No time for French wine and cordon-bleu cooking."

"We can think of something fun to do; you leave it to me," Stella said, still flirting. "I'm rather tired; I think I will turn in. That reminds me—when you have a moment, Sebastian, the main lightbulb in my bedroom broke when I was removing it. Some of it was left in the socket, and I couldn't replace it. It's rather dark with just my bedside lamp."

"My pleasure. Do you have another lightbulb?" he asked.

"I do. You don't have to do it right now."

"No problem. I will need pliers to remove it; they are in the garage. I'll go get them."

"Fine." Stella moved to the kitchen door. "I will leave my door ajar for you."

"Very good. I will see you up there."

She cast a glance his way as she left the room.

Stella made her way up the stairs and looked in on the older boys to make sure they were sleeping soundly. Slipping into her room, she left the door slightly ajar. She went to the window, pulled the curtains, and switched on her tiny bedside lamp. It shed a soft, warm glow across the room. She undressed quickly and slipped into her warm, fleecy long-sleeved nightgown. She turned on the gas fire, as the room was feeling a little damp. After placing a chair under the light for Sebastian to stand on, she sat down on her bed and waited.

She felt Sebastian was uncomfortable with the strong sexual tension that had developed between them lately. Tonight, however, it was overpowering. She could hear her heart beating in her ears and feel the thumping in her chest. Her mouth was dry as she felt the anticipation, knowing it was wrong. She hoped with everything in her that he would come through the door—she also prayed he would not.

Sebastian held onto his pliers, looking at Stella's open door, knowing what would happen if he walked through it. There would be no return. Hesitating, he looked toward the room where his sons were sleeping, waited for a few moments, and then popped his head around Stella's door.

"Bon jour. I am here with my pliers," he said, and he closed the door behind him.

After a time, Sebastian came out of Stella's room. He went to his own room and, moving around quietly, undressed in the dark. He could hear his three youngest sons breathing as they slept peacefully. He climbed into his matrimonial bed, looked up at the ceiling, and closed his eyes. Seeing Amelia's face, he whispered into the dark, "Oh dear God, what have I done?"

Stella awoke the next morning and lay still, collecting her thoughts from the night before. Was it a dream? As she lay under her blankets, a warm feeling radiated through her whole body. She closed her eyes and recalled the time she had spent with Sebastian.

Sebastian lay on his bed, working through his thoughts—how were he and Stella going to be together for the next few days, and what were they going to do? How would they behave when Amelia returned? Sebastian had done the unthinkable, and he had known what he was doing. The desire in him to feel like a strong, attractive man and passionate lover was overwhelming. When it was there for the taking, he could not resist. He was weak. Sebastian was aware of how devastating the consequences could be, yet he had not stopped himself—why? When it came to his own sexual desires, it was almost as if his love for Amelia stood alone, and then somewhere in some other time and space were his feelings for other women he was sexually attracted to.

As he thought about the situation, Sebastian became almost frantic. He could not imagine the repercussions if Amelia found out. He had to explain to Stella that last night was just a moment in time to keep to themselves. Anything else was unthinkable. He was, and would eternally be, in love with Amelia. He would love her until he inhaled his last breath—and no doubt thereafter—for she was his life, his love, and his all.

—23—

Helen arrived early on Saturday morning, as promised, with Abby and Cammie following behind her. She rang the bell and waited for a few moments.

"Ah, good morning, Helen. How are you?" Sebastian said when he answered the door. He stepped aside, allowing Helen and the girls to go past him. The triplets were sitting at the table, eating their breakfast of porridge with milk and treacle on top. Helen could see they were enjoying themselves, as it was Saturday morning.

"Are you having fun, boys," she said, "not having to go to school today or church?"

They all nodded, as their mouths were full.

Sebastian was busy dealing with their breakfast, as Leah was not yet home from her sleepover with Sally. Andre and Eugene were out working. Stella was nowhere to be found.

"Can I help with the breakfast?" Helen asked.

"No, thank you. I'm fine. Would you like some tea?"

"I really just wanted to drop off the girls and be on my way."

"Where's Stella?" asked Abby. "Can we go up and see where she is?"

"Non!" Sebastian replied.

Helen thought he'd reacted rather abruptly and frowned at him.

"Leave her be; she's going to be down here all day helping," Sebastian said. Just as he spoke, the kitchen door opened, and Stella walked in. It seemed to Helen she looked pretty compared to the last time they had met. Helen remembered her as a plain sort of girl.

"Hello, girls. Did you have fun with Auntie Helen?" Stella asked.

"Oh yes, we did!" Cammie answered.

"We had fish and chips and ate them in front of the telly, watching cartoons. Then Auntie made us homemade ice cream, just like Sally!" Abby exclaimed.

"That's nice. We should help Daddy get breakfast finished and wash up the dishes. Then maybe we can plan our day—what we are going to do to have fun."

The girls leaped with joy and turned in circles. "Yes, yes, please!" Abby said.

It was evident to everyone with eyes in his or her head, thought Helen, that young energy was an unusual thing around there. Poor Amelia was all out, and this young slip of a lass had an abundance—enough to spread around to all.

"How about if Abby helps Daddy do the dishes, and Cammie can help me with the boys?" Stella said.

Helen spoke up. "They are six now; they don't need help."

"It's more about organizing underwear and socks—that sort of thing," Stella replied.

"Amelia has everything well organized. She dresses them all the same on the weekend—their play clothes and dress clothes. She keeps nine of everything clean, doesn't she? And it really doesn't matter which one they get."

"Yes, but they still need help. Will that work for you, Sebastian?" Stella asked.

"Yes, that's good."

Helen noticed that Sebastian did not look up when he spoke.

"Sure you don't want some tea, Helen?" Sebastian said.

"No, I'm on my way. What time does Amelia get home on Monday?"

"Ten o'clock," Stella replied.

"Would you like me to pop in on Sunday?" Helen asked.

"No, thank you. We will be fine," Stella told her.

"Good enough. I will come by on Monday and see Amelia when she gets home."

Sebastian walked Helen out. "Good-bye, Helen. Thank you for having the girls last night."

"That's all right, Sebastian. Good-bye!" As Helen drove away, she thought Sebastian looked tired and subdued. Caring for eight bairns while his wife was away for a few days had given him an idea of what Amelia did day in and day out. Life was like a hamster on an eternal wheel—full of drudgery, with little time to just live their lives and no time to feel any joy.

Sebastian returned to the kitchen; Stella and the children were together, and the noise was overwhelming. He could barely hear himself think. He was about to yell at them, as he often did, to shut up, but he thought better of it.

As he watched his three young sons, it occurred to him that triplets were a wondrous miracle. Each of them was an individual, yet he could see that they were a reflection of one another, their other siblings, and many more who had come and gone before them. Why was he given such a gift and no means or wherewithal to embrace it? It seemed to Sebastian that to be able to indulge in them together or individually, one would sacrifice the means to provide for them. However, he had never looked at them as individuals. He could honestly say he had never spent time with them separately.

Today, he decided, he was going to spend some time reveling in the pleasures and joys of all his children and make the best of the day with them. Watching Stella, he could see she was good with them and kind. His thoughts went back to Amelia, and again, he felt guilt and sadness. What was he to do? Stella was looking back at him with a wistful, dreamy look in her eyes. Sebastian wished he could turn the clock back. The children were asking him something all at the same time, and they sounded like gaggling hens.

"I cannot hear you—one at a time!" Sebastian spoke over them all.

"Can we go to the seaside on the train?" asked Abby. "Stella said we should."

"What? Today? It's November and freezing!"

"Oh, please, Daddy!" Abby pleaded. "We can wrap up warm."

Sebastian thought for a moment. "Ah, oui, why not? Let's go. We can catch the ten o'clock train and be down there by ten thirty."

"Yeah!" They all jumped up, ran to the kitchen door, and pushed their way through in order to get coats, hats, scarves, and mittens. Nothing was as cold and damp as the northeastern coast on a day in November. The sky was gray at best. *How fitting,* thought Sebastian.

Looking at Stella finally, he said, "Well done!"

"Thank you. I'll go help them."

As they were getting ready to leave, Andre and Eugene arrived home, as did Leah.

"We are going to the seaside!" Abby said. "Do you want to come?"

"What? Now?" Andre asked.

"Daddy is taking us on the train, and Stella is coming."

Andre paused, as if to think for a moment. "Yes, that's a rare treat; I would love to go to the seaside. We'll have fun."

The ten of them made their way to the station and boarded the train. They seemed so excited that it was as if they were going to some exotic new world. Sebastian watched them—animated and involved with each other, looking out the windows as the train passed through small towns on the way to Tynemouth. Wall's End was the most interesting—the end of the Roman wall, as it was known. One of the few things about this place that Sebastian appreciated was the Roman history.

The train was like a dump site; Sebastian looked around at the empty beer bottles, chip bags on the floor, chewing gum stuck on the seats, and dirty windows. It was clear to him that the train had not been cleaned in some time. Someone had vomited in the corner the night before. *Drunk no doubt,* Sebastian thought. He opened the windows to remove some of the odor permeating the train.

They arrived at the station at last and headed toward the seaside.

"The children are so good together, Sebastian," Stella said. "They have a fantastic routine when they are out."

Sebastian did not wish to engage in chitchat; he just nodded.

Arriving at the ocean, the children took off screaming with delight and running in every direction. It did not seem to matter to them that the sun was not shining through the heavy, cloudy gray sky; that the northeast winds penetrated through layers of clothes until they reached one's bones like icy fingers; or that the North Sea looked angry—almost the color of phlegm, green and gray. To Sebastian, it all felt disgusting, bleak, cruel, and joyless. He longed to be back in France, standing on the beach, facing the Mediterranean Sea. It was as opposite to this view as one could imagine: blue skies dotted with fluffy white clouds, and warm sunbeams dancing across the blue-green sea, catching the diamond-like reflection of the water. Gentle breezes carried the scent from the mountaintops above Grasse, where they produced the best perfumes in the world. An enormous sense of joy filled one and made one happy to be alive. He ached to return and take all that was precious with him. Sebastian was aware that was not the answer, for he must right his wrongs.

As the children ran around playing, Sasha came up. "Daddy, can we make sand castles? Will you help us?"

"In a moment. I want to speak to Stella, and then I will come help you," Sebastian replied.

The older boys were kicking a football around the tidal flats. Sebastian could see the tide was out, making its way back slowly, giving the children room to run free. No one else was on the beach other than an old man walking his dog.

Catching up to Stella, Sebastian said, "We must talk."

"I agree. Are you angry with me, Sebastian?"

"Good God, non! However, I am very angry with myself, Stella. Last night was wrong."

Stella flinched at the harshness of his tone.

"I am sorry," he said. "Look at me; I am a married man who, believe it or not, loves his wife. I am middle aged and debt ridden, and I have eight children and a wife all looking toward me to protect them from anything that might hurt them and to provide them with the necessaries in life to survive. Amelia and I can barely cope, but we do, and we have. And I mean to continue. Last night happened, but we must move on. How do you think Amelia would cope with knowing if she found out? Can you imagine?"

"What am I supposed to do—forget it?" Stella asked.

"Yes, exactly. Forget last night happened."

"How can I? I think I am in love with you," she sobbed.

"Dear God, it's infatuation. You listen to me—Amelia adores you, and this cannot go on. If we cannot live together like we did before last night, then you must go."

Stella wept. "I can't. I won't. I must be near you."

"I will not sacrifice my marriage or my family. Do you understand?" Sebastian hissed through his teeth. "Forget me! Now, I am going to play with my children. We must not show any evidence of discontent between us." His voice rose with contained anger.

"I understand." Stella nodded, tears still running down her face.

"Ah," he said, rubbing his hands together as he went over

to his children. "Now, let's you and I make the biggest sand castle we have ever seen."

Sebastian looked at his children, feeling he did not deserve them—they were so trusting and precious—nor did he deserve the good wife he had in Amelia. After they finished the castle, they wrote their names in the sand, ran, and played half the day away, carefree and happy, as children should be. Then they all disappeared to scour the edges of the ocean to pick up what the waves had left behind—shells and the odd crab and winkle.

"Collect them for our dinner!" Sebastian shouted. "But be careful they do not nip you."

Andre took charge and pulled off his hat to collect the crabs they found.

Stella came up to Sebastian as he kicked the football back to Sasha. "I feel ill. I am going home to my mother from here. I will take the bus from the station, and I won't come back till after my shift on Tuesday. You should get Helen to help until Amelia comes back. I cannot face any of this," she mumbled.

Sebastian felt relieved. "Whatever you think—what is wrong?"

"I am sick to my very core."

Sebastian was about to reply, when Abby came dashing up to him. She was giggling and screaming breathlessly.

"Daddy, Daddy! Andre's chasing me with a crab!" she gasped. "This is so much fun. Can we do this again?"

"Yes, of course," he replied.

"Next time, can we bring Mammy? She would like it. It would make her smile, and I like it when she smiles; it makes my tummy feel warm."

Sebastian scooped Abby up into his arms. "We can, of course, and we will not leave until your mammy smiles."

Stella left them for the train station, explaining to the girls that she was feeling unwell.

"Go home with Daddy, and help all you can. Your mammy will be home soon."

Sebastian thanked his lucky stars; Stella's absence would give him time to sort out his head and work on bringing his family together when Amelia returned. That evening, they feasted on crabs and winkles. They'd collected ten crabs, so they had enough for each person to eat at least one. Sally came over and brought a dish of ice cream with chocolate flakes. They all went to bed content, looking forward to their mammy coming home.

—24—

Monday morning Sebastian sent Andre ahead of him to work to explain that Sebastian would be two hours late. After preparing breakfast with Leah's help, he organized the boys and got everyone ready for school. After sending Leah off to school with Eugene, Sebastian gathered the five younger children and walked them to the school gate.

"Your mammy will be home when you get back from school today."

They were all happy to hear that.

When he returned home, he wrote a note to Amelia, briefly explaining that Stella had been ill and gone home. Looking around the kitchen, Sebastian felt his guilt rising inside of him, and he knew he would have to work for a long time into the future to remove it. As for now, he would deal with one thing at a time. Closing the door behind him, Sebastian left for work.

Amelia enjoyed trains—the *clickety-click* rhythm lulled her into a relaxed state. She was almost home. Amelia had enjoyed her few days away; she loved visiting Edinburgh and her sister Deirdre. She had visited her favorite places: St. Margaret's Chapel; the lovely tearoom where she used to have tea with Sebastian on Sundays; and the Royal Mile, where she walked along, looking in the shop windows. For November, the weather was good—bright, sunny, and cool. She wondered how they had all managed and was grateful to Stella for giving her the opportunity to get away. Amelia wanted to give Stella something special for her time; she would think about that. Christmas was approaching, and maybe she could come up with a gift that would be appropriate.

Amelia arrived home, opened the front door, and called out, "I'm back! I'm home! Stella? Anyone here?" She put her suitcase in the bedroom and then went into the kitchen and looked around. All seemed to be in order. Then she saw the note on the kitchen table. She picked it up, read it, and was surprised.

How sick was Stella when she left? Amelia wondered. *She must have been very ill. Maybe not—how could she stay and risk passing it on to the rest of the family?* She would wait until Sebastian came home, and they would talk about it. She busied herself with her Monday jobs and started dinner, waiting for her young ones to come home. Soon enough, they rushed in through the front kitchen door and followed their mammy into the scullery, all chattering at the same time about their wonderful, adventurous day at the seaside with their daddy and Stella, including how they had gone on the train and run on the beach. Cammie was talking a hundred words a minute with Abby interjecting.

"Yes," Cammie said. "We caught crabs, and Daddy said that we could take them home."

"Crabs, yes!" Abby said. "Andre chased me with a crab all the way up the beach. He was pretending, of course." She giggled. "We brought them home, and Daddy cooked them. We caught ten, Mammy!" Abby held up all her fingers. "Sally came over and brought ice cream—we had a feast!"

Amelia's little boys clustered close to her as though they were trying to pick up her scent. She was somewhat overwhelmed by the five of them all trying to get a little piece of her. She was glad to be home, and as she looked at her children, she realized this was definitely where she belonged.

Amelia prepared tea for the children and then started making dinner for Andre and Sebastian, who would be coming in soon. Eugene and Leah came home and were happy to see her, regaling her with stories of their grand weekend. When Sebastian and Andre arrived home from work, Sebastian looked genuinely happy to see her; he came straight toward her and kissed her on the lips, something they normally did not do in front of the children.

"How was your trip?" Sebastian asked.

Amelia was surprised at Sebastian's greeting. "Ah, very nice—good weather, and Deidre and I had some good visiting time. I went to visit all my favorite places."

"Did you go to our tearoom?" Sebastian looked at her.

She smiled, astonished he would even ask. "Yes, I did, as a matter of fact—had a wonderful tea. Nothing's changed."

"I'll wash up." Sebastian calmly cast a glance toward Amelia as she was walking toward the sink. "You got my note about Stella, yes?"

"Yes, I did. What happened?"

Sebastian shrugged as he went toward the kitchen sink. "I really don't know."

"What's for dinner?" Andre asked as he hugged his mother, holding on for longer than usual.

"Are you okay, Andre?" Amelia asked.

"Yes, I'm glad you are back," he replied.

"Was everything okay while I was gone?"

"It was fine, Mam; we all managed well."

"I'm glad to be home," Amelia said. "Let's get back to normal." She ran her fingers through Andre's thick black hair, smiling at him. "Wash up, and come have some tea."

Tuesday afternoon arrived, and Stella came home after her day shift at the hospital. She could see Amelia was hanging around the door.

"Hullo, Stella. I'm so glad you are back."

"Oh, Amelia, you surprised me!" Stella felt edgy.

"My gosh, are you feeling better?" Amelia sounded concerned. "Come into the kitchen," she said as she held the kitchen door open. Stella could not wangle out of a visit.

"Okay, just for a minute, as I know it is time for Sebastian to come home for his dinner."

"He can wait; it won't kill him. I will put the kettle on."

"No, don't!" Stella shouted. "Sorry—I mean, no. I didn't mean to shout, but I had one at the end of my shift." She smiled weakly, patting her stomach. "I'll float away."

"Good enough," Amelia said. She sat down opposite Stella and looked deeply at her. "I feel so bad about all of this."

Stella tried to interrupt, but Amelia would not back off. Her deep, serious coal-black eyes gazed at Stella, who felt like jumping from her chair and running. She felt as if Amelia were looking into her soul and her conscience. Stella dropped her gaze.

"Amelia, please stop fussing. I'm fine." She swallowed. "We had no problems. Sebastian managed without me?"

"Yes, he did, and I can't tell you how relieved I am, Stella. I've had such an uneasy feeling the last few days." Amelia stood and put her arms around Stella. "I am delighted you are back."

At the same time, Sebastian and Andre came in the scullery door.

"I'm off, Amelia. I don't want to interrupt dinner," Stella said, trying to leave.

"Don't be silly," Amelia said, but Stella was gone, closing the door behind her.

Amelia went into the scullery. As Sebastian was drying his hands, she looked at him.

"Stella says she's fine and feeling better, but that girl is not right. Something is wrong."

"Don't be ridiculous," Sebastian said. "How can you say that?"

"I can tell; she was almost uncomfortable when she came in. Did you upset her, Sebastian?"

"Of course not. She's just tired after work. Don't worry. What's for dinner? I'm starving? Aren't you, Andre?"

Andre nodded, not saying a word.

"Well, maybe you're right; I will keep a close eye on her the next few days and see," Amelia replied.

"Stop fussing!" Sebastian shouted.

"Sebastian!" Amelia yelled back, surprising herself.

"I am tired of listening to you harp on and on—she's fine, she's back, and she's gone to her room! Now feed us!"

Amelia went quiet. After placing Sebastian and Andre's dinner on the kitchen table, she walked out, slamming the kitchen door behind her.

—25—

Andre was up early; he looked out the window and saw frost covering the ground. Delivering the papers would be cold work this morning, but he didn't mind. He wrapped up warmly. After he finished the papers, he picked up the other kids and took them out to the local fruit shop, where they chose the Christmas tree. His mam had put him in charge of putting up the tree and decorating it with his younger siblings. Soon he was in the front room, trying to place the tree between two bricks in a bucket and secure it with a piece of string.

"Is this straight, you lot?" Andre asked.

"Yes," answered Leah.

"Can we put the lights on?" Sasha asked impatiently.

"Not yet. Wait until it's fixed properly."

"It's too big on the top for the star!" cried Abby.

"That's okay; we will cut some off," Andre told her. He left the front room to go to the kitchen.

"It's a huge tree, Mam. I need the saw from the garage to cut off the top. We don't want you to come into the front room until we have finished decorating it. We all want to surprise you."

Amelia smiled at Andre. "You are such a big help, my son. I don't know how I would manage without you. I promise I will stay out until you call me."

As Andre was leaving, he saw Stella put her head around the kitchen door. "Can I come in?" she asked. Andre left.

Amelia was always delighted to see Stella.

"Of course. I was just going to pop the kettle on. You can sample some of my shortbread biscuits. Join me, won't you?"

"No, thank you. I really just came down to let you know that I will be going home for Christmas. I am working the day shift on the day of Christmas Eve, and I'll go straight from work and stay until after New Year's."

"We will all miss you," Amelia said. "You look tired, Stella. Are you working too hard?"

"Probably. Someone is off sick, and I have been doing longer shifts to cover."

"You must take better care of yourself, Stella. It's a very busy time of year, and we all have extra responsibilities and expenses."

"You should practice what you preach, Amelia."

Amelia took Stella's hands in hers. "I'll tell you what. I appreciate what you are saying, and you are kind to care. Let's make a pact—I will if you will."

"Thanks, Amelia." Stella pulled her hand away and cast her eyes anywhere but on Amelia's face.

"You'll be looking forward to spending Christmas in the country with your parents?"

"I am," Stella said. "It's always a beautiful time of year, and Mam and Dad's house lends itself to Christmas decorations."

"You must find time later to come see our Christmas tree. All the children are in the front room, working their magic."

"I would like that; I'll pop down later tonight when its dark and the lights are on. I am sure it will look pretty." Stella stood up to leave.

"It seems as if I have hardly spoken with you since my trip to Edinburgh," Amelia said. "Let's have a heart-to-heart after the New Year, shall we?"

"I would like that," Stella answered, anxious to get away from Amelia and her penetrating gaze.

Later, Andre came back into the kitchen to get his mam and bring her into the front room.

"Now, close your eyes, Mam." He guided her to the front of the tree and positioned her just so. Sebastian was behind her.

"Close your eyes, Daddy!" Abby told him. "Don't you peek until you are in front of it. Now open them, Mammy!"

Amelia opened her eyes slowly, allowing the image in front of her to focus. The tree was over six feet and a marvelous shape. The scent of pine permeated the air. The children had covered it with lights, glass balls, and some homemade garland. Beneath it, they had put a nativity scene with small lights around it. She looked at the figures of the little animals all slowly making their way to the baby Jesus in the stable with Mary and Joseph. The stable was centered under the tree, with a bright star above it in the tree. It looked delightful.

"Look, Sebastian—it is so beautiful!"

"*Tres bien,*" he agreed. "You have all done a fantastic job." Sebastian put his arm around Amelia's shoulders. "We have eight talented children."

Leah suggested they play some Christmas music. Amelia never felt such wonder as she did when she, her husband, and all her children were together. This was her favorite time of year—the anticipation and preparation lifted everyone from his or her winter sleep. After the dark, foggy November days, the house was filled with music, the smells of baking, and the children's dreams of what Santa Claus would bring them. Maybe things were looking up and life was improving. Christmas 1962 was going to be one to remember, Amelia thought with tears of joy in her eyes as she looked at the Christmas tree.

"Everyone had a wonderful day; it's been one to remember," she said to Sebastian.

"It has that; I cannot remember when we all enjoyed a day together as much." Sebastian looked behind the tree to make sure it was secure and firmly placed. As he came around to stand in front of the tree, he told Amelia, "It's splendid, Amelia. I am truly impressed with our children's abilities."

"They are clever, aren't they?" Amelia said.

Sebastian walked over to her and kissed her gently on the lips.

"You know, I am happier today than I have been for many years. I'm looking forward to Christmas and the future with you, Amelia, and our children. I know we don't have much in the way of materialistic things, but I am so proud of our children, and I love you, Amelia. I always will. You have instilled in the children the true meaning of Christmas. It is evident in their masterpiece." He looked at the tree once more.

Amelia stood, and they kissed tenderly.

"I will switch off the lights," Sebastian said.

There was a knock on the door, and Stella popped her head around the door.

"Come in," Amelia said.

"I've come to see the tree," Stella said.

"I was about to switch off the lights," Sebastian told her.

"No, don't do that. I'll go get some sherry, shortbread, and mince pies, and we can listen to some Christmas carols and enjoy the wonder of the season," said Amelia.

"I'm on an early shift," Stella protested. "I really just came in to look at the tree. I must say it's quite stunning."

Amelia smiled. "I'm so proud of them. Now, nonsense—you sit down. Sebastian, put some Christmas carols on the gramophone, and stoke up the fire. The three of us will enjoy some Christmas cheer." She left the room.

"Why did you come down here?" Sebastian asked.

"Because Amelia asked me to, and I need to talk to you."

"What about?"

"I think I'm pregnant."

"It simply cannot be! It's impossible. How do you know? Non, it's impossible!"

"It's not impossible—because I am four weeks late. What are we going to do?" Stella whispered in front of the grand Christmas tree.

"Nothing. You need to get rid of it; I want no part of it. Do you hear me?"

"I'm afraid that's not good enough, Sebastian. If I am pregnant, this is your responsibility as much as mine. It's not that simple; I'm really scared, and I don't know what to do. I expect you to stand up beside me and help me do something about this."

Sebastian was about to answer when Amelia came back into the room.

"Here we are. You didn't put on the music, Sebastian, or stoke up the fire."

"Yes, yes, I will!"

Amelia handed Stella her sherry and the plate of pastries.

"Try a sweet mince pie; they are delicious!"

Handing Sebastian his sherry, Amelia picked up her glass. "I wish to make a toast—a Christmas toast," she announced. As Bing Crosby sang "Silent Night" and the lights of the Christmas tree twinkled around the room like stars in the night sky, the smell of pine drifted through the warm room.

"To us," Amelia said. "May we have the best and happiest Christmas ever. I feel brighter than our beautiful tree!" She clinked glasses with Sebastian and Stella, and they sipped their sherry.

Stella suddenly put her glass down on the tray. "I am sorry, Amelia. I must go." She ran out of the room, slamming the door.

Amelia jumped up to follow her, but Sebastian blocked the door.

"Leave her be, Amelia; she needs to be alone."

"No, Sebastian, this girl is sick. She's not been well for weeks now; I can't ignore it." She tried to push Sebastian away from the door.

"She's young, Amelia, and she's just our lodger; it may be she doesn't want you invading her privacy. If she did, I think she knows you well enough to come ask. She also has her own parents. You need to put this in perspective, chérie."

Moving Amelia back so that she would sit down in her chair, Sebastian sat down in front of the tree.

"Sip your sherry, enjoy the tree, and if you feel the need to see she's all right, ask tomorrow. Things often look better in the daylight. Here's to you and me and new beginnings!"

Amelia smiled and raised her glass. The room was filled with the spirit of Christmas in the moment.

—26—

The following evening Amelia stood outside Stella's door for a moment, pausing before she knocked. She had cleared up her tea dishes, and the children were all in the front room, watching a Christmas cartoon on the TV. It gave her time alone. Amelia could see a shaft of light shining from under Stella's door, illuminating the dark hallway slightly so that Amelia was not standing in complete darkness. She knocked gently, and there was a silent pause.

"Yes, who is it?"

"It's me—Amelia." Amelia could hear the scuffle and shuffle of sounds like books falling onto the floor.

"Just a minute." After another pause, suddenly, the door opened, and the shaft of light became a floodlight shining onto Amelia, making her shade her eyes.

"Hello, Amelia. Come in. I had nodded off; I've not been home long from my shift."

"I heard you come in." They entered the room together.

"Sit down," Stella said. "Would you like some tea?"

"No, thank you. You must know why I'm here, Stella." Amelia decided not to beat about the bush.

"Yes, and I am so sorry about last night. I just came over so sick. I think it was the heat in the room and the smell of the pine from the Christmas tree. I—"

Amelia interrupted. "Stella"—she took her hands and held them in hers—"I am fonder of you than you know. I think you need to understand that." Amelia could see Stella's lips trembling. "I am a true friend, Stella, and I want to help you. Now, just let me say this. I ..." She hesitated for a second and then continued. "I have been pregnant enough times in my life to recognize when I see someone pregnant. I know every possible symptom like the back of my hand." She looked into Stella's face and, without hesitation, asked, "How far along are you?"

Stella looked dumbfounded; she stared at Amelia, her eyes wide and filled with tears.

She sputtered and stammered. "I don't know exactly. I just know I'm late."

"How late?" Amelia asked.

"I think six weeks or so."

"Have you told anyone yet?"

"No," she sobbed. "I don't know what to do; I just keep praying my period will start. Every day I pray that when I wake up in the morning, it will be there, and it never is. I feel sick all the time; I'm so scared."

Amelia smiled gently. "Is the father a student?"

"No."

"I know it's none of my business, but he does need to know, as you did not get into this situation alone, Stella.

You must tell the young man responsible for this as soon as possible. Do you love him?" Amelia asked.

Stella answered through her tears, "I don't know. I thought I did; now I just don't know what I feel."

"Could you talk to him before Christmas?"

"Yes, I think so."

"You need to do so, and when you go home, you must break this news to your parents. There are all kinds of ways you can have your baby whether or not you marry the father."

"I don't want to talk about this." Stella jumped up. "Not right now, Amelia. I feel sick. Would you mind leaving me alone?" Stella dashed past her toward the door. Amelia put her arms around Stella, stopping her.

"Remember, you are not alone in this; I am here, and I can and will help you in any way."

Stella burst into tears, pushing Amelia away and running past her into the bathroom, locking the door behind her.

The week before Christmas, Sebastian was upstairs fixing the drain in the bathroom. Stella opened her door, called him over to her room, and closed the door.

"You need to know, Sebastian, that I have confirmed I am six weeks pregnant. I am going home tomorrow; I have taken some sick leave. I shall stay with my parents until January first, and I will tell them everything; I must. You also need to understand Amelia guessed I was pregnant. It was awful; she wants to help, and she was holding my hand and telling me how much I mean to her. Amelia is going to find out, Sebastian; it's just a matter of time."

"Non, she must not ever find out!" He raised his voice loudly. Stella stared at him.

"Don't you dare raise your voice to me; I'm the one with the baby in my belly."

Sebastian looked at Stella and whispered, "I'm the one with the most to lose."

Stella sat down and, in a soft voice, spoke into the air, looking away from him. "Well, you should have thought about that before you took what you wanted from me. What do you think is going to happen? I will melt away into thin air, and it will all disappear? The reality is, we are pregnant, Sebastian—not just me—and you must tell Amelia. If you don't, I promise you I will."

Sebastian could feel his panic growing. "Yes, yes—all right." He stood in the dimly lit room, which now seemed cold and faceless. Six weeks ago it had looked warm and inviting.

"This is a disaster. I never imagined you would get pregnant. You are correct; it was all about sexual desire and gratification. You must promise me not to say or do anything—at least allow Amelia to enjoy her Christmas."

Stella looked at him coldly. "What for? Just to drop the bomb on her in the new year? You are a lying hypocrite, Sebastian. She will go out of her mind when she gets this news." Stella stood up and opened the door. "Get out of here, Sebastian; you make me sick."

"I'm sorry, Stella," he said as he looked back. "I did not mean for this to happen."

She closed the door and left him in the dark hallway.

The next day, Sebastian stepped off the bus, making his way home after work. The energy of the season was apparent in the local shops, which were all dressed with trees, tinsel, spray snowmen from cans, and angels plastered across the shop windows. The weather was fresh; there was a nip in the air, and the northeast wind, as always, howled around Sebastian's head, making him pull up his collar around his ears. He hated this weather and this country; how he longed for France. What was he to do? How could he have gotten himself into such a predicament because of his weakness? In his decision to gratify himself just one more time, he'd risked losing all that was precious and dear to him.

Maybe he could borrow enough money to give to Stella so that she could get rid of the pregnancy—that would solve everything. Whatever he did, he was going to make sure Amelia and his family enjoyed a wonderful Christmas.

Three days before Christmas Amelia purchased her Christmas food. The bulk had come in a large hamper that she'd paid for over the past twelve months at one shilling a week. She had a nice amount to spend on the hamper by the end of the year, which was a godsend, as she could prepare luxurious, extravagant, celebratory foods over the Christmas season, and the family looked forward to this treat every year. Amelia was about to go into the kitchen to sort out some of the groceries, as the children would be coming home from school in a couple of hours. This was precious time for

Amelia; she might even get a cup of tea if she was quick. She could hear footsteps on the staircase behind her.

Amelia turned. "Ah, Stella. How are you? I'm so glad to see you. Sebastian told me last night that you are going home for a week, and I'm so glad that we bumped into each other. Come in, and have a cup of tea with me, please, before you leave."

Amelia struggled with her Christmas shopping as she tackled the door to the kitchen.

"Here—let me help you." Stella moved toward the kitchen door, opened it, and held it so that Amelia could pass through with her bags of Christmas food.

"Thanks. Come sit by the fire, and have some tea with me."

"I don't have time, Amelia. I really just wanted to say good-bye before I go home. I've taken some sick leave."

Amelia sat and quietly asked, "May I ask—have you spoken with the father of your baby?"

Stella dropped her gaze, whispering, "Yes, I have."

Amelia said, "Well, that is very good; he knows now."

"He was very angry and upset—said he wants nothing to do with me or the baby."

"That's a normal reaction for a young man. He's frightened, no doubt; give him some time to think about it. He will come around. How old is he, Stella?"

"Amelia, this is not what you think. I am not, well, as innocent as you seem to believe. The father is, in fact, married."

Amelia took in a breath, feeling shocked.

Stella continued, "He was adamant that I do not interfere with his life, his wife, or his family. I informed him if he did not tell his wife, I would."

Amelia said, "Oh my, Stella, this is a different situation altogether. I don't know what to say to you. I am so terribly sorry this has happened to you."

"I know I made a big mistake," Stella said, holding back tears. "But I certainly didn't do this alone. I just don't know what to do; my parents will never forgive me."

Amelia stood up and went to Stella. "Of course they will; this is their grandchild. I'm sure they will be shocked and disappointed and maybe even disown you for a little while, but give them time. They'll get used to the idea. There isn't much else you can do; go home, and allow the dust to settle around this situation. Give the father time; he has a tremendous amount to contend with. I suggest you back off and allow him to handle it in his own way. Does he have children?"

"What does it matter, Amelia, what he has or hasn't got? How will it help me and my unborn baby?" Stella was weeping and angry. Amelia was somewhat taken aback at Stella's reaction.

"I'm trying to help you."

Stella jumped up. "Well, you can't! In fact, you have no idea how much you can't. It's a nightmare!" she cried, running away from Amelia and out of the kitchen along the dark corridor. Amelia followed her. Stella opened the front door. Helen stood there precariously with an armful of cakes, biscuits, Christmas treats, and one dozen fresh eggs perched proudly on the top. Stella pushed past Helen without even seeing her, knocking her sideways. Consequently, she sent Helen's gifts of the season tumbling to the concrete, smashing some of the eggs and all the treats and cakes to smithereens.

"What on earth? What in God's name?" Helen said.

It was useless to call after Stella, for she was running along the street toward the bus stop. Helen left everything on the ground as it was and stood staring after Stella.

"Oh, Helen, hello. I'm sorry!"

"I was bringing them to you. And that little"—Helen paused—"lodger of yours pushed past me, hysterical, and went flying along the street like a banshee."

"Yes, I will explain that in a moment. Let's see what can be salvaged." They both went about cleaning and tidying up, and amazingly, they rescued a few eggs, some of the shortbread and the broken cake, and some empire biscuits—Abby's favorite. They carried them into the kitchen.

"I'll put the kettle on; I know I could do with a cuppa," said Helen. Amelia put some of her groceries into the pantry and the cupboards. They eventually sat down to tea, broken biscuits, and cake. Even though the food was smashed, it was delicious.

"What is going on with that girl? I just don't know how to take her. I don't like her, Amelia; she gets right under my skin."

"She's a good, kind girl, Helen; I won't have you speaking about her like that. I'm very sorry that she knocked you over; she has a lot to contend with at this time."

"Oh?" said Helen. "How so?"

Amelia announced, "She's pregnant."

"Dear God." Helen looked flabbergasted.

Amelia continued, "I figured it out last week; she's been so quiet of late, certainly not herself. You know, I tried talking to her; it all seemed to start around about the time I went to our Deirdre's in Edinburgh. She has been very withdrawn since. I went to her last week and asked her if she was pregnant; she said yes—six weeks or so. We've discussed it a little bit; I suggested that she tell the father if she hadn't. And I said there were ways of working these things out."

"I'm in shock—absolutely."

"I can tell you it's put a real damper on my Christmas. I feel so sorry for her."

"Well, I must go, Amelia—a million and one things to do."

"You and Charles are still coming for dinner on Christmas Day, right?" asked Amelia.

"Of course, looking forward to it. I'll bring you a trifle. Don't show me out. See you Christmas Day."

Helen ran down the hall and out the door, gasping to get some clean, fresh air into her lungs. "Sebastian," she whispered under her breath, "your days of infidelity and abusing my little sister are over. I will personally put a stop to it if it's the very last thing I do," she added as she drove away from the Lavalle home.

—27—

Christmas Day arrived, and the Lavalle family celebrated as most families did in the early sixties—frugally. The children ran into the living room after Mass with anticipation, and the young ones each found his or her sock on the mantel over the fireplace filled with a tangerine, an apple, and some nuts. They all enjoyed their gifts, which were simple things, such as books, crayons, small toy cars, and brush-and-comb sets. They were happy and sat together playing with their new presents.

Andre and Eugene received a Monopoly game. They set up the board and started to play. Leah was showing her little brothers how to color and paint. Cammie was brushing Abby's long dark curls with a new brush set. They were involved with one another, and it taught them to work together and share.

"Amelia, sit by the tree and enjoy watching the children; I will go make you some tea," Sebastian said. When he was gone, Andre came up to his mam with a small blue velvet box.

"I've bought you a present with my window-cleaning money, and Eugene—he helped. We went in together."

"Oh, how wonderful. That's so special, Andre. Come over here, Eugene; sit beside me."

"We hope you like it."

Amelia held the blue velvet box, savoring the moment. She looked at her boys and smiled. "Well now, what have we here?"

"Open it, Mammy!" said Eugene.

Slowly lifting the lid on the box, Amelia was delighted at what lay inside: a glistening pair of crystal rosary beads, well made, with a crucifix beautifully embellished.

"Oh, boys! I can't believe it—they are so gorgeous. Oh!" She jumped up, clinging to her beads as though they were diamonds; they could not have meant more to her if they were. "Andre and Eugene, thank you." She kissed them both on the cheek with tears in her eyes. "I shall treasure these for the rest of my life."

"You really like them, Mam?" asked Eugene.

"Oh, they are the most beautiful rosaries I have ever seen. Where on earth did you get something so lovely?"

"We were looking in the gift cabinet at church," Andre explained. "We only had two shillings to spend, and there was nothing in the cabinet for that price. The lady asked if we were the Lavalle children, and we answered yes. She said she knew you.

"She said, 'Do you know that some rosary beads came in today exactly that price?' She told us to put the money in the box that said 'Offerings,' so we did, and she gave us the rosary beads. She said she hoped you liked them. We're really glad, Mam."

Amelia smiled. "What a beautiful story, boys; that makes them extra special." The other children gave her an enormous box of Black Magic chocolates. They had gone carol singing door to door and collected money until they had enough to buy a two-pound box of chocolates. Amelia said, "You are so good; we can open these after dinner when Auntie Helen and Uncle Charles come."

Sebastian came back with the tea. They all sat together around the Christmas tree, its soft smell of pine lingering around the room, as baby Jesus slept peacefully under the star of the Christmas tree. The warm coal fire glowed in the hearth, and some of the kids roasted chestnuts in the grate and tossed them back and forth to one another to cool them down. Westminster Abbey's choir was singing carols on the gramophone, and some snowflakes gently meandered their way past the window toward the ground. Amelia stopped and looked, taking it all in—impressing the moment onto layers of her memory, locking it in place, and keeping it there safely so that she could recreate it time after time for the rest of her life.

Sebastian watched his family playing with their Christmas presents; he felt sick to his stomach. Jumping up from his chair, he asked Amelia, "Would you like more tea?"

"No, thanks. Let's just sit and enjoy this special time, Sebastian."

He smiled and picked up the coal shovel to throw more coal onto the fire; sitting still was impossible.

"I think I will go baste the turkey," he said.

"Are you all right, Sebastian?" Amelia asked. "You look pale and rather tired."

"Ah, oui. I'm fine. I just didn't sleep well last night. Don't worry, Amelia. As you say, let's just sit and relax."

Helen and Charles arrived and joined the festivities.

The turkey was plump and juicy; Sebastian carried it to the dinner table, where he would carve it with his family. They all sat waiting with apparent appetite and anticipation. Amelia had put together an extraordinary Christmas feast—it was a miracle, if one considered how little she had to work with. The table looked festive, laid with one of Amelia's hand-embroidered tablecloths, covered with poinsettias in all different shades of red and pink; a small wreath homemade from evergreens in the front yard; and a candle in the center. Although the crockery, cutlery, glasses, and salt-and-pepper sets did not match, the display looked spectacular. The twelve of them sat around the misshapen table, each of them on a different-looking chair, but what mattered most to Amelia and Sebastian was that they were all together.

The dinner was fantastic—turkey with chestnut stuffing, small sausages wrapped in bacon, sweet mashed potatoes with whipped cream, roasted potatoes, brussels sprouts with butter, carrots with honey, turnips, Yorkshire pudding, and, of course, gravy. For dessert they had Christmas pudding and Aunt Helen's raspberry clotted-cream trifle. They finished off with Amelia's Black Magic chocolates. It was a grand affair.

Helen took Charles to one side after dinner and said, "Why don't you take the bus home early?"

"Whatever for?"

"I want to help clear up, and well, Amelia needs my help with something."

"Helen, I hope you are not interfering in something that simply does not concern you," said Charles.

"So do I, Charles. In fact, I pray I am wrong."

"What's going on here?" Charles said with concern.

"I can't talk to you about it—not yet. I shall explain in detail if and when I can. Charles, just trust me on this. Please go home."

"Fine, I shall do as you ask—under protest, may I add. I shall walk; it will be faster than waiting for a bus on Christmas Day."

"Good enough," Helen replied, not really listening to him. "Now," Helen said after seeing Charles off, "it's a nice day. Why don't the young ones go outside and play? The older ones can take them for a walk. Put your coats on, and go over to the park while your mam and I clear up."

"Non," Sebastian protested. "It's Christmas Day; we must all stay together. Leave the dishes; we can do them later."

Amelia spoke up. "Sebastian's right, Helen. What's going on with you? Why did you send Charles home?"

"Because I must speak with you."

"What about? Is it that important it can't wait?" Amelia asked.

"Yes, it is, I'm afraid."

"Helen, you're frightening me."

"That is not my intention," she said.

Sebastian looked at Amelia, and Helen looked at Sebastian.

Helen called Andre and Leah and shoved some biscuits and cake and the box of chocolates at them. "Here—take the young ones and go play at the park. It's a good day, and don't come back until they are tired. Wrap up warm."

"What's wrong?" Andre asked.

"Oh, nothing," Amelia said. "Don't fret. I want to talk to Aunt Helen about something. Now go play."

Just as Andre was about to leave, Cammie came in. "Guess who's come home to see us—Stella is here with a lady and a man. They've all gone up to her room, I think. I asked if she was coming to the park, but she said no, she couldn't, not today. She looked a bit sad."

"Andre, off you go. Have fun." Helen lined up all eight of them and watched as they walked down the dark hallway out the front door. The young ones were excited and skipping; the older ones were looking back, seemingly concerned. Helen waved. "Have fun." The children were gone.

Sebastian, Amelia, and Helen stood in the kitchen. Dinner dishes, pots, and pans were scattered in the sink, on the countertops, and on the table. Amelia went about starting to clear up.

"Put it down," Helen commanded with such force that Amelia dropped the plate she was holding.

"What is going on?" Amelia said.

"Just stop working and sit down, Amelia," Helen said.

Amelia sat. "What is wrong, Helen? Tell me, for goodness sake."

"I think Sebastian is the one you should be talking to." Helen glared at him.

"Amelia …" Sebastian's voice trailed off.

"Sebastian?" She stood up. "Are you ill?" She moved toward him, and as he was about to speak, there was a knock on the door. All three looked toward the door. Helen was the closest, so she opened it.

Stella stood in front of Helen with a small, stocky man wearing a cloth cap and glasses and a short, thin lady wearing a headscarf with messy salt-and-pepper-colored hair sticking out and a well-worn coat. Stella looked as though she had been crying.

"Yes?" Helen said.

Stella hesitated. "I've come to see Sebastian—er, Amelia," she said.

"On Christmas Day?" Helen said. "Could it not wait?"

"No." The man stepped up and said in a strong northern accent, "I'm her dad, and this is her mam. We would rather be someplace else, but we 'ave something that needs to be said."

Amelia pushed past Helen. "Move," she said. "Do come in, please, Mr. and Mrs. Cooperidge. The place is an awful mess; we've just finished Christmas dinner. Please sit, would you?" She indicated some chairs. "Can I get you something?"

"No, thanks," Mr. Cooperidge replied.

"Stella, how are you?" Amelia asked. "I'm concerned about you, the way you dashed off the other day."

"I'm so sorry, Amelia." Stella burst into tears.

"It's all right." Amelia went to Stella to comfort her. "I'm so glad your mam and dad are with you."

Stella's dad spoke up again. "Our only bairn is pregnant,

and she's going to 'ave a bairn of her own, and her not being wed and all makes it a bad kettle of fish indeed."

Amelia shook her head. "What has it to do with …" Amelia looked from one face to another. They were all somberly watching her. "You mean …" She looked at Sebastian, and tears began streaming down his face.

"Well, I hate to tell you, missus, but your fella's the father, and we've come to see what he intends to do about it."

"What are you talking about?" Amelia laughed hysterically. "I don't believe you; it's impossible." She was screaming at Mr. Cooperidge, moving toward him. It slowly started to make sense—Edinburgh, the long weekend in November, the change in Stella over the past few weeks. She went for Sebastian, throwing herself at him, beating him with both fists frantically, and swinging her arms at his face and chest. She wanted to hurt him.

"You bastard! You bastard!" she screamed, saliva dripping from her mouth. She looked at Stella. "And you—my friend. Look at you. Get out before I …" Amelia felt as though she were going to die. She heard herself wail; it was a loud, bloodcurdling cry filled with pain and disbelief that the two people she loved had betrayed her. She fell to the floor on her knees.

"It meant nothing—one senseless moment. It was a big mistake." Sebastian dropped to his knees beside her. "Everybody get out and leave us alone!" he screamed at Stella and her parents.

Stella rushed over to Amelia. "I never meant for this to happen. I am sorry."

Amelia looked at Stella. "My friend, I loved you. Get out. Get out of my house—now!"

Helen spoke up. "Please, could you give us some time? Amelia is clearly in shock. Just leave us be."

"Good enough," said Stella's dad as they got up. "We will be back." The mam and dad walked out with Stella between them.

Amelia lay on the floor in the fetal position, holding on to herself, rocking back and forth while weeping and whispering, "This is not true; it's a bad dream."

Sebastian watched in agony. He lifted Amelia onto a chair.

"I will make some tea," Helen said, and she went into the scullery to put the kettle on. She came back and held the cup up to Amelia's lips.

"Drink it, Amelia; it will help with the shock."

Sebastian heard the children coming in through the front door. They were yelling, laughing, running, and jumping along the hall toward the kitchen door. Helen glanced at him. "Go stop them from coming in here," she said. He instantly responded—not because he was obeying Helen but because he did not wish for any of the children to see their mother looking as she did. He needed some time alone with Amelia; Helen was not allowing that.

He turned his head from the door. "When I come back, I would appreciate some privacy with my wife."

"Yes, I'm sure you would," Helen snapped. "Go stop those children."

"Hello, bonjour. *Joyeux Noel*—did you all have a good time? Let's go into the front room and put the Christmas tree lights on. You can show me what you did with your coloring books and crayons and tell me what you did at the park. Let's go."

Andre was alarmed immediately; he could tell his father did not want them to go into the kitchen. He wondered what Stella had been doing there with what looked like her mam and dad before they went out to the park.

"What's wrong with Mam?" He looked at his dad.

"Oh, nothing; she's just very tired. Auntie Helen is helping her clean up the dishes and the mess. Just give them some time, please."

Andre did not believe him, and he intended to find out for himself. He was fifteen now and a working man; he could not be pushed around by his father or anyone else. The other children were just pleased to be spending time with their dad. They switched on the lights of the Christmas tree and put some coal on the fire; it caught, and the flame leaped to life, bringing a cozy glow to the room. The radio was playing Christmas carols.

"What did you do?" Sebastian asked them.

Abby jumped up. "We made up a dance in the park, a special one with nice moves and everything."

Andre slipped out of the room and went to the kitchen to find his mother. As he did, he heard his aunt talking to his mother about Stella having a baby. According to what they were saying, his father was its dad. It did not make any sense to Andre—how could it be true? That would mean his father had slept with Stella, not just eaten red meat and garlic and drunk red wine. He could hear great sobs heaving from his mother's tired, thin body, and he longed to go in and help. His father approached him, and Andre backed away. He was full of anger and shame.

"You fucking bastard!" Andre screamed, and he ran from his father out the door and up the street back to the park, where he cried and cried, for he knew that as of this day, his life would change, as would the lives of the rest of his family—and not for the better. He thought as he sat on the park bench. The sun was weak and feeble on this wintery December 25. It did not give color, grace, or warmth, only a chill. It looked as cold as Andre felt both inside and out.

—28—

Sebastian went back into the kitchen. Amelia was sitting in a chair, holding onto her teacup with both hands, staring into the warm, dark liquid. Her face was the color of parchment.

"Stay with the children, please. I must speak with Amelia," he said firmly to Helen. She hesitated, looking at Amelia for approval. Amelia looked up from her cup and nodded.

Leah, coming through the kitchen door, said, "Where's Mam?"

Helen stopped her and moved her out. "Just leave them be. It's all right; she's fine. Let's go look at your Christmas presents and the fantastic tree. I can't believe what a grand job you all did."

Sebastian knelt in front of Amelia, taking the cup from her hands and placing it on the table. He held her thin, fragile fingers in his, trying desperately to focus on salvaging his marriage and family and not on how the last few hours of this Christmas Day in their lives had aged and devastated his glorious Amelia.

"Look at me, ma chérie," he pleaded. Amelia's eyes stayed focused on the threadbare rug she had walked across many times to announce to him that she was pregnant. "What I am about to tell you may seem unbelievable, yet it is all I have to offer you at this moment—that is the truth." He stopped.

Amelia lifted her gaze for a moment from the rug; Sebastian felt she was looking through him, not at him. It made him shiver, although he could still feel some of the heat from the grate in the fire and smell the aroma of the Christmas turkey. There was a gentle hum coming through the wall—muffled Christmas carols. Her eyes went back to the rug.

"It was never, ever my intention to hurt you, Amelia; I don't believe Stella meant to either. It did not involve love, not in any sense of the word. It was only lust; you must believe me when I tell you."

Amelia stayed silent, keeping her melancholy gaze away from Sebastian.

"We did not set out to hurt you," Sebastian said. "You and I cannot allow all that we mean to each other—our lives, work, our children, the future—to be destroyed because of this one senseless mistake."

Amelia looked at Sebastian and sobbed out to him bitterly, "How can you imagine I would ever want you to even come close to me after what I have heard and seen this afternoon? Have you any idea what I am feeling inside? Everything I believe in has been smashed. The utter betrayal—the two people that I care about." Amelia dragged the sleeve of her sweater across her face to dry her tears as she continued. "I am to believe you—to let this all pass me by, to forgive and forget? I cannot even stand to look at you, Sebastian—get away from me. I feel sick to my very core!"

Sebastian stayed fast and did not move. "Amelia," he whispered, dropping his gaze, "believe me—we can work this out if you can find it in your heart to forgive me. We can rebuild this marriage. I know it will take time, but if we stick together and don't let others interfere, we can find a way back from this."

"I don't even want to think right now. I need you to leave me alone. Get out of my sight. Have you given any thought to this baby? It did not ask to be conceived in such a way."

"No," he whispered, "I have not."

"You disgust me, you selfish bastard! Just leave me!" Amelia cried. "Go to the children, and ask Helen to come back."

Sebastian turned and left the room.

Helen stood in front of Amelia.

"Why don't you go lie down, Amelia? I'll clean up these dishes."

"No, let's work together; I need to talk to you." They started cleaning up together, moving around the kitchen and scullery—soaking, washing, and drying. "Helen, Sebastian wants me to forgive him."

"I'm sure he does," said Helen.

"As I think about it, I have to wonder what else I can do; we owe it to our eight children. I don't know how to start, where to carry on, or who to trust or believe. Sebastian and

I have faced some hurdles together. I feel so weary, almost beaten down, as though I could not make another decision if my whole life depended upon it—outside of the decision that Sebastian thinks I should make. I made my commitment to him for better or worse twenty years ago. As betrayed as I feel, I see no other way out."

"Do you intend to stay with him after what we have all witnessed here today?" Helen said. Amelia was silent. They finished off the last of the dishes, and the kitchen looked as it always did—neat, tidy, and sparse. It was five thirty in the afternoon; Christmas Day was almost over.

"Sit down, Amelia. I must talk to you. I have a story to tell you. I always prayed it would go with me to my grave, but I cannot in good conscience allow you to make such a decision regarding your future with Sebastian without telling you what I know."

"Spit it out, Helen. Sometimes you really scare me!" cried Amelia, looking more frightened and tired as the day went on.

"I would rather cut my tongue out of my head than have to tell you what I am about to. Yet I must, as I believe it will definitely affect the decision you are about to make, Amelia." As Helen was about to start, she could hear the children in the next room through the walls. "I have to take you back to the night you gave birth to Malachi." Helen stopped, pulled out a handkerchief from her cardigan sleeve, wiped her nose, sniffed, and continued. "After I visited you in the hospital. When Sebastian was in France, looking after his sick uncle."

Amelia looked at Helen. "Yes, his uncle Phillippe—he needed help. I don't see what this has to do with anything that is going on here today."

Oh dear God, Helen thought, *this is impossible.* "Amelia, when I was coming home from seeing you in such a sad, desperate state in the hospital, I decided to take a taxi from the station. I could not believe what I was seeing. It was Sebastian, walking through the station, escorting a very attractive blonde woman. They were in deep conversation."

"Well, what of it?" said Amelia. "He was due back that night. Maybe the lady was somebody he'd met on the train."

"You must let me finish, Amelia; please don't interrupt. I continued to watch them. Before she climbed into the back of a taxi, they kissed like lovers."

"I don't believe you, Helen!" said Amelia with a gasp. "I don't believe you!"

"You must listen to me." Helen took Amelia's hands. "Dear God, listen. It's true. I confronted him at home. I told him you had lost the baby. He said it was over, that that was the last time he would be seeing her."

Amelia let out a cry. She sounded like a wounded lamb. "Oh dear God in heaven, no more!"

Helen continued, "I told him I would never, ever utter a word of this to a living soul. He swore to me that he would do everything humanly possible to help you and his children lead a decent life. I told him if he didn't, I would come after him." Helen broke down; she could say no more.

"How can I believe this—all that has come to me today? I feel numb; I can't think or decide what I am to do. I feel sick to my stomach," Amelia sobbed. "I don't even want to be in the same room with him—no, the same house. I want to leave, run, this minute—now!"

Helen tried to calm Amelia. "Shhh. We can work something out, but you must stay calm."

"Calm?" Amelia laughed hysterically. "Show me how. It's Christmas night, and I have no money and no place to go. I cannot stay, but I have eight children to take with me."

Helen interrupted Amelia. "Are you determined to leave here tonight?"

Amelia looked at Helen. "What reason do I have to stay?"

"I have an idea," Helen said. She went to the telephone in the corner of the room. After rummaging through her handbag, she pulled out a small address book, flicked through the pages, and stopped. Picking up the receiver, she dialed and waited for the ring tone. Helen listened. She could still smell a faint whiff of Christmas in the kitchen, but it was fading fast.

"Oh yes, good evening, yes. May I speak with Reverend Mother?" Helen inquired. "It's regarding Amelia Lavalle and her children. Yes, I will hold."

As she waited, Leah came to the door. "Is something wrong, Mammy? You look so sad. Come on in and sit with us around the tree, and listen to the Christmas carols. Daddy is going to put the TV on because *Going My Way* is the film tonight. I know you like that, don't you?"

Amelia stood up. "Leah, I want you to just go wait for me. I will be with you shortly."

"But, Mammy—"

"Shhh. Just wait."

"What's wrong?" Leah said.

"I'll explain later. Now, go." Amelia pushed Leah out the door.

"Yes, Reverend Mother, good evening. Yes, hello. It's—I understand this is a lot to ask of you on Christmas night, but my sister Amelia needs shelter for herself and the children."

The Reverend Mother was silent for a moment and then replied, "How old are the children now, Helen?"

"The older boys are sixteen and fourteen; the girls are thirteen, eleven, and nine; and the three little boys are seven."

"I see," said the Reverend Mother. "We can certainly do our best, but we cannot take the two older boys. Can you find somewhere for them to stay?"

Helen stopped for a moment. "Yes, I can take the boys."

"That's fine. This is rather a sad request on Christmas night, but we will be ready. So we are looking at three seven-year-old boys and three girls—nine, eleven, and thirteen."

"That's correct, Reverend Mother," Helen replied.

"And the mother?"

"Yes," Helen said.

"When can we expect you?"

"Within the hour," said Helen. "Reverend Mother, I thank you; we will explain. You have saved us." Helen hung up the phone, and Amelia stood watching Helen.

"I shall get the children," said Helen. "I'll put their coats and hats on and put them in my car."

"Do that," said Amelia. "And send Sebastian in here."

"Don't say too much," warned Helen. "The less said, the better."

"Go get him," she said. Helen went into the room; they were all watching the TV. "Sebastian, Amelia wants to see you alone." Sebastian jumped up and ran from the room. Helen told the children, "Don't ask me any questions, as I cannot answer them yet. Get your coats, boots, gloves, and hats; put them on; go to the car; and wait for me."

"All of us?" said Eugene.

"Yes, all of you. Where's Andre?"

"He's upstairs in his room."

"Well, go get him—now!" said Helen. Eugene ran out, and they all did as they were asked.

"And be quiet—do you hear me?"

"Yes, Auntie Helen," they said as they scampered out. All their clothes were in the hallway, and they began dressing, with Leah helping the boys. Then they all went outside to wait for Helen by the car. It was cold, and some flurries were falling softly upon the ground. The Christmas sky held no stars or moon; it was cloudy, dark, and dismal looking. The children were tired.

Andre came out of his room. "What's going on, Aunt Helen?"

"I will tell you when your mother comes out. Find some way for you all to get in this car. No, wait." Helen rummaged around and found some money. "Eugene and Andre, go find a bus, and make your way to my house. There's got to be one or two buses running tonight; if not, walk, and wait for me there—just do it."

"Okay—yes," Andre said as the two boys nodded. "We'll do it." They walked away together.

Helen told the others to climb into the back of her car, a Morris Minor van. They were scrunched, but they all fit. Helen started up the engine and put the heater on. None of the children uttered a word.

Sebastian opened the kitchen door as Amelia stood beside it with her coat and hat on. "Where are you going, Amelia, this time on Christmas night?"

Amelia glared at him and did not remove her gaze from his face. "I want to get as far away from you as physically possible." She hoped her voice would not break; she wanted to stay in control until she and the children were away from there. "You know, Sebastian, with a lot of prayer and faith, in time, it just might have been possible for us to salvage something from this marriage. However, Helen has enlightened me to your escapades in France when I was giving birth to Malachi."

Sebastian stepped forward to speak.

"Don't even open your lying mouth," Amelia said. The atmosphere in the kitchen was like that of a morgue—chilling. The fire had gone out, and all the pleasant, warm smells from the Christmas feast had faded, except for the smell of carbolic soap from the cleaning. Life had evolved for the past twenty years in this kitchen, tragedy and joy alike, but it was now empty and soulless.

"I am leaving this sham of a marriage with our children." Amelia swallowed. "I am never coming back."

"You cannot possibly mean that," said Sebastian.

"Oh no? Just watch me. Move your little mistress in, and have your baby." Amelia broke. "How could you? You bastard!" She went to open the door to leave, but Sebastian stepped in front of her.

"Amelia, I beg you—please do not do this."

"Move, or I swear, as God is my witness, I will swing for you." Her dark, smoldering eyes penetrated him with hatred. Amelia walked past him out of the kitchen, along the dark hallway, and out the front door for the last time.

—29—

The Reverend Mother was waiting at the entrance for the family when they arrived. There was hot cocoa for the children and shortbread biscuits, and she put some tea in her office for Amelia and Helen.

"I don't need reasons or explanations, Mrs. Lavalle," the Reverend Mother announced. "All you need to know at this moment is that you have shelter and food with us for as long as you need it. I have put you in one of the nun's rooms; it's small but adequate, as we are full to capacity. The six children will sleep in the sick bay until we can place them in dormitories."

Helen spoke up. "You are a godsend, Reverend Mother. I must leave now and go see to the two older boys who are waiting with my husband at my home. I'll see you tomorrow."

"I would really like to settle my children into their room, Reverend Mother, if I may," Amelia said.

"But of course. Let me show you to the sick bay." The children were all in there; they had been given sheets, blankets, towels, toothbrushes, and pajamas. Three beds were on one side of the room, and three were on the other. The children helped one another, and by the time Amelia arrived, they were settled in their beds.

Amelia switched off the lights.

"Good night. I will see you in the morning."

Leah spoke up. "Mammy?"

"Yes, what is it?" Amelia replied.

"Can we go home tomorrow?"

Amelia paused. "No, we will never go back to that house to live; it is not home now. This is home for the time being." With that, she closed the doors.

All the children were silent. Leah lay with her head on her pillow, watching the flashing red light of the Punchbowl Pub through the tops of the trees—on, off, off, on. *Some things stay the same,* she thought as she pushed her face into her pillow and wept until she slept.

—30—

One year later, on Christmas Eve, Amelia stood at the sink in her new home with Helen, peeling vegetables. They were looking out the window, watching a couple of robins dance around in the snow as if they were trying to keep warm. The fire crackled in the grate, Christmas carols were playing on the radio, and the house would have appeared to the outside world to be a normal family home.

"It's hard to believe that you have been living here for more than six months, Amelia," said Helen. "This is a perfect house social housing gave you—so close to the children's schools and their jobs and a good size at that. Do you ever bump into Sebastian and Stella?"

"No, thank God," said Amelia. "She keeps away from this side of the street and town, along with her baby. Sebastian comes to pick up the children, but he stays outside. He has visiting rights with five of them. It's been a hard year for everyone. This is the first Christmas since. Things have been really tight, and it will be a lean Christmas in more ways than one. I know I would never have managed without your help, Helen—baking, sewing, fetching, and carrying."

"All in all, I would say that your life is adequate. The bairns are in good health, as are you, Amelia; you have food on the table; and you are away from him, her, and that bairn of theirs."

"Yes, you are right, Helen." Amelia was drinking her tea, looking into the embers of the glowing fire, and listening to the Christmas carols on the radio. She felt an overwhelming sense of empty, hollow space. Shaking it off, she stood up.

"Let's get back to the vegetables, Helen. I am looking forward to Christmas in my new home."

Sebastian did not wish to enter the house yet. He had finished work early; it was three o'clock in the afternoon, and the factory was now closed for one week for the Christmas holiday. He was relieved, for he was desperate for time to think. Memories filled Sebastian's mind, mostly of Christmas a year ago. How could his life have changed so much? He looked around for somewhere to sit and noticed an old orange crate. He picked it up and dusted off the snow with his hands. After placing the box on a small patch of meager-looking grass and sitting down, he dropped his head into his hands. Sebastian was also full of remorse and deep sorrow. Was this his punishment?

He would not see his children this Christmas Day, as they were with Amelia. He would be able to pick them up on Boxing Day and spend two hours with them. His life was in chaos. He'd made poor decisions based on pleasure and lust, feelings lasting a fraction of a second, and a moment later, his feelings had changed.

However wrong, the result had been his daughter, the beautiful Jacqueline. She brought him a joy he had never imagined possible. She was bright and dazzling, warm like sunshine on his face after a cold, gloomy day. He felt reborn; she had brought new life into his home since that fateful Christmas Day a year ago, sweeping away some of the sadness and regret. He had more time to be with Jacqueline, a luxury he'd never managed with his other children. He had a little more money and a lot more wisdom. The older children had been deprived of much. He felt that Jacqueline was, in a way, a form of redemption.

He stood watching the dusk creep into the backyard. Sebastian walked along the path to perform his nightly ritual of washing his hands and chasing the cats away. Although it was cold, the cats were all curled up behind the dustbins. He stood still, watching the final moments of Christmas Eve daylight slip away forever. There was a dusting of snow on the ground, which made the dingy yard look almost magical. An odd star peeped through the clouds. The night was fresh, and the air was crisp, filled with the anticipation that only Christmas Eve could bring.

Resolving to put things right, Sebastian entered the house through the scullery door.

"Bonjour! Joyeux Noel," he said.

"Hello. You are home early," Stella said.

"Yes," said Sebastian. "And I am pleased because I am very tired. Where is Jacqueline?"

"Sleeping."

"Good," Sebastian replied. "I will get washed and cleaned up. I must speak with you, Stella, before she wakes and before we go to your parents' tomorrow. It is most important." Sebastian watched Stella.

"Fair enough," she said. "I will go put the kettle on."

They sat opposite one another in front of the roaring fire, which gave much-needed warmth to the room. Sebastian looked up from his mug of hot tea.

"I would like you to listen to me, Stella, and let me finish what I have to say to you before you comment."

Stella looked at Sebastian and shrugged. "Okay," she said.

"We are not together for any other reason than Jacqueline. You are not and never will be my soul mate, nor I yours, I am sure. We are going through the motions, and it is making me very unhappy. Eventually, I will resent you more than I do now, and in the long run it will be detrimental to Jacqueline." The heat from the fire was burning one side of Sebastian's face, forcing him to squirm in his chair. A piece of coal cracked and jumped out of the fire onto the well-worn rug. Sebastian stood, picked up the piece of coal with a small shovel, and placed it back in the fire; there was a smell of burning wool. Stella stayed silent.

Sebastian continued, "When we go to your parents' tomorrow, I believe you and Jacqueline should stay for good. It seems to me impossible to imagine my life without her, but I do know that we cannot go on like this." Sebastian's voice trailed off as he looked at Stella.

Stella jumped up from her chair. "I am so relieved, Sebastian. I can't wait to get away from this awful house full of sorrow and melancholy ghosts. It gives me the creeps."

Sebastian thought as he watched her that she was almost euphoric.

"I might as well tell you, Sebastian." She paced up and down, as she could not sit still. "I have met someone else at work, a male nurse." She rushed on. "He knows about Jacqueline and still wants to see me. I don't want to give up the chance of a decent relationship with someone my own age. I'm not sorry, Sebastian; everything you said is right. You can come visit Jacqueline on the weekends when you have time, when you are not with the others."

Sebastian thought to himself how young and insensitive she was. "Yes," he said. "We can work out the details. You can have full custody, and I will pay you child support and visit when I can."

"Good. Well, that's settled then," said Stella. "Let's start packing up, if that's all you have to say."

"Yes, for now," he replied. Sebastian could hear the sweet sounds of Jacqueline's voice coming from the next room. He felt a blanket of sorrow fall on him as he watched Stella leave the kitchen.

There was no Christmas magic in his home, Sebastian thought to himself—no Christmas tree, no manger, no singing of carols. Amelia and the eight children created that magic in their eager excitement to enjoy the season and all that it brought. He felt alone, even though he had his precious Jacqueline. He and Stella were up early on Christmas morning with no celebration and no ceremony.

They ate breakfast quickly; Stella was packed and eager to leave for her parents'.

Standing at the door of the kitchen, holding Jacqueline, she said, "I'm ready."

They left the house to catch the nine o'clock train. Sebastian stood on the platform, holding onto Jacqueline. The train arrived on time; the sky was gray, and the day was cold and damp. Any remnants of snow had disappeared overnight. It was as far away from a white Christmas as Sebastian could imagine. They rode the train together silently while Jacqueline slept in her push chair. He found his thoughts wandering back to Amelia and his children and what they might be doing—having their breakfast, helping clean up, preparing lunch while singing carols.

Sebastian decided to go for a walk through the train. He stopped to look out the window as the train approached Durham. An imposing sight passed before him: the cathedral high upon the crest of the hill, one thousand years old. Directly opposite was the castle, majestic and commanding as the sun shined behind it, spilling light upon the ancient city below. Sebastian loved when the train entered Durham; whether from the north or the south, it was always spectacular. He went back to his seat and sat next to Stella.

"I'd like to help you get to your parents' home with Jacqueline, but I do not wish to come in and go through the charade of a Christmas dinner. They do not like me, and I would rather not prolong the inevitable."

"You are right," Stella said. "I agree with you." It was a short bus ride to Stella's parents' home from the station.

"I will find a truck, and we can arrange to move all your

and Jacqueline's things from the house before I return to work," Sebastian said as they waited for the bus.

"I would appreciate that," Stella replied.

They arrived at the street on which Stella's parents lived. Sebastian was carrying Jacqueline; Stella went to open the push chair.

"Non," Sebastian said. "I would like to carry her. I am in many ways so sorry this is happening the way it is. I will miss Jacqueline more than you will ever know," Sebastian whispered. "But it is truly better this way." He kissed Jacqueline on the forehead gently and tenderly. *"Je t'aime beaucoup, ma petite fleur,"* he said with tears in his eyes. "Take her." He handed Jacqueline back to her mother. They had arrived at the front door. "I will say good-bye, Stella. I will be in touch."

As he walked away, Stella called out, "Good-bye, Sebastian, and thank you!"

Sebastian spent the rest of Christmas Day making his way home from Hexham; it was after four thirty when he arrived back home. He walked into the dark hallway and into the cold, bleak kitchen without fire or lights or the wonderful aromas of a Christmas dinner. He knelt, cleaned out the ashes and cinders from yesterday's fire, and laid a new fire. It caught quickly and was a roaring, welcoming sight; it helped. The heat from the fire warmed his bones and gave chase to the cold and the dampness. The kettle was whistling. He had not eaten since his early breakfast, but there was nothing in the cupboards or in the pantry. Stella was a poor housekeeper. He found some old cheese and dry bread, placed the food on a plate, made his tea, and sat on a chair in front of the fire, listening to Christmas songs on his old radio—"White Christmas," "I'll Be Home for Christmas," and more. He could not help himself—he wept until he could cry no more. He wept for all that had gone before him and for all everyone had lost because of his stupidity, especially Amelia and all his children, including Jacqueline. And there he was alone—one more devastatingly lonely Christmas night. He said out loud to the walls, "This will be my last sad and lonely Christmas!"

Amelia placed the turkey in the center of the table; it was plump, large, and juicy, with more than enough meat on its bones to feed the family for several meals. The St. Vincent de Paul Society had donated it to the family. The society had unexpectedly delivered a fantastic hamper to the door on December 24, filled to the brim with all sorts of delectable foods Amelia could not provide on the income they lived on.

The children were all sitting around the table, as were Helen and Charles. All the children provided exceptional help, and without question, Amelia would not have survived without their constant support.

Charles said, "This is an amazing dinner, Amelia; how do you do it?"

"With the help of my children, St. Vincent de Paul, and the good Lord," Amelia replied. "It has been a difficult twelve months, but we are all here to tell the story; we have survived and come together this Christmas Day to celebrate survival and one another."

Andre said grace, and everyone dug into the meat, potatoes, gravy, fresh bread, and stuffing. Amelia looked around the table, feeling a sense of pleasure.

"I wish Daddy was here," a soft voice said from the end of the table, stopping the conversation. Everyone looked toward the voice.

"I miss him," she continued. It was Abby, looking at her mam. For Amelia, her words were like a spear through the heart.

"He's with Stella and Jacqueline today. You will see him tomorrow; now, eat your dinner," she said matter-of-factly. Inside, Amelia felt a sting of guilt; the children kept their heads down, focusing on their turkey dinner—more than was necessary, she thought.

The Christmas Day was, all in all, a reasonable success compared to Christmas Day the year before. Amelia sat with her comfort tea in front of the fire at the end of the day, reflecting. It was late, all the children had gone to bed, and Helen and Charles had left two hours before, after eating Christmas cake with marzipan and royal icing, decorated to look like a magical Christmas snow scene. It was tradition to eat the first piece on Christmas night with a cup of tea after Christmas dinner. Amelia had baked it in September, as she always did, and soaked it in brandy for three months. Like most events surrounding their Christmas, this was a tradition that she and Sebastian had started many years ago, when they'd first married.

As Amelia looked into the embers of the dying fire, she finished the last drops of her tea and then wrapped up the Christmas cake to keep it fresh. She switched off the lights on the Christmas tree, turned off the radio, and closed the door on one more Christmas Day. With tears in her eyes, she whispered to the walls, "I wish he were here too."

— 31 —

The following July Sebastian had an abundance of work—he spent four nights a week teaching French to English students. With no one at home to take care of, he worked more. Keeping busy was good for him, as it prevented him from wallowing in self-pity and regretting his past mistakes. He was also renting the two rooms upstairs since Amelia and the children had left. The additional rentals produced more income, and because he had the opportunity to save after he paid his monthly commitments, he saved enough to purchase a well-used Citroen car. He felt like the king of the castle when he went to collect it; however, when he drove it away, the experience felt anticlimactic—there was no one to share the joy or the accomplishment with. The car did, however, afford him the opportunity to spend more time with Jacqueline on his days off, as he spent less time traveling to and from Hexham.

Jacqueline was ten months old now—almost a year—and she was a delight. He managed to visit her every other week on Sunday afternoons, and on the opposite weeks, he spent

Sundays with his other children. He knew the arrangement was far from perfect; however, it worked for now. Stella appeared to be a lot happier in her new life. She contacted Sebastian by telephone early in the week, asking if she could come discuss something important with him.

"Is Jacqueline okay?" Sebastian asked with urgency in his voice.

"Yes, there is nothing to be concerned about, Sebastian; I shall see you on Thursday at five o'clock."

"Would you like me to make dinner?"

"No, thank you," she replied. "I won't be staying that long. Good-bye. I'll see you then."

Sebastian was concerned. This upcoming discussion had an ominous feel to it, and Stella's phone call had been mysterious. He did not wish to guess what the matter was about—it could have been one of many things. He had no control; he must bide his time. Thursday would be there soon enough.

On Thursday Stella arrived at the door looking efficient in her white starched nurse's uniform underneath her damp coat. Sebastian helped her remove her coat.

"Shall I hang it for you?"

"No," she said. "Just put it on the back of the chair."

He had not been long home himself. It was not a cold night, as it was June; however, it was dull and wet. "Would you like a drink?" offered Sebastian.

"No, thanks."

The atmosphere in the kitchen was tense, Sebastian thought, reminiscent of many other occasions that flashed past his eyes, making him shiver as he spoke. "What have you come to discuss with me, Stella?" He pointed to a seat. "I am, to say the least, curious and also somewhat concerned." He sat in the chair opposite her.

"Well." Stella coughed to clear her throat as though she were about to make a speech, and then she blurted out. "It's very simple, really. I mean, well, you know I've been seeing Brian for, well, some time. We want to marry."

Sebastian broke in. "I think that is very good news. I must say—"

"I'm not finished, Sebastian. He—that is, well, Brian—wants to adopt Jacqueline," Stella continued. Her voice was shaking as though she might break down and cry. She cleared her throat once more. "We think—that is, Brian and my parents and I—that it is the best for everyone concerned, especially Jacqueline. I hope you will not prevent this, Sebastian." She tapered off almost to a whisper. "And give us permission."

There was chilling silence. Sebastian was shocked, and words banged around inside his head: *adopt, we, Brian, adopt.*

How does Brian know what is best for my chérie? Non, he does not. He could barely think clearly, as he was so stunned at such a request—the result of which would be him never seeing Jacqueline again. Sebastian didn't understand how or why he stayed calm; it was as though a thousand angels came to hold his tongue and keep him in his seat, calm and still, helping him to think before he erupted and terrified Stella out of her mind.

He heard himself reply, "I am happy for you both, Stella; it is a wonderful opportunity, and I congratulate you. I thank you for your direct approach to this"—he stopped and swallowed—"request. Obviously, I must give it some deep consideration. I will contact you next week maybe, and you and I can discuss it further. At this time, I will not say yes, Stella." Sebastian stood up and removed Stella's coat from the chair, indicating that the conversation was over.

"Good night, Stella." He opened the kitchen door to let her out.

"Good night," she said.

Sebastian walked over to his cupboard, took out his brandy, poured himself a drink, and sipped it slowly. The entire event from beginning to end had taken less than five minutes. *Rather like Jacqueline's conception,* thought Sebastian. He knew that the end result of agreeing to Stella's proposal would mean giving up the rights to Jacqueline for good. How life could change immeasurably in just five minutes; his life had proven that time and time again. He sat with the snifter of brandy, holding it and looking into the amber-gold liquid as though if he stared long and hard enough, it would magically show him the answer.

The truth was that Sebastian knew the correct answer to this request—he had known it long before Stella ever asked it of him. He'd secretly prayed for it, never expecting the prayer to be answered or such a decision to be thrust upon him so soon. He'd thought this might happen when Jacqueline was two or three years old, not yet. She was not even one year old. Sebastian thought of his little daughter—her sweet face; blonde curls; and big, round blue eyes. She looked like all the older girls mixed together; he could see whispers of them in her and often called her by one of their names. He had missed much of his children's lives when they were babies—all of it.

Sebastian finished his cognac with one last thrust of the snifter. Holding the liquid in his mouth, he felt it warm him, giving him a feeling of bravado. He could hold this adoption off indefinitely if he wished—why not? He decided he would like to get to know this Brian a little better. However, he knew he was kidding himself—Brian had been around for some time, and Jacqueline went to him as though she thought he was her father. Deep in the depths of his soul Sebastian knew Brian was a good man who could offer Jacqueline more than Sebastian—a middle-aged man—ever could. Brian could give Jacqueline a new young family, happy and energetic, and a future. To hold off this decision and prevent such a thing would be selfish. It would be in his best interest, not his daughter's. Yes, Sebastian knew what the right decision was. He stood up, resigning to call Stella sooner rather than later.

—32—

Amelia moved around her kitchen efficiently, as she always did on the day of Christmas Eve. There was a lot to accomplish. She was looking forward to Christmas Day, as all the children would be home. Andre was twenty-two and still working at the factory, but on weekends he worked cleaning windows, fixing bicycles, and delivering papers—doing any work he could find. He loved to work and save his money; he was still living at home. Andre was a fine young man, and he was courting a young lass from Durham. She was a nice-enough girl, but deep down, Amelia would never think anyone was good enough for Andre. The truth was she could not imagine her own life without him.

Eugene was now nineteen and had joined the navy like his father. Amelia felt the structure and discipline would be good for Eugene. He had been away from home for several months, but she was expecting him later that evening.

Leah, who was eighteen, was living in London, working at the Great Orman Street Hospital, training as a children's nurse, and she was made for it. She had been home for two or three days and was a wonderful help. Cammie, who was sixteen, was working as an office girl at a law office in Newcastle. Abby, her daydreamer, was fourteen and wanted to be an actress one day. Leah, Cammie, and Abby had gone out Christmas shopping.

Nathan, Sasha, and Noah, now eleven, were Amelia's pride and joy; they were in the local Dominican monastery choir as lead male sopranos. They were away practicing that afternoon for the midnight Mass.

Amelia finished peeling, chopping, and scraping her vegetables for the Christmas Day dinner, and she put on the kettle to make some comfort tea while allowing a nice shortbread biscuit to melt on her tongue. Amelia smiled into the dancing flames of the fire. It was a cold, frosty day with a howling northeast wind whining its way around the house. She wanted to provide a welcoming sight for the children coming home. She had made a large pan of mutton stew with some red wine and garlic, along with fresh bread rolls and butter. For the first time in four years, Amelia felt a genuine sense of joy within her and pride in every one of her children. The warmth of her comfort tea and the crackling fire crept into her bones. She looked at the clock. It was four o'clock, and she heard a noise in the hallway. Her boys had come home from practice, barging through the door, making lots of noise.

"Now," she said, "all of you sit down and take off your coats, and we'll have some dinner in an hour or so. You all need to have a bath and have a sleep before the midnight Mass."

"Oh, do we have to?" said Noah.

"Yes, indeed you do."

"You know," said Nathan, "Mam, you will really love this music tonight."

"Yes," said Amelia, "I am very excited and looking forward to hearing you all sing."

"Can we watch some TV for a little while before we eat dinner?" he added.

"Yes," Amelia replied. "I will call you." As they left, the girls came in through the back door, all chattering about what they had bought and where they were going to hide the presents. They headed upstairs to wrap their gifts away from the boys' prying eyes.

"Good. You all can go up," said Amelia, "and I will call you when dinner's ready." Cammie and Abby ran off, while Leah stayed back.

"Do you need some help, Mam?"

"No, Leah, I just finished the last of the vegetables, and we are all prepared. But if you like, you can set the table for our tea tonight."

Leah went about getting out the knives, forks, spoons, dishes, cups, and saucers. "It's really nice that we can all go to the midnight Mass tonight, Mam."

"Yes," said Amelia, "I think it's great that all our boys are singing at the Mass." Amelia watched Leah. "Have you something on your mind?"

"Mam?"

"Yes, Leah?" Amelia replied.

"When we were out shopping today, we bumped into Daddy."

"Oh?" Amelia made no comment. She allowed Leah to continue.

"Yes, he was Christmas shopping for the boys. He said that he was going to be seeing them on Boxing Day afternoon."

"Yes, that's correct."

"He was so happy to see us; we all went for a cup of tea and a cake with him. Abby and Cammie went off down the street to shop some more, and I stayed, and we talked."

Amelia knew Sebastian was now living alone; Stella had married and now had another child. Jacqueline was over three years old now, Amelia realized, calculating in her head. Sebastian had allowed Stella and her husband to adopt Jacqueline, meaning Sebastian had given up all his rights and would have no more contact with Jacqueline. According to neighbors and the local grapevine, Sebastian was devastated. She had not seen him for more than a year other than from the door when he dropped off the children; she had no reason to.

Leah continued, "I felt very sorry for him, Mam; he will be by himself on Christmas Day."

"Did he tell you that?" Amelia asked.

"No," said Leah. "I asked him how he would spend Christmas Day. 'Oh, don't worry about me,' he said. He asked me about my life in London and nursing work and said he was proud of me. When the girls came back, he gave each of us five pounds, Mam. Abby almost fell down! He kissed us all on the cheek and wished us joyeux Noel, and I know that he was crying when he walked away. We all thought you might be mad at us for taking his money, so we decided together that I would tell you what happened."

"Why on earth would you think such a thought?" said Amelia.

"It's just that sometimes you seem so angry when we talk about him."

"Just because I am angry with him does not mean you should have any problems with him."

"We all understand that, Mam. We just feel that—none of us ever want to disappoint you."

"How could you think that? I am proud of all of you." Amelia said no more.

"That's really good, but the thing is, Mam, I feel"—Leah burst into tears—"so sad and guilty."

"What are you talking about?" exclaimed Amelia.

Leah wailed, "I should feel so happy! I'm home with everyone for Christmas with food on the table and money in my pocket, celebrating midnight Mass with my brothers singing in the choir and everyone together—all of you."

"That's right—you and all of us are about to celebrate the best Christmas we have had in years."

"I know that, Mam, but I have a very sad, heavy feeling inside me when I think of all of us and what we have together with Aunt Helen and Uncle Charles tomorrow and Daddy all by himself. It makes me cry. Mam, can I ask Dad to come for his Christmas dinner with us?"

"What? No, absolutely not, Leah!"

"I knew you would say no."

"It's not that simple, Leah," Amelia told her.

"Why not? It's just dinner."

Amelia was taken aback. "The answer is no, Leah, and I do not have to explain myself to you. I am sorry you feel so sad, but sometimes life is just not fair. Now, go help your sisters wrap the gifts until I call you for your tea."

Leah walked away, mumbling under her breath, "I wish I had never told you."

Amelia sat in the front pew of the cathedral, surrounded by her family. Eugene had arrived home and joined in the Christmas festivities, beginning with the midnight Mass. Amelia looked around her; the cathedral was bleak, dark, damp, and in need of some repair. She felt chilled to her bones, yet as she sat watching and listening, warmth flowed through her. Amelia could see evergreens everywhere, cascading from the ancient pillars supporting the majestic church. Their scent was gentle to the senses. In front of her, on the high altar, was a life-sized nativity scene. It stood out, as it was bright, shiny, and new compared to the Gothic walls surrounding it; however, the scene successfully relayed its message, which was the importance of family.

Amelia closed her eyes and listened to the choir, allowing the music of the season to surround her.

Amelia thought of her boys singing—how proud she was and how blessed to be surrounded by her family. Amelia thought back to her conversation with Leah. Amelia stood up with her children to walk up to the high altar and receive Holy Communion. She went back to her seat and prayed for some guidance, for she knew Leah had been correct in her earlier comments. Down deep, Amelia was secretly glad Sebastian was alone. For her children, she knew she should reconsider letting him come over for the holiday—maybe. She thought of Helen's reaction and of Andre's, yet she was still overwhelmed with the thought and, yes, the desire to invite Sebastian to dinner. Maybe she should discuss the idea with the children first, she decided. The music from the choir rang out. Midnight Mass was over, and the processional moved into the vestry. Amelia and her family waited outside the choir room for the stars of the show.

"You know, I thought they sounded really smashing," said Andre.

"Me too," agreed Eugene.

"I really enjoyed the music," Leah said.

Abby announced, "One of the songs they sang was so nice I almost cried."

"Did you like it, Mam?" asked Camille.

"Yes, I did," Amelia replied. "It was wonderful—as special as anything I have ever heard—and I am very proud of them and also very happy to have us all together." Amelia stopped as the boys came out of the choir room, grinning.

"Well done," Amelia said. "You looked and sounded terrific. But you all look very tired, and we are walking home, as there are no more buses after midnight on Christmas Eve." They all started out of the great doors of St. Benedict's Cathedral. Standing outside, waiting in the bitterly cold early Christmas morning air, was Sebastian. He surprised all of them.

"Ah, bonjour. Joyeux Noel!"

Everyone stood still, unable to move, looking at Amelia for the next direction.

"Hello, Sebastian. I am rather surprised to see you out here."

"The boys told me they were singing at the cathedral at midnight Mass. I slipped into the back pew to watch and listen. I must say"—Sebastian looked at his three youngest children—"you were magnifique!"

"Thank you," the boys replied. They all felt uneasy, and no one knew what to do or say.

"We must get on our way; it's one thirty, and we are walking home," Amelia said.

Sebastian spoke up. "I have the car, Amelia—let me drive you home." It sounded more like a request than an offer. "You won't all fit in there, but the older boys can walk—non?" Sebastian looked at Andre and Eugene.

They looked at Amelia. "Yes, okay, I'll see you at home," she said.

They both headed for home. Sebastian walked everybody to the car, which he'd parked around the corner from the cathedral. "I think if you girls climb in the backseat and sit down first, the boys can sit on your knees, okay?"

As Amelia looked in his rearview mirror she saw a jumble of heads, arms, hats, and scarves and heard lots of comments, such as "Get off my knee," "You're killing me, Noah," and "You are sitting on my hand."

"Mam, Sasha is sitting on my new handbag, crushing it!" cried Leah.

Amelia turned around. "Settle down, all of you!"

Sebastian suggested they sing one of their songs from the service.

"Which one would you like to hear?" Nathan asked. "You pick it, Mam."

"How about 'Silent Night'?" said Amelia.

When they arrived home, the children all climbed out, happy to be back. They were all tired and looking forward to their beds.

Sebastian looked up at the sky. "Look up, children—the North Star is so bright it looks like the Star of Bethlehem."

"Wow, look at it sparkle," Abby said as everyone gazed at the beautiful stars.

"Good night, Daddy; thank you for the drive in your car," said Leah.

"You are welcome. Happy Christmas to all of you!"

"You too," she responded.

Amelia gave Leah the key. "Go on. I will be along shortly." The children all went into the house, leaving Amelia and Sebastian alone, standing together for the first time in years.

"I will say good night, Sebastian. Thanks for the drive home."

"Amelia, you are all still my family. I am happy to help."

"Good night, Sebastian."

"Merry Christmas to you, Amelia."

Amelia walked up the garden path to her front door, stopped, and hesitated before going into her home. She called out, "Sebastian!"

"Yes, Amelia?" Sebastian was standing next to his car, watching her as she walked away from him.

"Would you like to have Christmas dinner with us?" She did not turn to look at him.

"I would like that very much."

"Then I shall see you at twelve thirty, lunchtime. Good night." Amelia went into her home, closing the door behind her.

— 33 —

The next morning everyone in the Lavalle house worked to prepare the Christmas lunch. The turkey was stuffed and roasting in the oven—Amelia had used her mother's stuffing recipe, which involved sausage, roasted chestnuts, rosemary, sage, onions, and dried brown bread crumbs. The enticing aroma made its way to the dining room, where the table was set for twelve places.

Amelia announced to the children at breakfast on Christmas morning, "Last night, I invited your father for Christmas lunch today."

Leah shuffled in her seat and smiled. "Thanks, Mam." The girls were happy, Andre frowned, and Eugene shrugged.

Sasha asked, "Does that mean we still go with Dad tomorrow?"

"Yes, of course you do; nothing changes, and I don't want to hear your opinions. I have made the decision, so accept it, and remember to use your manners no matter what you think or feel." She shot a glance at Andre, who cast his eyes to the floor.

"I am looking forward to a wonderful Christmas Day. Do you all hear me loud and clear?"

"Yes, Mam, yes, we hear you," said Leah.

The older three children looked at one another and said no more. The doorbell rang.

"That should be Aunt Helen and Uncle Charles."

"Hello, all. Merry Christmas!" Helen said, and she gave each of the boys an item to carry into the kitchen. "Amelia, it smells delicious in here."

"Merry Christmas, Helen!"

"Look at what Auntie Helen has brought—cakes, sweets, biscuits, trifle, Christmas pudding, and Christmas crackers!" said Cammie.

"Oh, thank you, Helen," Amelia said. "Boys, go place the crackers on the plates at the table."

Helen watched them as they ran off. "They are growing into fine young lads," she said.

"They are a handful, though they are pretty good most of the time."

"Merry Christmas, Auntie Helen and Uncle Charles," Abby said as she kissed Helen on the cheek. She was like a gentle ray of sunshine, always happy and full of fun.

Helen's thoughts drifted to her son, Aiden, who was now living in Tennessee, married to Rosella, a lovely American girl. Aiden and Rosella wanted her and Charles to emigrate to be closer to them and enjoy their three grandchildren. Charles was in favor of the idea, but Helen was torn. Not seeing Amelia and her bairns, especially Abby, would be more than she could stand. Today she would put the issue out of her mind.

Helen jumped up from her chair. "What can I do, Amelia?"

"Nothing, Helen; it's all well in hand. The children have been marvelous. Go look at the table in the dining room, Helen."

"Come, Auntie Helen. I'll show you." Abby took Helen's hand, and they went into the dining room together. The table was made up of two tables pushed together, but one couldn't see that because of the wonderful table covering in red, green, and white, embroidered by Amelia. There were five chairs on one side, five chairs on the other, and one at each end. The table decorations were beautiful, including a centerpiece made of holly and red berries. All the plates matched, and each setting had a Christmas cracker on a plate and a wineglass.

"How very nice. What a marvelous job, Abby!"

"We all did it, Auntie Helen—well, my sisters and Andre. He helped with the tables and all the chairs. We needed one more, as Daddy's coming for Christmas."

Helen smiled at Abby, knowing she was mistaken. "No, Abby, you make a mistake there. Who's coming—Sally?"

"No, Auntie Helen, Daddy's coming."

Helen could not imagine what she'd heard. Abby recounted Christmas Eve the day before, explaining how she and her two sisters had gone shopping and accidentally bumped into their daddy. She told Helen how sad he'd seemed and that Leah had come home and asked Mam if he could come to dinner. Then she told about how they'd met at midnight Mass and how he'd driven them home in his car.

"Mam said at breakfast this morning that she was inviting Daddy for lunch and there was to be no more said. I'm happy he's coming; it will be nice for him not to be alone."

Helen's head was pounding; she went to Amelia in the kitchen. There was too much activity to confront Amelia.

Leah said to Helen as she was coming from the dining room, "Do you like it, Auntie Helen?"

Helen looked at Leah. "Like what?"

"The table—the Christmas table."

"Yes, it's very nice," Helen answered abruptly.

Leah asked, "Did Abby tell you Daddy's coming for lunch?"

"Yes."

Amelia was looking at Helen, and the whole room looked at Amelia.

"Are you out of your mind?" Helen asked.

Charles grabbed Helen and pulled her to one side, whispering to her with tight lips. He rarely said a word, but he was angry.

"Helen, mind your mouth, woman! Remember where you are and what day we are celebrating as a family." Charles dropped his voice. "All these bairns are looking up at you—do something now!" Charles held her tightly by the shoulders.

Helen knew she had indeed gone too far. She coughed and straightened herself up. "I am sorry, Amelia and everyone. I was just taken by surprise—you know."

"I know what you mean," Andre said. "We bumped into him last night at midnight Mass. It seemed strange to me—the first time the whole family had been together in four years. Rather awkward. He drove everyone home in his car, except me and Eugene walked. You know, if it's what my mam wants, it's okay with me."

Helen was about to say something when the doorbell rang. The younger boys ran to answer the door.

"Joyeux Noel!" Sebastian said.

At one point before dinner, Helen cornered Sebastian.

"Please do not make unnecessary conversation with me, Sebastian, as I have absolutely nothing to say to you," Helen whispered to him.

"I respect that, Helen, and I shall keep out of your way."

The Christmas dinner was splendid. Everyone participated and appeared to be reasonably relaxed under the circumstances. Sebastian had brought champagne and chocolates. As far as the children were concerned, it was normal to have their dad with them, and they thought it was fun. Abby went to sit with her dad after dinner, when the dishes were washed and the fire was roaring in the hearth. Christmas carols were playing on the radio, and the Christmas tree was sparkling.

Sitting close to him, she said, "Dad?"

"Yes, Abby?"

"I am glad you are here with us today."

"Me too. Thank you. I have missed you, you know—not just at Christmas and Easter but all the days in every way."

"You know, Dad, it was our idea—me and Leah and Cammie—to get Mam to ask you after we saw you yesterday. You looked so sad. We girls had a talk after you left, and Leah asked Mam before we left for Mass if you could come for dinner. I'm thinking that it was some kind of Christmas miracle that you were outside the church last night. Don't you think?"

"It must have been." Sebastian smiled. He took his daughter's hand, held it in his, and kissed it.

Helen stayed quiet and watched the children gravitate toward their father. Amelia appeared lighthearted also.

"I shall get out the Christmas cake. Let's have some sherry glasses out," said Amelia. They each had a piece of cake and a glass of sherry.

"You make the toast, Dad," announced Leah, and then she looked at her mam as if to ask if her suggestion was okay.

Amelia agreed. "Go ahead, Sebastian."

"To all, good health and many more happy family Christmases. Joyeux Noel!"

Helen put down her glass. "That's me—I am bushed, tired. Thank you for a delicious Christmas dinner, as always, Amelia. Let's go, Charles. Good night, all." Then they were gone.

"I shall be leaving also. I do not wish to overstay my welcome," Sebastian said.

"Oh, don't go yet," said Abby. "Have some more cake; I know you like it."

"Ah, oui, thank you. That is true, Abby. However, I am full—stuffed like that delicious turkey your mother served at dinner. I must go. It has been a long day—a wonderful one, may I add. Dinner was magnifique, Amelia. I thank you for such a warm and memorable family Christmas Day," Sebastian said.

Andre had left to go meet his girlfriend in Newcastle, and Eugene had gone out with one of his school friends for a pint at the local. The younger boys were watching a

Christmas film on TV and eating Christmas sweets from their selection boxes, lying on the floor. The girls all stayed in the kitchen with their dad.

"I will say good night, and I hope I can see you, Leah, before you head back to London. Maybe we can have lunch this week—non?"

"Yes, I would like that, Dad."

"Then call me and let me know when, because I have the week off." He kissed Leah on the cheek, and leaning over, he whispered in Abby's ear, "Thank you. I miss you every day also. Good-bye, Abby." He leaned in to kiss her and Cammie on the cheeks and then made a hasty retreat to the front door. Amelia followed alone. They stood together at the front door; it was dark, cold, and damp.

"Amelia." He took her hand, bowed his head, and kissed the back of her hand. "I simply cannot thank you enough."

"It was good for the children."

"May I call you, Amelia? I would like to take you out for a drive and lunch maybe. There are some fantastic pubs in Northumberland just along Hadrian's Wall. They also serve superb food." There was a silence between them that felt like an eternity to Sebastian; so much depended upon Amelia's response.

"If you like," she replied. "Good night, Sebastian."

"*Bonne nuit,* mon chérie." Sebastian smiled as he stepped out into the crisp night air and looked up at the star-filled sky.

—34—

On a cold afternoon in February, 1966, Amelia and Helen sat together on storage crates in Helen's empty living room, drinking tea.

"This is the end of an enormous part of our lives, Amelia. I can hardly believe Charles and I are leaving for the United States of America tomorrow for good. Hardest thing I've ever done in my life."

"Oh, Helen, how I will miss you. We all will," Amelia replied.

They sat silently for a moment.

"Are you excited about seeing Aiden and his family?"

"Of course I am," said Helen. "It's just the move; it's such a big decision to give up everything we know and own at this stage in our life. Charles is not well, as you know."

"Maybe all the more reason to be closer to your son," Amelia said. "It is important as we get older to keep those we love near."

"What are you going to do, Amelia? I know Sebastian is pursuing you and has been for some time."

"I honestly don't know, Helen," Amelia answered. "I can tell you this much: I am utterly exhausted—bone tired.

Andre is married and away from home, and Eugene is getting married and will be living on the base in married quarters. Leah is having a wonderful life in London, which I am pleased about. But I still have five children at home. I know Cammie and Abby are a big help—they work so hard, Helen, for young women. I ask so much of them and give nothing back. In truth, I am physically and mentally exhausted, with little or nothing in me left to give."

"Amelia," Helen said, "I am only concerned for you and those bairns; that's all I've ever been concerned with. I do not trust Sebastian, and I never will. Who can blame me? And now I'm leaving to go to the United States; I can't look out for you anymore."

"I know, Helen," Amelia answered. "And I understand—believe me. Honestly, I need him. I cannot manage on my own as it is now. He is a big help to me, and I am not saying we will get back together—I think we must try to be friends at least, for the family's sake. The boys are growing into young men, and they need a man's firm hand. They are his bairns too. I am ... I have gone as far as I can go. I can't imagine my days without you popping in with your arms full of something or other." Amelia looked into Helen's eyes. "Mostly care over these long years. And I thank you for being a kind sister."

Helen bowed her head. "As I said, Amelia, the changes in my life are going to be insurmountable. The hardest to bear is leaving you and Abby behind."

Helen placed the last of her things in her suitcase and closed it. The sisters embraced in the empty room and walked away together, closing the door. Amelia left her sister's house for the last time.

—35—

It was a bright morning in early May. Helen had been in America for more than three months now. Amelia had received a letter from Helen in the post that morning and was delighted. Amelia made herself a cup of tea and sat down to read her letter. It was the first she had heard from Helen since she had emigrated. She fumbled with the envelope, excited to pull the letter out and read it.

> Dear Amelia,
>
> I hope you and the children are well. Charles and I are enjoying our new home. It is so big—lots of space for the grandchildren to run around. Springtime is particularly lovely, with flowers and lovely fragrance everywhere. The weather is warm and sunny. We spend a lot of time with Aiden, Rosella, and our three wonderful grandchildren. We have meals together, and we go to church together on Sunday. I like to go on the

weekdays; it's a lovely church. I feel so very homesick, and I hope one day you can come here for a long holiday. Write back, and give me news of you and the family.
Love, Helen

Amelia closed her eyes, still holding the letter. How she would love to go to the United States of America one day—to Tennessee. Amelia decided to write back to Helen immediately; she knew it would be nice for Helen to receive a letter from home. After getting her paper and pen, she sat at the kitchen table.

Dear Helen,

I was delighted to find your letter in today's post and to hear your news. Sweet Hope Lake sounds like a beautiful place for you and Charles to be living. Things are much the same here; the children are growing fast. With the boys being teenagers now, they are a handful, let me tell you. I am finding it a struggle to manage—not just financially but the responsibility of it all. There is so much out there to tempt them—girls, drugs, and drink. I worry a lot. Sebastian has been coming to visit on a regular basis and is coming tonight. He's on his way back from France, a navy reunion. I am sure he is going to ask me to give it another try. To be honest, I've thought about nothing else, really. We've sort of

> discussed it in passing. I have told him I would never give up my house—between you and me, it's more about not moving back to the old house. Too many sad memories. I will keep you posted. We miss you—all of us, especially Abby.
>
> Love, Amelia

Amelia put down her pen and decided to heat the soup and start the bread. In spite of her reservations she found herself singing, something she had not done in a long time. The telephone rang and startled Amelia. She picked it up.

"Amelia, it's Sebastian."

"Oh, where are you?"

"I'm still in France. There is a strike." The connection was not good; Amelia heard lots of crackling. "There is a strike at the ferry crossing—customs or something. I am going to be delayed, only a couple of days or so."

"Are you all right?" Amelia asked.

"Ah, oui, yes. Sorry I won't make it tonight. Maybe Sunday before I get back. It is chaos here. I will be running out of time, Amelia."

"Yes, Sebastian, okay, I understand. Call me when you do get home."

"Yes, oui, Amelia. Can we talk about a holiday together when I come home? Will you think about that, Amelia?"

The phone went dead. Sebastian had run out of time, and he was gone; the line was quiet. Amelia placed the receiver back and went to the kitchen. She had a fleeting sense of disappointment and then shrugged and moved on to the next job, thinking about Sebastian's suggestion of a holiday. That was one step away from a trial reconciliation, and she was still unsure what she wanted.

She decided she would sit for a while, as she was tired. She had felt strange all day, with a dull ache in her head. She had taken a couple of headache pills, and she thought she would try to sleep for an hour; it was only one o'clock, and the boys would not be in from school until four fifteen. She swallowed some more pills, thinking to herself that it was the third time this week she had taken headache pills. Sitting in her chair, she closed her eyes, focusing on pleasant thoughts, such as a holiday with Sebastian.

Her thoughts drifted, however, and her headache became more intense. She was feeling sick to her stomach, as though she would vomit. She stood up to get to the sink, and as she went across the room, her head felt as if someone had hit it with an ax—as if there had been an internal explosion. The pain was so intense that Amelia cried out, vomiting all over herself and collapsing into a heap upon the kitchen floor, unconscious. Amelia's last thought before her world went black was Sebastian.

Andre, finished with work for the day, decided to pop in to visit his mam for a cup of tea, something he enjoyed when he had the time. He went through the yard, closed the gate, and entered through the back door, as he always did.

"Hello, Mam! It's me," he said.

She was not standing at the kitchen sink or at the stove, and he could not smell her delicious dinner cooking. In fact, the only thing he could smell was vomit. He heard a gurgling noise and felt a shiver run the length of his body, for he knew something was not right. He looked past the kitchen table and saw his mother on the floor. He rushed to her, dropped to his knees, and looked at her. Was she dead? She lay still. She was covered in vomit, her face was ashen, and she had blue lips. The stench was overwhelming, and Andre could not think.

"Mam?" He took her in his arms and tapped her cheek several times. "Mam, wake up." He knew if she heard him, she would wake. Amelia was making a gurgling sound. He had to do something quickly; he needed to phone the ambulance, but he did not want to leave her. Andre took off his jacket, rolled it up, and placed it under his mother's head. Just as he was looking around the kitchen for something to cover her and keep her warm, his young brothers came in through the back door from school.

"Hullo, Andre. Where's Mam?" Sasha said. They all came in at the same time, with Sasha in the lead. "What's wrong? Where's me mam?"

Andre stepped forward to hide Amelia from them. "It's okay; it's just that it looks like she might have—"

The boys looked around him and saw their mam lying on the floor.

Nathan screamed out, "Why is she making such a noise?"

"Calm down, Nathan," Andre said.

Sasha dropped to his knees and looked at her. "We should wake her; we should clean her up. She can't lie in sick like this."

"Just stay with her," said Andre to Sasha. "I've got to call the ambulance."

Nathan stood in one spot, crying his heart out. Noah moved slowly toward his mother and knelt beside Sasha.

"What's happened to her? Is she breathing? I'm scared, Sasha," said Noah.

"I know," Sasha said. "The ambulance men will help her when they get here." Sasha held his mother's hand; it was cold. Nathan was still unable to move.

"Let's all take off our blazers and cover her," Sasha said to his brothers. They took them off and placed them over Amelia, gently tucking them in around her to keep her warmer. Andre went to the front door to wait for the ambulance.

"Will they never get here?" Noah broke down in tears as he and Sasha stroked their mother's forehead.

"I hope they come soon," Sasha replied.

Andre came back into the kitchen with the paramedics.

"Hullo, lads," one of them said. "Now, stand back so we can help your mam."

"Don't you hurt my mam!" wailed Nathan.

"Not to worry, sonny; we're here to look after her. We need to give her some oxygen." Two paramedics knelt beside her, cleaned her face, and put a mask on her. "We need to give her some fluids, help her breathe better, and get her to the hospital as quick as we can."

They worked around Amelia, putting on a blood-pressure cuff, setting up intravenous fluids, and moving her onto a stretcher. Andre moved his brothers to the other side of the kitchen, and they all watched, tears coming from their eyes.

"Is she going to die, Andre?" Sasha asked.

Andre was taken aback. "Maybe. I don't know, Sasha. I just don't know."

The men carried Amelia out to the ambulance.

"I will go with her," Andre said. "Sasha, phone Abby and Cammie, and tell them what has happened. I will phone you from the hospital as soon as I can to let you know how she is." He climbed into the back of the ambulance and, looking up, could see his three younger brothers crying as the ambulance took their mother away.

Andre sat holding his mam's hand, listening to the sound of the siren as the ambulance rushed through the streets on the way to the hospital. He had often wondered what was going on inside an ambulance when it rushed past him on the street. He always felt sad for whoever was inside. *Now I know,* he thought to himself as he listened to the incessant gurgling from his still-unconscious mother.

Andre sat in the waiting room outside the emergency room. It was a new hospital with all the best equipment, and if anyone could help his mam, this place would, he told himself. He had been waiting all night, and it was late—ten o'clock. He had still not heard from the doctor. He had called home and said he would let everyone know how she was doing when he heard. Suddenly, a doctor in a white coat with a stethoscope around his neck came through the emergency doors. He looked at Andre.

"Are you Mr. Lavalle?"

Andre jumped up. "I'm her son Andre Lavalle."

The doctor steered Andre into a little room off to the side of the waiting room and offered him a chair. As the doctor sat opposite Andre, he said, "My name is Dr. Sandyford. Is there any other family?"

"Yes, they are all at home, waiting for news."

"And your father?"

"He is on his way home from France," Andre replied.

"I see," said the doctor.

Andre could feel his stomach turn, and the muscles in his neck and shoulders tensed. "How is she, Doctor?"

"We have done a lot of tests, Mr. Lavalle, and I am afraid the news is not good. Your mother has suffered a massive cerebral hemorrhage. That's a bleed inside her brain. It has flooded her brain, and the tests show that there is irrevocable damage. I am sorry." The doctor looked at Andre as he lowered his voice. "There is no hope."

Andre felt tears sting the back of his eyes. *No hope? Rubbish,* Andre thought. *You don't know my mam.*

The doctor continued. "She's now on a respirator, which is breathing for her at this time. If you wish, you may go in and see her, talk to her. We have no way of knowing if she can hear you or not."

Andre stood up, believing that where there was life, there was hope. He would talk to his mam, and she would recognize his voice—he knew it. He walked into the ICU room, listening to the beeping of the machine and watching the breathing apparatus go up and down. His mother looked as though she were cocooned in a blanket made of aluminum foil. As his hands spontaneously reached out to touch the blanket, the nurse behind quietly said, "To keep her warm." His mam looked as though her eyes were closed, yet when he looked closer, he saw that they were not quite sealed, as if there were a veil of tears underneath each eyelid. Should she be able to close them completely, it seemed tears would fall upon her pale, soft cheeks. It was as though she were trying to communicate to Andre how sad she was to be leaving him.

Andre coughed and cleared his throat. "Can you hear

me, Mam?" Amelia did not move. "Please don't go; we all need you so very much. Hold on tight, Mam, and stay with us. Hold on to my hand like you always have. The best is yet to come, Mam. You've come through the worst." He hung his head, bent over, and kissed her forehead, gently willing her to open her eyes. Andre looked at his mother—he saw life yet no hope. He felt overwhelming fear as he left the ICU room and closed the door behind him that he would never see his mother alive again.

Andre sat in his mother's kitchen, listening to the torrential rain bounce off the kitchen roof. It was Sunday morning, but it looked like night—dark and heavy. The ashes were still in the grate from last night's fire, the garbage was overflowing from the bin onto the kitchen floor, and there were dirty dishes piled up in the sink. The kitchen was in complete disarray, which was unusual, as it was normally neat. It had been thirty-six hours since the doctor had told him there was no hope. Eugene, Leah, Cammie, Abby, Sasha, Nathan, and Noah were sitting around the kitchen table, looking at one another or into their mugs of cold tea. Normally when they were all sitting around Mam's kitchen table, they were celebrating.

The telephone rang, startling Andre. Everyone looked toward him. He stood up, made his way to the ringing phone, and picked it up.

"Hello? Yes, this is he."

They all looked at him, frozen, their eyes on his face. They were tired, frightened, and fearful, listening and watching Andre's every move. He dropped his gaze, his lips parted as he drew them over his teeth, and his face folded inside itself as though he were in physical pain.

He listened, and his head shook frantically from side to side, yet his voice was amazingly calm. "Yes, I do understand, Doctor. Thank you, and good-bye." He put the receiver back, but his hand remained on it, not moving. He was unable to look up for a moment. Then he slowly raised his head.

"She's gone," he whispered. "Our mother is dead."

Sebastian arrived home late Sunday evening; it was almost midnight. He was exhausted; he had had a long day traveling back home. Everyone had been pushed into the trains and boats until they were overflowing. Some people had stood all the way home because there were not enough seats. He had not been able to use the hotel phone as he had wished, because the storm had brought down the lines. He did not concern himself too much, as he knew Amelia was aware of his situation.

He opened his door, picked up the mail off the floor, and went down the hall to the kitchen. After dropping everything on the table, he immediately went to put on the kettle and make himself some tea. He was to be at work at seven o'clock in the morning, and it was after midnight now; he was hungry, thirsty, and cold. He looked through his mail quickly as he waited for the kettle to boil, and he noticed a note with the word *Urgent* written in red letters across the front. Opening it, he read, "Call me as soon as you arrive home—urgent. Andre." He immediately went to the phone and called him.

"What is it, Son?"

"Dad, I will be there soon, okay?" Andre said, and he hung up.

Looking at the clock, Sebastian saw it was past midnight—too late to call Amelia to find out what was going on. He felt nauseated with worry. What was wrong? He made his tea, hot and sweet, and drank it; it did not help to calm him. The doorbell rang, and Sebastian ran to the door.

"Come in." He talked as he walked down the hall. "What is so urgent, Son? You have me frantic with worry."

"Dad, let's go to the kitchen and sit down."

"Non, non—stop this! Tell me!" Sebastian was shouting at the top of his voice, pleading.

Andre stood in front of his father, his voice breaking. "It's Mam—she died this morning." Andre could not continue.

Sebastian looked at his son. "I don't think I heard you right, Son. Tell me what is upsetting you so."

"It's Mam—she died this morning," Andre repeated. He stumbled through the events of the last two days as clearly and precisely as he could. Sebastian looked at his son in horror and collapsed onto the floor in front of him, howling, wailing, and clutching himself, convinced Andre was mistaken.

"Non, non!"

"Dad, it's true; it's really true." Andre managed to get Sebastian up onto a chair and pour him some brandy. Andre put on a fire and sat with his dad silently, listening to him sob from the bottom of his soul. When he was able to speak, Sebastian asked Andre about the children.

"About as shocked as you and I are, Dad," Andre said.

Sebastian looked at his firstborn—he was pale, heartbroken, tired, and tender faced. What a huge burden and responsibility for this young twenty-five-year-old to carry these past days alone. Sebastian suddenly felt overwhelmed with a desire to hold him like a baby. Sebastian stood up, topped off his brandy glass, and held it in front of his son.

"Here; this must have been almost unimaginable for you, Andre. I am so sorry I was not here for you and your brothers and sisters, but mostly for your mother." Sebastian broke down. "I simply cannot believe it. You know we were planning—"

"I know, Dad. I am sorry."

"No, Son, you have spent most of your life stepping into my shoes because I was not there or not available. I will not let you go through this alone. I want to come to the home tomorrow and see the children."

"They are all very distressed, Dad. I'm not sure if it will help."

"I am willing to take that risk, Andre."

"I will stay with you tonight if you like."

"Non, non, Andre, you go home to your wife and sleep in your own bed, where you belong. You must get some rest; you look so totally exhausted."

Andre did not protest. Sebastian walked his son out to the door; he longed to hold him in his arms.

Andre looked at his father. "I am truly sorry, Dad," he said, and he walked away without looking back.

The day was Wednesday. It was a half day, when all the shops closed at one o'clock. The sunshine had put a spring in everyone's step, and the mood on the street was happy. The front door opened, and Abby stepped out of the family home, followed by her siblings, each of them carrying his or her own sorrow like an invisible veil. As the procession moved toward the hearse, the coffin loomed. Abby thought it didn't belong there. She noticed the neighbors standing in their doorways with their arms folded and hands in their aprons; some of them were wiping their eyes and blowing their noses. Abby looked along the familiar street toward the shops. A bus drove by, and a lady got off. The elderly lady recognized a friend at the bus stop, and Abby could see them smiling at one another, one holding up a large bunch of bright yellow bananas as if she were showing a golden prize and pointing with a strong finger to where one could make such a wonderful purchase. It was evident no one should miss this bargain. As they were in conversation, Blind Mary passed by with her Seeing Eye dog, a black Lab, and one of the ladies patted the dog on the head. As she watched their faces smiling and heads nodding, Abby imagined they were commenting on the beautiful morning. The paper boy came out of the newsagent, eagerly tearing the wrapper off a large chocolate bar in anticipation of the first bite. The street was awake and buzzing early.

Abby watched, feeling within her an ache that was working its way up from her chest into her head. It sounded like a thunderous roar. *Stop, life on the street. How can you smile and eat chocolate bars or catch a bus? My mother is dead. The street should weep, not smile and shine. We are about to put her in a hole in the ground—a dark, wet, six-foot-deep hole. And yet the bus still stops, the dog wags his tail, and the sun still shines.*

Sebastian slipped his arm around Abby's waist and helped her into the long black car. A small whimper came from Abby's lips.

—36—

On a lovely Sunday morning in May in Georgia, Adam Gabriel Spencer, a young man known as Gabriel, stood behind the altar, looking out at the congregation, surrounded by loving family and classmates in this magnificent cathedral. He was celebrating the sacrament of his ordination. This was a day he had prayed for and looked toward for most of his life.

He used all his senses to savor every moment as the bishop anointed him, laying his hands upon his head and blessing him with the holy oil. Gabriel felt empowered, as if he had been touched by the hand of God. It was glorious; he believed he was a successor of the apostles—a living, organic link to them and, through them, to Jesus Christ himself. At the end of the service, the bishop said, "Go in peace, Father Gabriel, and serve the Lord."

Gabriel had been posted to a small country church, St. Michael the Archangel, in a little town outside of Memphis: Sweet Hope Lake. He had been to visit the pastor and liked the church and the community. Gabriel felt blessed and was looking forward to serving in his new parish.

Helen awoke feeling a deep, heavy sorrow. Three and a half thousand miles away they were burying her younger sister Amelia, her baby sister whom she had taken care of and looked out for all their lives. *Lord, how life is full of such twists and turns,* she thought. After getting out of bed she showered and dressed quickly and then prepared breakfast for herself and Charles. Looking across the small kitchen table, she could see how he had deteriorated since they had immigrated to America. He was losing weight, appeared to have difficulty breathing, and slept most of the day away. She felt she was losing him slowly.

"What are you going to do today?" Charles startled her with his question.

"I think I will go to Mass. It's all I can do—pray."

"That's a good idea, Helen," he said. "I'll spend some time with Aiden and the kids. It's a beautiful day to be outside."

"It is that," said Helen. "Everything here is new and big and beautiful. Yet I still ache for home, Charles, especially today." Helen stood up, wiped tears from her eyes with her handkerchief, and tucked it back into the sleeve of her cardigan. She cleaned up the dishes and left Charles sitting comfortably in his chair, looking out the window.

Helen drove her little Ford toward St. Michael's. It was not far and was a pretty drive. There were dogwoods, apple blossoms, cherry blossoms, magnolias, and lavender trees. On every street corner was a flowering tree or bush showing off its splendor to the world. The air was heavy with springtime perfume, and the Tennessee grass was blue. In spite of the amazing beauty of the day surrounding her, Helen wept.

She arrived at the little church; it was quaint, like something out of *Peyton Place,* a soap opera she used to watch back in the old country. It had a white steeple and a little churchyard. She was praying for some relief from the pain, sorrow, and dreadful feeling of helplessness. She entered the church and arrived just in time for the beginning of the Mass. She slipped into her pew, which was vacant, as not many souls were out at this time on a Wednesday morning. She recognized a few faces; however, she was not in the mood to be sociable. Kneeling, she kept her head bowed as she gathered her rosary beads in her hands and fingered each bead one at a time deliberately. *Hail Mary, full of grace, the Lord is with thee,* she prayed as she wept silently.

Continuing to pray, she realized there was a new face celebrating the Mass in place of Father Stephen. She dropped her rosary beads back into her coat pocket and paid more attention to the mass. She remembered an announcement last month regarding a new curate ordained recently. He looked young, Helen thought. He was fresh faced and had a million freckles and a head full of tight golden curls. His eyes shined; he had the face of an angel.

"The Lord be with you," the curate said.

"And also with you," the congregation replied. She liked his voice—it was warm and southern, and he spoke clearly with a slight drawl. His movements were reverent and precise, as though he were really living the Last Supper.

Helen could not take her eyes off him. *What a magnificent Mass,* she thought.

After Holy Communion she watched the young priest work his way gently around the altar, sipping the last drops of wine from his shiny new chalice. His cup of life was relatively empty, untouched by sorrow, pain, or disappointment. She envied his fresh enthusiasm and his shiny new chalice.

When Mass was over, she left the church. The new priest was standing outside in the warm sunshine; the air was heavy with the perfume of the May blossoms. He extended his hand.

"Hi. I'm Father Gabriel, the new curate at St. Mike's."

Helen smiled at him. "Hello, Father. My name is Helen Kennedy, and may I say—you celebrated a magnificent Mass this morning."

"Why, thank you." Gabriel threw his head back and laughed loudly as if he were directing his laughter toward heaven. "I am so delighted you think so and, may I say, humbled. Let me tell you a secret, Helen Kennedy." He smiled. "It is my second Mass ever and my first here at St. Mike's. I was nervous—I don't mind saying."

Helen smiled; she'd never met a priest so endearing. "Well, I am pleased to meet you, Father. Keep up the good work."

"Forgive me, Helen—I don't wish to be intrusive, but I do believe I saw you wiping tears away in church this morning. May I ask—what is it that saddens you so?" His question startled Helen but opened the flood gates.

"My sister is being buried today—far away in England. I wish I could be there for her children; I feel so helpless and alone."

Gabriel surprised Helen for the second time by placing his arm around her shoulders to comfort her gently, his voice smooth. "That is sad indeed, and I will pray for you, Helen; for your sisters soul; and for her children. Please don't feel alone. If you have a problem or just need a shoulder, mine is here waiting for you to cry on."

Helen felt comfort in Father Gabriel's words and sensed sincerity and concern beyond his tender years. She could not pinpoint her feelings; however, there had been a shift. The burden did not feel as heavy, nor did she feel so alone.

"Bless you, Helen."

Helen looked up at him in wonder. "And bless you, Father," she said as she walked away from the church.

Helen tolerated the Tennessee summer, although the heat was nearly unbearable. Worse than the heat was the humidity, something she and Charles were not used to. Fortunately, Aiden had air-conditioning, and she spent most of her time inside when she could, except when she had to take Charles to the doctor or for a hospital visit. He was suffering from several problems, the most serious of which was congestive heart failure. Life was lonely most of the time, and she kept to herself.

One day when they were upstairs having dinner with the family, Aiden asked her, "Would you like to come to the church picnic tomorrow, Mam? We're all going, and it's really fun—lots of organized games, hot dogs, hamburgers, barbecued chicken, salads of all sorts, and fantastic desserts.

Dad can come along and sit in the shade. He'll enjoy it—won't you, Dad? What do you say?"

Charles nodded. Helen thought, *You must be kidding in this heat,* but she found herself smiling, knowing she should accept; otherwise, she would seem ungrateful. Besides, it would be pleasant to see her grandchildren having fun.

"Yes, of course, we'd love to come, Son," said Helen.

The picnic was a fantastic success. Helen played with her grandchildren and drank cool lemonade with Charles. He enjoyed himself; although he stayed in his chair, he cheered his grandchildren in the games—tug-of-war, a three-legged race, and an egg-and-spoon race. Helen sat under a big tree draped with Spanish moss behind the church; tassels hung from its branches like spun green and silver silk, cascading toward the blue grass around them. A gentle, perfumed breeze meandered its way past them, softly swaying the foliage and Helen's hair. Helen sighed. One or two redbirds were dancing around in the grass beside them, picking up the crumbs left over from the hot-dog buns. The sun was soft, as it was late in the afternoon.

Charles said, "I hope you are feeling more settled, Helen."

She looked at him. "I suppose so, yes. This is where we need to be."

"We belong here with our son and his family. I believe we are more fortunate than many older folks I know."

"I'm not disagreeing with you, Charles; it's just that I've had a very difficult year—many losses and changes. I feel utterly lost sometimes."

"Me too," said Charles. "I'm sick, Helen. My health is not good, and it's not going to get better."

"Oh, don't talk like that, Charles."

Charles continued, "Helen, it's a comfort to me to know that we are settled here with Aiden and his family. Look at us. Look at this extraordinary place. Who would have believed?"

As he was talking, Father Gabriel came along. "Hi, y'all. Look at y'all—like a couple of young kids under the tree. You look like a Norman Rockwell painting."

Helen laughed loudly, something she rarely did. "Oh, you, Father," she said, giggling. "You are something else."

"It's true, Helen." He shook Charles's hand. "How are you, sir?"

"I'm fine. I can't remember when I've enjoyed a day so much," Charles replied.

"Well, I am pleased to hear that; this has been a perfect Tennessee day for our picnic." He pulled up a chair and sat between them. Silently, the three of them watched the late-afternoon sun slowly slip behind the Tennessee mountains, infusing the sky with a crimson glow. *What a feeling of peace,* Helen thought as she looked out at the breathtaking view. *Relaxing, yes,* Helen thought. *This is my life now, and it's a blessed one.*

The following week, Helen, to her delight, received a thick airmail envelope from Abby. She was thrilled and rushed into the kitchen in the basement of the house, waving the letter in the air.

"Look, Charles—a letter from Abby!"

Charles raised his head from the newspaper he was reading. "That's nice."

"I will make a nice pot of tea, sit outside in the swing in the garden, and enjoy every single word." It seemed to Helen that the kettle would never boil. Helen sat in the early morning sunshine; it promised to be hot summer day. Swinging back and forth in the chair she had grown so fond of sitting in, she took a sip of her tea and looked at the envelope. This was the first letter Helen had received from Abby. She waited some more in order to make the anticipation last longer. There were eight small, lined pages with writing on both sides. *Obviously,* Helen thought, *Abby had a lot to say.*

> Dear Auntie Helen and Uncle Charles,
>
> I am sorry for not writing to you before now. My goodness, so much has happened since you left for the United States, and I don't know where to begin. First of all, I hope you are both well and like living in America with Aiden and his family. Is it very different there? When I watch the television—*Peyton Place*—I think to myself, *I wonder if Aunt Helen's town looks like this. If so, then she's lucky.* I am happy for you if it is. Is it hot? Is everything as big as it looks—the cars, houses, fridges, bedrooms, gardens, trees, and flowers? Are people nice to you—friendly, I mean?

Helen stopped for a moment, sipped her tea, and smiled before going back to her letter.

> I think I'm rambling because I don't want to write about my mam.

Helen felt a sting behind her eyes.

> It is so sad. And it was a massive shock for all of us, my dad included. I have to say that nothing feels right or the same since she died, and the younger boys are feeling it a lot. Sometimes when I am going to my bedroom at night, I hear sobs coming from behind their door. One or the other of them is crying themselves to sleep, and I don't know what to do about it. I don't think they sleep very well, because I can't get them up for school in the morning. Cammie and I talked to the headmaster; he was very nice and told us not to worry. He said everyone was sad about Mam and would help in any way they could.
>
> At first, everyone was kind. Neighbors brought in food and cooked meals, ladies from the church helped us clean the house and do the washing and ironing, and it was very helpful. Four months later, it all seems to have slowed down almost to a stop, probably because of the summer holidays. The boys are off school till September. Maggie and Tom took them on a holiday camping to Scotland. They had a good time, and I think they felt better. I just feel so lonely and sad without my mam, and I feel sorry for them and my other brothers and sisters—not the ones so much who are

married but definitely those of us who live at home. Especially if they feel like I do.

Dad has helped. He wanted us to go back and live at his house with him, but no one wanted to. So he helps us here when he can. He looks somehow older since Mam died; he walks slower and with his head down.

I work a lot; I've changed my job. I work in a department store in Gateshead now. It's very busy, and I help Sally on the ice cream van on Sundays, serving ice cream, although I think I eat more than I sell; it's a lot of fun.

There's lots to be done at home, and everybody helps and does their best—shopping, cooking, washing, ironing. There isn't a lot of time for other things. Sally and I are saving up and hope to go visit her auntie in Italy. Maybe go to Rome and the Vatican and see the pope.

I hope you will write back to me, Auntie, and tell me all the fun new things you are doing and all about your grandchildren. Give my love to Uncle Charles and Aiden and his family—and especially you.

Love, Abby

PS Have you seen Elvis?

Helen placed the letter in the envelope and pushed it into her apron pocket. What a situation. She wanted to find some writing paper and reply immediately. Helen went into the basement, rushing past Charles.

"That poor bairn has a lot to contend with," Helen told him. "What a lot of responsibility for the young lass. Sad letter." Charles did not answer. Helen was rummaging around in one of her many boxes under the bed for some writing paper and an envelope.

"She says she's worried about the young ones—they cry themselves to sleep at night." Helen shouted, "Charles can you hear me?" Charles still did not answer.

Helen went back into the kitchen, clutching her writing paper and envelope.

"Charles, do you hear me? Those poor bairns. Charles—" Helen stopped, and her heart skipped a beat. She shouted in a louder voice, "Charles, are you asleep? Wake up." Helen went over to him. The newspaper had slipped to the floor and was in disarray at Charles's feet. His head was slumped forward, and his chin was resting on his chest as though he were sleeping. His arms hung lifelessly by his side, and there was no sound or movement. Helen dropped her papers and screamed, "Charles! Charles!" She dropped to her knees beside him. "Charles, wake up—don't you leave me now! Oh Charles, please." Helen wept.

Aiden had come downstairs to see what the noise was. He popped his head around the door.

"Hi, Mam—what's the noise?"

Helen looked up at Aiden and reached out her arms to him.

"Oh, Mam!" he cried. "No!" He went over to his father and checked his pulse.

"He's gone!" Helen wailed. "I'm so sorry, Son." Mother and son clung to one another, weeping. After a while, their sobs subsided. Aiden found a sheet, covered his dad, and led his mother out of the basement.

"Let's go upstairs, Mam, and make the appropriate phone calls and contact Father Gabriel."

The requiem Mass was both dignified and moving. Helen was touched by the kindness and thoughts she received from parishioners at St. Michael's. She had only lived there for less than a year, yet people packed the church for the burial and the reception in the church hall. The Catholic Women's League supplied the luncheon of sandwiches, cakes, tea, coffee, and cold drinks. Aiden, Rosella, and Helen's grandchildren all stayed close beside her as she moved from guest to guest, thanking them for their support and kindness. She felt as if she were in a slow-motion type of dream, watching something she was not part of. It felt strange to go through the motions of shaking hands, kissing cheeks, and introducing her family to strangers—kind strangers no doubt but still strangers to her. She felt numb from head to toe—empty. Father Gabriel approached Helen.

"You are a wonder," she said to him. "I don't know how we would have managed without you this week."

Father Gabriel sighed and looked at Helen, taking her hands in his. "That's why I'm here. Remember, Helen, my shoulder is yours if and when you need it."

Wiping her tears away, Helen nodded. "I know, Father. I remember."

Helen looked out the window. A light dusting of snow covered the ground on this cold January morning—unusual for Tennessee. It had been almost a year since she and Charles had moved to America. Much had happened. Helen heard a faint knock on her door. She was surprised when she looked at the clock; it was 11:15 a.m. *Who could that be?* she thought.

Opening the door, she smiled. "Oh, Father Gabriel, what a surprise."

"Hi, Helen. I thought you might like a visitor. I was passing this way."

"Come in, and I'll put the kettle on," she told him. Helen brought the tea and biscuits out and looked at Gabriel. "What brings you to me, Father?"

"Well, I have a confession to make, Helen."

"Really?" Helen smiled. "I thought it was the other way around."

Gabriel laughed loudly in spite of himself. "Aiden asked me to come by, Helen. He and Rosella are very concerned," Gabriel said. "They feel you are not recovering from Charles's death—or Amelia's, in fact. I'm here because I have to agree with them."

"How so?" snapped Helen. "How so?"

"He tells me you are not participating in family events. For Thanksgiving and Christmas, he said they had to drag you upstairs. You prefer your basement. You really do look pale, thin, and tired, Helen. I have missed you at Mass both this month and last. I've come to see if I can help you, Helen."

"And how do you think you can do that, Father? Can you take me home or bring back Amelia or Charles?" Tears poured from Helen's eyes. "I'm so lonely I could die!" she cried.

Gabriel took Helen's hand gently in his own. "That is absolutely normal under the circumstances," he said. "You have experienced more loss in the past year, Helen, than anyone should have to carry. Be patient, Helen, and kind with yourself, and allow the family in. They are grieving also and wish to be close to you."

"I can't let them see me like this!" Helen wailed.

"Yes, you can, and you must. They worry more when they don't see you, Helen. Would you mind if I came and visited a couple of times a week? We can talk or not—whatever you feel like," said Gabriel.

"Whatever you like," Helen replied.

"I must be off. Blessings upon you, Helen," he said as she showed him to the door, and she watched him walk away. She closed the door and went to clean up the dishes. Somehow she always felt lighter after she spent time with Father Gabriel.

Gabriel visited Helen twice a week for a month, and she felt much better. He suggested she start driving to the presbytery office to see him.

She was driving that day for the first time. Gabriel opened the door and welcomed Helen into his office at the top of the stairs. It was a large, bright room with a huge window looking out over a field with a beautiful racehorse grazing in the February sunshine. A large desk, bookcases, a football on top of one bookcase, family photos, and two leather high-backed chairs filled the room.

"Sit down, Helen, please, and welcome. Would you like some tea?"

"No, thanks, Father." She smiled. "Your office looks like you."

"How's that?" said Gabriel, throwing laughter up to the heavens.

"Warm and welcoming," Helen answered.

"Well now, ah, thank you. How are you doing?" he asked.

"Better than I was. I've stopped feeling so sorry for myself. I've been thinking a lot about Amelia's children and how hard it must be. I write to Abigail; she's a wonderful child and the youngest girl. I miss her a lot, and I wish I could help her and be with her. I think I would like to go back and spend some time with them and Abigail." Helen noticed Gabriel's eyes widen. "Are you surprised?"

"Well, yes. Have you suggested this to anyone?"

"Not yet," said Helen. "I wanted to discuss it with you first."

Gabriel was quiet for a moment. "I believe you should wait a full year at least. Everyone is still grieving. Remember, a lot has happened since you left, and things will not be the same. I would think on it—give it some more time. That's the miracle of time—it heals."

Helen thought for a moment. "I will give it more time, Father; you're right."

"Good," Gabriel said. "Will I see you in church on Friday?"

"Yes," said Helen, "you will."

"Then I'll save you your favorite pew." Gabriel smiled. "Bless you, Helen."

"And you, Father. And you."

A few days later Gabriel opened the door and welcomed Aiden into his office.

"Thanks for coming to see me, Aiden."

"My pleasure, Father. I can't believe the difference in my mam since she started counseling with you—it's a miracle."

"I am pleased and relieved she is moving through her grieving. I wanted to discuss something in confidence that she has made mention of several times without betraying her confidence. It's a niece in England—Abigail."

Aiden spoke up before Gabriel could say any more. "She seems to have an attachment. Abby always was her favorite."

"She's discussed going back to be with her and the other children. I believe it's too soon for her, and who knows what situation she might find? It occurred to me you might try asking Abigail to come here—maybe surprise Helen. Would that be a possibility?"

"You are correct; they are very close and have quite a history together. What a fantastic idea, Father. It might be good for both of them—just what they need. I'll call Abby and see what is possible, if anything." Aiden stood up and shook Gabriel's hand. "Thanks for everything, Father."

"I'm glad to help in any way I can," Gabriel replied. "Good luck."

— 37 —

Sebastian and Abby sat in the kitchen of his home, sipping tea. The room looked brighter; he had painted the walls a cream color and hung some pictures of Paris. He had put down a new carpet, and the fire was crackling in the grate.

"I had a phone call from Aiden, Dad," Abby said.

"Really?" said Sebastian.

"Yes, he's asked me to find my way out to visit Aunt Helen. She's in a sad state, apparently—very depressed. He seemed to think that I could help. I've looked into it, and I can get the time off work, and Cammie says she can manage. He suggested that I come for six weeks. The problem is that I don't have enough money for the ticket, Dad. I wondered if you could lend it to me."

"How much do you need?" Sebastian asked.

"One hundred seventy-five pounds seems to be the best price I can find. It's a long way—from Newcastle to Heathrow in London, to Chicago, and then to Nashville."

Sebastian looked at Abigail. "You are a very kind girl for considering this. It's a lot to ask of you."

"It's an exciting thought to go to America, and I would never have considered it if I were not invited."

"It's a whole new world—that's for sure," Sebastian agreed. "You know, you are not only kind but also wise." He smiled. "Yes, Abigail, I will lend you the money. Helen was very kind to your mother and to this family, and we owe her a lot."

Abby jumped up. "Thanks, Dad. I'll organize the ticket, passport, visa, and smallpox vaccination immediately. It will all take a little time."

"Good," said Sebastian. "You make the most of it. As you say, it's a wonderful opportunity."

Abby kissed her dad on the cheek. "I couldn't do it without you," she said, smiling.

Three weeks later Abby sat in the lounge of Heathrow Airport, waiting to hear an announcement for her flight to Chicago. She could not believe she was going to America. Abby stood up and paced around, checking the information board. She went back to the bathroom for the umpteenth time. She had butterflies in her stomach. Abby bought a pack of cigarettes. Although she didn't smoke, she thought it might make her feel calmer. She drank yet another cup of tea and watched all the people coming and going in the airport—some were smiling and happy, and some were crying, sad to be leaving loved ones.

Abby boarded the airplane and found her seat by the window. There was no one sitting beside her. As the plane made its way down the runway and the engines roared, Abby had a sensation of wonder. She was roaring toward a new world different from the one she had lived in up to today.

Nashville's airport was enormous. Abby thought she would never find the exit or Aiden. She found her luggage and went through customs. Suddenly, there was a crowd of people, and she could see Aiden coming toward her. He looked much the same as she remembered, with a little less red hair maybe. It had been ten years since they had last seen each other.

"Hi, Abby. How wonderful you look." He held her and kissed her on the cheek. Aiden took her suitcase and her arm and guided her effortlessly through the airport to his car.

"Hop in," he said, pointing to the passenger seat. It felt strange to get in on the wrong side, Abby thought—on the left. Aiden's car was like the airport—large.

"I must say, Abby, you have grown into a beautiful young woman. You look like Aunt Amelia."

"Thank you, Aiden," she replied.

"How was your flight?"

"Very exciting—it was long, but the stewardesses looked after us with good food, wine, and a nice film."

Aiden smiled. "It's all very new for you. You must be exhausted; that's a long time to be on the way. We will be at my home soon. Mam does not know; we have not told her. We've only told her we're having a friend for dinner. I can't wait to see how happy she will be to see you, Abby!"

Abby looked out the window at the new world flashing past. She saw beautiful homes, cars, and tall glass buildings that seemed to stretch up to the sky. As they approached Aiden's home, it looked to Abby like a giant bungalow with a large garage attached to it. Leading up to it was a winding driveway surrounded by what seemed to be a hundred trees.

"This is so beautiful, Aiden." Suddenly, the garage door opened, as though it knew Aiden was coming. Abby's eyes widened. "How does that work, Aiden?"

"It's magic," he said, laughing. "Magic. It's going to be great fun having you here with us."

Everyone sat at the dinner table. Abby was feeling tired and dizzy, as though she were floating. She would have loved to lie down and go to sleep; it was only six o'clock in Tennessee, but to her, it was midnight. Rosella, Aiden's wife, had made lasagna for dinner. The children sat beside Abby, all asking her different questions about England. Aiden had gone downstairs to bring Aunt Helen up. Abby could hear them coming through the kitchen door.

"Now, close your eyes, Mam. I will hold your hand and guide you to the dining room. We have a surprise."

Abby watched as Aiden led his mother toward her.

"Keep them closed—no peeking!"

"Okay, Son," Helen replied. "What are you up to?"

"You will see," he told her. He stopped and maneuvered his mother so that she was facing Abby. "Now you can open them."

Abby stood up. Helen opened her eyes and looked at Abby in disbelief.

"Oh! Oh my! Oh Abby!" Helen burst into tears and threw her arms around Abby, almost knocking her over. Helen kept drawing back and looking into Abby's eyes.

"I don't believe it—I just can't believe it." She touched Abby's face to see if she was real. Helen's hands were shaking.

"Come on, Mam; sit down beside Abby."

Helen held Abby's hand throughout the entire dinner. It was a wonderful surprise.

The Sunday after Abby arrived the family was getting ready to go to Mass.

"After church today, I will introduce you to Father

Gabriel, Abby. He runs the youth group. I think it would be a nice idea for you to meet some people your own age."

"Yes, I would like that very much." She liked it at Aiden's house, but as she would be there for some time, it seemed a good idea to meet some young people and see their way of life. After the Sunday Mass Abby walked through the church grounds. She looked up at the white steeple, which stood out brightly against the blue sky. The white headstones in the graveyard and the manicured green-blue grass shined—what a contrast to the ancient, dilapidated cemetery her mother was buried in. *This place is unbelievable,* Abby thought.

She sat on a bench and looked up at the giant tree beside her; she had never seen such a magnificent tree in her whole life. It looked like a weeping willow dressed for a ball. The branches hung from the tree, reaching for the earth, glistening in the sunlight. Beautiful bright red birds played in the grass; the contrast of colors was like art—bright and lovely. Aiden came up to her; he was walking with someone.

"Abby, this is Father Gabriel. Father, this is my cousin from England," Aiden said.

"Well, hi, and welcome to St. Mike's. How are ya?" He took both of her hands in both of his and held them. Abby was astonished that this man was a priest—he didn't look or sound like a priest. His voice was warm and infections—Abby loved it and wanted to respond with the same warm, lazy southern drawl. His voice was like a warm cup of cocoa on a cold night by the fire. He resembled a brown bear that had just stepped from the pages of the story of Goldilocks. Gabriel wore a brown suede coat, and his curly hair was the same beautiful golden-brown color. Golden-amber eyes filled with light looked back at her, and his face was completely covered with freckles. If a face without freckles was like a night without stars, Gabriel's face was a brilliant starry night.

Abby was captivated by him from the first word. She was half listening as she studied him.

"We would just love having you come to our little group on Friday in the parish hall at seven o'clock. I am sure we will all enjoy getting to know you, Abby."

"Thank you, Father. I would like that," Abby answered.

"How are you enjoying Tennessee?" he asked her.

"Very much. I haven't been here very long, Father. I only arrived on Thursday and am still feeling jetlagged. Everything is so different—very beautiful, nothing like my home."

"How is it different?" Father asked.

"It rains a lot," Aiden said, breaking into the conversation. Abby wished he had not. She was enjoying every word and wanted Father Gabriel to continue. He was amazing; she did not want the conversation to end.

Abby had been in Tennessee for just over a week, and she felt as if she belonged.

Abigail was helping Rosella with dinner—it was spaghetti night. They were making meatballs, and Father Gabriel was coming.

"We are all enjoying you so much, Abby," Rosella said as they worked together in the kitchen. "And I just can't believe the difference in Helen; she is so bright and involved since you came. She's downstairs making an English trifle for dinner tonight. She's not cooked in months!"

"I am really pleased she's feeling better," Abby said. "I must say I love it here, Rosella; everyone is so kind to me. They make me feel special, different. I feel like the center of attention. I am lucky if I am ever noticed at home, let alone acknowledged."

"Well, we're only too happy to have you," Rosella told her. "We want you to feel at home and be comfortable."

"Honestly, Rosella, I feel like I have landed in paradise. I can't believe the beauty of the homes. Everything you have is amazing—central vacuums that come out of the wall, intercoms outside the front door, refrigerators that are enormous, and my own bedroom with a bathroom with a shower in it. I feel like I'm a film star living in Hollywood or some such place. At home in England, I'm lucky to have a bath once a week, and the rest of the time, we do a body wash with a cold flannel. There never seems to be enough of anything. There is always too little for too many. We don't concern ourselves—it's the way things are. Until now, I didn't know things were different."

"It's a whole new experience for you," said Rosella. "You enjoy it while you have the opportunity. Now, would you mind setting the table for me?"

Dinner smelled wonderful—homemade spaghetti with meatballs. Abby loved the dining room, which had a long table with a sparkling crystal chandelier over the center. The crystals reminded her of icicles on a cold winter day. Aiden was an amateur artist, and he had painted a mural on one of the walls—a picture of Lindisfarne Castle, looking out over the holy island and beautiful Northumberland coast.

"We're all ready. You can go shower and change," Rosella told her.

Abby was afraid to use the shower, in case there wasn't enough hot water to go around. Rosella explained that there was always sufficient hot water, as they had a large tank to accommodate the house.

Abby stepped into the shower; as far as she was concerned, it was pure luxury. Every time Abby closed her eyes and felt the water spill over her head, onto her back, and over her breasts, she shivered because it felt so good. She felt an excitement and anticipation she had never felt before. She stepped out of the shower, dried herself, dressed, and joined the family for their spaghetti dinner with Father Gabriel.

Gabriel enjoyed the short drive from the presbytery to Aiden's home; it was a nice area. The homes were custom built; each had a two-acre lot and many beautiful trees, and a creek ran through most of the backyards. It was luxurious—not that he was used to luxury in his own home or in the seminary, which were frugal and sparse. He was enjoying his life in his new parish, and he appreciated all the kind parishioners who invited him for dinner.

Everyone sat around the dining room table: the three children, Aiden, Rosella, Abigail, Helen, and Gabriel. Father Gabriel said grace.

"Tell us some of the things that are different in England," Gabriel said to Abby.

"Many things are different—the houses, the cars, the road, the sheer distance between places, the gardens."

"You mean yards." Gabriel started to laugh.

"Yes, I do."

"And when you say 'fridges,' you mean refrigerators. I love some of your words, Abby—tell me some more differences."

"Believe it or not"—she hesitated—"Mass is different; we don't drink wine ever. It was amazing to me to be offered wine at Holy Communion."

"Is that right?" said Gabriel.

"I must say it was delicious," she replied.

Gabriel threw his head back and let out a peal of laughter that shook his body. "Oh, Abby, you are so funny. Tell you what—let me know when you are coming to Mass again, and I shall put a little extra in the chalice for you."

"I must say, Father, that's not exactly ..." Abby hesitated. Gabriel looked at her. The conversation stopped as she tried to find the right word. "Reverent?"

Gabriel laughed his big laugh again. "You know, Abby, you may be correct. I like to believe God has a sense of humor, don't you?" Gabriel raised his eyes to the heavens and blessed himself. In doing so, he knocked his glass of wine over onto Rosella's white Irish linen tablecloth.

"Oh, I do apologize!" Gabriel jumped up.

Abby jumped up at the same time. "Don't worry, Father; I'll get it." They both reached for the spilled glass at the same time, and their hands brushed.

"I have it, Father; don't worry." Abby dropped her napkin over the spilled liquid and removed the glass.

Aiden broke the moment. "How about telling us about your trip to Rome with Sally?"

Gabriel was amazed. "You have been to Rome?"

"Yes," Abby replied. "For one week in October last year. My friend Sally has an aunt who lives in Italy, near

Rome, up in the mountains. We went to Trevi Fountain. It surprised me, as I'd imagined it to be in the center of Rome, surrounded by many tourists. And yet it is located on a quiet little street, which was odd. There were lots of kids standing around with magnets attached to long strings, collecting the pennies the wishers threw in. Legend has it that if you close your eyes, turn around three times, and throw a penny over your right shoulder with your left hand into the water, you will return to Rome."

"A nice legend," Gabriel said.

"I ate spaghetti that burst into a symphony of flavor in my mouth, and there was no need to swallow, as it melted upon my tongue."

"Which way to that restaurant?" Gabriel laughed.

"It's up in the mountains. It's Sally's auntie's home—she was a fantastic cook. We experienced endless wonders in that village—picking olives, washing our hair in fresh rainwater collected in vats amongst the houses."

"Did you go to the Vatican?"

"We did," Abby said.

"Oh my Lord, you lucky girl!" Gabriel was mesmerized. "I want to hear every single detail." He sat opposite her as she spoke.

"Vatican City was the highlight of the trip."

"How long were you there—at the Vatican?" asked Aiden.

"Only half a day. We could have done with a month. But it really is a city; every part of it was exceptionally special. St. Peter's Basilica—for me, the most magnificent was the Sistine Chapel. It is indeed miraculous, covered from ceiling to floor—every part—with the most fantastic frescoes.

Somehow they look real, as though one could reach out and touch them. Michelangelo was a genius."

"I am envious beyond words," Gabriel said. "You are indeed a fortunate young woman to have been to Rome."

Helen spoke up. "Not something I have done yet."

"I felt truly blessed—close to God somehow. For several days after, I had an extraordinary sense of peace, as though God were holding my hand."

"Did you see the pope?" Rosella asked.

"No, I did not, but I bought some rosary beads that he had blessed, and I keep them in my pocket. I can show them to you."

Gabriel was touched by Abigail's sincere description.

"What a fantastic story," he said. "I shall pray that someday I will be as fortunate as you, Abby, to visit that holy place."

"I hope you do, Father; you would love it!"

"Let's make some tea," Aiden said.

"No, not for me." Helen stood up. "I'm rather tired," she said curtly. "I shall say good night." She left.

"I will make it," said Abby.

"No," Rosella said. "You go sit with Father Gabriel. We will bring it along shortly. We must get the children ready for bed, as spaghetti night has gone on much later than usual."

Abby and Gabriel cleared the table and tidied up, working in unison. Then they went into the family room, which was cozy, and he found himself pleased to have some time alone with her.

"Do you like music, Father Gabriel?"

"Why, yes, I do," Gabriel replied. "I love music. I like to listen to it whenever and wherever possible."

"What music do you like?"

"I like all kinds—classical piano, country, Elvis, the Beatles, and more."

Abby stood in front of Gabriel, looked into his eyes, smiled at him, and said, "I am glad." He felt intoxicated as he continued watching her. "I'm going to play an LP on the stereo. Aiden has a wonderful sound system, and I brought this with me. I am enjoying it very much; this is Andy Williams—the album is called *Happy Heart*. It has lots of different songs. My very favorite is the third track, 'Bridge over Troubled Water.' Do you know that song, Father?"

"Know it?" Gabriel replied. "Why, it's my all-time favorite."

"Ah, me too." Abby jumped up and gave him the sleeve so that he could look at the tracks. "It has such wonderful lyrics—'Like a bridge over troubled water, I will ease your mind.'" Abby sat down, silent. Gabriel noticed sadness wash over her. It was powerful and tugged at him.

"Abby?" Gabriel said. "Do you have a need to ease your mind and talk? I'm a good listener."

"Thank you, Father. I may just do that sometime."

"I am available anytime." Gabriel suddenly felt an urgent desire to get away back to his room to be alone with his thoughts. He stood up. "I must be leaving now."

Abby looked at Gabriel, and her brown eyes widened as she moved toward him and placed her hands on his arm. Looking into his eyes, she said, "Must you go so soon, Father? 'Bridge' has not even played yet."

Gabriel felt her disappointment. "That will give me good reason to come back and listen to it with you."

"I'll go find Aiden and Rosella." She walked past him,

and he could smell her shampoo, fresh in her clean hair. He headed for the door.

Aiden and Rosella came from the bedrooms. "Thanks for coming, Father; we always enjoy your company."

"I had a fantastic evening. Thank you all for the food, conversation, and friendship. It's been good to be with you." He raised his hands, blessed them, and walked out of the door, relieved to be outside heading toward his car, though he could not say why. He did not understand himself or his behavior—maybe he was just tired. *Let me get home and relax in my rooms,* he thought as he started his engine and drove away from the Kennedy home.

— 38 —

Abby was to be ready for a ride to the church in order to participate in the youth group; it was Friday night. She found herself suited to the American way of life and didn't miss Newcastle or her siblings at home. Aiden was going to drop her off and then pick her up at nine o'clock; youth group usually lasted for approximately an hour and a half. She made a special effort to look good this evening; she wore blue jeans and a brown turtleneck sweater. She had washed her hair that morning, and when it was still slightly damp, she'd put some rollers in it. Her hair was now soft, shiny, and smooth. Abby liked it like that; it made her look more mature, she thought. She never wore makeup, but she decided to put on some mascara to lengthen her already-long eyelashes and some soft beigey pink lipstick. She looked back at her reflection and was satisfied; she told herself she wanted to create a good impression with all the other young people at the youth club.

Aiden knocked on her door. "Ready, Abby?"

"Yes." She picked up her purse and coat and came out.

Aiden whistled. "You look smashing, Abby; you will knock those lads over. Come—let's go, or we'll be late."

"Bye, Rosella. Bye, Aunt Helen."

"You look beautiful, Abby," Rosella said.

Aunt Helen looked right at her. "Don't you think it's a bit too much? It's only a church basement with a group of young high school kids."

Abby was a bit shocked at Aunt Helen's comment. "I did not know what to wear; it's my first time. I thought it would be appropriate."

"It isn't what you are wearing; it's how you look in it, my dear," said Aiden, smiling. "Come—don't worry. Let's go, or you shall be late."

Ten minutes later Aiden walked into the church hall with Abby.

"Are you all right, Abby?" asked Aiden.

"I'm fine, just a little nervous not knowing anyone, and it is something new and different."

"Well, if it's any consolation to you, in my humble opinion, any eighteen-year-old young lady who can travel from Newcastle, United Kingdom, to Tennessee, USA, changing three flights in three different airports, is rather gutsy. Don't you think so?" Abby grinned at Aiden. As far back as she could remember, he had been present in her life, always kind and encouraging. "How about I come in with you, just the first time?" he said.

"That would be a good idea, Aiden." They entered the church hall, which had a small stage at one end, a piano, and a tiny kitchen of sorts. A group of young people were standing around talking, sharing stories, and laughing. Father Gabriel was in the center of the group. Two of the young people had guitars, and they were strumming a tune. Father Gabriel was deeply involved with a young woman looking at some sheet music. It was nice to have the opportunity to observe him when he was not aware of her presence. Abby found herself staring at him, watching his every move; he looked comfortable with all of these young ones around him. He was enjoying the conversation with deep interest; suddenly, he threw his head back and let out a booming sound of laughter.

"Oh my Lord, I don't believe that!" He continued to laugh freely and helplessly; something had certainly amused him.

Abby and Aiden did not interrupt; they waited for an appropriate moment to catch his attention. Father Gabriel turned and headed toward them and shook Abby's hand.

"Well, hi. You have come to our little group. We are both delighted and honored to welcome you." He was brimming with enthusiasm as he walked Abby over to the center of the group. Fifteen or so young men and women all looked at her as Father Gabriel introduced her. "Folks, we are fortunate enough to welcome a special guest this evening to our meeting. This is Abigail Lavalle from the United Kingdom. She is visiting with her cousin Aiden and his family for six weeks." He glanced at Abby, smiling. "Nice vacation—or holiday, as you call it." He gave a chuckle. "Let's give her a warm Tennessee welcome, folks, and show her that southern hospitality is the best around." He held her hand throughout the introduction.

"Thanks. When should I come back?" Aiden asked.

"Around nine," Gabriel replied.

"Bye then. See you later. Have fun."

Father Gabriel dropped Abby's hand as suddenly as he had taken it in his, and she felt strangely alone.

Everyone moved around her and bombarded her with questions.

"Where in the United Kingdom do you live?"

"Have you met the queen?"

"Do you know the Beatles?"

"How long was your journey?"

"Do you like it here? Is it very different from your home?"

Abby politely answered everyone's questions as appropriately as possible. As she did, she found herself looking out of the corner of her eye to see if she could see Father Gabriel. It appeared the others were fascinated with her, particularly the young men.

"Hey, Abby, how about a group of us take you out to a movie and grab a pizza one night?" one young man said.

"I'd like that very much."

"We can pick you up."

"I don't have the address."

"I'll give you my number, and you can call me. I'm Scott. We all live pretty close, as we are all in the same parish. Do you like music?" he asked.

"I love music."

"Do you like the Beatles? Let's sing some Beatles songs to help Abby feel right at home."

They all sat on chairs and started strumming at the guitars, singing "Yesterday" and "Hard Day's Night." Abby was having a wonderful time; they all were. These young people were no different from the folks back home, except they could all drive and all had their own cars. The girls were pretty; they had lovely clothes and long hair. Most of them were blonde; there was one girl with bright red hair. They all had introduced themselves, and Abby was starting to wonder how she would remember all their names.

Father Gabriel came back into the hall. "What about fundraising ideas to help one of the families in our parish? The father has lost his job, the mother has been sick, and there are three young children. Do you have some ideas?"

"Car washing!" shouted Scott.

"Garage sale?" suggested someone else.

"What about a bake sale after Mass?" Abby added shyly.

"All very good ideas. We can look at them individually and decide how and when to appropriately present them. It's nine o'clock, folks; let's do our closing prayer."

They all bowed their heads, and Father Gabriel said the prayer.

"Good night, y'all. Thanks for coming, everyone."

Scott gave Abby his phone number. "Call me," he said.

"Yes, I'll do that; it sounds like fun."

Father Gabriel walked toward the door, showing everyone out, as he was about to lock up. Everything went quiet, and Father Gabriel and Abby were the last two left in the big, empty room. Abby could hear her heart beating. She did not know what to say but did not want to leave.

Father Gabriel broke the silence. "You look like you had fun tonight, Abby."

"Yes, I did, Father. They are very nice, warm, and friendly."

"Well, of course they are; they are from Tennessee. Did I see Scott slipping you his phone number?"

"Oh yes, well, I—he, um, said that we should all go to the pictures and eat pizza."

"Splendid," said Father Gabriel, laughing his big, lovely

laugh. "Go to the pictures—I tell you, Abby, you crack me up with your English words. I love it." He turned and smiled. Just as he was about to say something, Aiden appeared, seemingly from nowhere.

"Hey, did you have fun?"

"Yes, I did. Thank you."

"Nice of you to invite her, Father; we'll see you on Sunday. Good night."

"My pleasure," Gabriel replied.

Abby looked over her shoulder. "Good night, Father Gabriel."

"Bye, Abby; y'all come back now," Father said softly as he walked away.

—39—

The next morning Abby awoke feeling restless and agitated. She climbed out of bed and paced around the room for a while, looking out the window. She decided to go take a shower. Feeling the warm water washing over her body helped her unwind and relax. She stood with her face toward the showerhead, willing the restlessness to leave her; to her surprise, she felt worse. The water was awakening feelings in her she was not used to.

Abby climbed out of the shower, dried herself, and dressed quickly in blue jeans and a white sweatshirt, which would keep her warm, as she intended to go for a walk. It was only six thirty in the morning. She tiptoed out of her room, past her cousins' room, out the back door, and through the garden. The scent of the early morning perfume hit her; the air was heavy with it. The mist was rising up from the valley like a cloud shrouded in silver morning light.

Abby headed out toward the little village. No one was awake; it was too early. She passed some fantastic custom-built, raised two-story ranch bungalow homes with huge walls around them. One house had two lions at the front door, and a wrought-iron gate surrounded the property. *This place is like a dream,* she thought. *Imagine—people living and working in such luxurious settings.*

Abby breathed in the fresh air of the morning and listened to the redbird singing his February song; it was still chilly, yet she could smell the promise of springtime. Abby continued her walk, enjoying the trees and the solitude. Her anxiety was subsiding a little. Why was she feeling restless? She had enjoyed the youth meeting. Abby was looking forward to a night out with the other teenagers. She was interested in seeing how the young people of the United States of America had fun.

She stopped to watch a beautiful horse behind a white picket fence. It was a little too early in the year for the grass to be blue, but Father Gabriel had told her it really was blue. She whispered his name, and her restlessness returned. Abby flushed at her thoughts; she was feeling both excited and ashamed at the same time. What on earth was she thinking? She knew her thoughts were sinful.

As she continued heading toward the town, she walked alongside a stream. The water looked like liquid crystal as it danced over the rocks and pebbles in the sunlight. Abby decided to sit on the grass beside the water to look at some of the colors of the early morning. Sunlight dusted the water. *How lovely,* Abby thought, putting her finger into the stream. She was trying to touch the rainbow of colors running through the water, which felt refreshing and cool. She placed both hands in the water up to her wrists, closed her eyes, and breathed in, enjoying the tingling sensation and the rushing sound of the water running toward the lake.

Ah, that feels better, she thought as she opened her eyes. Several joggers passed her; they either ignored her or just nodded.

She thought maybe she would take a closer look at the footpath to see where it began and ended. From where she was sitting, she could see through the trees, as there was still no foliage, though the evergreens were heavy. The pines stretched up to the sky, and the holly bushes were full. There were many leaves on the ground from last autumn's trees. She saw a bicycle coming down the footpath, but the cyclist went right past her.

She stood and turned to start walking back toward her home. She smiled at a jogger approaching her, and then she imagined she could hear Father Gabriel saying her name.

"Abigail, is that you?"

She looked around, and there in front of her was Gabriel. He said, "Well, hi. How wonderful to find you in the middle of my jog in the woods on this beautiful February morning."

Abby was flustered. "Oh, I was walking, and I don't know the path, so I was heading back to the house. I, um, I'm sorry, Father; I'm surprised to see you."

"Me too," he said. "Let's walk together. I always jog on Saturday early and on Tuesday and Thursday if nothing stops me. Keeps me from gaining weight on spaghetti nights, you know." He threw his head back and let out his infectious laughter; it echoed around them, bouncing off all the beautiful trees. She adored Father Gabriel's laughter.

"What are you doing all this way from home?" Gabriel laughed.

"Oh, I don't know," Abby replied. "I couldn't sleep, and I thought it would be nice to just wander toward the village.

It's so lovely here; there's always something that catches my eye. This morning, I sat by the little stream and watched it dance its merry way to wherever it was going—so special." She smiled at Gabriel. "I was thinking how different it is from my home. Back there, we have the North Sea crashing up against the cliffs on King Edward Bay with the imposing sight of the ruins of the old Benedictine monastery towering over it all. On a cold winter's day, my favorite time to visit the ruins is when the tide is in and the northeast wind is howling, whistling, and whispering its old stories through the stone and rubble of the monastery. Even though I am high above the bay, sometimes I can feel the ocean spray upon my face; it is so invigorating and stimulating. In a very bleak way, it is beautiful. I feel so alive there. You know, for a split second, I actually felt lonesome for my home."

"That sounds like something I need to see and feel for myself. You know what I think, Abby? It is you that is special—how you see things. You are looking at a brand-new world, and your response is so refreshing, as are your words. I can't tell you just how much I enjoy your company."

"Oh, Father Gabriel," Abigail blurted out, "I feel just the same way; you are so different—your laughter, your enthusiasm. You fascinate me, like almost everything else around here. You are not at all like our priests at home."

Gabriel grinned at her. "Oh no? And what are they like?"

"They are all fuddy-duddies!"

Once more, Gabriel roared with laughter. "There's another one—what is a fuddy-duddy, Abby?"

"You know, Father Gabriel—old fashioned, strict, and no fun. Everything you are, they are not. If our priests were just a wee bit like you, Father Gabriel, people would go to church because they liked it and not because of mortal sin, the fire of hell, and damnation if they should miss Mass on Sunday," said Abby. "Talking with you is like having a conversation with one of my brothers."

"You know," said Father Gabriel, "I was just thinking about how you remind me of my sisters."

They both asked at the same time, "How many brothers and sisters—"

They stopped, laughing.

Gabriel made a bow. "After you, ma'am," he said, chuckling.

"I'm one of eight; we have five boys and three girls in our family. I fall in the middle somewhere," Abby told him.

Gabriel stopped in his tracks. "I don't believe it—I am one of eight. My family has five girls and three boys, and I'm the eldest. How amazing—what a coincidence."

She smiled at him.

"Here is where we have to part company, Abby; that's the road to my home, and the opposite is the way to yours. Ah, I am so delighted I stumbled across you this morning." He smiled at Abby, making a salute gesture.

"See you in church."

Then he was gone, leaving Abby breathless, speechless, and euphoric. She looked up toward the sky through the magnificent trees and knew she was experiencing something special.

Abby arrived home; she had walked quickly in order to arrive before the family awoke and missed her. She did not want them to worry; she should have left a note, yet she had been so restless and in such a hurry to leave that she'd run out the door before doing so. What a wonderful morning—she felt alive and glowing. The walk was lovely, and bumping into Father Gabriel had been exciting. How she liked him. She felt as if she had known him all her life, as though he had always been there. Her mind was racing with thoughts and ideas, words and feelings; her body was alive. As she opened the door to the mudroom, as the family called it—a special room for coats and shoes to keep the house clean and free from clutter—Abby smiled to herself. *They should see our house,* she thought, *full of junk at the front door, with so many folks using it and no mudroom.*

"And where have you been?" The words broke her thoughts. Aunt Helen was glaring at her, waiting at the kitchen entrance.

"Oh, I'm sorry, Auntie. I was out early for a walk. I could not sleep. I was very restless, and well, I—"

"We are all out of our minds with worry. Aiden is about to take the car and go looking for you. You were very irresponsible, Abby, not to tell us where you were going. What were you thinking?"

"I am so sorry, Auntie Helen; it was very wrong of me. I wasn't thinking. I do apologize, and I will speak to Aiden." As she was explaining to her aunt, Aiden walked into the kitchen.

"Hey, Abby, where did you get yourself off to?" He looked at her, smiling, not seeming upset at all. "Mam is worrying about you. You look just fine to me. In fact, you are positively glowing; share your secret." He winked at Abby, making sure Helen didn't see him.

Abby was embarrassed. Could Aiden see by her face that she had bumped into Father Gabriel?

"Eh, just a lovely walk along the footpath, and I sat beside that little stream—you know, the one near the town—for quite some time. It was such a beautiful morning, quiet and cool."

"It's sure put a glow on your face. You should do it more often; it will give you some color before you go back to the waterlogged northeast coast of England. All's well that ends well, Mam. Let's have some pancakes; it's Saturday. We can pig out on a nice big breakfast, and then we can all drive to Daniel Boone country and go for a walk on one of the trails. What do you think? The kids would love it, and we can show Abby some of the state."

"Yes, that's fine," said Helen.

Aiden winked once more at Abby. "How about you help me with this breakfast, Abby?"

"I would love to," Abby replied, smiling, keeping her unexpected meeting with Father Gabriel to herself.

— 40 —

Gabriel always looked forward to Monday, his day off. He was driving his little VW Beetle, heading up the highway toward his family home. He was from a small town nearby called Lakeville, one of the few places with its own lake.

His parents owned a small wheat farm, and they'd raised all eight children in a three-bedroom farmhouse. He was used to living away from the farm but looked forward to his day off, when he made the fifty-minute drive back to his mother, father, and siblings; home cooking; the smell of the farmyard; and all that was familiar. His mom would have fresh coffee and his favorite blueberry-cinnamon bran muffins ready for him when he arrived at ten o'clock. He could smell them now as he imagined her preparing them. Gabriel's visits with his family were his mainstay—they helped him focus, relax, and replenish. Most of all, his time with his mother was special and nourishing. She listened to everything he had to tell her with a passionate interest, asking him questions and always remembering stories he'd shared with her from his last visit. He usually arrived at ten;

stayed until after dinner, around eight o'clock; and arrived back at the parish around nine.

He didn't do anything exceptional on the farm; he just enjoyed the ordinary, familiar routine of the life. He used to help collect the eggs from the henhouse. Sometimes he would work in the vegetable garden, but as it was still winter, there was nothing to do there. His father enjoyed wood carving and had his own little shed at the bottom of the farmyard, where he could indulge in his hobby. Although his dad was a man of few words, Gabriel knew and understood he enjoyed those special quiet times they shared together. He pulled up into the farmyard, and his mom was at the front door to meet him. He walked straight into his mother's arms; seeing her always made the visit worthwhile. His mother's hug was filled with love and worth the drive.

"Come in, Gabriel. It's so good to see you."

"You too, Mom. What's new? Is Dad in the shed?"

"Yes, he is, and you can take him some coffee and a muffin later—he'd like that."

"Is Amy home?"

"No, she's in school, studying for some exams this week."

Gabriel sat at the old farmhouse's kitchen table, which was pine and long enough to seat ten. His mother scrubbed it clean every day. She was pouring coffee from the old blue coffeepot; it was the best coffee one could taste anywhere.

"So what have you been up to since our last visit, my son?" Edna looked into her son's eyes with pleasure, waiting to listen to his stories.

"Mrs. Nesbith is much better—the lady who I was telling you was sick last time, remember? I gave her your cookies, and she thought that they helped her recover, so she has named them healing biscuits."

"Oh, I am so glad," said Edna, chuckling. "Have you been busy?"

"No, not really, not much going on. Same daily routine, although one of my parishioners has a cousin visiting from the United Kingdom. Do you remember me telling you, Mom, about the older English lady who was having trouble coping with her grief?"

"Yes, I do, Son."

"She was not doing too well, and her son asked that they bring her favorite niece over. They thought the company might help, as she is a child of the sister she lost, whom she was so close to."

"How nice—is it helping?"

"Not sure yet, although I am thoroughly enjoying her company."

Edna looked up. "Really?" his mother inquired.

"Yes. Abigail—Abby for short. She reminds me of Amy. I love to listen to her talk with all her funny English sayings. She has the most melancholy eyes and hair like golden chestnuts. Spaghetti night at the Kennedys is even more interesting and fun. She's so different, Momma; she seems to see things in ways no one else does."

"How old is she, Son?" asked Edna.

"Eighteen—and very lovely. She looks at life and this state of ours with new eyes. She fascinates me, though I do see a deep sorrow within her, Mom; she is definitely troubled."

"In what way?" asked Edna.

"She is still grieving the loss of her mother, I expect. We have not discussed that at all; I only know this because of her aunt Helen and the grief counseling that she and I have done together. I ran into her on Saturday morning when I was out on my jog. She seemed flustered."

"How so?" asked Edna.

"I don't know—just surprised to see me and stumbling over her words. We walked and talked, and we really connected. You know, Mom, she is one of eight. I told her how amazing that was, as I am one of eight. How we have so much in common."

"Quite," said Edna, getting up from the table and walking away. "More coffee and a muffin?"

"Not for me; I will take one out to Dad, though."

"Good idea. How long is Abby to stay in Tennessee with her family?" Edna asked.

"Six weeks. She has five weeks left, and already I think I will miss her presence," Gabriel replied.

His mother had produced a wonderful dinner, as she always did when he was home for the day—a feast fit for a king. Today she had prepared a turkey dinner with all the fixings—all his favorites.

"What a meal, Mom. Thank you so much." Gabriel got up to help her with the dishes, but she told him to be getting on his way, as it was seven forty-five, and she did not want him to be late.

"Thanks for a great day, parents." He hugged his mom and dad. "I'll see you in two weeks."

His mother escorted him out to his car. "Son," she said hesitantly, "this young girl ..."

"Who? Abby, you mean?"

"Yes. You are limited with how much you can help her, you know, regarding time and even knowledge of the situation."

"Ah, don't worry, Mom. I know what I'm doing."

"Yes, well, um—I'll see you in two weeks, my son. Bless you."

Gabriel embraced his mother and left.

Abby had been in Tennessee for three weeks; she was halfway through her six-week stay. She and Rosella were on a late-afternoon walk; they stopped to sit by the creek Abby loved so much.

"I can't believe how quickly the time is passing. I feel like you have always lived with us," Rosella said.

"I wish I did. I can't imagine going back."

They sat on the grass.

"Look how beautiful that is," Abby said, watching the sun slowly descend. She had a sinking feeling, although the beauty of the sunset was astounding, with the huge winter ball of fire bursting with a cool yet warm energy, its last for the day. The sun slipped past the horizon quickly now, as though it were in a hurry to leave, creating a spectacular array of colors in the clouds—mauves, pinks, purples, and oranges. The cloud formation created the illusion of long streaks, as though the fingers of God himself had penetrated the clouds to create such a magnificent sunset.

"It's mesmerizing to me," said Abigail.

"Yes, that is beautiful," Rosella agreed.

Suddenly, the sun was gone, and it was dusk.

"We had better get up and walk back before it gets too dark," Rosella said. "How was your evening last night with the youth group?"

"It was great; I had a good time. I'm amazed how they drive around in those enormous cars. They seem to take it in stride. When we go out to the pictures back home, we take the bus."

"What did you see at the movies?"

"*Man of La Mancha*. The cinema was in an old church—great atmosphere. I loved it. Halfway through, Scott started pawing at me, trying to get fresh, kissing my mouth and slobbering. There was a very strong smell of lunchtime salami!"

Rosella started to laugh. "Eww, disgusting! I hope you put him in his place."

"Definitely!" Abby assured her. "I told him I was not interested. I told him a fib: I said I certainly hoped my boyfriend back home was not necking with a girl in the back of the pictures. I suspect he won't call me to go out again, and I hope it doesn't affect our involvement next week, when we do the big bake sale."

"I'm sure it won't," Rosella assured her. "You are funny. What are you going to do when you go back home?"

"Honestly, I don't know. I know I have something to reach for—a different world. I've learned a lot in my short time here, Rosella." As they walked, Abby could see the silhouettes of cardinals heading back to the nearest tree for the night.

"Look at that," she said to Rosella. "It must be wonderful to be as free as a bird. I love watching those cardinals perform their magic dance every morning outside your kitchen window after you have fed them. The males are so bright and beautiful, and the females are so dull. You know, I read somewhere cardinals are lifetime partners. Doesn't that seem amazing to you—that little birds with such tiny brains could be that smart? I think we as humans could learn a lot from watching the little birds. What a life—to dance freely on the grass with your partner, eat, drink, and then fly away together to a safe and magnificent tree somewhere and set up house with someone you choose."

Rosella looked at Abby and spoke softly. "You have feelings for Father Gabriel, don't you?"

"I'm afraid so; it seems so complicated."

"It's not that complicated," said Rosella.

"I know Aunt Helen is upset with me—disgusted, in fact. She's hardly talking to me."

"She feels a secret claim to Father Gabriel, as though she discovered him. She feels rather protective of him. He used to shower her with attention until you arrived. I suspect she is maybe a little envious."

"It's not my intention to hurt her or upset her. I came a long way to be with her," Abby said.

"If you have fallen for Father, I would think it is inevitable, I'm afraid," replied Rosella.

"We have done nothing to be ashamed of; I don't even know what he feels."

Rosella looked at her and smiled. "Then you are blind," she told Abby as they arrived at the front door of the house.

—41—

The Sunday morning of the bake sale finally arrived. Abby did not sleep well the night before—for several reasons. She was heading the bake sale and was anxious. Also, she would be seeing Father Gabriel. She showered and dressed, choosing her clothes carefully. She put on a white blouse and a black skirt and tied her hair up on top of her head. She thought she looked rather professional as she checked herself in the mirror.

Helen and Rosella had been amazingly helpful, baking and freezing all week, making every possible kind of pie one could imagine. Rosella handed her a basket laden with peach pie, huckleberry pie, apple pie, and rhubarb-strawberry pie. There was also pound cake, chocolate cake, and Dundee fruitcake. The best, of course, was Aunt Helen's melt-in-your-mouth shortbread. The boys had done a car wash the week before and raised $150.

"How amazing this country is—the way people come together for one cause. No one would think to suggest such an event back home at my church. I believe this parish, town, state, and country are filled to the brim with youthful energy, imagination, and opportunity. If you believe and work hard, if you want something enough, I think in time, you could accomplish almost anything!" Abby exclaimed.

"I think you are right," Rosella said, smiling.

"Let's go," said Aiden. "The car is filled with goodies, and we don't want to be late for the ten-thirty Mass." Off they all went.

Abby knelt in her pew, watching Father Gabriel say Mass. She enjoyed the moment, observing him uninterrupted as he read the Gospel and listening to every word of his sermon. She especially enjoyed the consecration of the Mass, when he blessed the bread and wine. He was beautiful, and she longed to get closer. She sighed.

Her friend Mary Jo asked, "Are you okay?"

"Yes, I'm fine, thank you," Abby replied.

"I thought you were gasping for air or something. Did you need to go outside or get some water?"

"No, I'm fine," Abby assured her.

"We will need to leave soon to set up the tables," Mary Jo whispered.

"After Communion. Then we can head out," Abby replied.

"Okay," said Mary Jo.

Abby and the youth group set up the bake sale; everyone from the parish brought something. When they had finished setting up the hall, it looked amazing and professional—under Abby's direction.

Gabriel came by Abby's bake table. "Well, I must say I am impressed. Have you done fundraising before, Abby?"

"No, Father Gabriel, this is all new to me."

"Then you are a natural at it, and I wish I could keep you here with me forever, Abby," he whispered. "Now, you show me what you baked that is English, and I will purchase one of everything that you made."

Abby smiled at him. "Oh, we saved some for you for spaghetti night, Father; I was going to share it with you then."

"Then all the more reason for me to sample your fare now."

"There's shortbread that Aunt Helen made, and I helped. She's so good at that. And there's a great selection of delicious cakes."

"Abby, you just fill me a box with some of everything, and I will come back and pick it up. I must go meet and greet, or tongues will be wagging that I am spending too much time with the English baker. You look very professional—and lovely. See ya!" He was gone.

The bake sale was over within an hour; not one crumb was left unsold. Father Gabriel came back into the hall and addressed the youth group in front of the parishioners.

"How about that, y'all! You should be very proud of yourselves; you have worked so hard. I am sure we will have enough money to present to the family to purchase groceries for at least two or three months. Well done! I have to thank the parents and parishioners for all their support and participation. I would particularly like to thank Abigail, our visitor from England. You come out here, Abby—I know she will be embarrassed, but I think a rousing round of applause is in order for the effort she has put forth in organizing this bake sale. We are happy you came to our little town; you have been a true inspiration!"

Gabriel stepped up in front of her and, to her astonishment, took both of her hands, looked into her eyes, smiled, and kissed her gently on her left cheek and then on her right cheek. Stepping back, he led everyone in the applause, and everyone crowded around to chat with her. Abby was overwhelmed. Gabriel had kissed her, and the moment was powerful in her mind. She could still feel the tingle inside her cheeks. She was warm with desire. Abby excused herself from the circle of people. Fortunately, the washrooms were empty, and Abby rushed over and splashed her face with cold water several times to cool off. Mary Jo came in.

"Well done, Abby—you're the best! That was so much fun. You okay?" she asked.

"Yes, yes, I'm fine, just a little warm. Come on—let's get cleared up and go for the pizza that Father Gabriel promised us."

"I can drive you, if you like," Mary Jo told her.

Abby and Mary Jo returned to the hall. Aiden, Rosella, the children, and Aunt Helen helped with the cleanup.

"I can't thank you enough—all of you—for your help and support," Abby said as she handed over a bag of tablecloths to Aiden to take home. "You've all been so wonderful, especially you, Aunt Helen. Every crumb you baked was sold."

"You are welcome." Helen nodded and said nothing more. Rosella kissed Abby on the cheek, as did Aiden.

"We are so proud of you. This bake sale was a real achievement, and you have endeared yourself to the parish of St. Mike's," Aiden said.

Mary Jo was anxious to get going, pointing to the door.

Abby told Aiden, "We will be doing something afterward; Father Gabriel is treating us to pizza. We may go back to someone's house and listen to records or something like that."

"Come on then," said Mary Jo. "Let's all go for that pizza Father Gabriel promised us on Friday. That was sure some speech he made there—and kissing you on both cheeks."

Abby and Mary Jo arrived at the pizza place. Abby looked at the long table, which was full except for three seats at the far end.

"Come in, Abby. We've saved a seat at the top of the table, just for you, and Father is on the other top, as he's paying!" one of the youth group members said. They all laughed. She was as far away from him as possible, and she felt disappointed and relieved at the same time. She seemed to be experiencing that feeling a lot these days. Someone interrupted her thoughts.

"Smile—you are out having fun, celebrating how well we did. What a morning!"

The pizza was delicious, and they all chatted and enjoyed stories through the lunch.

"I am so full," Abby said. "I've never had pizza like that—I never imagined so many choices."

A beautiful redhead flounced in, windswept and breathless. Her hair was bright auburn, wild, and curly, and her face was covered with freckles. She looked somehow familiar.

She approached Father Gabriel, announcing at the top of her voice, "I made it, Gabbie!" She planted a big kiss on Father Gabriel's cheek. His mouth was full of pizza, and he pointed to the seat next to himself, mimicking with his head and hands that his mouth was full and he was unable to speak.

"Who is that?" Abby looked at everyone, trying not to sound indignant.

"Hi, Amy!" everyone said.

She high-fived everyone all the way down the table.

Mary Jo called out, "Hi, Amy. Come sit down with us." She told Abby, "This is Father Gabriel's sister." Her red hair was all over the place, and her big, round amber eyes had long lashes; she was energy from top to toe.

"You must be Abby—right?" She put her hand up for a high five. "Put it there. My brother talks about you nonstop when he comes home." Then she whispered behind her hand toward Abby, "Got my mother's knickers in a real tizzy, may I add. I came out today especially to meet you, girl. How was the sale? How much did you make? You know, that was a fantastic ideer, Abby. How much did you raise?"

Mary Jo piped up. "With the car wash, over five hundred dollars."

"Wow, wow!" Amy jumped up and, holding her Pepsi glass, said, "I raise my glass to you, Father Gabe and all the guys and gals. Well done!"

"Thank you, Amy. Cheers!" said Gabriel.

Abby was having so much fun; this girl had endless energy, and she liked her instinctively.

"Whenever they have a party in the group, I try to come to them. It's a far drive from our hometown, but I had to come check you out, Abby girl. My mother will be waiting at the door for me, wanting to know if I think you are a Jezebel or a Virgin Mary." Amy's eyes flashed. "So how long are you staying?"

"Six weeks," replied Abby.

"When do you return back to little ole England?"

"Two weeks' time."

"I would love to visit, see the queen and the Beatles, and tour London, Carnaby Street—all those great places. Can I come visit you? I'd love to do that."

"You would be very welcome, Amy."

Amy looked at Abby with her amber eyes. "You mean that, don't ya?"

"Yes, of course I do. Write and let me know when you are coming, and you will be made welcome. There will be somewhere for you to stay."

"I like you a lot; you're a good sort. What time is it?" She jumped up. "I gotta go—meetin' some friends in town. We're going to go to a university basketball game." She shot a glance at Abby. "It was nice meetin' you. I'll be in touch with you again—Mary." She threw her head back and giggled just like Gabriel. She dashed to the end of the table where her brother was sitting, kissed him on the cheek, and ran out the door like a windstorm.

As Abby watched her, she thought Amy probably had more energy than Gabriel because she was younger and a girl; she seemed a bit more free spirited. Abby found her just as captivating as her brother.

Mary Jo broke into her thoughts. "Well, come on, Abby. We're all leaving now. I thought we may be moving to a party in someone's basement, but it seems we're all going different ways."

Father Gabriel stood up. "I don't know about y'all, but I have had the best time. What an example of how to enjoy oneself and at the same time be productive. Well done, y'all.

My suggestion would be to congregate in the parish hall next week and do a farewell bash for our little English rose. What do y'all say?" Everyone cheered, agreeing.

"When do you head out, Abby?" Gabriel asked her. These were the first words that had passed between them since she had arrived at the pizza house.

"March twenty-third. It's a Thursday, Father."

"Well, how about we all get together on, let's say, March eighteenth, Tuesday, at seven o'clock in the hall? I'm sure it's free, but I'll check the book and see. I'll provide the pizza, and the rest of you can bring what ya like." He raised his hand and made the sign of the cross. "God be with you all." Everyone said amen and good-bye, high-fiving.

Mary Jo tossed her lovely, long blonde hair over her shoulders. "Come on, Abby Road. Think I'll call you Abby Road—that's the Beatles' new album, and I love it. Have you heard it?"

"Yes, I have. Let's go," Abby replied, laughing.

Father Gabriel was at the door of the pizza house, saying his good-byes, just as he did at the church on Sundays. He shook the boys' hands and kissed the girls on the cheek, thanking them all. Abby felt both happy and sad once more to see him do this, as it meant he had not singled her out, which somehow removed the special significance and her secret euphoria. She could still feel a gentle tingle.

Mary Jo nudged her. "Will you get a load of Father Gabriel, Abby Road? Look at him—he is kissing up a storm." She giggled.

Abby smiled at her, secretly wishing she would shut up.

Mary Jo stopped in front of Father Gabriel. "Hey, Father, do we get one?"

Father threw his head back and laughed. "Are you kidding, Mary Jo?" He bent over and pecked her on the cheek.

"It's been a blast, Father," Mary Jo said as she passed.

Abby stood in front of him and smiled.

"What can we say to you, Abigail? Thank you! How are you getting home?"

"Mary Jo is driving me. Thanks."

"That's out of your way, Mary Jo. How about I drive you? I'm passing the Kennedy house to get home."

Mary Jo smiled and shrugged. "Okay, I will leave her in your capable hands, Father."

Abby's heart was doing cartwheels in her chest; her mind was racing a hundred miles an hour. She imagined him pulling over his car into the trees near the footpath by her special place at the babbling brook and her opening up and telling him how she loved him, wanted him, needed him, and couldn't imagine how she was going to leave him behind. He would kiss the tears from her face, put his lips on hers, and kiss her deeply. She physically ached for more of him; anything he was able to offer she would receive and reciprocate with all of herself.

—42—

"Let's go, Abby." Father made her jump. "Where were you?" He laughed. "A million miles away?"

"Oh, nowhere special." That was a lie, and she flushed and turned her head away.

"My car is over this way."

"Ah," she said, "a VW Beetle. Do you like this car, Father?"

"Yes, I do. It is reliable and economical, and I love the color—red is my favorite."

Abby laughed. "You know, you won't believe when I tell you this, Father Gabriel, but my brother Andre—he's your age, and he also has a Beetle."

"I don't believe you."

"Yes, he does. He rebuilt it from the wheels up, going back and forth to the scrapyard. He loves it—feels the same way as you do about yours—except his is black." They both laughed. As they were driving, it was silent—a soft silence, not an awkward one, with both of them deep in their own thoughts.

"Abby?" Gabriel spoke first. "Are the Kennedys expecting you home at a certain time?"

Abby hesitated. "No, no, I told them not to worry, that I may be late and would find my own way home."

"I wonder," he continued, "if you would like to come back to my office at the rectory. Do you remember when we first met and you talked about the song 'Bridge over Troubled Water'?"

"Of course I do," she replied almost sharply.

"I hope I'm not being intrusive, Abby, but I feel we know each other well enough for you to confide in me, if you wish to."

"Yes," Abby blurted out awkwardly—anything to be alone with him.

"That's good. I can make us a nice cup of tea, and we can talk privately and uninterrupted. Time is moving so fast, Abby. I can hardly believe you go back to England in two weeks. Has the time gone as quickly for you?"

"Oh yes, Father, I can barely believe I have spent one full month here in Tennessee, although I must say it's as though I always lived here." Abby went silent. Gabriel did not say anything more until he drove the car into the car park at the rectory.

"Here we are; this is where I call home at this time. C'mon in, and I will make us tea and give you the grand tour. Father Stephen is away for two days on a retreat, and the housekeeper has the day off." He walked her around the rectory; it was simple, with not much clutter.

"What a view," she said, looking out the window.

"Isn't it?" Gabriel replied.

"I would sip my coffee in here every morning if this is what I called home." Abby sighed.

"In a way, I do. My office is straight above this room, and I have the same view, only better because I'm higher."

"How lucky." Abby smiled.

"Yes, I'm blessed."

The rest of the home was simple and clean. It was not as fancy as some of the homes she had visited, especially the one where her cousins lived, yet compared to her home in England, it was luxurious. The coffee smelled good. Gabriel poured two cups, and they went upstairs to his office.

Abby was impressed; the room was enormous. She crossed to the window.

"Oh, look, Father—there are two horses cantering around in the back field." He came up beside her, and they sipped their coffee together silently, watching the horses move around the field, eating and standing in the late-afternoon sunlight.

"I spend a lot of time looking out this window; helps me think, Abby. Have a seat. I'm just going to take my jacket and collar off. Make yourself comfy, and I shall return in a jiffy, as you say." He laughed as he went through the door and closed it. Obviously, that was his bedroom. Abby tried to block out the thought that they were together just a whisper away from his bed. She looked around the room, which was so Gabriel—full of photos. She looked closely at the pictures on the wall, which featured his mam, dad, and siblings. She recognized Amy in the group; they all looked alike. There was a beautiful crucifix on the wall; a big green plant in the corner, which looked as if it had been with him for a long time; an American football on a shelf; and a large framed print of an angel. She looked closer—it was the angel Gabriel. *How appropriate,* she thought, smiling. He also had a bookcase with lots of books, most of them philosophy, psychology, and theology, though there were one or two novels. The bedroom door opened, and he came out.

"That feels a whole lot more comfortable. Would you like to use the bathroom, Abby?" She was a little startled. "You can use the one at the top of the stairs, if you wish."

"Yes, thank you, Father. I think I would like to do that."

He opened his office door and showed her the door to the bathroom. She brushed past him and felt the familiar tingle rush through her body. He had taken off his jacket and collar and put on a sweatshirt, which was open just enough at the neck to show that he had a little chest hair. The shirt was dark green and looked good on him; it made his amber eyes look like liquid gold to her. Abby opened the door and went into the bathroom. She washed her hands and splashed water on her flushed face; her head was aching. She decided to let down her hair. She brushed it, and it fell loosely upon her shoulders. Her head felt a lot better now. She went back to Gabriel's office with a feeling of anticipation.

As she opened the door, he looked surprised. He said, "Ah, you took your professional look away."

"Yes." She smiled. "If I keep my hair up too long, it gives me a headache."

"I can understand that. Do you want a Tylenol or something?"

"No, no, I'm fine now, and the coffee is really helping." There was some background music playing.

"I put on a record, as you call it—Elvis sings gospel, nice and soft. I know how much you like your music, Abby. Come sit down and relax and talk to me." They sat opposite one another.

Abby felt tense. She was not sure what to say to him. "I really don't quite know what to say or to tell you, Father."

"If you don't mind my saying so, Abby, you are a very beautiful young woman in every possible way with extraordinary gifts. I think you have a bright future, and yet when I look at you sometimes, you are wearing a melancholy mask. What's troubling you, Abby?" Gabriel asked.

Abby sat back in the big, comfy chair and allowed its crevices to embrace her. As she started to relax, words began tumbling from her lips. She was hesitant at first, and then it was as if someone opened a floodgate—everything poured from her. She wept, laughed, and sighed deeply as she told the story of her troubled young life up to that point.

Gabriel sat back in his chair to listen as Abby purged herself. He thought that for someone so young, she had experienced much sorrow. He desired to go to her, sweep her away, hold her under the stars, and kiss away her sorrow. He had never felt such a strong longing in all his life; it was tormenting and painful. He watched as Abby sat forward in the chair. He studied her golden curls falling forward and the smoothness of her skin where the white virginal blouse opened slightly at the curve of her chest.

"Father. Father?" Abby was calling him. "I'm sorry, Father; I have upset you."

"Oh no, Abby, no, no. The sadness of your story moves me. You must continue telling me what's on your mind." Gabriel sat on the end of his chair, observing Abby with every sense he was capable of using. He prayed in his head for the strength he required to help her, keeping his own feelings out of the equation.

"You look so tired, Father Gabriel. I think maybe you should drive me home."

"Only if you really feel you want to go," replied Gabriel. "I am truly interested in everything you have to say, Abby; I have been from the very moment you were introduced to me. Please, I beg you to continue."

"Very well, Father. There's not much more to add. You know, after the death of my mother, we all struggled to cope. Oh, we all survive and do the best we can. But having lived here in Tennessee for the past four weeks, I don't know how I can even think of going back; it feels like I've arrived in some perfect place. I can't explain it. Everyone is so kind to me—they treat me as though I am someone special, help me, explain things to me, and congratulate me. I love the comfort of the life, the luxury. If you reach for the moon here, I think you can touch it. I simply don't want to leave; my cousin wants me to stay. He wants me to try to emigrate; he's even offered to sponsor me."

Gabriel broke in. "Now, that's the most sensible thing I've heard—a fantastic idea. I agree, and if there is anything I can do to assist, Abby—"

"How can I, Father? I simply can't walk away from my responsibilities at home. I am needed."

"Your sisters are there," he assured her.

"We all work together hand in hand, pay the bills, and help look after my three younger brothers. Leah is going back to London to live and work. I have to go back. I already work three jobs."

Gabriel shook his head. "Abby, you have your own life to live."

"Father, whatever I decide to do, I must return in order to apply for emigration. I have to apply from within my own home country. My brothers—they are only fourteen years old, and it has been very hard on them. My mother spent a lot of time with them, and I know they miss her terribly."

"How about you, Abby? Do you miss her?"

"Yes, of course, but she was not that close to me, Father. I was much closer to my auntie Helen, though somehow or other, she's got herself upset with me now."

"That surprises me, as I know of her fondness for you, Abby."

"How can I guess what's going on in her head? Maybe nothing, but it feels like she would like to get me out of here and back to England as quickly as she can. I must go back. You know, Father, I just would not be able to settle here and be happy if I left my family high and dry."

Gabriel smiled and shook his head. "Oh, Abby."

Tears rolled down her cheeks. "How can I be in two places at once? How can I go back, but how can I stay?" As they sat together opposite one another, each of them was sad for his or her own reasons.

"I think maybe I should be making my way back, Father, if that's all right with you."

"Of course it is, Abby. Why don't you go down and just wait by the car? I shall be there in just a moment. Use the ladies' room on the way if you wish to splash your face with some cold water."

"Yes, thanks, Father. I think I'll do that—perk me up a bit."

Gabriel threw his head back. "Oh, Abby." He laughed loudly. "I just love that one; it gives me such a visual—all perked up, nice and tall. Oh, you make me feel so good. I love ..." He hesitated. "I love those little phrases of yours. Let's go get perked up a bit." He went to his room, laughing as he closed the door behind him.

They drove home in silence most of the way. "Will you come to spaghetti night on Tuesday, Father?"

"I'll try, Abby."

"It is my last one before I go back to England."

"Yes, I know." The VW pulled up outside the Kennedy house, and Gabriel switched off the ignition.

"Would you like to come in, Father?"

"No, thanks, Abby. I would like to have a chat with you regarding your conversation with me this afternoon. I thought it better to say this to you outside of the office, as we were both quite exhausted. It would seem to me that you have a tough road ahead of you, Abby. The life experiences you have lived have brought you to become an amazing woman way beyond your years. I suspect they have given you insight and strength to accomplish all that you wish to do." Gabriel took Abby's hand in his and placed it over his heart. "I truly believe, Abby, one day you will come back. I shall pray daily for your safe return." He let go of Abby's hand. "Good night, Abby. See you soon."

"Good night, Father." She climbed out of the car, but before she closed the door, she looked into Gabriel's eyes. "No matter where I go throughout my life, I shall never forget you for as long as I live." She smiled and closed the car door. Gabriel drove away.

—43—

Abby walked toward the house slowly; she wanted to savor her feelings and the time she had just spent with Gabriel. She opened the door to the mudroom and took off her shoes. Abby decided that wherever she lived, one day she would have a mudroom. She smiled at herself. She felt as if her whole inside was a smile that must come out and be seen.

Abby went into the kitchen. "Hello! I'm home!" she called. She was later than she had anticipated; however, she had told Aiden and Rosella not to worry, as she might be late. Aunt Helen showed up.

"Hi, Aunt Helen. Where is everyone?"

"Not here," she replied curtly. "Where have you been?"

"I was out with the youth group and Father, having pizza."

"Till this time? It's after seven. It was a luncheon, wasn't it?"

"It lasted for a few hours." Abby did not want to tell Aunt Helen that she and Father had gone back to the rectory and spent several hours together talking. She lied. "We all went to Scott's house and listened to some records."

"I saw you with Father Gabriel in the car. What were you doing?"

Abby was starting to feel defensive, as Helen's tone of voice was rising and she was looking at Abby accusingly.

"Have you been watching us, Aunt Helen?" Abby regretted the tone she used, but she was upset.

"Don't you dare use that attitude with me. I invite you to come to my son's home, to my home, and you show up like a femme fatale, batting your eyelashes and flirting with the newly ordained curate—from the first time you laid your eyes on him. You have no right turning that young priest's head. My God, I can hardly believe my own words, Abigail. You are a female version of your father, Sebastian—no morals." Helen shouted the words into Abby's face. "Your poor mother would turn in her grave!"

Tears welled up in Abby's eyes. "What are you saying to me, Aunt Helen? How can you say such things?"

"Never mind your sniveling; it will not work with me. I am responsible for your being here. You have two weeks left until you go back, which cannot come soon enough for me. You are unbelievable; this is how you repay kindness and hospitality? I am ashamed to call you my niece." She turned on her heel, leaving Abby stunned.

Abby ran to her bedroom, slammed the door, and threw herself on top of the bed, sticking her face into the pillows so that her sobbing could not be heard. Several hours later, she awoke to the sound of knocking in the distance.

"Abby?" She could hear her name being called. "Abby?" It was Rosella. "Can I come in?"

"Oh yes." Abby scrambled into a sitting position. "What time is it?"

"It's nine o'clock."

"Oh, I must have fallen asleep."

"Are you okay, Abby?"

"Yes, tired—all the excitement of the day, I suppose." Her voice was quivering, and she kept her head down.

"Abby, go take a shower, and put your pj's on; I'm going to make us some hot tea and bring it back here. I can see you are very upset." Abby burst into tears. "Oh, Abby, darling, what has upset you so?"

Abby dabbed her eyes. "I can't tell you."

"Yes, you can; I will be back in a minute, and you and I can have a nice long chat."

Abby did as she was told; she stripped off her clothes and climbed into the shower. She had grown to adore the habit of standing under the warm water and allowing it to wash away her sorrows. However, tonight she continued to weep. She was not sure what made her the saddest—Auntie Helen being so mad and angry, the thought of leaving this wonderful place, or the thought of leaving Gabriel. Her sobbing increased at that last thought. She stepped out of the shower, dried herself, slipped into her warm pajamas, tied her hair up, and went to sit on her bed. Rosella came in carrying a tray with cups, a teapot, milk, sugar, scones with jam and butter, and homemade shortbread saved from the sale.

"You know, Abby, Aiden, the children, and I are so proud of you—especially today. You were fantastic."

Abby dropped her head, and tears fell from her chin onto her bedsheets.

"What has made you so sad?" Rosella poured Abby her tea and handed it to her. Abby sipped it; the warm golden liquid felt soothing and refreshing. She was thirsty and hungry. Abby wrapped both hands around the teacup and crossed her legs.

"It's a lot of different things."

"Start at the beginning."

Abby told the long story of what had happened throughout the day. Rosella sat silently for a moment.

"More tea?" She topped off Abby's cup. "You know, Abby, as wise as you are and as much life as you have seen that has given you a wisdom and an ability way ahead of your years, at times, you are a little naive."

Abby looked up. "What do you mean?"

"I can see this from the outside looking in; that gives me an advantage." Rosella smiled at Abby. "Aunt Helen has, in the last twelve months, lost so much—her home, her friends, her country, you, her darling Amelia, and, to top it off, her beloved Charles. You are a young person, Abby, and you cannot possibly imagine how devastated and lonely Helen must feel; no one could unless he or she was in her shoes. She was severely depressed, Abby—that is why we called you. Then Father Gabriel came to St. Michael's. His first Mass was the day your mam was being buried back in the UK. Helen was distraught over not being able to be there for her sister and her sister's children. She came home and talked about Father incessantly. Her first few months here after his ordination, he was so good with Helen—patient and kind—and he was more so after Charles passed away. He did the requiem Mass and continued to grief-counsel her." Abby sat up straight, and her weeping eased off as Rosella continued.

"I strongly suspect she envies you somewhat. She expected to see the little girl she'd left behind, and instead, you showed up—a beautiful young woman. She feels a certain kind of love for Father Gabriel, a loyalty. I think we all can be accused of loving Father Gabriel. The difference with you, Abby, is it appears he loves you equally as much as you love him."

"Oh, Rosella, I just don't ..." Abby gasped.

"Shhh. Listen—I can see it in him whenever you are around. On spaghetti night, he never takes his eyes from you. At Sunday Mass, I watch him scan the congregation until his eyes fall upon you, and I can see him relax. It has been amazing watching the two of you thinking no one else can see it, not even each other. Am I correct?"

Abby burst into tears once more. "Oh, Rosella, what can I do? How can I leave him? I love him so much. We are doing nothing wrong. God forbid we should be."

"You are not the first—nor will you be the last—young lady to fall in love with a priest, Abby. I strongly suspect this will resolve itself through distance—three thousand miles—and time. You may not get back here for several years, by which time Father Gabriel will be long gone. Sadly, that is the way things are. Abby, life throws curveballs at you from time to time; how you catch them can determine the quality of your life. Don't you worry about Helen; she will forgive you in time."

"I hope you are right."

Rosella hugged Abby. "Now, dry your eyes, Abby, and dream sweetly. You surely deserve it."

"Good night, Rosella." Abby slipped in between her sheets, closing her eyes. Her mind filled with thoughts of Gabriel and how she could return to Sweet Hope Lake for good.

Gabriel drove back home with his radio on as loudly as he could stand it. He wanted to take his mind off his own thoughts. He could still feel her about him. Her energy, her essence, was unlike that of any other woman he had ever met, and he found her to be intoxicating. As he went to switch the radio off, Simon and Garfunkel came on, singing "Bridge over Troubled Water." Abby would have told him that was a good omen—serendipity. He loved to listen to her chatting away to him. Though she spoke mostly of unimportant things, she had an uncanny knack of capturing him with her words.

Gabriel arrived at the rectory and sat in his car for a few moments until the song finished. Rather than walking toward the rectory, he walked over to the church. As he pushed open the large oak door, it creaked loudly, announcing that someone was entering the sanctuary. Gabriel loved this church; it was beautiful. It was small, yet it had a cathedral presence—county and Renaissance combined. The sanctuary candle flickered, reminding Gabriel of why he had come in. He went down upon his knees, looked around him, and started praying out loud.

"Hi, Lord. I need your help. Quite simply, I have, I believe, fallen in love—earthly love—and I'm looking for all that goes with it. I don't know what to do about it—I am not at ease no matter how I look at it. Seems to me to be a lose-lose situation. I am questioning everything I have learned and the way I have lived—right up to this point in my life—and my very foundations are shaken. Abby is all I could wish for, and when I lay my eyes upon her, when I am with her, I feel complete—yet I am terrified, and I can't make any decisions. Help me." Gabriel felt a lump in his throat as he knelt and prayed. Tears fell freely for all that he was about to lose no matter which path he decided to choose.

—44—

Time passed faster than Abby had ever imagined possible; it was her second-to-last day, and she was packing her suitcase. As she moved around the room, taking clothes from her dresser, the surroundings felt like hers now. The room was beautiful and familiar; she knew every part of it—the American quilt on her bed and the lace curtains at the windows, which allowed the light to come in. As she looked out the window, hugging the clothes she was about to pack, her heart was heavy. She looked out onto the front yard, as they called it there in Tennessee. In northeastern England, they called it a park. There was a knock on her door.

"Come in."

The door opened, and Rosella came in with two cups of tea. "I thought you could use some refreshment." She smiled. "Come sit; let's drink our tea. I can help you finish. You do want to look your best for the big farewell bash tonight. What are you going to wear?"

"Oh, I don't know. I was thinking of jeans and a nice jumper, as it's the church hall, and I don't want to overdress."

"Nonsense," replied Rosella. "It is your good-bye and thank-you party; you are the guest of honor. It's your night, Abby! You need to pick the best outfit you own and wear it with passion. I understand you are feeling sad that it's time for you to leave here, but I think you should save the melancholy for when you have gone, not your last days. Live it up, enjoy, and leave them with the memory of your beautiful sparkle, Abby, so they will never forget you. Remember to make the best of your last few days. Father Gabriel called this morning."

"He did? What did he want?"

"Just to remind us to bring you to the party tonight and not to concern ourselves about your ride home, as he would love to drive you back this evening."

"I feel so excited—and sad."

"That is understandable. Now, let's finish packing and do the fun stuff—find you an outfit for tonight."

That evening Rosella and Helen sat at the kitchen table, and Abby came out dressed and ready to go to the church. She had chosen to wear her favorite dark-blue dress with a white collar and cuffs, and she wore her hair down, the chestnut curls tumbling down her back.

Helen said nothing, not a word. Rosella jumped up from the table and said she would like to drive Abby that night.

As they were leaving, Abby looked back. "Good-bye, Auntie Helen."

Helen looked up and, with a joyless, flat tone, said, "Good-bye." Abby and Rosella left for the church hall.

"I am so disappointed and hurt, Rosella. Why is Auntie Helen behaving this way?"

"I wouldn't worry yourself too much, Abby. I've told you

what I think the problem is. Time will work it out once you have returned home—it will all disappear."

Abby decided not to ask what would happen if she returned to the United States one day, which she fully intended to.

"Now, go enjoy a wonderful evening. You look so beautiful, Abby. Go shine your light," Rosella said as they arrived. "Don't worry about what time you come home. I will leave the mudroom door unlocked, and I will get Auntie Helen to bed before you arrive."

"Thank you so much, Rosella." She gave Rosella a hug.

Scott was just arriving. "Wait up, Abby. I'll escort you in!"

"Thanks, Scott." Abby smiled. He offered his arm, and together they walked into the church hall. Abby was speechless; there were kids all over, dressed up beautifully, and the hall was full of helium balloons with various messages: "Good-bye," "Good luck," "Thank you," "Come back soon," and "We love you." The Beatles were playing on the record player. "You say good-bye, and I say hello—hello, hello. I don't know why you say good-bye. I say hello," they sang. The table was filled with all sorts of beautiful foods, and the pizza had just arrived. As Scott walked her in, everyone clapped and cheered and then started singing "For She's a Jolly Good Fellow," followed by saying, "Hip, hip, hooray!" Abby felt useless, unable to collect herself. She stood in the center and watched, smiling.

When they finished, she smiled. "Thank you so much. I feel like a film star."

They all laughed together. "You mean movie star. Come on—let's eat. We're all starving," said Scott.

Abby could not see Father Gabriel. Where was he? She

kept looking around in every corner. Was he not going to show up at her farewell party?

"So, Abby Road, what are you thinkin'? Sorry to be leavin', or happy to be goin' home? It's a long time to be gone, six weeks."

"Yes, I know. It will take me some time to get back into a routine. I start work next Monday; that will be difficult after six weeks' leave of absence."

"We wish you could come back to live in Tennessee, USA."

Abby smiled. "Me too," she said. "Where is Father Gabriel?" Abby blurted out the words. She was devastated not to see him as soon as she walked in the hall.

"Oh, I'm sorry; I forgot to tell you," said David. "He came by earlier to give you a message; here it is in my pocket. He was called away on some emergency—too bad. Still, he kept his word on providing the pizza."

"Yay!" they all cheered together. Abby summoned every resource within her and cheered feebly; with every fiber, she wanted to rush off into a corner and tear open the envelope with his handwriting and his message to her, but she did not want to look desperate.

"Yes, let's go sample his donation—maybe save him a slice if he's lucky," said Mary Jo.

The night passed quickly; it was a lot of fun, though she missed his presence. She went to the washroom sometime after she received the envelope, locked herself in one of the bathroom stalls, and tore open the note.

> Abby, dearest, I am so sorry. I have been unavoidably detained, an emergency at the hospital. I will not be able to make your

farewell party. I feel so sad. Please wait for
me after in the church. I will drive you home.
Love, Father Gabriel

Oh my gosh. She could not imagine saying good-bye to him. She was in tears.

Mary Jo came in. "Abby Road, are you in there?"

"Yes. What's up?"

"Are you crying?" she asked.

"No," Abby replied.

"Yes, you are; get out here."

"Oh, Mary Jo, I'm so sorry to be leaving this wonderful place."

Mary Jo hugged Abby. "Now, don't you be messing up that fantastic face of yours with tears, girl. Come on—we have a presentation to make!"

Mary Jo linked arms with Abby and escorted her back into the middle of the room. All the kids from the group circled around her. Scott stepped up, coughed, and then said, "Well, we had planned for Father Gabriel to present this gift to you, Abby, but I guess I'm going to do it. It is my pleasure to present to you a small token of our friendship. We have all enjoyed getting to know you, Abby, and we hope this will remind you of the fun times we have all shared." He walked up to Abby and gave her a big card and a small gift. The small gift was wrapped in silver paper with a blue bow. She opened the card. It was a farewell card with several different versions of farewell—*ciao, so long, bon voyage*—and inside, they all had written messages to her and, underneath, written their addresses and phone numbers.

"How wonderful. What an idea!"

"Now there's no excuse not to communicate with us, is there?" said Scott. "We all have your address—it's on the church bulletin board. Father Gabriel put it up there last week. Too bad he's not here, Abby; he was so disappointed. Anyway, looks like he ain't going to make it, so open the gift." Abby put the card down and gently opened the silver paper and removed the blue bow.

"So pretty," she said.

"Oh, come on," said Mary Jo. "I am dying to see what you think."

Inside the paper was a small hinged velvet box. Abby held it for a moment and then slowly opened the lid.

"My goodness." She gasped. "It's so ..." She could hardly speak.

"Do you like it? We all pitched in, although we must tell you Father Gabriel gave the lion's share—that's why we were able to buy you a gold one and not silver. We did try to find Michael the archangel—the church name," Scott said.

Mary Jo jumped in. "But there it was, Abby, sitting in the middle of the jeweler's cabinet with your name written all over it."

Scott said, "It was a unanimous decision; we all agreed—an Angel Gabriel pendant. Father is overjoyed, and we loved it, though it did cost a lot. We phoned Father, and he said, 'Get it—just get it gift wrapped, and you just bring it on home.'"

"Oh, it's so lovely."

"We know how you two have a real connection, and we thought it was more feminine than Michael the archangel, even if we could have found him."

"I absolutely love it with all my heart; I shall cherish it

forever and ever, as I will the memories and friends that I have made here. Thank you all."

Everyone hugged, kissed, and shook hands, and some of the girls cried. They all promised to keep in touch and write, and they all told her, "Y'all come back now."

Mary Jo came up. "How are you gonna get home, girl? Do you need a ride?"

"No, I'm fine. Thanks. I do want to see Father if he gets back, and he'll drive me home."

"I know." Mary Jo opened her arms wide. "You have been such fun. Keep in touch. One day I may come see you."

"Anytime, Mary Jo; you would be so welcome."

Scott hugged Abby. "I hope to see you back for good, Abby; I would like that. You okay out here alone?" He locked the church hall door and put the key in his pocket.

"I'm fine."

"Well, travel safely." They all climbed into their cars, and she waved to them. They disappeared; all was quiet.

Abby walked toward the church; it was dark except for some lights from the porch. She pushed open the door and stepped inside. There was one small light on, keeping the place from being in complete darkness, and the sanctuary candle flickered. The atmosphere was inviting, calling her to walk up the aisle; Abby made her way along the aisle, looking at the beautiful stations of the cross. She arrived at the front pew, genuflected, made the sign of the cross, and slipped in, holding onto her golden angel and waiting for Father Gabriel.

Abby was not sure how much time passed. She was in a daze—not sleeping or praying, just sitting and allowing herself to enjoy the moment of quiet; it felt good. The door of the church creaked open, and then she heard it close. Abby waited, held her breath, and listened for the voice that was like a warm cup of cocoa to make its way up the aisle. She heard footsteps and forced herself not to turn until she heard him speak.

"I am so glad you received my note and waited. I was praying all the way home you would be sitting in that front pew, waiting for me."

"Of course I would wait for you." Abby turned, stood, and walked toward him.

"I am so pleased we are going to have some time alone together—and in one of my favorite places." Gabriel took Abby's hand in his and led her to two large chairs facing the altar, near the choir stalls. Abby sat in one, and he sat next to her. With her hand in his, he started to pray out loud.

"Hi, Lord. Here I am, and I am excited to introduce you to Abigail Lavalle. You know her, because I have been talking to you for some time about her. Please help me—help us both. I feel so connected with Abby, and I don't want to disconnect. The thought hurts me too much."

Closing his eyes, he continued, "This is and has been one of the most difficult of experiences, because I have been unable to express my love or show any outward sign of affection for her. Oh, I know what needs to be done. Please enable me, Lord, to stay focused as a priest and lovingly support Abby, as she must go home to finish the job her own mother could not do. I must say this out loud, for if I had not taken the sacrament of ordination, I would surely now be hoping to take the sacrament of matrimony one day with Abigail, who, for some reason, you have sent across my path. Keep her close to you, as I surely will in my heart, as she travels back to her life and leaves me with mine."

Standing together on the altar, they clung to one another. Abby felt Gabriel's lips upon hers—softly and gently at first and then with passion and desire, as though he were reaching within her for something so deep she was not aware of it. She responded, searching for something to satisfy the longing inside her. Abby gave herself up to the moment, feeling her first taste of true love and praying it would last for an eternity.

"I love you, Gabriel," she whispered as she pulled away. "With the very best of me, with all that I am. I cannot believe this is it. Will I ever see you again? Why have we found one another just to lose each other? Answer me." Abby wept. "It's unfair; I feel so alive with you, as though you can see and feel parts of me that no one else can. I shall die of a broken heart if we must part for good."

"I can only tell you what I believe to be true, Abby. We cannot do this; we will regret it. We are damned if we do and damned if we don't." Gabriel enfolded Abby in his arms and held her close to him. "Abby, cry and let out the pain, for there is nowhere else to go with this."

After she could cry no more, Gabriel walked Abby out of his church. As they drove home, he held Abby's hand in one of his while steering the car with his other hand. The only noise was the radio—"Bridge over Troubled Water" was playing. They arrived outside Aiden's home.

"I can't stand this," Gabriel said. "I will walk you to the door now."

"No, please, Gabriel, not yet," Abby pleaded. "I want you to do something for me. Will you bless my angel, Gabriel?"

"Oh, I am so sorry, Abby. I forgot all about the night and the gift—forgive me. Do you like it?"

"I love it with all my heart and soul."

Gabriel took it out of the box, placed it in the palm of his hand, blessed the little golden angel, and placed his lips upon it tenderly.

As he brought the gold chain around Abby's neck to fasten it, he whispered. "Abby, whenever you touch this angel, know I am with you."

"Then know I shall never take it off." His hands were laying softly upon her shoulders. She could feel him inhaling her scent as deeply as his lungs would allow. Nuzzling his face into her hair, his tears were falling onto her warm skin. "Gabriel please stay in the car, I will wave to you from the front door." Abby lifted his hands to her lips and kissed them tenderly. She opened the car door, slid from her seat and made her way to the door blinded by her tears. As she waved goodbye, Gabriel smiled at her through his tears and drove away.

Abby collapsed onto the front doorstep and pushed her face into her arm to quell the sound of the sobs racking her small frame. She wrapped her other arm around herself, rocking back and forth for as long as there were sobs within her. After some time her tears subsided, and she stood and went quietly into the house from the mudroom. As Rosella had promised, the door was unlocked. Abby tiptoed past the shoes and into the large kitchen she had become attached to, thinking about how, the day after tomorrow, she must leave it all behind her. She decided to make herself a cup of tea and sit outside to drink it, as she could not sleep yet. Abby could barely sit still; her mind was full of the evening's events. She walked over to the kitchen sink, filled the kettle, placed it on the stove top, switched it on, and moved toward the cupboard to find a cup. Suddenly, she jumped. In the shadows in the corner of the dining room sat Helen in the dark silence. Abby was startled.

"Aunt Helen, what are you doing here," she whispered, "sitting alone in the dark?"

"I was waiting for you," said Helen. "You didn't think he would give it all up for you, did you?" Although it was dark, Abby could see the satisfied grin across Helen's face. "I was willing to sit here as long as it took to see this. He's gone back to his church—am I right?" Helen did not wait for an answer. "I'm so happy you can return to Newcastle and let us all get back to life before Abigail Lavalle appeared." Helen pushed her chair back and stood up to leave.

"I'm so sorry you feel the way you do, Aunt Helen. Father Gabriel had no intention of leaving the church. I don't understand why you think so, and I won't try to change your mind; hopefully, time will do that. It was never my intention to cause you such distress in your life, as I know how you have suffered this year. All I ever wanted was to bring comfort to you. I am deeply saddened at some of the things that you have said and believe. I shall be gone the day after tomorrow, maybe never to return. But let me tell you this: I will be forever grateful for my time here, the lessons I have been given, and the love I was allowed to freely give and receive. Not even you, with your anger and disappointment, can take that away."

Helen glared at Abby, marched out of the kitchen to her own apartment, and slammed the door behind her.

—45—

Abby held Rosella tightly. "Good-bye, and thank you for everything."

"We will miss you so much," Rosella said with tears in her eyes. "And look forward to the day you come back to us."

Abby kissed each of the children. She went to Aunt Helen, hugged her, and kissed her on the cheek. Helen did not respond.

"Auntie Helen, thank you for everything. I am sorry it turned out to be such a disappointment for you. I hope one day soon you will feel better about it."

"Good-bye," Helen answered, and she said no more.

Abby cried as Aiden drove her to the airport.

Aiden shook his head. "You know, Abby, I'm so sorry about Mam. I don't understand what's got into her. Maybe she's homesick and wishes she was coming with you, or she's missing my dad."

"Don't worry, Aiden," said Abby, blowing her nose. "I would not have missed this for all the world. I can't thank you enough for the opportunity and the kindness you have shown me. It has inspired me to consider many new options in my life when I am able."

"You are a good girl, Abby," said Aiden, "and I want you to know if there is anything Rosella and I can do to help you achieve those goals, you just call my name."

"I know, and I shall be ever grateful to you both."

The airport personnel were announcing Abby's flight; it was time to say good-bye to Aiden. They hugged, holding on for a moment before Abby walked away to board the plane. Passengers began handing tickets to ground staff, and lots of family members and well-wishers stood behind the ropes to keep the main area clear for passengers to walk through. Families were waving, crying, and blowing kisses. Aiden stood behind the rope. Abby let go of him and walked away toward the gate. Unconsciously, she touched her angel. As she turned to wave to Aiden, she stopped, catching her breath. Behind the rope, waving to her frantically and calling her over, was Father Gabriel.

She ran toward him. "I can't believe you are here!"

Gabriel took her hand in his. "I needed to see you. I wanted to look at you and hold your soft, gentle hands in mine and tell you …" He stopped. "To come back to us one day, Abby. I shall always think of you and cherish the moments you and I have shared." He held a small blue envelope, blessed it, kissed it, and gave it to her. "God go with you, Abby."

"Thank you for coming to see me. I'm so happy." As she moved toward the gate, she waved to both Aiden and Gabriel until she turned a corner and was out of sight.

The hustle and bustle of the departure of the long-haul flight from Chicago to Heathrow had somewhat subsided. The lights had been dimmed; all seemed calm and serene.

Abby lifted the window shade; it was a perfect night with a dark blue sky scattered with a multitude of stars. A full moon with a glow bright enough to read by hung over the plane.

Abby pulled out the blue envelope Gabriel had handed to her. She touched her angel pendant. She sat silently for a while before opening it, looking at the silver light pouring into her window from the luminous moon. It seemed appropriate to read Gabriel's letter by moonlight—it felt mystical, secretive, and romantic. She held the envelope and relished the moment, imagining what might be inside. The moonlight shined on the wing of the aircraft, making it look like the giant wing of an albatross, covering the metal in a beautiful silver veil. Abby felt as though she were flying toward the heavens. She watched the stars and could almost feel the wind in her hair, blowing away her fears and sadness.

Slowly, she opened Gabriel's envelope, which contained a note, a photo, and a small card. She looked at the note.

> Hey, Abby, by the time you read this, you will be high in the sky, winging your path far away from me—physically at least. On a spiritual level, I shall never be far away from you.

Abby stopped reading, looked out at the silver moon, and wondered if Gabriel was looking at the same moon. It was ten thirty in Sweet Hope Lake; maybe he was lying in his bed, feeling the same as she. Looking back at the contents of her envelope, she continued to read.

> We both understand that. I have enclosed a photo. Mary Jo took it—remember? The

two of us together at the bake sale. I like it,
and I hope you like it also.

Abby looked at the photo; they were indeed standing together side by side at the bake sale, talking and smiling at one another. The photo had captured their genuine appreciation for one another. Abby stroked Gabriel's face with her finger. *You are lovely,* she thought, and then she went back to reading the letter.

I have framed mine, and it is on my night table. I see you as I wake, Abby, and when I fall asleep, which is exactly how I want it. Travel safely, and sleep well. I have included a Mass card for tomorrow morning. I am saying the eight o'clock mass and shall offer it for you, Abby, my cherished friend. God bless.
With love, Gabriel

Abby looked at the Mass card—it was a picture of the Virgin Mary holding baby Jesus in her arms. Written on the back was "For Abby. From Gabriel with love." Abby slipped her photo, letter, and card safely back into the envelope. She was about to place it in her bag but decided to pull the photo back out. She propped it up on her pullout table, retrieved a pen and paper from her bag, made herself comfortable, looked at the photo, and started to write.

With you all of the way,
As the sun rays warm your face in the morning,
And you kneel at your bedside to pray,
Remember somewhere in the distance,

I'm with you all of the way.
As you are offering Mass at the altar,
And you look toward heaven and say,
"Dear Lord my cup runneth over."
I'm with you all of the way.
Deep in the depths of your slumber,
With dreams of tomorrow today,
Remember somewhere in the distance,
I'll be with you tomorrow forever someday.

The moonlight streamed through the window, lighting up Abby's verse as she reread and signed it—"For only you, Gabriel. Always yours, Abby."

As Abby looked upon the moon-drenched night, she resolved to make some changes in her life. She would work harder, save money, and find a better job. Suddenly, the dark sky appeared to light up as the aircraft flew beyond the moon and stars toward the new day. A warm red sun was rising; the jet was quickly approaching the daylight. Its vibrant colors, a myriad of prism sensations, were so bright that Abby had to shade her eyes. *How breathtaking,* she thought. Abby felt it was a special sunrise performance only for her. Move from the dark to the light—that was what she was going to do. One way or another, she would go back to Sweet Hope Lake someday, even if it took a lifetime. She would find a way.

Abby arrived home in Newcastle the next day. After searching for her key, she unlocked the door, knowing that because of the time of day—two o'clock in the afternoon—no one would be home. She had been traveling for almost twenty-two hours, and she was weary. As she walked along the hallway it felt dark, dreary, and gloomy. Abby put her suitcase down at the bottom of the stairs and stopped for a moment, feeling a desire to sit down in the dark. She was exhausted, yet somehow she was filled with a sense of joy.

"Gabriel," she whispered as she closed her eyes and touched her necklace. How she longed to reach out for him. Abby had never imagined in her life that she could feel such a deep love for another human soul.

She went to the kitchen, and as she slowly opened the door, her eyes searched around the room. Everything looked smaller, darker, and grimier. She saw ashes in the grate, dishes overflowing in the sink, rubbish in the bin and on the floor, and dirt everywhere. Somehow even the dirt looked dirtier than it did in Tennessee. It never looked like this there; they had dishwashers, gas fireplaces, garbage-disposal units, and central vacuums. Abby sat down in a chair in the middle of the kitchen. Looking around the room, she wondered how in heaven's name she would ever adapt to living in this house again. She thought it was as far from her idea of a home now as one could ever imagine. Abby put her head into her hands and wept, partly from weariness and the anticlimax of returning home but mostly from the sense of reality that was hitting her. The situation she found herself in made her soul ache. She must, with all that was within her, find the resources to pay back her father and return to where she knew with her every breath she belonged—Sweet Hope Lake, Tennessee.

—46—

One year later Abby arrived at the front door of her house, breathless. She had run all the way back from her job in the hairdressing salon; she'd had a long day and no lunch, which was not unusual, as it was always busy on Fridays. Ladies anticipating their weekend activities threw money at her boss on Fridays—money that Abby received little of. She knew how to look after the customers, remembering little details about their likes and dislikes. Mrs. Whitehouse loved black tea with lemon and the dryer on medium; Mrs. Whitby drank coffee with milk, preferred plain biscuits, and liked the dryer on high. Abby made it her business to know her customers, and she was so good that she accumulated more money in tips per week than she earned in her wage.

Tonight she had to rush because it was her turn to make the tea for her three younger brothers. They were still in high school, and Cammie and Abby shared the responsibilities of running the home. It was Abby's turn to cook dinner; tonight she would make something quick, such as beans on toast. She did not have much time, as she had to change and leave for her second job. On Mondays, Wednesdays, and Fridays Abby worked as a barmaid at the pub at the end of the street, the Queen's Head. It was usually filled with locals, and some of the men would stand at the bar all night, drinking one pint after the other. All of them had sad looks on their face as they looked into the bottom of the empty glasses and told her, "Put another one in there, pet, and have one for yourself." She was not sure what held them fast to that bar night after night. It was beyond Abby's understanding; all she could do was be kind, listen, and then watch them stagger across the bar floor. Working there taught Abby a multitude of lessons, the least of which being that she knew she must get away from this place no matter how much time or effort it took.

Sunday was Abby's favorite day of the week, as she worked with Sally on the ice cream van, and they had fun talking about how they would travel through Europe, working in France and Italy, picking olives and grapes.

"Do you really think we can?" Abby asked.

"Of course," Sally replied, switching on the van's chimes. They played "Pop Goes the Weasel."

After they stopped there was stillness; then the doors would open, and all along the street, the young and old alike would spill out toward the van, clutching vessels of all different colors, shapes, and sizes, including jugs, vases, and plates—whatever they could use to hold their soft, smooth, sweet vanilla ice cream. *Everyone is a child when he or she is licking ice cream,* Abby thought as she watched a young man walk away licking his ice cream cornet so as to stop the raspberry sauce, called monkey's blood, from running onto his sleeve. Nothing in the world mattered at that moment other than the first taste.

At the end of the day she finished her chores and collapsed onto her bed, exhausted, in the small room she shared with Cammie. Lying down, she slipped her hand under her pillow and did what she had done every night for almost one year: read the letter. It had arrived one month after she had returned home. Abby closed her eyes and recited the contents to herself, as she had read it so many times that she knew it by heart.

> My dearest Abigail,
>
> How I have longed to reply to your beautiful poem before now. I must start by offering my heartfelt gratitude for such beauty and grace. It took me several attempts to read it through in its entirety, as tears blurred my vision. Abby, I have not allowed one single day to pass without reciting it, as it is impossible not to do so. When I speak, it tumbles from my lips like a prayer; it is inscribed upon my soul. I carry you within me always.
>
> There is so much I want to say to you. After you left my parish, the priest approached me. There have been some concerns within the parish regarding my relationship with you during your visit. I was most distressed at such a suggestion and expressed to him that we had done nothing to hide, regret, or be ashamed of. He is a good man, and I did confide in him as to how I felt regarding my vocation and

questions around my feelings for you. He has been most understanding, suggesting a change. The Kennedys have asked me several times to supper. I went once but could still feel your presence. I believe you to be my soul mate and yet it is not to be—not at this time.

I have requested a move away from here. They are moving me to a small parish outside of Memphis. I have been counseled to give it some time, maybe a year or two. I can only give you the same advice—in time, Abby, you will feel the freedom to move on and live your life. Always remember me as someone who touched your life as a kind person. I do know that is not what you want to hear. I cannot give you my forwarding address; however, I will be sending you my eternal love. I do not know why our paths crossed, but I do know you have given meaning to the words *life, love,* and *laughter.* For this, I shall never forget you.

With you all the way, Gabriel

She was as sure as the sun would rise and set that one day, somewhere, they would meet again. Abby closed her eyes and fell into a gentle sleep.

— 47 —

It was Monday morning, and Abby was late to her job at the hair salon, as she often was. Geri, her friend who worked with her, was covering for her. Geri was fun loving and looked a lot like Twiggy—tall and blonde.

"You work too hard—all those extra jobs," Geri said when Abby dashed in the door late. "When did you last have a good night out? I swear you carry the weight of the world on your back sometimes."

Abby just smiled.

"Come out with me tonight," Geri said as they were folding towels in the back room. "Just to the local pub. There's a good folk band on; they are called Lindisfarne. Come meet some new young people."

"Oh, I don't know." Abby sighed. "It's my only night free this week, and I have a thousand things to do."

"Hush," Geri said. "Come out with me. I have this friend. He's really very nice; he's just split up with his girlfriend of two years. You know, he looks just like that singer and songwriter you love that you are always playing—the one who sings the sad songs. Gilbert and Sullivan."

Abby smiled. "Oh, Geri, you know it's Gilbert O'Sullivan."

"Well, he looks just like him—I swear. His name is David, and it's taking him some time to get over his old girlfriend, Desiree. I think you would be good for each other."

"Oh, all right." Abby gave in.

She arrived at the pub late. When introduced to David, she was amazed at his likeness to Gilbert O'Sullivan.

"See? I told you," said Geri, smiling. "Now, I'm going to the bar to get us some drinks. You look after her, David. Be nice."

Abby and David sat together awkwardly, as people did on all blind dates. Abby was not interested, and they were trying to make small talk. As the night wore on, she was enjoying the music, and the drink of wine seemed to relax her a little. Though Abby behaved indifferently, David appeared to be having fun.

"Can I see you again?" he asked. Abby was getting up to leave; Lindisfarne had finished singing "Fog on the Tyne."

"If you like," Abby replied.

"We could go to the pictures," he said. "There's a good Burt Reynolds picture on next week at the Apollo. That's near where you live, right?"

Geri jumped in. "We can all go; I'll bring Simon along."

"Can I call you?" asked David.

"You can call her at work," said Geri. "I'll give you the number."

"Okay, I'll see you," said Abby as she left.

Geri walked her to the door. "He likes you, Abby; be nice to him. You need to have some fun in your life, lassie."

Abby and David started going out a couple of times a week, and she found herself enjoying his company more as time passed. She thought of Gabriel a little less; she felt more lighthearted. Geri and Simon and she and David would go out as a foursome, walking on the beach in Bamburgh and then stopping in quaint little pubs on the way home. They went bowling in Newcastle, played darts at the local pub where she worked some nights, or went to the pictures on Fridays, sitting in the back row, necking. After they had been going out together for a few weeks, Abby was starting to feel quite attracted to David. He was a lot of fun, not serious, and liked to drink lots of beer, play darts, and drive his car fast. Other girls looked at him when she was out with him, and that made her feel good.

On New Year's Eve they were all going to go to a dinner dance out at one of the big hotels in the city. David had invited her; Geri and Simon were going also. They were all going to go back to Geri's house afterward, as her parents were away in Spain for the week.

"You must get all dolled up. New dress, shoes, handbag—everything! It's a big deal," Geri said as they chatted between clients.

Abby took the advice and took advantage of the after-Christmas sales and the good tips she had made over Christmas. She found a beautiful silver dress that swayed with her when she walked; it was low cut for Abby. She also found a pair of shoes and a handbag to match—all for 50 percent off. On the day of New Year's Eve, Abby packed her small suitcase with her new outfit, a pair of pajamas, a toothbrush, a hairbrush, and makeup. Before she went to work for the day, she told Cammie she was going for a night out and staying at Geri's.

"Have fun. Be careful," said Cammie. "Happy New Year."

"Happy New Year to you too!" Abby replied. For the first time since leaving America, she felt free and excited and was looking forward to something with anticipation. She knew what was going to happen, and she was ready. She longed to love and be loved, and David was her answer; Abby was sure of that.

Abby and Geri left the salon after a long, busy day. They were not tired in the least. They linked arms and walked along the cobbled street toward the bus shelter for the number 37 bus. Giggling and having fun, they compared notes on the outfits they would wear that night. Once they arrived at Geri's, they spent time together in Geri's little room, in front of the tiny dresser with one mirror, helping one another with hair and makeup.

"Oh, you look like a film star in that dress, Abby!"

"Do you like it?" Abby smiled.

"I can't believe how well you dress up," Geri said.

"I love your red dress," Abby told her. "Let's hope we have a good time."

When the girls met David and Simon at the bottom of the stairs, David let out a slow whistle. "You look smashing," he said.

"Yes," said Simon out the side of his mouth.

"Look at that huge Christmas tree; it touches the ceiling, and there must be a million lights and ornaments!" Abby exclaimed when they arrived at the hotel.

"Yes. The band sounds wonderful, too. Great—we have Christmas crackers, party hats, and favors," said Geri.

Abby and David danced, drank champagne, and kissed, and at midnight, David kissed Abby as no one had ever kissed her before—long and hard. It made her tingle. Maybe it was the champagne, but whatever it was, she felt wonderful inside and out.

They arrived at Geri's home in a taxi at three o'clock in the morning, a little worse for wear. Abby felt dizzy and not sure what she was doing.

Giggling, Geri pointed up the stairs to Abby. "That's where you're sleeping!"

David took Abby's hand and led the way into the room, closing the door behind them. It seemed to Abby that David had his clothes off in a minute. He was standing in front of her, naked. She was unsure of herself and not able to take her eyes from him. David came closer to her.

"Let me help you get that fancy dress off." He unzipped the back of the dress quickly. The dress fell to the floor. "Wow, what a bod! I've wanted you for a long time; you've been a bit of a tease, you know." As he felt her breasts, he added, "You need to be nice to me; tonight cost me a bloody fortune."

Abby stood like a statue. He pushed her onto the bed roughly. She felt lightheaded yet ached to feel David's arms around her. She wanted him to hold her, kiss her softly, caress all the parts of her body, awaken everything in her, shed her virginal skin, and help her become the loving women she longed to be.

He shoved his tongue into her mouth with such force that Abby felt like retching. Lying on top of her, he pushed his hand between her legs, shoving his fingers inside her so hard that the sensation made her jump. David rolled off her to get something from his pants on the floor. Fumbling around, he turned and told her it was a safe. He was hard and enormous, and she was terrified and transfixed; she could not move or cry out. She just lay there and gave herself up to David, hoping he knew what he was doing.

"What's up with you?" David asked as he let out a long, satisfied groan. "Oh, did you not come?"

She turned her head away. "I am fine," she lied, holding in her tears. "Go to sleep."

He did just that, passing out on top of her.

Abby awoke with the moonlight streaming in through the window. It was January 1, 1970. She wasn't sure at first where she was. Quickly, memories of the night before came to her. David was still on top of her with his mouth open, snoring, smelling like last night's dinner mixed with champagne, beer, and bad breath. She looked at him and remembered the events that had taken place just a few hours earlier. It had been a disaster, and she had not been prepared for any of it. He had been fast and thoughtless; she had cried because it hurt her so much.

Abby gently slid out from underneath him, feeling dirty. She found her dressing gown and went to the bathroom. As she went to flush the toilet, she noticed something in the toilet bowl: the condom David had put on before he pushed himself in her. She felt sick. How could he have not removed that thing? She frantically wiped herself clean, washed, and dressed as quickly as she could. Abby left before anyone was awake. She arrived home feeling sickened by her own poor decisions. She ran up to her room and closed the door. Later, she went to the bathroom, filled the tub with scalding water, and soaked herself in it for a long time.

There was a knock on the door. "Abby, are you in there?" It was Cammie.

"Yes. Yes, I am," Abby replied.

"What are you doing? Other people want to use this room, you know."

"I'm just having a bath. I'll be out soon. Just really tired—had a late night."

"Was it fun?" Cammie asked.

"Oh, it was all right," answered Abby. "I drank far too much champagne. Feel rather sick today."

"Ah, well, you'll think on next time, won't you?" said Cammie.

"Yes, that's right," Abby replied, biting her lip and holding in her tears.

Abby went to work the next day, and Geri was upset. "What the hell happened to you yesterday? We woke up, and you were gone!"

"I am sorry," said Abby. "I just felt very sick and decided to go home."

"David was mad as hell—said he was finished with you."

Abby dropped her gaze.

"David told Simon you were no good in the sack." Geri dropped her voice. "He told Simon it was like shagging a kid. He said you cried like a little baby."

Abby was too upset to answer.

"Are you a virgin, Abby?"

"Not anymore!" Abby cried.

"Oh my God! If I had thought—"

"I understand you meant well, and it really was fun while it lasted. But I feel so ..." She wanted to say *used* and *dirty*, but the word *stupid* came out. "I really don't want to talk about this anymore. If David's finished with me, well, that's good because it saves me from finishing with him."

"I don't think that's very nice of you, Abby," Geri said.

"Maybe not, but he is not what I thought he was. Let's leave it at that."

"This is going to be awkward, working with you. David is a good friend of mine. After all I have done for you, I'm not sure we can still be friends."

The manageress opened the back room door and called down the long corridor, "Your nine thirty is here, Abigail. Get a wiggle on."

Abby was on her knees, her head leaning over the toilet bowl, at home in the dingy little bathroom, retching until her insides ached and her ribs felt bruised. She stood, splashed her face with cold water, and opened the bathroom window to allow the chilled February air to slip over the windowsill, giving her some fresh air to inhale, even though the day was damp and foggy. Abby was grateful for the limp breeze on her face. As she held a damp cloth to her forehead, the shock of what was causing this sickness suddenly hit her. She was desperately ill most mornings, sometimes all day, and she had been for several weeks. Her period was now ten days late, and her breasts felt tender and swollen. Sitting down on the toilet, Abby wept, filled with a morbid sense of fear and isolation, for she could share this news with no one.

Later on in the day, Abby was sitting in Dr. O'Malley's waiting room. The doctor was still working, and she hoped that because of his connection to the family, particularly her late mother, he might in some way be able to help her. She looked around and saw that the holes had been plastered, and the walls had been painted, but the room was still as dingy as she remembered from her childhood.

"Abby, you can go in now; the doctor's ready for you," the nurse told her.

Abby sat on a chair opposite Dr. O'Malley. He looked exactly the same as he had years ago, though maybe a little shorter and chubbier and somewhat bent over. However, he still had the same kind eyes.

"Abigail, look at you—certainly all grown up." He smiled. "And if you don't mind my saying, you look the spitting image of your dear mother when I first met her many, many years ago." Smiling at Abby and looking over his glasses, he made her feel a little more comfortable.

"Hello, Doctor. No, I don't mind you saying so. Thank you. That is very kind, for she was a very beautiful lady," Abby responded.

"How can I help you today, Abigail?"

Abby lost all her courage; she started to stammer and cry softly.

"What is it?" Dr. O'Malley asked. "Take a deep breath, and tell me what's troubling you."

There was a long silence, and Abby collected herself, taking a deep breath, as Dr. O'Malley had suggested. "I think … I am pregnant, Doctor." She broke down, releasing more tears.

"Now, why do you think so, child?" he said, pulling himself up and using his desk to support himself.

Abby recited all the symptoms like a bad story as the doctor listened.

"Well, you may be right; however, it could also be the

anxiety that has caused this delay in your cycle and the vomiting and indeed the sore breasts. Now, I want you to bring me a small sample of your urine; bring it to the office tomorrow." Dr. O'Malley passed her a small vial. "And leave it with the nurse. Come back in a week, and I will have the results. We must confirm before we can make any decisions, Abby. Try not to worry."

She nodded and rose to go.

"Abigail?" the doctor called as she was leaving. "Have you talked to the father?"

"No!" Abby cried. "And I don't want anyone to know, Doctor."

"I should hold off for now anyway," said Dr. O'Malley, "until we know for sure."

Abby closed the door behind her.

One week later, Abby sat in the same waiting room, thinking of the conversation she had had with Geri that morning. Geri had hardly spoken to her in the last several weeks, but she had been full of herself that day. While they folded the clean towels in the back room together and stacked the shelves with the new order that had come in, Geri stopped and put on the kettle to make some tea. She came back and shook a towel hard, making it smack in the air, before she folded it much more precisely than was necessary.

"I thought you might like to know David and Desiree are back together. Remember the girl he had finished with just before he met you, Abby?" Geri said, taunting her.

Abby looked at Geri. "So what?" she said.

"They are in love with each other, and they are getting engaged on Desiree's birthday, April fifteenth. I am pleased for him. Des has asked me to be one of her bridesmaids. You know, I was a good friend to you, Abby, and you let me down, just walking out that morning without a word. If you had told me you had not, well, done it before, I could have"—Geri hesitated, looking for the right word—"advised you on things that would have helped it not hurt so much. And I might as well tell you now: I have a fantastic new job; I'm leaving this place. Big department shop in Newcastle—more money and commission."

Abby stayed silent for a moment. "I wish you all the best, Geri. I hope we can still be friends."

"Not likely," said Geri. "We won't be moving in the same circles."

"You know, Geri, you are very disappointing, and I am sad, as I thought you were a better friend than that. You are right; I will not be moving in the same circle of friends if they include David. He is a selfish, self-centered creep. If that's who you choose to be with, then good luck to you, for you will need it one day—believe me." Abby turned away from Geri and slammed the door behind her as hard as she could.

Abby's thoughts returned to the wretched waiting room at the doctor's office. She had been waiting for what seemed like an eternity—seven days and an eternity. She prayed the results would show anxiety, not pregnancy.

"Miss Lavalle?"

She jumped at the calling of her name.

"Doctor is ready to see you."

"How are you feeling, Abigail?" Dr. O'Malley asked.

"Oh, just about the same, Doctor, maybe a little worse."

The doctor looked over his eyeglasses kindly at her. "You are indeed pregnant. About six weeks or so."

"What am I to do?" Abby gasped.

"You must tell the father; maybe he will marry you."

"No!" Abby blurted out. "I've just heard today that he's getting engaged."

"He must know, Abby; it is his right, and you must discuss it and talk to your family."

"No, Doctor, I do not want to talk to him; I do not want my family to know—no one."

"You cannot handle this alone, Abby; a baby is a lot of responsibility."

Abby jumped from the chair. "I understand."

"Abby, go talk to the father, and see what he feels; it might all work out. Come back in one week. I would like to see you on follow-up." The doctor patted Abby on the shoulder. "Try not to worry. It will all work out for the best."

Abby waited in the park for David, sitting on a bench. He was late. Eventually, he showed up.

"What's so damn important?" he asked. "Make it snappy; I don't have all day."

Abby looked at him. "I'm pregnant."

"How the hell can that be? We only did it once, and I used a safe. It's not mine." He started to walk away from her.

"You fell asleep on top of me, remember? And when I went to the bathroom, it came away from me."

"I don't care. I want nothing to do with this. My plans are to get engaged to Desiree." David paced up and down the path. It was early afternoon but already dark, wet, and miserable. "The best I will do is give you half the money to get rid of it for sure. I do not want it. I shall send you a money order in the post. Don't talk to me by phone or any other way. I will not help you. Do you get it?"

Abby looked at David; he looked frantic with fear and showed no concern for her or the baby. She stood up from the park bench and walked toward him. "I do not want your money; in fact, there is nothing I want from you. As the father, you had a right to know that I was pregnant with your child. Now you have told me in no uncertain terms how you feel. I have absolutely no desire to see you or hear from you ever again." Abby turned from him.

"Is that a promise?" David shouted after Abby. She continued to walk away and did not look back. Tears spilled from her eyes.

The following week Abby met with the doctor.

"There is only way to go, and that is abortion," she told Dr. O'Malley.

"Have you thought about this?" he asked.

"I have thought of nothing else for the past week, Doctor."

"Are you absolutely sure?" the doctor asked once more in earnest. "There are other alternatives."

"I have considered every possible angle—everything from suicide to adoption. Believe me."

He jumped from his chair, walked around the desk, and paced up and down the surgery. "Abigail, please—you must try to stay calm. If this is truly what you want, I will book you into the Northwest Clinic, behind the big park up in Baker. Because of your extenuating circumstances, we can put you in as a D&C. I do wish you would talk to someone in your family. Share this burden, Abby."

"No, Doctor, I want to get this over with as soon as possible."

Dr. O'Malley dropped his head, shaking it from side to side, and went back to his chair.

"Very well. Please see the nurse on your way out, and she will instruct you as to what to do. We can book you into the hospital. Under these special circumstances, it will all be paid for by the National Health. It's a fairly simple procedure, Abby," the doctor told her. "You will be in the hospital for a day or two, and you should take a week off work. I shall give you a sick note along with instructions. Can you find somewhere to stay after?"

"I'll think about that later," Abby said. She thanked the doctor and walked out of the office, feeling nothing.

A week later, as she lay on the gurney waiting to go into the operating room, Abby's thoughts raced. She had lied to almost everyone she cared about, telling Cammie and her boss that she was going for a week's rest to a friend's cottage in Brighton Beach.

"Seems like a good-enough idea to me, Abigail," Cammie had said. "Are you feeling all right?"

"I'm fine. Why do you ask?" Abby had said.

"You look rather pale, and you've been quiet the last few weeks. I think you've even lost some weight."

"Just busy. You know how it is with the house and work and jobs. I'm fine."

"I think getting away for a week will be good for you; maybe I will go somewhere when you come home," Cammie had said. "I could use a change myself."

"You know, that's a really good idea. I must go." Abby had dashed out the door and walked to the bus stop, from which a bus would take her to the hospital.

The staff were efficient, abrupt, and bordering on cruel. It was clearly their intention to make sure that special D&C cases did not return. Abby was pushed, poked, and manhandled for her pre-op care. She was in a ward with several other girls who were in for D&Cs—some of them for the second or third time. Abby shared her information with no one. She kept quiet and to herself.

"Have you got no family coming to visit you today, Miss Lavalle?" one of the younger nurses asked her.

"No, I have not," Abby replied.

"Well, maybe tomorrow."

Abby looked back and shrugged. She had been given a sleeping pill to help her rest that night. The next morning she was the sixth operation scheduled, and a nurse woke her at six thirty. She had to go without food or water until twelve forty-five, when she was still lying outside the OR. The big doors swung open, and a nurse pushed someone out; it looked like the girl who'd been in the bed next to her. She had told Abby last night that this was her second D&C. She looked childlike lying there; her face was small and deathly pale. Two IV bottles were hooked up, one on each side, with one holding blood and the other holding clear fluids. The white sheet covering her was covered with blood on the bottom half. Abby gasped as she looked, and then the girl was gone. Another nurse came and pushed Abby through the doors; Abby's heart was racing, along with her thoughts. Should she jump off the gurney and run from this cold, empty, soulless room? Should she flee toward life and save her baby, not kill it? How could she do this?

Someone pulled at her arm, turned her hand, slapped the back of it, and shoved in a needle. It stung, and she cried out. Everyone worked around her efficiently, wearing their green garb—hats, masks, gowns, and rubber boots. There was a strong smell of disinfectant. They talked around her as though she were asleep or not even there: "Female, twenty, eight weeks pregnant." Someone lifted both of her legs up and placed one foot and then the other into a stirrup. Abby's gown fell away, revealing every part of her. She felt like one of the sides of pork that hung in the butcher shop around the corner from her house. When she was waiting in the queue for her meat or pies, she stared at them, feeling sorry for them as they hung on hooks, dead, with everyone looking at their insides.

If I do jump and flee, what can I give this baby? I have nothing. I am nothing.

Someone placed a mask over her mouth and nose. "Count to ten backward," she heard him say.

How can I not do this? was her last thought before blackness overtook her.

Abby slowly opened her eyes, lying flat. A nurse was talking to her.

"It's done. Wake up. How do you feel? Do you feel cold or sick?"

Abby heard sobs. Someone close to her was crying, letting out heart-wrenching sobs.

"Miss Lavalle, stop crying! You must calm down. You are fine."

It was strange, as she felt as though she were listening to someone else.

"Why are you crying?" asked one of the nurses. "Are you in pain?"

"Yes." She did not recognize her own voice.

"Where does it hurt?" the nurse asked impatiently.

"Everywhere—all over me." Abby sobbed.

"What do you mean everywhere?"

"My body is wracked with pain from top to bottom, heart and soul!" Abby cried out. "I've just killed my baby."

Abby wept day and night. Finally, when it was time for her to be discharged, the tears stopped.

"Is someone coming to collect you?" the nurse asked her.

"No," Abby replied. "I'm going to take the bus home; it's not too far."

"Then you should go home to bed and rest for a couple of days. If the bleeding becomes heavy or there are clots, come back or contact the hospital or call an ambulance," the nurse told her.

The specialist came by and looked at Abby, pushing on her stomach.

"You are feeling strong enough to be discharged, Miss Lavalle?" It seemed more like a command than a question.

"Yes, I am, Doctor," Abby replied. She wanted out of there.

"Then I shall discharge you; I do not wish to see you back here again. Is that clear?"

Abby stared at him. The doctor turned his gaze and walked away.

Abby had rented a room at the YMCA in Newcastle; it was warm and quiet. She had brought a hot water bottle for the cramps and a thermos, which she filled with hot tea from the café, where she bought a sandwich. Wrapping herself in a warm blanket, she climbed into bed at eleven o'clock that morning and slept until nine thirty that evening. Abby awoke feeling disoriented in the dark room; it took her some time to figure out where she was. She felt better, rested. She climbed out of bed and, moving around the room, found the light switch on the wall. She went to the bathroom, washed up, filled her hot water bottle, and went back to her room. She poured herself some tea from the thermos; it had stayed surprisingly hot. She sat down and ate the sandwich; it tasted good, and she was pleased she had an appetite again. After taking two of the pain pills the doctor had given her, she lay down in the bed with the hot water bottle across her tummy. Abby felt a great sense of loss. It was as though some light had gone out, leaving her in a dark, cold, solitary place with an ache that could not be removed.

She remembered feeling something similar when her mother died. People who knew things—or were supposed to—such as priests, doctors, aunts, and friends, had told Abby that in time, she would feel better, that her mother was in heaven now. Abby remembered wanting to scream at them to go away. Abby started to cry softly. What would her mother have thought? After Malachi died, her mother had been devastated; she knew Amelia would have disowned her and would have been heartbroken. Abby understood now some of what her mother had felt when Malachi died.

Why was she going through this? It was all because her arms had reached out to the wrong man. Lying in a dark, dingy little room away from everyone she knew and loved, she vowed never again to make the same mistake. She was not the same girl; Abby was a woman now—a broken one, but she would come back stronger. She would move onward from this horrible time in her life with a strong resolve. Abby was aware down in the deepest parts of herself that something had changed forever.

— 48 —

Several weeks after Abby returned from the hospital, she and Cammie were washing and drying the dishes after dinner.

"Let's finish up, and I'll make some tea. We can sit down. I'd like to have a chat with you, Cammie," Abby said.

"What's wrong? Are you sick?"

"No, I'm fine. I just need to talk to you."

Abby made the tea, and they sat together at the kitchen table.

"Cammie, I must do something different with my life," Abby began.

"What do you mean?"

"I can't go on with the same old pattern day in and day out. I've been back from Tennessee now for over a year. The whole experience was amazing, but in a way, it unsettled me, as now I know there is something better out there, and I can't stay here."

Cammie looked at Abby. "I know you've been very unhappy over the past year."

"I've been so torn. Part of me doesn't want to leave you

handling all the responsibilities. I've seen an ad—World Airways is hiring airline stewardesses, and I've sent for an application, Cammie."

"Wow," Cammie said, "that's a big leap. You're reaching high."

"I know; I believe there are three interviews to get through. But I must try, or I will regret it if I don't."

"You know what? I don't blame you. I wish I had half of your courage and guts. I would do the same thing. Good luck, I say. The boys are leaving school in the summer, and they will be heading on their way. Don't worry about us. You go live your life. If it's time for you to fly away, then you go, and the best of luck to you!"

When Abby received the letter, it fell onto the floor through the letter box in the dark passageway. Three envelopes lay on the floor—one of which could change Abigail's life for good. The other two were an electric bill and a letter addressed in what looked like her cousin Aiden's handwriting. The biggest envelope lay faceup. It was from World Airways, addressed to Miss Abigail Lavalle. She bent down to pick up the three envelopes; the envelope from World Airways was heavy and thick. She knew with a leap in her heart it was an acceptance with more information. She was aware that rejection letters were light and thin.

She tore the envelope open with shaking hands and began to read.

> Dear Miss Lavalle,
>
> We are happy to inform you …

Abby walked to the stairs and sat down, crying with joy and disbelief. She moved the tips of her fingers over the words as she sat, closing her eyes as though she were reading braille, imagining the changes this letter was going to bring to her life.

From today, I shall be different. I am about to begin pursuing my dreams.

Abby moved to London two months after she received the letter for training. The trainers told her and her classmates that they were all special. Abby could not get used to that word—it was not something she was accustomed to hearing. But as the weeks passed, she discovered that she was as special as the next one. Her confidence grew throughout the ten-week training program, which was rigorous. She was to learn the aircraft inside and out. She had to know all the safety procedures and every door, and there were eleven on the large aircraft. Each attendant received a number from one to eleven, which determined where she would work within the aircraft and how she would execute her responsibilities for evacuating the aircraft, should the occasion arise. Every possible scenario was considered, and they were trained to handle it.

Over the following six weeks, they had their inflight training for cabin service. They learned about food preparation, drinks, duty-free regulations, babies, mothers, movies, vomiting, nervous passengers, first aid, drunks, heart attacks, and inflight deaths. Abby was trained for it all. She traveled between London, New York, Los Angeles, Montreal, Toronto, and the Canary Islands. Staying in five-star accommodations, she met wonderful people who were fun, energized, interesting, and interested from all over the world.

One day Abby was working in the first-class cabin, flying from New York to Gatwick. As she was seating passengers, taking coats, and giving out newspapers, she noticed a tall, handsome man with wavy dark hair and tan skin. He was impeccably dressed—he was gorgeous. As Abby watched silently, one of the girls who worked with her came up behind her and whispered across her shoulder.

"You wish!" she said. "I've seen him before—gorgeous, isn't he?"

Abby smiled. "I don't know what you mean."

"Lucky you—he's in your section. Good luck."

Abby found his name and addressed him professionally. He asked her name, and she told him. She gave him as much attention as she gave all her other passengers, although most slept through the night, thankfully. He did not, which gave Abby more opportunity to pamper him and just look at him; he was exquisite. He called her over. "I would like a cup of coffee, Miss Abby."

"Certainly, sir. How would you like that, Mr. Oliver?"

"Hot, black, and strong."

"May I bring you some breakfast?"

"No, it's too early—just coffee."

She brought him a tray with a china mug full of hot, steaming, fresh coffee; two homemade oatmeal biscuits; and a hot steamed towel to freshen up.

"Enjoy, sir." She smiled.

He dazzled her with a response. "You know, Miss Abby, I travel this flight quite regularly, but I have never had the pleasure of meeting you."

Abby smiled. "I am new in first class, Mr. Oliver; this is, in fact, my first flight."

"Well, let me tell you, I have never had such attention—pleasant, professional service. Well done. And I truly hope to see you more often." Smiling, he went back to his notes and coffee.

After a smooth landing, the passengers disembarked.

As he left, Abby thanked him for flying World Airways. "Have a wonderful day, Mr. Oliver."

"You too, Miss Abby." He smiled at her and was gone.

She sighed, and all her fellow stewardesses sighed with her.

Abby left the aircraft quickly. She was rushing to catch a flight leaving from the other side of the airport, flying home to Newcastle for the weekend.

"Hello, Abby. Heading home?" the attendant said as she boarded the plane.

"Yes." She smiled. "Here's my boarding pass—15C." Abby went to her seat, and as she was removing her jacket, she heard a familiar voice.

"Well, hello again to you, Miss Abby."

As she looked down at the seat beside hers, the charming Mr. Emerson Oliver stared up at her.

"What a wonderful surprise this is. Are you 15C?" he said.

"Yes, I am." Abby smiled, taking her seat next to him. She soon discovered he was the president of an oil company and traveled all over the world. He lived in Durham City and was heading home for a few days to get away from it all. He flew out to Dubai next week.

"Tell me about yourself, Miss Abby. Are you flying to Newcastle for work or pleasure?"

"My home and family—they are there."

"Ah. Married?" he asked, raising one of his eyebrows to show interest in her response.

Abby hesitated for fun; she was enjoying flirting. Looking down at her finger, she held it up in front of him. "No ring!"

"Would you be free to have dinner with me this evening?" he asked.

Abby smiled; she really liked him. "I'm sorry, but I have plans this evening."

"Of course you have; all I can say is lucky fellow." He backed down gracefully.

"Yes, he is a lucky fellow; it's my younger brother. We are having a farewell party for him. He is leaving for France next week to work for a year."

Emerson sat up. "How wonderful—marvelous news. I am delighted for him. How about tomorrow?"

"I would love to," she told him.

Abby and Emerson were together whenever they could be when they weren't traveling for work. Emerson wined and dined her. On their third date, he took her to Paris for the weekend. They stayed at the Hilton on the Champs-Élysées and strolled through the parks during the day, visiting all the wonders of Paris, including Sacré-Cœur, Notre Dame, and the Louvre; eating divine French cuisine; drinking beautiful French wine; and making love. Emerson was an expert. His lovemaking was extraordinary. He enjoyed Abby's shy ways and naïveté as he taught her the ways of love. She had never known in her wildest dreams that two people could share such pleasure. She became a different person. She longed for him to kiss her and touch every hungry part of her. Abby was longing, starving, aching, and searching for love. She had been for most of her life—searching for something to calm the storm within her.

Abby lay on the satin sheets, looking out at the moon as it cast its glow through the lace curtains, creating delicate patterns across the bed. Emerson lay sleeping like a satisfied, beautiful cat, stretched out, his tan skin shimmering in the pale moonlight. *He is gorgeous,* she thought, *sleeping or awake.* In the stillness, she lay watching Emerson. It was a thrill to her, for she knew he had transformed her from a girl to a sensual woman. Abby closed her eyes, drifting into a dreamy sleep. She knew in the deepest part of her that something was still missing.

— 49 —

Abby opened her eyes, unsure of her whereabouts; she sat for a moment, recognizing slowly the feeling of the familiar rhythm of the train carrying her northward toward home. It was Christmas Eve 1975, and the train was full to overflowing with excited, happy, stressed people from all corners of the world, trying to make it home. Abby was as eager as the next one to get home for the first time in several years. Her father, all her siblings, and their spouses and children were congregating at Amelia's house for Christmas. Six Christmases had come and gone since their mother had died. Six Christmases had passed since they had all been together.

Two of those Christmases she had spent in the family home with Cammie, Noah, Nathan, and Sasha. They'd invited Sebastian for Christmas lunch, and everyone had sat around the splendid table, unsure what to do. The scene had reminded Abby of a poor play in which the actors knew their parts but did not remember their lines. Abby had spent the third, fourth, and fifth Christmases in London or traveling around the United States and Canada, enjoying the festive season with work colleagues and friends.

Looking out the window, Abby could see the green English fields covered with a soft frost. The milky white heat of the winter sun was slowly warming the day. The clouds parted slightly, and the light caught the frost; there was a slight twinkle.

The train had come to a stop in York. *What a fantastic city,* Abby thought. It was rich in heritage; its ancient walls provided a mosaic background to York Minster Cathedral, built one thousand years ago. Three or four generations had labored tirelessly over one hundred years to erect it. Looking through the window of the train, Abby could almost hear the echoes of the stonemasons' chisels. It amazed her that it still stood in all its majesty and many splendorous facets. Generation after generation, past, present, and future, was able to enjoy it.

The train pulled out of York, and Abby looked at her watch. In forty-five minutes they would be in Durham City; however, Emerson was not there. They had met in London for dinner three days ago. He had made plans to go skiing in Vancouver for ten days over Christmas and New Year's. As they were enjoying their coffee and liqueur, Emerson spoke.

"I have an early Christmas gift for you, Abby." He smiled as he handed her an envelope tied with a red ribbon.

Abby looked at it. "What is it?"

"Open it, and you will see."

She untied the ribbon, and inside the envelope, she found an air ticket to Vancouver and reservations and ski lessons at Whistler Mountain Resort.

"This is truly amazing." She was stunned.

"I knew you would be astonished. We will have a fantastic time, and I can't wait to ski with you."

"How did you think I would be able to come with you?"

"What do you mean? You have the time off, you told me, because of this family reunion. I figured you could wangle your way out for a fantastic holiday like this." He flashed his handsome smile at her.

"You obviously did not understand how important this Christmas family reunion is. Not only to me but to every single member of my family."

"Oh, you are making a big fuss," he told her.

"I know you have no special attachment to Christmas, Emerson. Probably because you don't have children or siblings and spent most of your time in boarding school or skiing when you were a child. I am truly sorry, but I will not be coming with you." Abby was upset. "We are so different, Emerson—in every way."

"What are you talking about, Abby? We have a great time together. I am happy. Aren't you?"

"Honestly, Emerson," Abby responded, "no. We have been together eighteen months, and our relationship hasn't developed beyond three months. It seems to be going nowhere."

"What do you want from me? We travel, have fantastic meals and wine, have great friends, and go to the theater, and our lovemaking is sublime."

"I want more, as ungrateful as that may sound," said Abby.

"What more is there?" Emerson asked.

"Marriage, children, home—"

"Oh, that. Spare me the white-picket-fence speech. You

want to spoil our relationship. I'm twice divorced, remember? You know how I feel."

"That's why we must separate, Emerson, before we become resentful. I have loved our time, and I won't ever forget you. You have given me confidence and taught me the ways of love."

"Me too, Abigail." He looked at her. "I am sorry."

Abby wiped tears from her eyes as she recalled the dinner with Emerson. Durham City was approaching, her favorite place. One could see the cathedral and castle on opposing sides, commanding the view of the city, as the train approached going north or south. It was the most spectacular view, with the working Roman viaduct outside the station. Abby had many happy memories of Durham with Emerson.

It was sad that the relationship was over. Abby closed her eyes as the train left Durham Station. It was like closing a door on a special time in her life.

—50—

On Christmas Day, Sebastian sat at the large table, surrounded by his family. He was grateful to be part of this amazing celebration, the coming together of all his children and grandchildren for the first time in six years.

"You have all prepared a fantastic feast," Sebastian said, looking around the table. "Thank you for inviting me. I must say everything looks as it did in Christmases past. The food, the tree, the crib, the music, the crackling fire—it is wonderful."

Looking around the table, Sebastian observed his children and grandchildren with wonder and pride.

Abby stood up. "Listen, everyone—I would like to say grace, if that's okay."

Everyone nodded in agreement. Sebastian watched his youngest daughter; how she had blossomed in the past years into a confident woman.

"I would like to do something very special—different but special. Amelia's prayer." She cleared her throat and touched the pendant she always wore—her angel Gabriel. "Mother

Mary, bless this day. Keep us safe in every way. Guide me to a peaceful place. Fill my heart and soul with grace. Enfold us in your tender care. Mother Mary, this is my prayer." Abby finished and smiled at everyone.

Sebastian could barely hold his tears in.

"Good one, Abby!" Andre called out. He lived just outside of Newcastle, where he had recently opened his second shop dedicated to maintaining and taking care of small engines. He and his wife had a sweet little daughter who was almost two years old.

Eugene was still in the navy, a second lieutenant based in Germany. This was his first Christmas leave in six years, which was one of the reasons they had all come together. He too was married to a local girl, and they were expecting their first child in the spring.

Leah was happy living in the south of England, working as a nurse at the Children's Hospital. She was married to a dentist who worked at the same hospital. They had been married for three years and had a wonderful little boy who was now fourteen months old.

Sebastian picked up his glass and took a sip of his fine red wine while watching his two grandchildren, who were sitting side by side in their high chairs, playing with Christmas crackers and conversing in baby language.

Cammie was sitting between the two high chairs, apparently enjoying every moment of her job as auntie. She was still living in Amelia's home and was the person most responsible for bringing this spectacular feast together. She worked in the city in a large lawyer's office. Cammie was courting a nice young man. Sebastian wanted to see them married, but Cammie was not ready.

Sasha, a chef, lived at home with Cammie. Noah was a teacher in France. Nathan was still at university—the perpetual student.

Andre stood up and cleared his throat, tapping his spoon against his glass to make a pinging noise. "As I am the eldest, the smartest, and the best looking," he said, laughing. His siblings all moaned, groaned, and laughed at him, throwing broken pieces of Christmas crackers and their party hats his way. He did not let it bother him as he continued.

"Behave yourselves," said Andre, "as I'm about to make a Christmas toast." As he spoke, they settled down, and a gentle silence fell over everyone, except for the little ones. It was perfect. Andre looked around the table; the jocularity had left his voice and his eyes. He looked more melancholy, which was his usual look—he was like Amelia in that way. "Welcome. A merry Christmas to everyone. As I was thinking about what I would like to say, it occurred to me Mam would have called this family reunion nothing less than miraculous. As siblings, we have, over the years, experienced some rather difficult times. It is true, I have discovered, that adversity does make one stronger. As I look around this table, you prove it. I am very proud to call you brother and sister, and I would like you to know if you were not part of my life by birth, I would seek you out in order that I may call you my friend."

Andre stopped, cleared his throat, and looked toward his father. "Dad, I know this has been difficult for you in many ways, and I cannot pass judgment. I would like to say that in becoming a father, I have learned to understand many things that I did not. We appreciate your commitment to us all, and I know how much Mam loved you. Amelia would be overjoyed to witness this Christmas celebration with all of us here. I thank you for your presence. Let us raise our glass to the family—our family!"

They all stood up and said, "Cheers!" Sebastian knew there were not many dry eyes around the table.

Sasha shouted out, "Well done, Andre! Hey, Abby, where are you flying off to next? You lucky duck—will you take me in your suitcase?"

Abby replied, "I'd love to. Come the new year, World Airways is adding three new routes: Chicago, Miami, and Nashville."

"Nashville is in Tennessee, right? You'll be able to go see Aunt Helen and the family there."

"I certainly hope to." Abby smiled softly.

Later, after the turkey, pudding, and other goodies, Sebastian sat around the tree, looking at the manger, counting his blessings. Sitting upon one of his knees was his beautiful granddaughter, Amelia, and on the other knee was his handsome grandson, Malachi. Although Amelia was not physically present, as Andre had said, the beauty of their grandmother shined from within these two amazing grandbabies, leaving a fantastic legacy of loving strength and presence for all those who came after her to follow. Drawing his two grandchildren close to him and closing his eyes, Sebastian could hear Amelia's soft voice: "It's Bastille Day today, isn't it?"

About the Author

Christiane Banks was born in Newcastle-Upon-Tyne, in the north east of England. She was raised in an industrial area and began working at 14 years old, as a stylist/beautician apprentice. At this job she met many women who had lived during the world wars and, was inspired by their vivid stories of those periods.

Banks is a storyteller herself, and these accounts helped to inspire her to become an author and ultimately became part of the story of "Amelia's Prayer"

Christiane now lives in Milton, Ontario, Canada with her husband. Amelia's Prayer, Which took six years to write, is her debut novel. She is currently working on writing a sequel.

CPSIA information can be obtained
at www.ICGtesting.com
Printed in the USA
LVHW041451040319
609421LV00001B/8/P